The Hidden Wife

Joanna Rees, aka Josie Lloyd and Jo Rees, is a bestselling writer of fifteen novels, including rom-coms, blockbusters and big-hearted adventures such as *The Tides of Change* and *A Twist of Fate*. Based in Brighton, Joanna is married to the author Emlyn Rees, with whom she has three daughters. They have co-written several novels, including the *Sunday Times* number one bestseller *Come Together*, which was translated into over twenty languages and made into a film. They have written several bestselling parodies of their favourite children's books, including *We're Going on a Bar Hunt*, *The Very Hungover Caterpillar* and *The Teenager Who Came to Tea*. As Josie Lloyd, Joanna has also written the novel *The Cancer Ladies' Running Club*. When she's not writing, she likes running on the seafront with her dog. Joanna is always delighted to hear from her readers, so please visit her Joanna Rees Books Facebook page, or find her on Instagram @jorees22 or on Twitter @joannareesbooks.

BY JOANNA REES

As Josie Lloyd

It Could Be You
The Cancer Ladies' Running Club

As Josie Lloyd, with Emlyn Rees

Come Together
Come Again
The Boy Next Door
Love Lives
We Are Family
The Three Day Rule
The Seven Year Itch
We're Going on a Bar Hunt
The Very Hungover Caterpillar
The Teenager Who Came to Tea
Switch It Off
'Twas the Flight Before Christmas
The Joy of Socks
Shabby: The Jolly Good British Guide to Stress-free Living

As Joanna Rees

A Twist of Fate
The Key to It All
The Girl from Lace Island
In the Shade of the Blossom Tree
(previously published as *Forbidden Pleasures*)
The Tides of Change (previously published as *Platinum*)
The Runaway Daughter
The Hidden Wife

The Hidden Wife

Joanna Rees

PAN BOOKS

First published 2020 by Macmillan

This edition published 2021 by Pan Books
an imprint of Pan Macmillan
The Smithson, 6 Briset Street, London EC1M 5NR
EU representative: Macmillan Publishers Ireland Limited,
Mallard Lodge, Lansdowne Village, Dublin 4
Associated companies throughout the world
www.panmacmillan.com

ISBN 978-1-5290-1887-5

1 3 5 7 9 8 6 4 2

A CIP catalogue record for this book is available from the British Library.

Typeset by Palimpsest Book Production Limited, Palkirk, Stirlingshire
Printed and bound by CPI Group (UK) Ltd, Croydon CR0 4YY

For Tallulah, my party girl, with all my love

The
Hidden
Wife

1

March 1928

Vita Casey stood in the wings of Les Folies Bergère, a couple of silk robes hanging loosely over her arm. She heard a collective gasp and leaned forward to see the bright platinum hair of Julianne as she flew in a languorous arc, her knees hooked over the trapeze. From the shadows, Vita could see only a small section of the enthralled audience, but the sheer *joie de vivre* – as the French reviewers put it – was palpable in the air. It was hardly surprising, Vita thought. Ever since Josephine Baker had performed her sensational dance two years ago, wearing nothing more than a skirt made of fake bananas, it was one of *the* Paris night-spots.

Vita quickly ducked back as the new section started and the line of bare-breasted dancers ran in from the back, down the central aisle and up onto the stage, to the sound of the slurring, raucous trombones. The girls whooped now, high-kicking and moving shoulder-to-shoulder in their perfect line, and the audience – as many women as men – clapped and cheered. Vita saw her best friend Nancy whizz past, the red ruffle skirt revealing her toned legs. She winked at Vita, her

1

cheeks highly rouged, her lips glossy, the giant white feather headdress bobbing.

Vita waved dutifully, but she missed the Nancy of old – not this crazy Folies girl who was high every night, as if she had a duty to be the most daring . . . *the* most outrageous.

Has Nancy always been like this? Vita wondered. She supposed she had, but she missed the days when it had been just the two of them against the world. Back then, when Vita had raced onto the train out of London at the last possible minute, running for her life from her crazed, vengeful brother, with only her friend Edith's passport and the clothes on her back, her head had been in a complete spin. But Nancy, ever practical, had turned their terrifying flight to the continent into a real adventure.

They hadn't even stopped in Paris, which was as far as Vita herself had ever dreamt of going. Nancy had insisted that they go properly to ground for a while, and so they'd changed trains straight away at the Gare du Nord, to travel south with Mr Wild, Nancy's little dog.

They'd kept going all the way to Rome, and then on to a glorious villa of some old family friends of Nancy's on the Amalfi Coast for Christmas and New Year – until, having drunk the cellar dry, they'd thoroughly outstayed their welcome. The pair had scrimped by on Nancy's diminishing trust fund, although they'd never turned down a free meal from fellow travellers. And since Nancy was such an incorrigible flirt, and Mr Wild managed to make friends wherever they went, their self-imposed exile often bordered on something very much like fun.

But then the money had run out, and Nancy had declared

that the best place to re-establish themselves would be Paris. Vita didn't want to go there, but Nancy was insistent. Vita was terrified that her brother Clement would still be looking for her, but Nancy had argued that after all these months Clement was almost certainly tired of hunting for her and Vita had nothing to be scared of.

With her knack of putting a positive glow on even the worst situation, Nancy reasoned that they'd been on the run long enough, and Vita wasn't Anna Darton any more – the girl who'd fled her abusive family. She didn't need to be that downtrodden, scared little daughter of a Lancashire cotton-mill owner, but could fulfil her destiny as Vita Casey, a designer and all-round fabulous girl-about-town. 'Because Paris, *darling*,' she decreed in her American drawl, 'is the *only* place to be.'

So Vita had relented, telling herself that even though she'd changed her name once before, hidden in the heart of the metropolis and Clement had still managed to find her, Nancy was right and it wouldn't be the same here in Paris, surely? Not in the heart of the most changeable city in the world. Besides, Nancy had been so good to her. Who was she to dampen Nancy's dreams of taking Paris by storm?

When they'd first arrived, fizzing with excitement, Vita had assumed that Nancy wanted to come good on the promise she'd made in London to help Vita establish a business here in Paris, the home of lingerie. She'd said she would pull in favours from her family contacts, but soon it became clear that none of these contacts were going to materialize, leaving Vita feeling that Nancy's promises had never been anything more than hot air.

Instead Nancy had headed to Les Folies Bergère and, with puffed-up claims of their experience as dancers in the Zip Club in London, it wasn't long before she had talked her way into the troupe. Vita herself wasn't so lucky. She didn't pass the audition, the director claiming that even though she had *jolis* blue eyes and golden-blonde hair, her breasts were far too large and she wouldn't fit in with the current line-up of girls.

Nancy, who firmly believed that everyone would eventually bend to her wishes, said this was nonsense, and it was just a matter of time before she could bring Vita in, too. She decreed that she'd done it before in London and would do so again in Paris. And then, once they'd saved some money, they could start thinking about Vita's business.

But now more than a year had passed and Vita was no closer to setting up her fledgling underwear business, Top Drawer, again, or joining the dancers, for that matter – not that she really dared to. Nancy seemed to have forgotten that Vita had never really been a trained dancer in the first place.

Instead, Vita got by, helping the dressers backstage for a pitiful wage, under the watchful gaze of Madame Rubier; but for the most part her purpose was waiting in the wings: waiting for Nancy, ready to be at her beck and call. She knew that some of the other dancers referred to Vita unkindly as Nancy's 'wife' – a joke that Nancy herself was happy to perpetuate – but Vita wondered, as she did more frequently now, how long she was going to be stuck as Nancy's companion when she was longing to strike out on her own.

She stepped back as the dance ended and the girls careened towards her, led by the Brazilian beauty Solange and the fiery

Sicilian Collette, who tottered quickly past Vita so that the other ten dancers could bunch into the dark wings, their wide-armed poses deflating as soon as they were out of the lights. The girls brought with them a pungent smell of sweat and perfume, and a waft of the smoky electric lights.

The applause from the audience was deafening, but the girls weren't doing an encore tonight. Instead across the stage, Tibor, from Russia, was preparing to go on with his contortionist act.

Vita quickly handed out the robes to the girls, with encouraging smiles and little words of congratulation: '*Bien joué*, Adrienne', '*Quel spectacle formidable*' for Rosa, '*C'était magnifique*' to Madeleine and Simone; and the last robe held out for Nancy. But Nancy's chest was glistening, her long strings of beads stuck beneath her pert bare breasts, and she shrugged it away. Instead she shook out the tall feather headdress and handed it to Vita, before flicking her fingers through her short black hair.

'Get changed, kiddo,' she said, looking up and down disparagingly at Vita's neat shirt tucked into flared trousers, which Vita had no intention of changing out of. Next to the half-naked exotic dancing girls, she did look a bit urbane, but Vita liked her stylish look. She'd made these trousers from some material that Madame Rubier had been about to throw away, basing the style on an advert she'd seen for a similar pair by Coco Chanel.

'What's wrong with this?'

'We're going out first to Solange's and then on to a club,' Nancy said, with a raise of her eyebrow. 'It'll be so much fun. And *he'll* be there . . .'

2

A Dare

It was usual for 'the gang', as Nancy called their group, to go to a club to dance after the show. They often went to Nancy's favourite, 'The Rodent' – or Le Rat Mort, as everyone else knew it – which was owned by the Corsican mafia and had a seedy late-night atmosphere, where they could all get drunk on cheap red wine and dance themselves into a frenzy. But Vita's favourite was Le Grand Duc, which was known as Bricktop's because of its red-headed owner, the larger-than-life Ada, who had taught anyone who was anyone in Paris how to do the Charleston. Vita loved the spontaneity of their late-night sing-songs at Bricktop's and how Ada joined in with the girls, dancing across the sticky floor.

Tonight they'd all congregated first at Solange's apartment, which was conveniently located a few blocks away from Les Folies, at the bottom of the rue des Martys near the Notre-Dame de Lorette church, on the attic floor of what had obviously once been a grand – but was now a decidedly shabby – apartment block.

Solange herself was still in one of the backless dancers' dresses, a sequinned band around her coiled black hair, her garters and seamed stockings on show. She had exotic dark skin and was exceptionally supple, having joined the Ballets Russes when they'd been on tour to South America, before finding her way to Paris. She was petite, but had a fierce voice and an intense brown-eyed gaze that meant people usually did as she commanded.

As usual, she was holding court in the midst of the crowd in the drawing room. Some of the dancers sat, lolling on the round, deep-pink velvet banquette beneath the crumbling plaster rose and dusty chandelier, which seemed to be hanging by a rather dangerous-looking wire. The others were on the fainting couch next to the floor-to-ceiling windows. Rosa was reclining, one long leg stretched upwards against the frayed curtain, the blue shot-silk fabric faded where it had been bleached by the sun. It seemed to Vita that even when they were supposed to be resting, the dancers were always moving – forever stretching and flexing.

Maxwell, their friend, who looked very smart tonight in immaculate tails, was changing the record on the gramophone. There was a very large crackle as the needle started at the beginning of the next song.

Vita suppressed a yawn. Unlike Nancy, who stayed in bed most of the day, she was an early riser – thanks to the demands of Mr Wild – and now, at coming up to midnight, she felt tired, longing for her bed, rather than a trip to a club. But leaving was impossible. Not yet. Not when Nancy was just getting started.

Vita watched as her friend took a long slurp from the 'coquetele' she was holding: a 75, by the look of it, Vita thought – a lethal gin-and-lemon drink. To be fashionable, they all drank cocktails, with Nancy often leading the charge in ever more heady concoctions, and the 75 was one of her favourites. Vita couldn't even have one without getting head-spins.

'You want some?' Nancy asked, taking a long slug and then holding out the glass. 'It's not that strong, I promise.'

'No thanks,' Vita said, but Nancy was ignoring her. The music suddenly kicked in – an upbeat number, the clarinets and trumpets high above the banjo and bass. The girls all jumped up from the sofa with a collective shout and started dancing. 'Oh, look – look, they're here,' Nancy trilled, flapping her hand towards the open door of the apartment.

Six or so men were filing through the door, squeezing past the people chatting in the small foyer, and Vita recognized them as the Les Folies house band. Her heart did a little skip as she saw Fletch at the back, heaving Bobo's double bass up the last flight of stairs.

'Hold this, darling,' Nancy shouted above the music, pressing the cocktail into Vita's hand, before trotting across the parquet flooring, her arms out wide as she whooped with greeting. She got away with being so brash and loud, Vita thought, because she was American, but it was really who she was – an attention-seeker and fun with it, loving every second of it, as her skirt rode up. She kissed Bobo and then Fletch, who laughed at their effusive welcome.

Vita had only had a few brief conversations with Fletch, the new trumpet player, but she liked his easy confidence as he stood up in the band in the orchestra pit in front of the stage, his trumpet raised towards the balcony. There was something so slick, so modern about him, and exotic, too.

8

She saw him looking bashful as he rubbed Nancy's lipstick from his cheek.

As they all moved towards the drawing room, Nancy trotted back to Vita, dancing to the music. 'Don't look like that,' she scolded Vita.

'Like what?'

'Like you want the floor to swallow you. This is not England – it's Paris. It's totally fine to like men of colour. What do the French call it? *Négrophilie*. A love of all things black.'

'Shhh,' Vita said, worried that someone would hear. Nancy really did have no idea how to be subtle. She wished now that she'd never let slip how she was developing a crush on Fletch.

'Don't be coy, darling. It's so obvious you like him. In fact I dare you to *have a fling* with him.' She threw down the gauntlet, and Vita remembered their dares of old.

Vita pulled a face at her. 'That's not going to happen.'

'Why not?'

'Because . . .'

'It's what you need, Vita. I've told you before, you need to get back on the horse and stop moping after that dreadful Archie Fenwick.'

'I'm not moping.'

'Besides, you know what they say about trumpet players?'

'What?'

'The embouchure makes them good kissers . . . and other things,' Nancy said, raising her eyebrows, her eyes flicking downwards to the crotch of Vita's trousers.

Vita gasped at her bawdy suggestion, but Nancy only

smiled, grabbing the cigarettes and matches from beside the lamp on the table. 'Now, shoo!' she commanded, kneeing Vita in the backside so that she lurched towards the newcomers.

Vita glared at her over her shoulder, annoyed that Nancy was following close behind, with that mischievous grin Vita knew so well plastered over her face.

3

Fletch

Fletch was dressed in a black suit with an open-necked white shirt. He held his felt hat in his hand, along with a brown case.

'Fletch darling, you remember Vita,' Nancy said, waving a lit match between them, then lighting the cigarette between her teeth. 'The one I was telling you about. She's our costume girl,' Nancy added suggestively, blowing out smoke towards the ceiling. 'She's quite the seamstress. She makes bras, and all sorts.'

Nancy had spoken to Fletch about her already? And made her out to be so much lower down the pecking order than the dancers, Vita noted, feeling that all-too-familiar sense of being tethered to Nancy.

'Hey, Vita, nice to see ya again,' Fletch said in a rather charming old-fashioned way. He had an American accent – from the South, Vita guessed – and a disarmingly honest smile. He was probably no older than her, Vita thought, looking at his smooth young skin. He pressed back his oiled hair with his hand.

'So, ladies, what's happenin' here?' he asked.

'Nothing much yet. We were waiting for you. The night's

young,' Nancy trilled, twirling away, the fringing on her dress jumping. She winked at Vita over her shoulder.

'She's quite something, your friend,' Fletch said. He had a very neat thin moustache above his full lips. She had a sudden flash: picturing him shaving in the morning and how he might look half-naked . . .

'Isn't she,' Vita agreed, alarmed at her flight of fancy.

Fletch looked towards the drawing room and started to move. 'I could do with a drink. You want a top-up, Vita?' He nodded to Nancy's nearly-empty glass, which Vita was holding, and she followed him. She liked the way he said her name: *Vida*.

What had she expected, she wondered, in her vague musings about Fletch? He was so different from anyone she'd met before, but once again she found herself warming to his easy charm. Although she couldn't begin to imagine what her mother, Theresa Darton, might say if she could see her now, chatting to this handsome black man.

But Nancy was right. This was Paris and, with the city 'awash with foreigners', as she'd read in the papers – especially Americans, as far as Vita could tell – she'd got used to all manner of skin tones and accents. And she loved the diversity all around her: each new face bringing a different story to the vibrant city. So perhaps it wasn't the colour of Fletch's skin that made her feel flushed and girlish, but because Fletch was a man . . . and a very attractive one, at that.

They walked together through the drawing room, squeezing past the dancers with their windmilling arms and over to the mirrored sideboard, where there was an impressive array of bottles.

'Help yourself,' Solange called as she skipped past in Maxwell's arms, raising her voice over the music. 'We're out of beer. Tomas was making cocktails, but he's gone for some more ice.'

'Ah, shucks,' Fletch said, looking at the bottles. 'It's a little early for absinthe,' he joked, replacing the bottle and choosing another green one. 'Pernod. That'll do. You want some?'

Vita nodded and he pulled an approving face, before taking the last of the ice from the ice-bucket and putting several cubes in two of the cut-glass tumblers on the dented silver tray. Then he tipped in an inch of amber liquid, before picking up the carafe of water and holding out the glass to Vita. 'Say when.'

'That's fine,' she said, watching the liquid turn an opaque yellow as he poured in the water. Fletch handed the glass to her, his fingertip accidentally brushing against hers. She felt her cheeks flushing as he looked into his eyes.

'*Salut*, as they say,' he proposed, once he'd made a drink for himself.

As the liquorice-flavoured drink burnt against her tongue, Vita turned away, flustered as they stood side-by-side for a moment, watching the dancers. She wasn't used to flirting, and this unspoken attraction between them made her feel tongue-tied and bashful.

And then the moment was suddenly gone and Fletch was being pulled onto the dance floor, Collette stealing his hat and using it as a prop to dance with, putting it on and off her head. Vita watched, mulling over what had just happened. She hadn't experienced this tug – this pull of attraction – since Archie, and now she felt flustered and unsure of herself.

She couldn't help thinking back to what Nancy had said. Archie wasn't 'dreadful'. Did Nancy really think that? And was it really so obvious that Vita had been moping over him? Maybe it was. She felt guilty now, as if she were betraying Archie by finding Fletch so attractive, although the notion was utterly ridiculous.

Archie was gone for good. The love of her life was married off, to dull and boring Maud, and he'd never know how much he'd broken her heart. It was so broken still . . . after all this time. Why couldn't she forget him and move on?

Maybe it was because she couldn't help dwelling on the what-ifs. What if Archie had known who she really was? Might things have been different if he'd known that she was so much more than the wild flapper girl his mother had assumed Vita to be? It was too late now, though. Archie was out of her life forever.

So maybe Nancy was right. She *did* need to get the ghost of Archie out of her head. And maybe Fletch was the best way to do so.

4

City of Lights

It was over an hour later before Vita had the chance to talk to Fletch alone again.

'That thing is so loud,' she said, nodding to the huge horn on the gramophone, which was belting out a Scott Joplin rag. Solange was making Maxwell play dance records back-to-back. 'Someone should put a sock in it,' she added – the popular trick that she and Nancy knew for dampening the sound.

'I could do with some air. You want to join me?' Fletch asked, nodding to the window.

Outside on the balcony Vita shivered. Fletch closed the door and the party was muted and her ears had to readjust to the quiet. Above, stars were sprinkled across the black sky, the half-moon bright and yellow. Far below she could hear the clip-clop of a horse on the cobbles. A motorcar honked in the distance.

She leant on the ornate cast-iron balustrade and looked down the narrow street, where the white shutters on most of the buildings were closed now. Across the street the railings were crowded with bicycles, but the neighbourhood was quiet.

'Here, take this,' Fletch said, taking off his jacket and putting it round her shoulders.

'Thanks,' Vita replied, hugging the unfamiliar material around her. It smelt reassuringly manly – of smoke and pomade.

'Come on,' Fletch said, hopping up on the stone wall that separated Solange's balcony and the next-door apartment. 'Let's go see the view.'

'Really? You want to go up there?' Vita asked. Now that the cool air hit her, she was drunker than she realized, and climbing up the stone facade of the building looked rather precarious.

'Sure. This is the only reason Solange got this apartment. Come,' Fletch insisted, his brown-and-white shoe already getting a foothold on the next stone balustrade. He was carrying his trumpet case under one arm and his drink in his hand.

'You're taking that with you?' Vita asked.

'Mabel? I never leave her,' Fletch said, reaching up to put the trumpet safely above him on the flat roof. 'And certainly not in a room full like that. Don't trust any of them.'

Vita glanced through the gap in the curtains and could see Nancy dancing across the parquet floor, her legs kicking out. He had a point.

'Your trumpet has a name?'

'Of course. Now pass me your drink,' he instructed and she did so, amazed at his easy strength as he clambered onto the heavy stone coping, reaching up and putting their drinks out of sight above him. Then he leant back, holding on and stretching out a hand for her, and Vita clambered up on the wall and hung onto the bulky stone. From below, she had a view upwards of Fletch's trim body.

She hoisted herself up, laughing with the effort and glad that she hadn't listened to Nancy, but was still wearing her long flared trousers. Then she reached up and took Fletch's warm hand and he pulled her towards him, their hands still clasped, her body pressed momentarily against his. A long-forgotten flush of sexual desire pulsed through her now, and she remembered the first time she'd ever felt it.

And in her mind vivid images sprang up of her swimming in the lake at Archie's stately home, how their bodies tangled together and then – although she tried hard to banish the memory – how they'd made love in the boathouse, and how her body had responded.

She knew it was wrong then, and she knew it was wrong now, but she seemed powerless to fight these feelings of longing and desire. But was it longing for Archie or desire for Fletch?

'Wow!' she said, breaking away and seeing the view for the first time, as she stepped down from the stone facade onto the flat lead roof. In one direction she could see part of the illuminated sails of the windmill of the Moulin Rouge up in Pigalle; and in the other – way in the distance – the Eiffel Tower, lit with hundreds of lights, dazzling against the night sky. She breathed in, listening to the distant cars and the pulse of the city.

She remembered how she used to go to the roof in London with the girls from the Zip Club. And then there was that other night on the roof: the night she gave herself to Archie Fenwick. *Don't think about him*, she told herself. *Don't.*

Archie Fenwick had used her, and had let her down. That night on the roof? Well, it had all been lies. But even so, with all these memories, she couldn't help feeling that being alone up here with Fletch was intoxicatingly intimate.

'You sure can see why they call it the City of Lights,' Fletch said, coming to her side. 'It's magical, don't you think?'

She smiled, looking out over the city. When she'd thought about Paris before she'd arrived here, Vita had imagined that it would be staid and closed off, but it wasn't like that at all. It was vibrant and teeming with life, and each new moment, like now, felt like a revelation.

5

An American in Paris

They walked over towards the grey chimney breast where there were two low chairs, with a table between them. There was a plant pot with some sort of creeper snaking up the wall, and a battered novel splayed open on the table, with an empty glass next to it. By day, this was clearly a suntrap.

Vita sat down in the chair, hugging Fletch's jacket around her as he put their glasses down on the table. She liked being up here, with the music from the party below them only faint, and the sound of laughter above it.

She picked up the book, turning over the brown paper cover to see the red marbled inner pages. It was an Agatha Christie novel, *The Mysterious Affair at Styles*, and Vita smiled, remembering the tale of the detective, Hercule Poirot. She had given a copy to Nancy, who only took an interest when the writer went missing. There had been a huge manhunt, which had been reported all over the press. Sir Arthur Conan Doyle had given a spirit medium one of Miss Christie's gloves in order to find her, and she'd eventually turned up in a hotel in Harrogate. Nancy, who was a firm believer in clairvoyants, had been convinced it was the glove that had solved the mystery.

'Do you like reading?' Fletch asked.

'I love browsing through bookshops. There's this place – Shakespeare and Company – that I go to. Do you know it?'

Fletch shook his head. 'Books ain't my thing, I'm 'fraid. I guess I'd like to read more, but I tend to sleep in the days. And Mabel takes up my time.'

Vita nodded, realizing how different his life was from hers. How being a musician was more of a life choice than a profession. 'How did you get to be in Paris?' she asked.

'Same as just 'bout everyone else. I fought in the trenches, then couldn't bear to go back home. Not with the way things are there.'

'How do you mean?'

Fletch sighed. 'It's hard for you Europeans to understand. Especially here. But where I come from, being here with you now – a white woman – would get me arrested.'

She felt ashamed that she had felt a frisson of . . . not prejudice, but excitement at his difference.

'I had no idea it was that bad.'

'Oh, it's worse than you can imagine,' he carried on. 'But I like it that in Paris I can walk down the street and people will call me *Monsieur* – not something much worse. And you and I can share the same water fountain, whereas back home I could be slung into jail for that. But here . . . here I can be a musician on my own terms, and Mabel can work her magic and I can earn good money with the band.'

Their eyes met for a long moment and Vita felt her gaze stray to Fletch's full lips, and the memory of Nancy's earlier comment suddenly made her blush. Embarrassed, she nodded towards his case. 'So, will you play something for me?'

'If you like,' he said, opening the case. The bell of the brass trumpet glinted in the moonlight as he pulled it out of the velvet-lined case, licking his lips, his fingertips waggling over the three pistons, pressing them down in quick succession so that they clicked softly. He pressed his lips into the small mouthpiece and played a note, then adjusted the tuning. 'Well, what do you want to hear?'

'Anything – anything at all,' Vita said, watching him.

He smiled, then reached into his case and pulled out a rubber dome.

'What's that?'

'I use it as a mute, but actually it's a plunger for a lavatory,' he said and she laughed. 'I stole it from a hotel.' He started with a jazz tune, using the mute in one hand to change the sound, so that it made a 'whah-a-whah' kind of noise.

'Oh, don't stop,' Vita said, when he pulled the trumpet away from his lips and smiled bashfully at her.

'What else do you wanna hear?'

'Play something you like. Something I haven't heard before. Surprise me.'

Fletch put the mute back in the case, closed his eyes and was silent for a moment, as if waiting for the music to come to him, then he started playing a haunting melody that seemed to soar over the rooftops. It was such a romantic tune – somehow both exuberant and elegant at the same time.

When the final note ended, he still had his eyes closed and there was a dazzling moment. Time was suspended as the music stopped and finally drifted away. Then Fletch lowered the trumpet and grinned at her.

'Oh, goodness,' Vita said, impressed. 'That *is* beautiful. What is it?'

'It's a work in progress by this guy Gershwin. I just got hold of this melody . . .' He played part of it again. There was something so attractive about how Fletch himself admired it. 'He's writing it at the moment – *An American in Paris*, it's called. You know he went and bought all the car horns he could, so that he could replicate the sound of rush hour at the Place de la Concorde.'

'Wow,' she said, wishing he'd play more. 'I could listen to that all day. You're so talented.'

Fletch shrugged. 'Everyone has a talent. You have a knack for sewing, so Nancy was saying . . .'

'It's hardly in the same league.'

'My grandma is a great seamstress, too,' he said, placing Mabel back in the velvet-lined case. 'I could never even attempt any of the things she does.'

He seemed so good, so decent, that Vita felt embarrassed now at how far removed her Top Drawer underwear must be from the patchwork quilts she imagined his grandmother making.

'It's not really a great talent. I help out with the costumes for the girls, but . . . well, I would like to do my own designs.'

'So why don't you?'

And then, because he seemed so honest and because the drink had loosened her tongue, she told Fletch her story – about running away from home and how Nancy had found her in London, and how she'd helped Percy with the costumes for the dancing girls at the Zip Club, and how she'd designed a brassiere. And as she told him, Vita remembered the first

22

bra she'd made for Nancy, and how Nancy had strutted around sticking out her chest, declaring it to be 'the bee's knees'.

And for a while Vita had been borne aloft on Nancy's wave of enthusiasm – getting a contract to make the bras for Nancy's dressmaker, Mrs Clifford-Meade, and even getting her Top Drawer underwear into a department store. She'd been so elated, so sure that she was on to something.

'But, you know, it's over now,' she said. 'It was just a little thing.'

'Why is it over? Sounds to me like you still have a dream,' Fletch said.

'Yes, I suppose I do,' Vita admitted, amazed that Fletch seemed genuinely interested – and that she'd found it so easy to be candid with him. 'But it's hard, you know. There's rent and . . . Nancy and . . .'

She fizzled out. What was her excuse for not doing here in Paris the one thing she'd loved so much in London? Was it that she was annoyed Nancy seemed to have forgotten how much she wanted Vita to succeed? Or was it because she was afraid of doing something on her own, now that her costumier friend Percy wasn't around to help her? Or because, even now, she looked over her shoulder whenever she was walking down the street, as she was sometimes convinced that Clement might be following her.

Fletch's chocolate-brown eyes locked with hers for a long moment, and she felt another tug stirring inside her.

'If you ask me, it sounds like it's time to stop hiding in the shadows, Vita,' he said.

6

The Slow Walk Home

Vita had hoped that walking from the party to their apartment might sober Nancy up, but it seemed to have done quite the reverse. The plan to go to a club had been abandoned after Tomas had returned to Solange's apartment with several more friends, who had come armed with bottles of vodka, gin, cassis and vermouth to make cocktails. They'd all got terribly drunk and merry and the music had blasted all night.

'I told you. Didn't I tell you?' she bellowed, slipping off the kerb and laughing. Vita ducked Nancy's lit cigarette, which she waved haphazardly. 'I *knew* Fletch liked you.'

Vita was annoyed now that she'd told Nancy about Fletch and their time on the roof. He'd let her play Mabel – or try to, at least – but her attempts at getting a tune out of the instrument had only sounded like rude noises, and she'd got the giggles. She'd been so disappointed when Solange had called out from the balcony and demanded that Fletch come inside and play with the band, rather than wake up the whole neighbourhood, and they'd rejoined the party like naughty schoolchildren.

'Why didn't you kiss him, when you got the chance?' Nancy demanded.

'We just talked. And he played. Oh, Nancy, it was so lovely.'

It had been a fun night, and for the first time in ages she had really let her hair down, loving the way Fletch occasionally caught her eye. A short time ago, when everyone had decided to call it a night and started to slink off home, he had kissed her hand, telling her that he hoped they'd see each other again soon.

Now, shortly before dawn, it was chilly and Vita pulled her coat more tightly around her, wishing that Nancy would hurry up, but she was very drunk. Her heels wobbled on the cobbles. There was a faint smell of fish in the air as they passed the *poissonnerie*, its display cabinets scrubbed clean; and they moved on up the street towards the artisan *pâtisserie*, where there was a light in the back kitchen, the chefs already making those little vanilla choux buns that Vita often drooled over in the window.

'And now you'll have men *falling* over you by the dozen,' Nancy said, making another grand sweep of her arm.

'Don't be silly.'

'It's true. It's the rule. You just need one. Once *one* man finds you attractive, then every other one does, too. Like him – I bet he likes you, too.'

Vita noticed a man crossing the road ahead, coming out from the rue de Navarin.

'You like my friend?' Nancy called, but the man tutted and hurried away, his shoes echoing on the cobbles.

'Come on, it's time to get home,' Vita said, rapidly sobering up herself, now that she had to manhandle Nancy before she picked a fight with a stranger. When she was this tight, Nancy could be volatile or, worse, maudlin – and Vita was keen to get her inside and into bed before she caused a scene.

'I should get married, you know. I should have done what my mother said. I could be rich. I *should* be rich,' Nancy slurred as they walked on. She had a habit of stopping and pontificating, and progress was slow. 'I don't like men that much, but you'd think I could find *one* who would do. Especially here,' she continued. 'But it's not so easy. It is for you. Men like you. But not me.'

'That's not true,' Vita said, keen to keep Nancy on track. She tended to do this – spiral off into jealous comparisons, the ultimate goal of which was to make Vita acquiesce and declare undying loyalty. 'Anyway, shouldn't you marry for love?'

'Pah! Rubbish,' Nancy said. 'Nobody marries for love any more. That's the biggest mistake you could make.'

Vita put her arm firmly round Nancy's shoulder and they headed towards the leafy avenue Trudaine, with Nancy all the while lamenting her single life and Solange's wonderful apartment. Vita let it wash over her as she looked at the shut-up restaurants, their wicker chairs upended on the tables, the ornate lamp posts lighting the empty pavement. A milk cart clanked by, the horses' hooves clopping on the cobbles.

Soon they arrived in the Square d'Anvers. Usually, school-children played here and there was a little street market on a Friday, where Vita often bought discounted flowers at the end of the day. Now a fox crossed the misty patch of lawn.

They walked along the side of the square, past Le Grand Comptoir, the lively oyster restaurant they sometimes went to when Nancy got her pay cheque from Les Folies. Ahead, in the distance, way up on the hill, the white domes of Sacré-Coeur basilica glowed sepulchrally in the moonlight.

Finally they were on the boulevard de Rochechouart, which was usually crowded, but now it was empty as they carried on past Anvers, their local metropolitan station, with its fancy gold-and-green Art Nouveau signage. They usually walked everywhere, but Vita adored occasionally riding on the metro, the novelty of it not yet having worn off. She was very proud that she'd mastered the metro map all by herself and was fascinated by the names of the stops on the Nord–Sud line from Montmartre to Montparnasse.

'We should go to a club,' Nancy said, suddenly clocking where they were. 'Why are we going home? I don't want to go home. Let's go party.'

'No, come on.' Vita pulled her across the road, past the black wooden frontage of Sympa, the *chemiserie* on the corner, and up the steep cobbles to their apartment building on the rue d'Orsel.

Out of breath now, Vita took the key out of her bag and quietly opened the faded blue doorway of their building.

'Shhh,' she warned Nancy, who lolled against the wooden frame. 'Don't wake up Madame Vertbois.'

7

Madame Vertbois

Vita poked her head around the doorway of their apartment building and looked past the office to where the stone staircase began. Then, pulling Nancy inside and closing the door as quietly as she could, she glanced upwards: the black ironwork of the stairs wound like a Fibonacci coil into the darkness. Hopefully they had time to make it to the stairs.

But it was too late. The light clicked on in the office and Vita winced as the brown wooden door clattered open and the ferocious concierge stood in the office doorway.

Madame Vertbois was wearing her usual shapeless black dress, a crocheted shawl around her shoulders, a brown scarf tied over her hair. She'd been a teacher a long time ago and, much to Nancy's disapproval, Vita came to her office twice a week to practise her conversational French, in an attempt to soften the cold-hearted old woman. Unlike Nancy, Vita was rather in love with the French language and hadn't got over her delight at the novelty of picking up little phrases and idioms. Over the last few months Madame Vertbois had gradually cracked, worn down by Vita's enthusiasm, and they had developed a relationship of sorts, so she couldn't risk Nancy blowing it now. They relied on Madame Vertbois to let the various neighbours in to their apartment to walk Mr Wild occasionally, when they were both at the club.

There was an electric fire in the office and now the cat, which had been sleeping in front of it, came to the old woman's feet, its back arching. Vita was reminded of Mrs Beck's cat, Casper, in the boarding house she'd shared with the girls from the club, and with Percy, in London. Casper had had a soft spot for Vita, but this cat let out a low hiss.

'*Bonjour*, Madame,' Vita said, reverentially.

'What time do you call this?' Madame Vertbois snapped in French, her face puckered into a disapproving scowl. Her wrinkled neck sagged beneath a gold crucifix. 'It's very late,' she added pointedly. '*Très tard.*' She rolled her 'r' for effect.

She looked Vita up and down and then stared at Nancy, pushing her glasses up her nose to get a better look. Vita dug her elbow into Nancy's ribs, to make her behave.

'I heard you. All the way down the street.'

'Not us,' Vita lied, in her best French. 'We just came from a cab. There are lots of people out tonight.'

'*Bad* people,' Nancy added in English.

Madame's eyes narrowed and she flicked her chin.

'Do not wake anyone up.'

'We won't. Goodnight.'

'*Bonne nuit, chérie*,' Nancy said in a loud stage whisper.

'Shhh,' Vita cautioned, manhandling her from behind.

'Shhh,' Nancy copied her, giggling.

'I mean it,' Vita said. 'Don't antagonize her. She'll throw us out.'

'She won't throw you out. She likes you. You're her pet.'

Vita hurried Nancy up the stone stairs, knowing the

electric lights wouldn't be on for long and that they needed to make it to the fifth floor. By the time they got to their corridor, Nancy was heavy on her arm. Vita could hear Mr Wild barking his usual welcome.

'I hate this place,' Nancy moaned. 'It's so poky. And it smells of boiled beans.'

'It's perfectly fine. And we're hardly ever here. We're out in Paris,' Vita reminded her. 'We only need a small place.' She was keen to get Nancy through the door and inside.

She fumbled with the key, then groped in the dark for the switch and the light flickered into life. She pulled Nancy inside, before slumping back against the door, relieved they were home. Mr Wild jumped up and down and ran in circles, and Nancy picked him up.

'Oh, my baby, my baby.' She nuzzled the dog, then set him down and he jumped up at Vita. She tickled the white dog, but didn't pick him up. She could only really show affection to him when Nancy wasn't around, otherwise she got jealous of the fact that Mr Wild liked Vita best. But that was probably because Vita was the one who remembered to feed him and give him water, not to mention the fact that she was always the one to walk him in the mornings. Mr Wild, who had clearly been waiting anxiously for them, curled up in his little bed and let out a sweet, contented sigh.

Vita kicked off her shoes, putting the keys on the small half-table in the hall, but Nancy swayed uncertainly, looking at her reflection in the silver mirror above it, as if she didn't recognize herself.

'Mr Wild doesn't love me any more,' she said.

'He does. He's just tired. Look at him,' Vita said, nodding

affectionately at the dog. 'It's way past his bedtime,' she added pointedly.

'Do you love me?' Nancy asked, her voice plaintive. In the light, Vita could see that her eyes were bloodshot, her lipstick smeared. No wonder Madame Vertbois had given them such disapproving looks.

'Of course I do,' Vita said, recognizing the onset of the maudlin stage.

'You don't love me enough. Not like I want you to love me.'

Vita felt her cheeks flushing. She'd once got absolutely blotto with Nancy in a bath, and the details of the drunken physical intimacy that had ensued still shocked her. She had always been aware that Nancy wanted more from her. She'd even told Vita, when they'd left London, that she'd been in love with her for a while. She was pretty sure that Nancy's ridiculous infatuation was over, but sometimes – like now – she felt as if she were on quicksand, unsure of what it was that Nancy really wanted from her.

'Kiss me,' Nancy slurred, closing her eyes and trying to grab Vita. 'I want to be kissed. I had your first kiss, and now you owe me.'

'You need to sleep,' Vita said, embarrassed and ducking away.

'Oh, I'm going to be—' Nancy said, lurching forward, and Vita grabbed the furry stem of the potted palm, yanking it from its large china pot, which she thrust below Nancy, just in time.

'Do you have to drink so much?' Vita asked, rubbing Nancy's back as she wretched. She hated Nancy being in this state. She looked for a place to put the palm down, before the dry soil scattered all over the floor. She laid it gently on the hallstand.

'Pass me a cigarette,' Nancy said when she'd finished, straightening up and hiccupping. She smoothed down her short hair, shaking her head haughtily, as if she'd been doing something far more glamorous than being sick.

'You need water,' Vita said, heading for the tap, but knowing the pipes would clank loudly at this time of the morning.

'Cigarette,' Nancy insisted. 'And that. The *eau de vie*,' she insisted, jabbing her finger towards the clear bottle of pear brandy on the tiny kitchen table. She lurched after Vita to the small kitchenette and grabbed the bottle, before Vita could grab it first, taking a swig and wincing.

'Please,' Vita begged. 'Stop. You're going to make yourself even more ill.'

'You're not my mother,' Nancy said, stabbing the bottle in Vita's direction. 'Stop being bossy.'

'I'm trying to help you.'

'Well, you're not. I'm bored of you. I'm going out,' Nancy declared, spinning on her heel and staggering back towards the door, bottle in hand.

'You can't. It's too late. Madame Vertbois will have a fit.' She raced to intercept Nancy before she reached the door. 'No, Nancy. No,' she said, sternly, barring the way. 'Not tonight. Come to bed. I'll sleep with you.'

Nancy's bloodshot eyes looked defiantly into hers and then the fight seemed to drain out of her.

'Don't leave me.'

'I'm not going to leave you.'

'Everyone leaves me.'

'Come on,' Vita said, gently, taking the bottle and then half-carrying Nancy into the bedroom, where she flopped face-first diagonally across the bed. Vita slipped off her shoes and pulled the part of the eiderdown that was visible across her friend, then she went back to the hall and cleared out the china plant pot and tipped away the brandy in the sink, for good measure.

She sighed, exhaustion hitting her – not just from the late night, but because she was so tired of being constantly jolted emotionally one way by her friend and then the other. But what could she do? She was stuck with Nancy, and *someone* had to look after her when she behaved so recklessly.

She checked on Nancy one last time, then headed for her own tiny box room, which really only had room for a single bed and a chair. She lay on her back, knowing that she should get up and close the shutters, now that it was getting light, but instead she gazed through the glass at the small patch of pale-pink sky, remembering Fletch's soft trumpet playing. And, as she fell asleep, she wondered what his hands would feel like on her body.

8

The Deathbed

From the other side of the tall mahogany bed, Edith Darton watched her mother-in-law, Theresa, wringing the embroidered white handkerchief in her hands, twisting it one way and the next.

'It's just I wondered if you knew where she is? I think Darius would so want Anna to be here,' she whispered in her cowed, birdlike voice. 'Do you know? Surely you must know?'

'No,' Edith said, 'I wish I did . . . truly. I would like to help, Theresa – so much.'

Edith had a very good idea where Vita was, of course. She'd given Vita her ticket to Paris – although she'd told Clement that Vita had stolen it from her. He'd been there to look for his sister twice, but so far he hadn't managed to track her down, and Edith was glad. She didn't want Vita coming back to Darton and ruining everything she'd built up here. Including her relationship with Darius Darton.

In the last words he'd uttered just over a week ago, his mouth lolling from the second stroke he'd suffered, he'd told Edith that she was more of a daughter to him than Anna had ever been. Well, that's how Clement had interpreted the slurred words, and Edith had considered it a moment of absolute triumph.

Now she leant over her father-in-law's bed, masking her revulsion as she covered his cold hand with her own, noticing the purple patches that sprouted on his crinkled skin like mould. He was nearing death; she could sense it, and she longed for the release for him – and for her. Because without him, her ambitious plans with Clement for the Darton Mills could become a reality. And without Anna, or Vita, as Edith still thought of her ex-friend, then the business – everything – would go straight to her husband, and, of course, to her.

Feigning anxiety, she looked across the bed to Theresa.

'Should I fetch Clement from the mill?' she whispered and her mother-in-law nodded, her hand fluttering to her mouth.

'I don't think it'll be long. I just wish Anna would come home.' Theresa's eyes filled with tears. 'Why must she stay away?'

'It's dreadful, I know,' Edith nodded. 'How she could be so thoughtless at a time like this . . .'

She stood and walked over now and gently squeezed Theresa's hand, thinking that her mother-in-law was like a gramophone record with a scratch, her mind always jumping back to Anna. Edith was sick of it. And so she could totally understand why Clement was so incensed with his sister. He'd done everything for his family – and yet they only seemed to want their daughter.

If Edith had her way, though, Anna would never come home. And *should* never come home. Not after she'd almost been responsible for Clement being permanently scarred, and very nearly paralysed for life. Clement had told her all about how his unruly little sister had never toed the line, had never respected him or his father. Which is why Anna had run away to London, although it baffled him how she'd ever survived there.

Edith knew exactly how Anna Darton had survived in London. She'd reinvented herself as Vita Casey and had lied and cheated her way into the Zip Club. Which is where she'd stolen Nancy, Edith's best friend.

And then, if that wasn't bad enough, it had been Vita whom Nancy had taken to all the parties – Vita who'd got all the attention. And Edith had *known* . . . she'd known all along that the Vita girl was a fraud, an imposter. She'd been able to smell it, right away. She couldn't even dance! But everyone else had thought she was wonderful. Vita with her sassy outfits and crazy sense of style, thanks to Percy giving her so many free costumes. She'd just taken, taken, taken, with no concept of how hard it had been for the rest of them.

Downstairs, glad to be away from the vigil in the stuffy bedroom, Edith examined herself in the mirror, admiring her sleek blonde hair and the expensive black dress that Clement had brought her back from his last trip to London. She admired the collar and how it showed off her pale neck. With any luck, she'd get the Darton pearls before too long, and then the look really would be complete.

She had a sense that her life was on track at last – the track it should have been on all those years ago, when she'd come out as a debutante in London with Nancy. Back then, her world had been full of promise and she'd been convinced she was going to marry well and make her parents proud.

But that was before her affair with the Askew chap had heaped shame on her family and she'd been cut off. At the time she'd been convinced that she and Quentin were in love, but she'd soon learnt the bitter pain of empty promises. Not enough, however, not to make the same mistake again, because – much to her frustration – it had been the same with Jack Connelly, the proprietor of the Zip Club. He'd promised her the earth and, if not that, that he'd certainly leave his wife, but that had never happened, either.

So when Clement had turned up unexpectedly in London, asking after his sister, Edith had been at a rather low ebb. After the police raid, the Zip Club had folded, Jack Connelly had vanished whilst the police looked into the books, and the girls scattered around the country. Edith, sorely regretting giving her train ticket to Vita, was penniless and pounding the West End pavements looking for a job as a chorus girl, when Clement knocked on the door of her apartment, explaining that it had taken a while to find her. And whilst her instinct had told her firmly never to trust a man again, something about Clement's obvious attraction to her had been irresistible.

The girls at the club had always been so soppy and romantic; and Edith, who seemed to find only unattainable men attractive, had panicked at the notion of a straightforward romance. She knew that girly gushiness wasn't her forte, but Clement hadn't seemed to want that. And so, for once, she'd found herself playing hard-to-get, which had worked surprisingly well, because after an indecently short time Clement had proposed, along with a prize that was far more attractive than the opal ring he had given her: a promise to

37

take her away from the cut and thrust of London to a new life.

Of course he hadn't realized the enormity of the lifeline he'd offered, and Edith had kept up the narrative that she'd been doing *him* a favour. But for once in her life, a man had been true to his word, and she'd married Clement at Marylebone registry office, with two strangers for witnesses. And then he'd brought her home here to Lancashire, showing her off as if she were *his* prize.

And now she'd won. She was married. She was a *wife*. She'd had great satisfaction in writing to her family to gloat about what a good match she'd made for herself, without their help. Her mother had even invited her for lunch in Surrey next month, an olive branch that Edith considered to be a real victory.

She stroked Victor, the kitten Clement had given her as a present, for a moment, knowing that Theresa would be horrified that he was inside. He'd already had three of her new canaries and had seen off the dogs. Edith opened the door that led to the conservatory a crack, letting the large tabby kitten through. Victor liked to paw Theresa's silk sofa and eye the birds in the aviary; and if she didn't open the door, he'd start mewing loudly and then that dreadful woman, Martha, would be up the stairs to complain.

Now Edith picked up the heavy Bakelite telephone in the hall and was put through to the mill office. She could hear the clank of the machines in the background as Clement said: 'Great news,' and she could hear the jubilation in his voice. 'Another Top Drawer order has come through.'

Edith clenched her fist in a moment of triumph.

'That's marvellous. Didn't I tell you?' she asked, knowing it was too much, knowing that her husband didn't like being asked for the affirmation she craved.

He might never say it, but there was no denying that their recent success was due to Edith's cleverness. When she'd told him all about Vita's designs and explained how she'd got an order for Vita's Top Drawer underwear – thanks largely to the girls' presentation and, most importantly, to Edith closing the deal – Clement had come with her to meet Lance Kenton at Withshaw and Taylor, the department store in London. Mr Kenton, impressed by Edith's vision and Clement's clear knowledge of the textiles trade, had agreed on an even larger order and a timeline for the brassieres. Edith had no trouble convincing Mr Kenton that she had been the one in charge all along.

Those first bras they had made for W&T had been a huge hit, and this year the orders had got so large that they'd started manufacturing them full-time at the mill. Edith had convinced Clement that this new direction would save their business, when so much of their textile trade was being lost to competitors abroad. Malcolm Arkwright, who had shifted his business out to India, had decimated the mill workers' communities on the other side of the valley. And the same thing would happen to the Darton workers unless they found a new niche – a new direction for their business. Fortunately, with Darius Darton ailing and out of the way, Clement had really started to see things from her point of view.

And I was right, Edith thought, allowing herself a satisfied smile. Now that Top Drawer was taking off in London and in Manchester, too, the underwear business was well on the way to making them rich. So what if it had been Vita's designs that had got them to this point? Without Edith's vision and determination, this venture would never have become a reality.

'How's Father?' Clement asked.

'Oh, fine . . . well, the same,' she said. 'I was missing you, that's all.'

Edith heard her husband's voice soften. 'Should I come?'

'No. No . . . it's more important that you stay there,' she said. She didn't tell him that his mother had been asking after Clement's sister. No. Edith liked to control the flow of information, and it was more important to make herself indispensable here.

She thought wryly of Vita now, missing her father's passing. She might be in Europe having fun with Nancy – a fact that still made Edith occasionally smart with jealousy – but Edith knew that being here was the better option.

No, Vita might be living a carefree life, but soon Edith would be in charge of Darton Hall and instrumental in the future of the business – the business opportunity that Vita was too stupid and hedonistic to protect. Yes, she thought, whatever Vita was doing now, good riddance to her.

9

La Carte Postale

Click-clunk. Vita pushed down the shutter on the black box camera, satisfied she'd captured the famous twin towers of Notre-Dame cathedral in the viewfinder. She let the camera hang on its long leather strap around her neck and pulled down her sunglasses from where they were wedged over the polka-dot silk scarf in her hair.

'Mr Wild, don't go too far,' she called out to the dog, which was sniffing around a bench. He liked being off the lead in wide spaces like this and, hoping that he wouldn't run off, she looked up at the wonderful cathedral again, taking in the magnificent stonemasonry, the line of carved saints above the sculpted door arches. One day she'd climb up one of the towers to see the view. She was a big fan of Victor Hugo and had just read *The Hunchback of Notre-Dame* for the second time, the tragic story of Quasimodo and Esmeralda capturing her imagination even more the second time round. And here she was: staring at the very tower where Quasimodo had finally pushed Frollo to his death.

She turned now to look out at the Seine beside her. The river sparkled in the bright sunlight, a thin barge sliding beneath the bridge, where she could see three men sitting on the far bank chatting, their fishing rods connected to long lines leading into the water. One man stood, reeling in a wriggling fish, its iridescent skin flashing in the sunlight, then unhooking it and throwing it into the bucket. She and Nancy ate those little goujons sometimes at the café, coated in flour and deep-fried, and her stomach gave an involuntary growl of hunger.

She lined up the view of the fishermen in the box camera and pressed the shutter. Perhaps it was because her new connection to Fletch continued to make her feel womanly and sensual, or maybe it was that spring was in the air, but she felt the sense of a new beginning – as if she were a bud on one of the trees, bursting into bloom. She was aware, too, of a creative buzz inside her: a desire to *do* something, and taking photographs felt like a start.

It had been two weeks since Solange's party, and she'd been to several parties and nights out at Bricktop's when Fletch had been there. They hadn't managed to be alone together much, but there was an ever-growing closeness between them, and now she looked forward to going to Les Folies Bergère in the evenings just to see him. Yesterday he'd given her a posy of spring flowers that he told her he'd collected in the park next to where he lived. He said he'd show her it someday, and she'd replied that she'd like that.

She called Mr Wild now, and he came obediently. He trotted beside her on his lead as she walked over to the wide square in front of the cathedral, where a man in a red beret was playing a dance tune that she recognized on the accordion. Two old women sat on a bench crocheting with fine yellow wool, and a young artist arranged some rather good charcoal sketches of the Paris landmarks against the wall, the one of Notre-Dame behind him catching Vita's eye. But when he gave her a hopeful look, she shrugged and shook her head sadly. She had no money for such frivolities.

In fact she only had five francs and a few centimes to her name – apart from the banker's draft Archie had given her, which was folded up in her sewing box. She'd never cashed it; after what he'd done, she never would, but she remembered now how – despite everything – he'd believed in her and in her vision for Top Drawer.

As had dear Percy. He'd been the first person to believe in her dreams and had helped make them a reality. He'd been such a true friend, and it still hurt terribly that Clement had almost ruined him . . . all to get at her.

Clement. Ugh! How the thought of her unhinged, dangerous brother made Vita shudder to her core. Even now.

When he'd found her at the Zip Club, she'd run away from him in London so fast, grabbing the lifeline Edith had offered her – the ticket to Paris with Nancy – that she'd hardly had time to process the shock of seeing him again. It had taken months for the truth to sink in: Clement wasn't dead.

He wasn't dead.

When she'd locked him in a stable with Dante, her horse, she thought her brother had been kicked to death. And now Vita didn't know whether to be happy that she wasn't a murderess, or terrified that her brother was still alive. Because, alive, Clement would never give up until he'd destroyed her. She knew that. He'd told her as much.

She remembered the last time she'd seen him, his pale, angry face blazing with hatred and with a bigger, meaner burning desire to make her pay for the injuries he'd suffered. But Clement was in England, she reminded herself – miles away, with the English Channel between them. He had no way of finding out where she was; and even if he did come looking for her, he'd never find her here.

Now she took the coins from the pocket in her skirt and went over to the stand of postcards by the kiosk, then plucked one out, paying for it. She knew the address of Percy's studio in Soho and hoped he'd still be there. But it was a risk. Clement knew perfectly well where Percy's workshop was, too, and might somehow intercept her postcard.

Or maybe not. Maybe, just maybe, Nancy was right and Vita was being unnecessarily paranoid. Clement must surely have got tired of looking for her by now. Mustn't he?

She decided it was worth taking a chance. Percy was the only one who understood how close she'd come to making a success of Top Drawer, and perhaps he could help her resurrect her dreams now. She had so many questions churning over and over in her mind: did Percy have a copy of the prototype bra they'd created together – the one she'd given, along with all the plans for the business, to Edith? Was it really too late to try to contact W&T, the department store that had given her an order? Might she be able to go back to them and see if she could still find a way to make it work?

She'd often thought about that moment: swapping her plans and designs for Edith's passport, trying to puzzle out what had been going through Edith's mind. Had it been an act of friendship? Because, if so, Vita was grateful. Or had Edith genuinely wanted to do something with the business herself? And what if she had?

'*Edith?* Don't be ridiculous. How could she?' Nancy had said more than once. 'She'd need more designs, and she really doesn't have what it takes. No, she was just doing you a favour. And she didn't have the bottle to come to Paris – that's all. You know what a disaster she is with men; she'll still be hankering after that awful Connelly man.'

She was probably right, but one thing was certain, Vita mused now: she couldn't wait for another year to slip through her fingers. However, it was so long since she'd contacted Percy, and she felt a pang of genuine guilt.

Then she remembered his kind face, and his mews studio behind Covent Garden where she'd been so happy. Sitting on the low stone bench, with Mr Wild jumping up beside her, she turned over the postcard and wrote:

> *Dearest Percy,*
>
> *Alive and well. Want to start Top Drawer again, but need your help? We're where you predicted we'd be: FB. Write to me there.*
>
> *I miss you. x*

10

The Fancy Car

After posting the card, Vita set off with Mr Wild along the rue de la Cité, crossing the river and heading south. She watched waiters laying out the crisp white tablecloths on café tables below the awnings, and a boy riding a bicycle with a huge basket on the front filled with flowers.

She loved walking around Paris like this, looking longingly in through the windows of the elegant apartments, her imagination running away with her about the lives of the inhabitants.

On the corner, she crossed in front of a very fancy white car, with a chauffeur sitting in the front in a white peaked cap. It probably belonged to some impossibly glamorous woman from one of the grand apartments. Perhaps she was getting ready right now for a day of shopping. But she wouldn't be window-shopping wistfully – *faisant du lèche-vitrines*, which amusingly, Vita thought, meant 'licking the windows'. No, the grand *madame* would actually be shopping on those great boulevards. Or taking an appointment with one of the glamorous designers that Vita read about in the magazines. Oh, how wonderful *that* would be.

Or maybe the car belonged to a foreigner – one of the rich Europeans who came to Paris to be seen. Nancy said that amongst 'that' set, the women came to buy clothes and get a French maid, and the men came for the brothels and to buy art, but Vita always sensed a little jealousy in her scorn. She sometimes wondered if she'd held Nancy back from being part of that set herself. Because perhaps, if Nancy hadn't needed to be responsible for Vita and look after her, she would now be married to someone rich. Perhaps she might be living a life where *she* was the one buying couture clothes and bossing a maid around.

But instead they were both poor and making the best of it. After all, it was a common thread of conversation amongst the people she and Nancy talked to, in the cafés around Montmartre and the Rive Gauche, that if you were going to be poor, then Paris was *the* place to be so, as if there were some kind of badge of honour in going hungry.

Vita always agreed with such conversations, not pointing out that Nancy hardly qualified as a starving artist. She had a sought-after dancing job and she wasn't really poor – not in the way Vita herself was. Nancy was just careless with money, and every penny she earnt went on partying, something that Goldie – her lawyer, Larry Goldblum – was becoming increasingly cross about.

Vita herself asked for very little and survived on almost nothing, but she was secretly so bored of scrimping and saving and trying so hard to be invisible. It was easy for Nancy to see the glamour in being poor, but Vita had so much less than she did, and sometimes felt she was hanging on by a thread.

And now, alone and free to let her imagination soar, Vita wondered what it might be like to live *properly*, with real money – her *own* money – here in Paris and not beholden to someone else, as she was to Nancy.

What would it be like to have her *own* home filled with beautiful things: paintings and furniture and ornaments? She imagined herself in a light-filled drawing room, and how it might feel like she'd really arrived. And she could picture it: she *could* see herself as a person of consequence, her life meaningful and fulfilled. But as soon as she conjured up the image, it blurred and vanished, like smoke. The reality of who she was, and how she was living, was so very far from that.

But she so wanted to *be* someone. Someone in her own right. Talking to Fletch had reminded her of how ambitious she had once been, and she'd started to dream again. She sighed, wondering if these thoughts were more of a hindrance than a help, pondering on whether contacting Percy was a step in the right direction or asking for trouble.

Now she glanced idly up at the window of a room jutting out to the side of the corner building. It was clearly a drawing room in a fancy apartment, and had long windows that faced onto the street in both directions. From her vantage point on the street, her attention was caught by two figures near the window: two men. She couldn't see them clearly, but one man – the taller one – leant in to embrace the other. The taller man kissed the shorter one on the cheek, then held his face, and Vita felt as if she were spying on a very intimate moment. Then the shorter man pulled away and yanked the curtain across the window, and she suspected that he was admonishing the taller man for kissing him in full view of the street.

Vita felt a frisson of shock, remembering how she'd once walked in on Percy and his friend Edward and had realized they were lovers. Were those two strangers in the window lovers, too? Nothing shocked her these days, and certainly not the idea of men being together. But she saw the curtain twitch and felt as if she were being watched.

Not wanting to be caught out as a voyeur, she called out to Mr Wild and, taking him by the lead, hurried across the street.

11

Shakespeare and Company

Shakespeare and Company was already busy, with a man and a woman browsing the wooden crates of books outside. In certain circles this was a place to be seen, and Vita could tell they were wondering who she might be. She tied Mr Wild's lead to the lamp post on the pavement and told him to be good, and the couple smiled at the little white dog.

The bell above the door chimed pleasingly as Vita made her way inside, the smell of bound books and dusty air lending a magic to the space. Dust motes swirled in the shafts of golden light coming through the window, illuminating the floor-to-ceiling shelves crammed tightly with books.

Sylvia Beach, the proprietress, whom Vita had seen here before, was halfway up one of the tall triangular wooden ladders, adding books to the top shelves. Like so many gamine women in Paris, Sylvia was slim and trim and wearing a short skirt and jacket over a white shirt with a large turned-down collar. A flouncy brown silk bow was tied at her throat, and although Vita liked the look, she was reminded of a schoolgirl dressed up as a librarian.

Sylvia glanced over her shoulder and smiled down at Vita, before calling out, '*Bonjour.*'

Vita loitered by the table, running her fingers over the spines of the books, remembering how Archie had confided in her about his dreams of writing a novel. She wondered whether he would achieve his dream, now that he was married to the awful Maud. She thought about how they'd gone boating on the Serpentine and had bumped into one of his friends, and how Archie had confided that he longed to reinvent himself. *Don't think about it*, she told herself. *Don't think about him. Think about Fletch . . . about Paris. Not Archie.*

Soon Vita was absorbed in her browsing, each book a fresh delight. There were so many wonderful stories, so many worlds to escape to, but her attention was caught by the tinkle of the shop bell and she looked up to see a dark-haired man coming through the shop. As his eyes met hers, he smiled and lifted his hat. She noticed that he had a short, stubby pencil tucked behind his ear.

Vita dropped her gaze to the book, her cheeks flushing, but couldn't read any of the words, embarrassed that the man had seen her staring at him. Now she walked slowly, pretending to read, until she was hidden by a shelf. She positioned herself so that she could look through it, and saw the man's face light up in a smile.

'Sylvia,' the man said, kissing the proprietress, now that she'd descended from the ladder. He was American – or at least American by way of Dublin, judging from his accent.

'Paul, you old rascal,' Sylvia said affectionately, holding on to his shoulder. 'You back for a while?'

'No. It's only a flying visit. I'm going out to the country-side later this week.'

'You keeping out of trouble?'

'Just about,' he said, smiling, and Vita saw Sylvia's eyes crinkle at the corner.

'That looks like the end of a shiner to me,' she said, holding the man's face and turning it to the light.

'What can I say? My boxing career is not taking off,' he joked, and Sylvia laughed.

'Did you read *Ulysses* yet?' she demanded.

'I confess I haven't. Too busy.'

'No such thing. Anyone who is anyone has read it by now.'

'I know, I know,' Paul said, with an apologetic shrug, and Vita smiled to herself. The bell on the door went again and Sylvia went to greet a pair of women, both dressed in suits – right down to the waistcoat and watches. And now Vita's heart beat a little faster, when the man – Paul – looked directly at the shelves and his eyes met hers, and she realized that he knew she'd been watching him the whole time. His face lit up in a big grin.

She looked down studiously at the book as he approached.

'She always tells me off for not reading that damned book,' he said in a stage whisper. He had blue eyes – as blue and clear as the sea – and brown curly hair. He was small and wiry, probably no taller than her. She noticed a gold signet ring on his little finger and wondered if he had money. But then she saw that his tweed suit was fraying at the cuffs. An artist then. Or maybe a writer. Probably a writer, with that pencil behind his ear, she concluded.

'What's *Ulysses*?' she asked, amused. That's what she loved so much about Paris: the way it was so easy to strike up a conversation with a stranger.

'Oh . . . Sylvia published it for her author friend, Mr Joyce,' he said, coming closer to her side of the shelf. He lowered his voice again, putting his hat in front of his mouth, confidentially. 'He's usually around here somewhere. You can't miss him. He looks about ninety and wears dirty sneakers. His book has been quite the sensation, but between you and me, I can't make head or tail of it.'

Vita laughed, liking Paul's honesty.

'You come here often?' he asked.

'Yes,' she said.

'Me too. Great for watching people, I find,' he said, teasingly. She knew that he was referring to her watching him and she blushed. 'But anyone who loves books like I do is a friend of mine.' He grinned broadly. 'I say, why don't I take you for lunch?'

'It's not lunchtime,' Vita said, thrown by this sudden invitation.

'It will be soon. If we stroll down to La Coupole, it'll take half an hour and that'll be perfect timing,' he said, looking at his watch.

'But . . .'

'But what?'

'We're strangers. You don't even know my name,' she said, with an amused laugh.

'But I will, any second now.' In two strides he was back in the centre of the room, plucking a book off the table.

'Sylvia, I have a customer,' he said. 'She heard us talking

and has been longing to read this, so I'm going to buy her a copy.'

'Really, there's no need,' Vita said, following him.

'I insist, Miss . . .'

'Casey. Vita Casey.'

Paul reached into his pocket, but was out of money. 'Put it on my tab,' he said and Sylvia tutted at his audacity, before putting the book in a paper bag, her eyes dancing with amusement as she handed it to Vita.

'Thank you,' Vita said. Then, awkwardly, she thanked Paul, too. 'I've got to go,' she said, pointing to the door. 'I have to get back to my friend.'

He nodded and saluted to her and she turned back to smile at him, expecting him to say something, but he didn't and she left the shop.

Outside, cheered, but also perplexed by the encounter, she untied Mr Wild and set off down the street, remembering only now that she'd been planning on buying Fletch a book. But it was too late to go back and she set off at a quick pace, feeling guilty for leaving Nancy alone for so long without any food, when she'd meant to return hours ago with croissants. What was she even thinking of – talking to a man who was clearly another writer. She didn't need another one of those in her life. Not after Archie.

'I'm Paul Kilkenny by the way.'

She turned to find that the man had followed her. Couldn't he take a hint? Hadn't she already made it clear that she was on her way somewhere else? But now she felt obliged, because he'd given her a book. 'I see. Well, thank you for the book, Mr Kilkenny.'

'Paul, please. Everyone calls me Paul.'

Mr Wild barked and jumped up excitedly, and Paul crouched down to pet the little dog, which licked his hands. 'Hey, fella,' Paul said, laughing as Mr Wild rolled over onto his back to have his tummy tickled. Vita looked on, amused. This Mr Kilkenny seemed to have a knack of charming everyone – even dogs.

'Come on, Mr Wild,' she said, yanking at the lead and setting off again, but Paul Kilkenny followed her, matching her steps.

'Are you following me?' she asked, turning round to face him. He raised his eyebrows and put his hands out in a boyish gesture that reminded her of a silent-movie actor. He grinned widely and shrugged.

'It's just that you're going in the right direction for lunch.'

She gave him an amused look. She'd already turned down his invitation, but he was clearly a man who didn't take no for an answer.

'I hate dining alone. You'd be doing me a favour. Anyway, how harmful can I be? They say that dogs are great judges of character – and yours likes me. So how about it, Vita?'

12

Le Jardin du Luxembourg

Vita was very aware of Nancy's word of caution that there was
no such thing as a free lunch, but she didn't know how to turn
down Mr Kilkenny – or Paul, as he insisted she call him – and
he seemed so happy to be falling into step next to her.

'What have you been taking pictures of?' he asked,
nodding at the camera on the leather strap that hung across
her body, like a satchel.

'Things that intrigue me. Although everywhere you look
in this city there's a photograph opportunity.'

'You're not wrong there. Paris in the spring has to be one
of the finest places on earth. Makes you feel good to be alive,
doesn't it?' he said, taking a deep breath in, before swinging
around one of the wrought-iron lamp posts, with his arm
stretched out.

Vita smiled. 'It does.' She sneaked a sidelong glance at
him, intrigued at this irrepressible young man. He seemed at
once very boyish and yet also wise. She was dying to know
how he'd come by his black eye, but maybe he really was
training as a boxer.

The large white motorcar she'd seen earlier had moved
now to the other end of the street, and Vita watched as the

chauffeur got out. She looked up at the large building, wondering who would emerge.

'I saw that car earlier,' she said. 'It's quite something.'

'How about that?' Paul sighed longingly, following her gaze to the car and putting his hands in his pockets. 'You like it?'

'I do, although . . .' She paused, embarrassed at appearing too materialistic. She thought about her earlier musings on wealth and how she could never share them with someone like Paul. And now, thinking about it, maybe he was a good reminder of the better, more noble path that she'd taken in life.

'It's just, I was thinking . . . Much as I would love to have all of that – all the trappings of wealth, a car, a fancy house – I think rich people are,' she thought of her father, of Archie and of the set she'd never been allowed into, 'often mean. Mean-spirited, I mean. I think it's better to be poor and true to yourself. Authentic. You know?'

'Well, I . . .' Paul said, rubbing the side of his face.

'I mean there's really no shame in being poor,' Vita hurried on, trying to clarify what she meant and hoping she hadn't offended him. 'All I'm saying is that being artistic and creative is surely so much more important than being rich?'

'Sure. But it's still a fancy car. Hey, you know what? Take a picture of me with it,' Paul said suddenly, as they got closer. 'That's a photographic opportunity, if ever I saw one.'

'No! We'll get into trouble. It's rude.'

'We won't. Pretend you're photographing me.'

Vita relented eventually, letting go of Mr Wild's lead and lining up Paul in the viewfinder, with the chauffeur behind him staring straight ahead, deliberately taking no notice.

As they passed, Paul tipped his hat to the tall chauffeur. 'Top of the morning to you,' he said, accentuating his Irish accent. The chauffeur didn't flinch.

'Stop it,' Vita laughed, shocked at his audacity, and they hurried around the corner together and set off down the rue Saint-Jacques. Mr Wild barked happily, keen to join in the fun.

'Are you not a risk-taker, Vita?'

'I'm taking a risk now, aren't I?' she countered. 'Going to lunch with a perfect stranger.'

'That you are,' Paul grinned. 'But come on – you must have done something. What's the most daring thing you've ever done?'

Running away from Darton Hall – leaving her family and everything she'd ever known and hiding on a steam train – had been pretty daring, but Vita didn't want to talk about that with Paul. She didn't want to have to explain where she'd come from, or how Clement had set out to ruin her life.

'I said hello to the Prince of Wales once,' she said, suddenly remembering that night in the Café de Paris with Nancy. It had been the first time she'd ever set eyes on Archie Fenwick.

She shuddered inwardly, seeing him in her mind's eye on the grand staircase and how his eyes had locked with hers.

'How do you mean "said hello"?' Paul asked, mimicking her English accent.

'Just that. I was in the Café de Paris in London with some friends and I got dared into it. So, bold as brass, I went up to him and said hello.'

'And what did he do?'

'He kissed my hand,' she said, smiling at the memory. 'He has very nice eyes,' she informed Paul and could tell that he was impressed.

Soon they were cutting past the Sorbonne, the famous university building. Vita and Paul had to separate to let a gaggle of students through, in their flapping gowns. Vita saw many young women amongst their ranks, holding piles of books against their chests.

'Do you wish you'd been a student?' Paul asked, picking up on her look.

'Sometimes.'

But that was all a fantasy, she reminded herself. Darius Darton would never have allowed her to go away to study. And her mother . . . well, her mother was only interested in her caged birds. She'd never stood up for her daughter. She thought of home now – of the slow, ticking clock in the dining room. How her mother and father and Clement would be exactly the same as they always were. She imagined how they would have carried on with their rules and their judgements and their dull mill business without her, as if she'd never been there in the first place.

'In my opinion, universities are overrated,' Paul declared.

'Is that so?'

'The University of Life,' Paul said, proudly, tapping his temple. 'That's the only one that counts. They can't teach real life from books. Most learned people I know don't have a clue.'

Vita laughed and they continued to chat easily. Paul told her about his family in Dublin and about going to New York on a steamer, and his narrow escape from being on the *Titanic*;

but he said his heart belonged in Paris and extolled the virtues of the city and how he adored Sylvia at Shakespeare and Company.

Vita was happy to listen to him chat away, enjoying the way he noticed things that she didn't. They made their way into the Jardin du Luxembourg, entering the park near the Marie de Médicis fountain, and Vita stopped to take pictures of the long, thin lake in front of it. Mr Wild scampered happily over the gravel. Above them the birds chirruped, busily building nests in the overhanging trees; and in the lake the fish kissed the surface of the water, making circles amid the reflections.

They strolled along the wide path, past the palace where an artist was standing in front of an easel, painting the lake. The marble figurines in the fountain gleamed white in the sunshine, the spray making a hazy rainbow. All around the lake, people were sunning themselves in low green chairs. A child ran across in front of them, chasing a hoop.

Further on, a group of men played pétanque in between the avenue of plane trees, and women strolled with large black-and-cream prams, chatting. A couple of horses passed, their flanks glistening, the *gendarmes* atop them touching their hats to Paul and Vita, who picked up Mr Wild and tucked him under her arm. She wondered what kind of picture she and Paul must make, strolling along through the gardens as if they were a couple without a care in the world. *Is that what other people must think of us?* she mused. And would they think the same if it was her and Fletch walking through the gardens?

13

Champagne at La Coupole

Vita had been to the cinema several times in Montparnasse, and everyone had been to Le Dôme Café. Whatever the time of day, there was always a crowd: groups of men and women drinking carafes of wine at the wicker tables beneath the red awning, all of them artists, writers, dancers or models. It was the kind of place where everyone looked at everyone else and, needless to say, Nancy loved it.

As they passed now, several people got up to greet Paul, including two very beautiful women in long fur coats, who looked like sisters. One of them looked Vita up and down with curiosity, but Paul didn't introduce her.

A few doors down was La Coupole, a famous restaurant amongst the girls at the club, although Vita had never been able to afford to dine there herself. Now she was both nervous and excited and, more pressingly, very, very hungry. It had been a long time since she'd eaten a decent meal.

'In or out?' Paul asked, gesturing to the terrace, which was already fairly full of diners.

'We should go outside with the dog,' she said, nodding to the remaining table in the corner.

'We'll go in. There's heaps of space inside.'

'But won't they mind Mr Wild?'

'Not at all. Leave it to me.' Then he added in a stage whisper, 'They think I'm a reviewer for the *Michelin*.'

'What's that?'

'It's a guide that rates restaurants. One star for simple and well run; up to three stars for high-class places. They caught me with my pencil and think I'm an anonymous reviewer. I find the trick is to be whoever people want you to be.'

So *that* was what the pencil was for. He wasn't a writer after all. Vita laughed as Paul held the door open for her, and she picked up Mr Wild and walked through into the fabulous interior of the restaurant.

'Ah, *bonjour*, Monsieur Kilkenny,' the maître d' said, his mouth forming a smile beneath his bushy moustache.

Paul leant forward and spoke quietly in his ear, then turned and raised his eyebrows at Vita. A moment later they were being led to a table.

The restaurant was pleasingly modern and light, with green leather banquettes encircling a large metal sculpture, the small, neat tables in front of them already filled with diners. Large, square painted pillars rose to the ceiling.

'They're all by local artists,' Paul said, pointing upwards. He smiled in a dreamy sort of way. 'I'll be up there one day.'

Oh? So maybe he *was* an artist after all, Vita surmised, smiling to herself that her first guess about him had been right. *Should I have heard of him?* she wondered. Was he famous, and she had no idea?

They were seated with a good view of the gold bar, with Mr Wild under the table with a silver bowl of water that the maître d' carefully placed down. Vita was impressed by the large mirrors behind the bar and the array of bottles on display. The waiter brought over the menu card, but Paul waved it away.

'Let's have the menu of the day, and save ourselves for the crêpes Suzette. You've had those?'

'No. What are they?'

'You'll see. A tiny piece of theatre. Oh, and wine. White wine? Or champagne? Let's have champagne,' he decided, without waiting for her answer.

Paul spoke to the waiter in French and he bowed and left, backing away.

'So are you a successful artist?' she asked, realizing as she said it how rude she must sound, but Paul intrigued her. How could he afford to bring her here and order champagne? Most of the artists she and Nancy had met were starving, for the sake of their art.

'Me? Oh no. Not yet. But I do all sorts of things to get by, so that I can paint.'

He smiled at Vita, his eyes holding hers for a second, and she thought he was going to say more, but he didn't.

'So what do you paint? Not this modern stuff that is all the rage?'

'Nothing wrong with modern art,' Paul said defensively. 'Some of the greats have left their mark up there.' He nodded towards the pillars.

'So who are your influences?' she asked, trying to sound knowledgeable, although she really didn't follow the art scene as much as she should, but everyone talked about Picasso.

'Renoir, Matisse, Monet. But the greats too – they're all . . . *great.*'

She laughed.

'To be honest, I'm a man of simple tastes,' he continued. 'I like pictures of girls. I even like the *Mona Lisa.*'

'I've never seen it.'

'You live in Paris and you have *never been* to the Louvre?'

'No,' she laughed, embarrassed that the nearby diners who were sharing a large platter of *fruits de mer* had paused momentarily.

'Then I insist that we go. After lunch.' Paul banged his fingers on the tablecloth.

It was outrageous enough that he'd invited her out to lunch, but was he now suggesting that they go and see a painting?

'Say you will,' he insisted. 'It's a cultural emergency.'

'I can't. Not today. I must get home to my friend.'

'Who is this important *friend*?'

'Nancy. She's a dancer at Les Folies.'

'Ah . . . Les Folies Bergère. I'll admit that I'm more of a Moulin man myself.'

Vita raised her eyebrows, wondering just what kind of man Paul Kilkenny was, if he was a regular at the Moulin Rouge.

'I work there too . . . at Les Folies,' she said.

'You're a dancer?'

'I was – back in London – but not now. I help backstage, with the costumes.' Why was it so important that she wanted Paul to think well of her? 'I'm hoping I can do that for a living. Designing, I mean. One day I'd like to make proper

64

clothes – of all kinds,' she said, surprising herself by how passionate she sounded and how good it felt to voice such an ambition. 'I started a business selling brassieres in London. "Top Drawer" I called it.'

'That sounds fun.'

'It was, but . . . well, it didn't happen.' She shrugged, embarrassed to admit that her once-bright ambition had guttered out, like a candle.

'Then make it happen.'

'But how? I mean, it's very hard. Anyway, I can barely sew and I don't know—'

'Then learn,' Paul interrupted, waving his hand as if her excuses were pathetic. 'Learn your trade. Work in a fashion house, if that's what you want to do. You're in the right place.'

Vita laughed. 'It's not that easy, believe me.'

Paul pulled a face at her. 'On the contrary, it's all about recognizing your opportunity and then bashing down doors.' He faked a punch.

'Sounds very violent.'

'There's nothing wrong with demanding what you want,' he said. 'See, it's the first thing you need for the University of Life.'

'What's that?'

'Tenacity.'

'I shall remember that,' Vita said, thinking it was probably good advice.

'Just get through the door,' Paul said. 'That's the most important thing. Once they get to know you, the rest will be easy.'

'Easy?'

'You gotta seize the moment.' He sounded so sure.

'I'm not so good at that,' she said, although she remembered now how she used to be braver. How she'd tell herself that she only had to get through the next sixty seconds. It had been a mantra that had helped her get out of a few tricky situations. 'I was once, but I don't know . . . Maybe I've lost my confidence.'

'You're over-thinking things, Vita,' Paul told her. 'Live in the moment. Stop worrying about the past or the future. It's only now that counts.'

'It's that simple?' she laughed.

'Sure. Oh . . . will you excuse me for one moment?' Paul asked, his attention caught by something behind her.

She watched as he walked towards the kitchen door and, when it swung open, she saw him shaking hands with a swarthy-looking man in a sharp suit, slapping him on the shoulder, before the door swung closed and they were both hidden from view. He certainly wasn't kicking down any doors, she thought, but walking right through them.

He was very mysterious, this Paul Kilkenny. He was an artist, but clearly he had money – or at least the knack of *living* like he had money. It was fun being with him, and it had been so long since she'd had someone other than Nancy to confide in. She hadn't had a friend like this, since Percy.

A few moments later Paul was back, but he didn't elaborate on where he'd been or who he'd been greeting. She watched him replace the pencil behind his ear and tuck a book in his inside jacket pocket.

'Ah, champagne,' he said, as the waiter brought the bottle

and twisted it skilfully so that there was a subtle pop. He poured it into two glasses. She knew enough French to understand from the waiter that it was vintage champagne, and it was somehow on the house.

'What are we celebrating?' she asked, as Paul picked up his glass, ready to salute her.

'Life,' he said. 'And new friends.'

14

A Date with Fletch

Nancy was fast asleep when Vita got back to the apartment and was grumpy when Vita insisted that she get up, even though they should already be at the theatre.

Eventually Nancy sulked into the kitchenette, slumping at the table, lighting a cigarette and grudgingly taking the glass of salts that Vita pushed towards her. Mr Wild barked, waiting to be picked up, but Nancy only put her hand on his head in a lazy way, so he continued barking and, annoyed at the high-pitched noise, Nancy kicked him away. Vita gave the poor little dog a sympathetic look as he scurried back to his basket.

She knew Nancy was impossible when she was in this state, so she smiled and flapped the paper bag of croissants that she'd scrounged from the *boulangerie*, just before it closed for the day. They were slightly stale now, and she felt guilty for enjoying the delicious lunch she'd had with Paul. The crêpes had been served on a trolley, with the chef coming out of the kitchen to light the brandy in the heavy copper pan. It had been an absolute treat.

Paul had walked with her afterwards as far as the metro station, and as she'd sat on the train coming back, Vita thought about their parting. He'd told her that he was going on a trip to Cognac, although he didn't tell her who with, or why.

'I'll see you,' he'd said assuredly, giving her his card, a white rectangle with his name in raised black lettering and a telephone number, 'when I'm next back in Paris. A fortnight or so. We'll go and see some art.'

'I'd like that,' she'd replied honestly as they'd shaken hands, as if making a deal.

'Goodbye for now, Vita Casey. Don't go getting into any trouble . . .'

She shook her head, smiling at the memory, and then, worried that Nancy had seen her expression, turned away to open the cupboard and look for the jam. It felt thrillingly illicit to have a new friend all of her own. She thought of Paul's card in her purse and wondered if she'd ever call him.

He hadn't given her any indication that he found her attractive, and there certainly hadn't been a spark, like there had been with Fletch, but it was still very flattering that a man had taken her out. Maybe Nancy was right: perhaps she was giving off some kind of aura, and she had to admit how wonderful it felt to be noticed. Oh, and the lunch . . . the lunch had been *divine*.

'Eat,' Vita instructed, seeing Nancy's pale, sallow complexion. 'You'll feel better.'

'Where have you been?' Nancy sounded suspicious, before being stopped by a bout of coughing. Vita winced at the rumbling, phlegmy sound, and Nancy thumped her chest, her eyes watering as she tried to recover. 'You look very . . .' she groped for the right word, 'fresh.'

'Out for a walk, with Mr Wild.'

She made it sound as if her jaunt this morning had been commonplace, hating herself for not mentioning Paul and the lunch, which even a few months ago Vita would have insisted Nancy joined in with. Back then, Nancy had always come out with Vita in the mornings, keen to explore and see everything. In fact, today's events, and lunching with a perfect stranger, were the sort of thing Nancy adored. It was on the tip of Vita's tongue to tell her how much fun it had been, but something in her friend's prickly, hungover state stopped her.

Instead Vita said breezily, 'It's a lovely day. I took some pictures on the camera. I hope you don't mind. Oh, and I sent a postcard to Percy.'

'Did you? I thought you said it was too risky?'

'It's just . . .' Vita started and then, feeling on a high after her day, decided that maybe, if she couldn't tell Nancy about Paul, she could at least admit how she'd been feeling. 'I'm fed up with treading water. I want to do what I did in London. I want to get paid to make things: underwear again.'

'Well, it'll be tough. You're a nobody here, Vita,' Nancy said nastily.

Vita pressed her lips together. She knew all too well that Nancy could be as mean as hell when she was hungover, and it was always Vita she chose to lash out at, but describing her as a *nobody* was a bit low. Usually Vita jollied her out of her bad mood, but she was too annoyed with Nancy's nasty words to bother.

Nancy delved inside the bag and turned up her nose at the croissants. Then she put her hand into the pocket of her robe and pulled out the small silver case that she kept her cocaine in.

'Really? For breakfast?' Vita asked.

'Don't let me stop you leaving, if you disapprove,' Nancy said nastily.

'But we're already late for the theatre.'

'So? I can be ready in two minutes,' she said, taking a bump of white powder from her hand.

Vita watched her, wanting to snatch the powder away. She couldn't bear the way Nancy was so addicted. She was such a good person, such a good friend, but this habit of hers put a barrier between them, and they both knew it. These days Nancy always chose the drugs over Vita; and the more she took, the more Vita pulled away in the other direction. And now Nancy didn't meet her eye as she got up from the table and went to her bedroom.

'Five minutes,' Nancy called, as if proving a point.

But it was ten minutes before they left, and Vita felt annoyed that Nancy was trying to pretend everything was normal, when she was high.

'Why are you being a sourpuss?' Nancy asked, as they hurried to catch the tram.

'I'm not,' Vita said, annoyed. Nancy knew perfectly well how she felt about her taking so many drugs, but it was even more annoying that she was turning it round, making out that Vita was the one with a problem. Nancy was astute enough to pick up on Vita's disapproval and, despite denying it, they both knew that Nancy's behaviour *had* upset Vita's mood. She'd had such a wonderful day, so full of possibility; and meeting Paul and going to lunch with him had been so much fun. But now she felt sucked down into the emotional quagmire that Nancy created, and she longed for a way out.

Fortunately, the tram was crowded and they couldn't speak. And then they were both rushing to get to rue Richer.

The theatre, originally built as an opera house, had an imposing facade, the blocked letters of Les Folies Bergère carved above an elaborate stone engraving of a reclining naked woman, dancing through waves.

As Vita got nearer, she could see that the ornate wooden doors of the foyer were being opened by the front-of-house staff, ready for the early theatre-goers who came to see and be seen in the huge reception hall, beneath the fancy alabaster work, and to stroll through the galleries above it.

Fletch was waiting on the corner, his brown trumpet case in his hand. A gaggle of pigeons pecked at the pavement by his feet, and Vita saw that he'd emptied out the paper bag he was holding.

He grinned widely and lifted his hat as Vita and Nancy approached, and Vita felt so relieved to see him. She waved back at him.

'So . . . Vita, I'm glad I caught you,' he said, blushing, as if he might get away with this being a chance encounter, when they both knew he'd been waiting for her. 'A few of us, we're going to the Chez Joséphine later, after the show. It'd be mighty fine if you'd join us?'

Nancy looked at Fletch, her eyebrow arched. 'Yeah. Sure, we'll come,' she said, even though the question hadn't been directed at her. 'It's a date.' Then she walked off through the pigeons, which scattered. 'Oh, revolting things,' she cursed, flapping her arm to shoo them away. 'Come on, Vita.'

Vita looked desperately at Fletch. She wondered if Nancy was ever going to let them be alone together. She'd been all for Vita having a fling, but she seemed to have changed her mind, now it was becoming a reality. *But to hell with her*, Vita thought. She was sick of Nancy's sudden mood swings, and the way she tried to wrong-foot her all the time.

Vita thought of the girls laughing, referring to her as Nancy's 'wife', and she remembered what Paul had said about being who people wanted you to be. But she didn't want to be some kind of hidden wife any more. She wanted life on her own terms for once, and she was not going to let Nancy ruin tonight.

15

Chez Joséphine

After the show Vita dressed in one of the dancers' outfits for the night out, and Antoinette did her make-up, filling in her eyebrows and outlining her eyes in kohl.

'It's a bit daring for you, isn't it?' Nancy asked, as they went out of the stage door.

'Aren't you always telling me to be more daring?' Vita countered with a bright smile, licking her teeth to make sure that Julianne's best Helena Rubenstein red lipstick hadn't left a smudge. She was trying to be breezy, but she still hadn't forgiven Nancy for being so mean earlier, and it felt good to assert herself, for once.

They caught a taxi from Les Folies up to the rue Fontaine with Julianne and Antoinette, Fletch and the boys following in Bobo's car, the neck of the double bass sticking out precariously from the back window.

Vita had only been to the club once before and was intrigued by the proprietress, Josephine Baker. She'd been to see the silent film *Siren of the Tropics* twice with Nancy, and afterwards they'd tried to impersonate Josephine's kamikaze dancing – the crazy chicken-strut she did, along with that spectacularly loose Charleston, her legs appearing to be made

74

of rubber, as if she had the very essence of jazz under her skin.

There was something so beguiling about a seemingly ordinary girl from a humble background achieving such stardom, though Vita had heard rumours about Miss Baker's wild sex life. It seemed she'd had scores of both male and female lovers, and there were rumours about her apartment, too, which she'd filled with animals, some of which she took onstage with her. It was said that her pet cheetah quite often tried to make an escape into the orchestra pit.

'Do you think she'll be here?' Vita asked Fletch as they edged forward in the short queue, wondering if she might get to meet her in person.

'Josephine? No, she's left to go on tour.'

'You know her?'

'Sure,' he said. 'We all do. She poached us from the Imperial, when this place opened. Bobo and I were waiters there for a while, before we got a break in the band.'

This was certainly news. 'What's she like?'

'Well, put it this way: she ain't got time for us no more,' Fletch said with a shrug. 'She moves in different circles these days, with that manager of hers, Pepito. They say they're setting up a Chez Joséphine in each city that she's visiting.' He gave Vita an unimpressed look.

'It sounds like you don't approve?' she said.

'I think it's important to remember where you come from. I see a whole load of folk get into trouble when they pretend to be somethin' they ain't.'

Vita felt the truth of his words like a sting. What would he say if he knew that she was pretending to be someone she wasn't? That she, like Josephine, had escaped her roots, determined to build a better life for herself?

She thought of Paul for a moment, and how his philosophy was so different. He believed in going out and grabbing every chance and making what you could of yourself, and Vita had felt enthused with his view of life. She'd wanted Paul to believe whole-heartedly in her being Vita Casey, because she *was* Vita Casey, wasn't she? That's who she'd become. Who she'd chosen to be.

But now this conversation with Fletch felt unsettling, because it made her remember who she'd been, not so very long ago. And she wondered whether he'd have dared ask her out, if he knew that she was actually Anna Darton.

It was very confusing sometimes, Vita thought, working out where she fitted in, all whilst this urge to break away from Nancy and the life she was currently living – to break out and *do* something daring – was getting stronger and stronger.

Fletch and Bobo knew the doorman and, now they had neared the front of the queue, they skipped ahead and greeted each other warmly with a manly handshake, then stayed chatting for a moment as Vita wandered inside.

'What was that about?' she asked, when Fletch caught up.

'It's easy to get in tonight, now that the party has left.'

'The party?'

'You know . . . Le Monsieur and his set.'

'The who?'

'There are always hotshots hanging around here,' Fletch said. 'And Le Monsieur? He's da man,' Fletch laughed. 'Runs the gambling scene, so I heard.'

Vita was intrigued by this 'Le Monsieur' and was about to ask more, but inside the club the music was bouncing and she gave her coat to Nancy who went off to the cloakroom, declining to go with her. Vita wanted to be with Fletch, not watching Nancy snort yet more of her never-ending supply of cocaine. Nancy's heavy-lidded eyes already had that milky, opaque look Vita knew meant trouble. She didn't want to be responsible for Nancy tonight or pander to her moods. She wanted to have fun.

The club, according to Fletch, served food from 'back home' – the best black-eyed peas and rooster-combs – but tonight Vita wasn't hungry, and anyway, the diners who'd been here earlier, keen to get a table, were all up on the dance floor. The club was crowded and the atmosphere was buzzing, even though 'the set' had left.

'Let's dance,' Fletch said, and she felt him slide his arm around her waist. In the crush they were pressed together and she felt his hips against hers. His body felt lithe and strong.

'You smell good,' he said, breathing her in, and she was glad he'd noticed. She'd borrowed some of Simone's little pot of oud, which she'd been given by her Moroccan boyfriend, the scent of which had immediately made Vita feel much more womanly and courageous.

She smiled up at him and their eyes locked.

'And you sure look good, too. You hide those legs away, Vita, but you got a fine figure . . . if you don't mind me saying.'

They did the whole dance, then another and another. They should have broken apart to go to the bar, but Vita didn't want to, and neither did Fletch. When she saw Nancy waving her over, she deliberately swerved around, out of her line of sight.

'You avoiding Nancy?'

'Tonight, yes, I certainly am.'

'She sure likes to party,' Fletch said. 'They say she's the biggest snow-queen at the club.'

Vita felt both defensive and embarrassed. She knew Nancy had a reputation, but she hoped Fletch didn't think *she* was the same. She never touched the stuff – not after what had happened with Nancy in London. Vita never wanted to feel that out of control ever again.

'She's got worse,' she said. She couldn't talk to any of the girls about how things were with Nancy at home, and she suddenly felt the need to confide. 'She parties far too hard and, to be honest, she worries me. And she's positively vile when she has a hangover.'

'But it's not your problem,' Fletch said, and Vita pulled a face, because it *so was* her problem.

'Just don't let her see us,' Vita said, glad to be out of Nancy's clutches for once.

'Shall we take a breather then?' he asked and squeezed her hand, and she knew that this was the moment – that they were going to make this unspoken thing between them real. 'You know there's a room here . . . I mean, the place where the orchestra sometimes—'

'Take me there,' she whispered.

He manoeuvred her around the dance floor to the far corner of the room, where Vita noticed a small corridor leading backstage. With one glance to check that Nancy wasn't anywhere near, she followed Fletch a little way down the corridor. He looked both ways, then opened a wooden door with frosted glass panels.

Inside he flicked on the lights, but only one worked, although it was enough to show that the room was stacked with piles of wooden chairs.

'It's a bit crowded,' Fletch said apologetically, as he shut the door.

'I don't mind.'

'It's just . . . I wanted a moment to be alone with you.'

'Me too.'

'Oh, Vita, Vita,' he whispered, pulling her into his arms. And then, gently, he stroked her cheek and leant down towards her and kissed her.

16

The Woman Behind the Hearse

In the front pew of St Hugh's, the church in Darton village, Edith looked down at her best black shoes from underneath the veil draping her hat, and wriggled her toes, feeling rain-water squelch between them as they all stood for the final hymn. She'd been the one to choose this hymn for the cere-mony, but the congregation rammed into the pews were doing a poor job of droning it out above the distant claps of thunder and the rain lashing against the leadlight windows. Why couldn't anyone around here *sing* properly? What a turgid cacophony for a send-off.

The past week since Darius Darton had drawn his last, gasping breath had been long and arduous. Secretly, she'd wanted to celebrate his passing and what it would mean for her and Clement, but there were so many funeral arrange-ments, and she had to keep up the decorum of being a grieving family member in front of her mother-in-law, who seemed to have fallen apart completely. From what Edith had observed, her in-laws' marriage had hardly been a joyous one, so why Theresa Darton was so distraught was baffling.

Beside her, Clement mumbled the hymn as he leant on his stick, whilst on the other side of him, his mother's shoulders shook as she cried silently. Edith nudged him and made eyes at him, to make Clement put his arm around his mother, knowing that such affectionate gestures were completely unnatural to him. Finally understanding her meaning, Clement let Edith take his stick and put his arm around his mother, who slumped against him gratefully. Such a show would do wonders for their reputation with the onlooking congregation behind her.

Clement had rigid views about the role of women – an entrenched view inherited from his father, which Edith was on a daily mission to change. He, like his father, believed that a woman's place was to subjugate herself to the better sex. Clement had no time for the women in the newspapers who were achieving everything that men could, or for the ordinary women in the mill who were the lifeblood of their business. Slowly Edith was starting to make him see that a little bit of respect went a long way. Now she looked at the wooden box in the middle of the aisle. There lay a man who had put his wife down so often that she could barely speak a sentence without second-guessing herself, and Edith silently thought, *Good riddance*.

Because, with Darius's passing, it was time to change the tone of the draconian management up at the mill, and making the workers – particularly the females – see Clement in a new light would be the key to their success. Yes, things were going to be different around here at the mill, and they'd better start getting used to the modernization Edith had planned.

So far they'd improvised in order to make the bras, but they needed new machines and seamstresses. The old looms needed replacing anyway, and Edith was trying to persuade Clement to turn the space into a proper factory, and then they could really ramp up production. He didn't agree that there would be the demand, but Edith knew that every woman, once she tried one, would want a brassiere. And not just one, but several. In different colours and styles.

Edith's head was buzzing so much with her plans that she was surprised when the service was over, and she and Clement filed out of the pew to walk out of the church behind Father McDougal and the coffin. She allowed herself to smile graciously at Theresa, who took a moment to thank Edith for organizing a perfect service. Edith was glad to be going up and up in her mother-in-law's estimation.

Outside the porch of the church the crowd from the mill, who had shuffled in a silent group behind the hearse, were lining the gravel path next to the tall yew trees. Edith saw Harrison, the foreman, shadowed by Meg and Ruth, step back deferentially to let Darius Darton's coffin pass. He caught Edith's eye and she saw in his gaze the look she often encountered in the factory – the kind of longing adoration that men reserved for women who were forever beyond their reach. Edith knew full well the status she'd earnt as the new Mrs Darton. She'd overheard whispers on several occasions amongst the workers and had savoured their comments about how beautiful she was and how nobody in the factory could fathom how Clement had managed to woo and marry someone so elegant. These moments were reassuring. She'd always enjoyed an audience as a dancer and she felt, in a way, that the workers were her audience too. And it was only right that they should look up to her. She was a cut above them all and one day she would prove that it wasn't just her beauty they should be in awe of, but her business mind too. She eyeballed several more of the familiar faces in the crowd, seeing a few flushed cheeks as the men doffed their hats.

And that's when Edith saw her: the woman who'd been in the front row behind the hearse on the way here. The one with the small child, who had held eye contact with her for a moment too long earlier on. Edith had noticed her because, unlike so many of the mill workers, she was blonde. She was also very pretty, if a little stern-looking, her hair coiled in an elegant bun beneath her hat. Unlike some of the others, she wasn't carrying an umbrella and she was soaked now, her eyes blinking in the heavy downpour, but her gaze was not leaving Edith and Clement.

'Martha, who is that woman?' Edith asked the Dartons' housekeeper, whom Theresa seemed to treat like family and who had sat in the pew behind them.

'She's the Chastain girl,' Martha said. 'Marianne, she is. They call her Marie.'

'Chastain? That's an odd name, for around here.'

'Her mother was French. A milliner, so they say.'

Edith saw the woman – Marianne – step forward now onto the gravel out of the crowd, as the coffin passed. Her eyes blazed at Clement, and Edith saw him notice her and shake his head.

And in that moment Edith understood: the blonde woman and Clement had some sort of history. Marianne, her jaw set firmly, clutched the little girl's hand and walked right up to them, and Edith knew there was going to be a confrontation. Clement, clearly keen to avoid it, suddenly veered away, taking his mother's arm and leading her away from the coffin, stumping determinedly on his stick across the sodden grass towards the grave. Indignant tears smarted in the woman's eyes at this deliberate snub, as she watched him go.

The small girl stared up at her mother and then at Edith. She had a grey wool coat on, which looked too big for her, and a solemn, wise look to her, despite the fact that she could only be about six or seven. And that's when Edith realized why her face seemed so familiar: *she looked exactly like Clement.*

Edith had only just computed this dreadful fact when the woman spoke, confirming her worst fears.

'She has a right to be here,' the Chastain woman said, in a shaky voice.

'I beg your pardon?'

'Darius Darton was her grandfather.'

'What?' Edith hissed.

'You heard me.' The woman's tone was defiant.

'You stay away from here, do you understand me?' Edith said, stepping towards her and pinching her arm, so that she was forced back towards the crowd.

'But if you only knew how badly he's treated us.'

'It is not my concern. This is neither the time nor the place. *Go away.*'

'If only we *could*. If we could only get away from here . . .'

'Go away!' Edith repeated, keen to shut this woman up. How dare she cause a scene like this.

'He won't make you happy, Miss,' she said, leaning in close to talk in Edith's ear. 'He's not a nice man. He'll let his own daughter starve; but then he still comes to me, you know. He can't help himself.'

'Don't you *dare* speak like that of my husband.'

'You might as well know the truth. He's a horrible man. The worst. It's just as well Mistress Anna got away.'

Edith drew herself up, her cheeks burning, but the woman grabbed the child now and dragged her away. Edith bent her head and walked quickly on, keen to catch up with Clement.

He avoided looking at her as they stood around the grave, but she stared straight at her husband as the coffin was lowered. Clement was standing next to Theresa, who was clinging on to his arm, and together they watched the rain pattering on the heavy oak casket. Father McDougal read from the Bible, with one of the mill workers holding a large umbrella above his head, but Edith hardly heard his words.

Why hadn't Clement told her about Marianne? Or her whey-faced bastard child? And what if everyone knew? God knew how many people had witnessed that little scene. She felt humiliated and angry, but frightened too, by what the woman had said about Clement. What had she meant, about him being the worst kind of man?

Then Theresa Darton threw a small handful of earth on top of the coffin and turned away. Clement went to follow her, but she shook her head, accepting Martha's arm instead.

Edith pounced on the opportunity and walked quickly to her husband's side. He didn't move as the crowd around the grave filed away.

'I will not tolerate you being unfaithful to me,' she hissed. 'That was not part of our arrangement.'

Clement blushed and looked angry, but Edith gave him a stare. He could not have an outburst here, not today.

'I shall make Darton great again with you,' she said. 'But I have to be respected. Do you understand?'

He nodded mutely, his eyes downcast on the grave. 'I shall deal with the situation,' he said. 'With her . . .'

'No, you will not. You will have nothing to do with that woman or child. *I* will deal with it. We will not speak of it again.'

17

Sacré-Coeur

It was early in the morning as Vita stepped out of the dark apartment building into the glorious spring day and headed up to the basilica of Sacré-Coeur, its gleaming domes making Vita think of whipped cream. Mr Wild skipped happily past the Italian carousel and into the gardens, knowing the route up through them to the church, where Vita always liked to go on a sunny day to admire the view.

Daffodils and tulips had sprung up on the grass verge, and she remembered the poetry book Archie had given her with the Wordsworth poem in it, and how she'd had to leave the book behind in London at Mrs Bell's boarding house. She supposed that Mrs Bell, who had been so furious when Percy had been arrested for homosexuality, must have burnt her box of possessions by now.

Vita examined herself for the dull ache that she felt in the pit of her stomach whenever she thought back to those 'Archie days', as Nancy called them, and realized that it didn't feel the same. Maybe Nancy's advice to 'get back on the horse' was working, after all.

She still hadn't told Nancy that she'd kissed Fletch, or

that the first kiss had turned into a full *patin* – the French-kissing the girls at the club talked about. And as the days had passed, she was glad she hadn't. She knew Nancy would do her own trumpeting from the rooftops, and would turn the secret that Vita wanted to savour into salacious gossip.

Now, days later, she was still turning the whole experience over and over in her mind, as if she could still taste it, and she couldn't help blushing at the thought of what might have happened, if someone hadn't opened the door of that room in the club. She remembered so clearly how her heart had been pounding as she and Fletch had sprung apart; and as she'd stolen a guilty look at him, she'd seen that Fletch was as breathless and as shocked by their passionate clinch as she'd been.

Because it hadn't been just the kissing – which, Vita had to admit, had been amazing – but the very fact that it had been *Fletch* she was kissing. It felt so daring . . . so thrillingly *naughty* to break all the taboos she'd grown up with. She couldn't imagine what the young Anna Darton would say, if she'd known that in a few years' time she'd be living in Paris and kissing a *black* man. It was dizzying to think about how far she'd come.

She wondered if it was the same for Fletch, because he'd seemed shaken, too. Back on the dance floor, his eyes hadn't left hers and, when Nancy interrupted, demanding that Vita dance with her, it had felt as if they'd shared a monumental secret.

But since then, despite desperately wanting to talk about what had happened between them, and Vita secretly longing for another of Fletch's sensational kisses – the memory of which seemed to turn her insides to liquid – they hadn't had a moment alone together. And now her head was in even more of a spin, with endless questions pricking her conscience.

Had she made a terrible mistake? *Should* she feel guilty? And what was going to happen now, when just one kiss between them had made her feel so . . . well, so *undone*? If only she could tell someone. If only she had a friend to confide in – other than Nancy. She thought of Paul's parting words: *Don't go getting into any trouble*. Well, that's *exactly* what she'd done, and she really didn't know what to do with herself.

She was out of breath by the time she'd climbed the final steps and stood on the wide, white stone stairs. Pigeons flapped at her feet, picking up the grain that someone had thrown; and, reminded again of Fletch, Vita turned and looked out at the breathtaking view of Paris. In the morning haze all the buildings were in soft-focus. She could see the Panthéon, the Arc de Triomphe, the Eiffel Tower and all the streets in between.

She felt herself filling up with wonder at the view, because sometimes she wanted to pinch herself that she really was in Paris. Wonderful, glorious Paris, and it was all out there – whatever 'it' was. But she sensed something . . . a new life. Could it be because she'd taken a risk with Fletch that she felt a new surge of confidence? A new-found passion?

Because she *did* feel different. And if she carried on feeling like this, then who knew what might happen? She couldn't begin to imagine, but she felt a strange kind of excitement building in her as she turned towards the cathedral, still half-smiling to herself. Secretly, she wasn't a great believer in the religion she'd been force-fed as a child, but she wasn't going to take any chances on incurring the wrath of God – whoever He might be. It would be wrong to come all the way here and then not visit the church.

She told Mr Wild to be quiet and tucked him into her wicker shoulder bag, then walked inside through the high wooden door. The church was dark and cavernous, the pews empty at this early hour, except for a few people praying. She knew that for the past thirty years there had been a constant adoration – people who prayed around the clock for the church, for the world and for peace. She admired their dedication and looked up at the giant mosaic of Jesus inside the main dome, His arms outstretched, His golden heart reaching out, and she wondered if His love would extend to her, now that she'd kissed Fletch.

She sat on the pew, staring up at the inscription, wanting to think spiritual thoughts, pondering on the nature of faith. Nancy was still a believer in her clairvoyant, Mystic Alice, who had once told Vita that 'the dark stranger' was coming. At the time Vita had thought she'd been prophesying Archie Fenwick coming into her life, but maybe she'd meant Fletch. And now her mind wandered back to how her body had felt when they'd been kissing. Was it a sin to feel this aching desire?

She stared up at Jesus, waiting for some kind of sign, but then she saw an old clergyman walking past in his long robes, his head bowed as he swung the metal ball full of smoking incense. Something about his profile reminded her of her father so much that she did a double-take.

She deliberately tried not to think about her parents, but

the man was such a dead ringer for Darius Darton that now her father sprang vividly into her mind. For a second Vita remembered him kissing her cheek when she was a small child, when she'd given him a drawing for his birthday, and she felt the first pang of homesickness that she'd experienced for a very long time.

Maybe she should go back to Darton? Just once. To see her parents. To show her father the kind of woman she'd become. But then she remembered that her father would be horrified by her association with Nancy and the Les Folies girls . . . not to mention with Fletch. He wanted her to be a woman, but not the sort of woman Vita herself ever wanted to become.

And, of course, there was Clement. She shuddered as she remembered his temper – the way he'd wanted to thrash her in Dante's stable, and how he'd always ruined everything for her.

No, she reminded herself. She'd never go back to Darton. Not now, not ever. That was the price of her freedom.

But that was fine, she told herself, standing up. Her life was here now, and it was time to get on with it. She left the church quickly, an unsettling feeling coming over her as the priest walked away, his eyes watching her.

18

An Encounter at Dreyfus

Deciding to take a detour home, Vita veered down the lesser-known steps from the lofty cathedral, with Mr Wild sniffing happily through the rockery, until they came out on the rue Charles Nodier and headed to Dreyfus, the fabric emporium on the corner. It had a royal-blue canvas awning over the doors, with 'Coupons' in white writing and 'Dreyfus' in architectural block-letters up the side of the building. She left Mr Wild tied up outside and walked inside.

This was Vita's favourite treasure trove, and she often came here to wander up and down the rickety wooden stairs to the different floors, where the tables – skirted in red material – were piled high with colourful bolts of material from around the world.

There was everything from candy-striped upholstery fabric to the most delicate white lawn, along with rolls of smooth silk and satin in every colour, not to mention the tweed print in thick wool.

Perhaps it was being around the fabric like this that gave her a small taste of home, because standing amongst the lovely printed cottons, she couldn't help thinking about Darton Mill, and of the fabric that Ruth and Meg would be making right now. Did they ever think of her, she wondered, as she thought of them?

She strolled over the wooden floorboards, touching the fabulous materials, feeling the different textures between her fingertips and letting her imagination run wild. It was as if she could see the unmade garments floating above them, like ghosts.

In the corner there were stiff, headless mannequins draped in fabric – just a suggestion of clothing – and Vita was drawn to one with a sequinned silver sheath, a boa wrapped around the shoulders. How she would love to make herself an outfit like *that* for a party. If only she had the money. Or a smart party to go to, for that matter.

Up on the second floor she saw that a shop assistant – one of the many knowledgeable young men who waited, poised with a yard-long wooden measuring stick to help customers – was serving a girl in a smart navy cape. The girl wasn't that much older than Vita, but Vita could tell from the involved conversation that she was buying some special fabric.

'Excuse me. Would you help me choose?' the girl called over in French, holding up two long, thin bales of fabric. 'Which colour do you prefer?'

'They are both beautiful,' Vita told her, pleased that she could reply in French and that her lessons with Madame Vertbois were paying off.

The fabrics the girl was choosing between were the same: both silk adorned with appliquéd flowers that looked so romantic, Vita wondered if it might be for a special occasion. She could imagine the fabric being cut on the bias, the flowers in a cascade down the front of a beautiful dress – maybe some cap-sleeves or contrasting chiffon. And a ruffle hem, perhaps?

She walked around the table of fabric bales, keen to get a closer look.

The assistant was shaking his head. 'It won't hang as you wish,' he said.

'You think? Perhaps you are right,' the girl said, looking critically at the fabric. 'It's a shame.' She stroked the material as if wishing it a fond goodbye.

'Wouldn't it be better like this?' Vita asked, in English, unable to stop herself butting in.

The man seemed annoyed at being interrupted, but the girl looked at Vita, a curious expression on her face. 'Go on.'

'Sorry. I don't know the French.'

'I speak English,' the girl said.

'If you were to drape it on the bias,' Vita said, 'then the line would be perfect.' And she held the fabric up against the young girl. 'See.'

'Actually you're right. Maybe it will work,' the girl said. '*Merci.*'

'Oh, and I prefer the pink,' Vita said, in French.

'*Moi aussi,*' she replied, smiling, then she nodded to the man and issued instructions for the fabric to be cut. Vita watched him pull sumptuous wafts of fabric from the roll, before measuring it with his stick. Then he drew out a large pair of shears from his apron pocket and cut the cloth, the blades zipping through it.

But the girl was ignoring this fascinating part of the

process and was busy consulting her list. She was clearly buying a lot of material, and Vita felt a jealous pang, thinking what an enviable task that must be.

She watched as the girl and the assistant chatted and walked purposefully away towards the stairs. Vita had to resist the urge to follow them. Helping the girl make up her mind had felt so satisfying, and she thought of Percy and his incredible collection of theatre costumes, and how much he would love it here, too. Still wishing that she could follow the girl, but realizing it would be rude, she wandered over to where the lace was displayed in rolls.

'Would you like some?' another assistant asked. Unlike his colleague, this one was an older man, and he looked at her disapprovingly as she tested the weight of the different lace between her fingertips.

'Oh no, I'm just browsing . . . Well, actually, yes, I'll take a little piece.' An idea was forming in Vita's mind. She wandered over to the basket of offcuts and, at the bottom, found some baby-blue silk that would be perfect. And she had just about enough money.

The till was upstairs, and she had to go up with her meagre purchases to pay. At the booth the teller – a woman in a long-sleeved frilly blouse with a high collar, with a pince-nez perched on her nose – was sitting behind an ornate till, with a glass top and patterns on the brass sides. Suddenly she gasped and called out to the assistant Vita had seen with the girl. The teller was holding up the pink appliquéd fabric, which the girl had clearly forgotten. The assistant rushed to the window and looked out, from three floors up. 'Oh no, she's gone,' he exclaimed.

Vita looked at the fabric, suddenly remembering Paul's advice.

'Could I help?' she asked. 'Maybe I could take it to her?'

The teller, who was clearly furious with the assistant and considered the overlooked fabric to be his mistake, peered curiously at Vita through her pince-nez.

Vita, aware that she was being scrutinized, settled on a thoughtful frown, looking wistfully towards the window and the embarrassed assistant. 'Your customer looked familiar,' she lied.

'Oh? Well, she works for Madame Sacerdote. You know Jenny Sacerdote?' the woman at the till asked, in a confidentially low tone.

'Jenny Sacerdote?' Vita asked.

'She's quite the rage in Paris,' the assistant said, joining in the conversation between Vita and the woman at the till. He said it as if part of the girl's association with this glamour was attributed to him. He was clearly annoyed that Vita was involved in the situation. 'She makes beautiful dresses. She has offices on the Champs-Élysées,' he said, as if Vita were an idiot for not knowing such common information.

'She dresses Suzy Solidor,' the woman by the till added.

Vita nodded at this obvious name-drop. 'The artist's muse? I've met her,' she said, although this was rather an exaggeration. Nancy had pointed out the tall, blonde woman who'd been dining at Les Deux Magots.

The woman by the till nodded, as if Vita had passed some kind of test, and she saw a look pass between the woman and the snooty assistant.

'I'm going that way,' Vita said, suddenly seeing an

opportunity. Isn't that what Paul had told her to do? But no sooner was the offer out of her mouth than her mind started to race, about how she'd get to the Champs-Élysées. 'I could take the material,' she said, sounding way more confident than she felt. 'It would be such a shame if Madame Sacerdote's assistant got into trouble because of an oversight.'

'That would be very kind, Mademoiselle,' the woman at the till said, staring down the assistant, who was about to object.

19

The Champs-Élysées

Twenty minutes later Vita pushed through the metal turnstile of the metro station and walked up the steps into the sunshine, with the package wrapped in Dreyfus paper and string tucked firmly under her arm. She'd quickly taken Mr Wild back to the apartment building, leaving him with Madame Vertbois to deliver to Nancy.

Now she stood on the wide pavement for a moment, taking in the splendour of the Champs-Élysées. She'd driven down here once in a cab before, but she'd never really appreciated the scale of the majestic cream stone buildings that lined the pavement, or the leafy avenue of horse-chestnut trees that cast shade onto the passers-by.

In the parts of Paris that she frequented everything was squashed together, but here everything was taller and more spacious. And the people were different, too. She watched several elegant women strolling in the shade of the trees, their heads held high, and the men, all dressed in sharp suits, admiring them. Smart motorcars passed on the road and there was a sense of commerce – of business being done. There was no doubt about the feeling that she'd arrived at the beating heart of Paris.

She walked along the pavement, looking up at the doors and their fancy signage. Even the *tabac* looked terribly smart, with its fan of artistic glasswork above the door. A man came out in a fawn overcoat, lighting a small cigar, and smiled at Vita.

Everyone here was so well turned out, and she was aware of her scuffed shoes and her frayed coat. She'd flung on her blue-and-white striped dress this morning and had crept out of the apartment, not wanting to wake up Nancy, but now she wished she'd chosen a smarter outfit and pulled her coat across her dress, self-consciously.

She looked at the piece of paper in her hand with the Dreyfus logo on it and the address of Jenny Sacerdote's building, hoping that she was going in the right direction, following the numbers on the buildings. As she got towards number seventy, the shop fronts became more and more impressive, and Vita became increasingly nervous.

She stopped, looking up at the huge, pale stone buildings ahead of her, adorned with lion heads, until she saw the glamorous shop front of Louis Vuitton, then walked slowly past and saw that Maison Jenny's building was equally grand and just next door. Two large tricolour flags fluttered in the breeze, and Vita looked up to see more flags outside the windows above. The word JENNY was emblazoned on the balustrade of one of the grand balconies, so she must be in the right place.

The archway to the building had huge black iron gates, which were adorned with a gold-leaf pattern and the word JENNY in gold capitals above them. A liveried doorman stood by the gate in a smart cap, keeping guard.

'Goodness,' Vita exclaimed to herself. It had seemed like such an inspired idea at the time, to follow the friendly girl who'd been buying material. But now she felt nervous as she walked to the far edge of the pavement next to the road and stood in the shade of a tree behind an ornate street lamp, hoping that from her vantage point she'd be out of sight of the doorman. Spying from behind the lamp post, she watched the building, trying desperately to think of a plan and to recall the optimism and confidence she'd felt earlier outside Sacré-Coeur.

A young couple walked out of the building, chatting and laughing arm-in-arm, and exchanged a few words with the doorman, who tipped his hat to them. The woman was wearing a fur stole around her neck, and the man was wearing a very dapper pinstriped suit; they walked off down the street, both of them the very essence of chic.

A grand car drew up alongside the wide pavement, a little further up from Vita, who moved to the other side of the tree trunk. She watched as a chauffeur got out and opened the back door. A small, sturdy woman in a dark suit came out of the building, her arms outstretched, ready to greet the passenger who was now alighting from the back of the car. She was wearing a magnificently cut coat with a fur collar, and her curly hair was neatly arranged under a modern hat with a diamanté brooch. She had a small white poodle tucked under her arm, and Vita did a double-take. It couldn't be . . .

But it was. It was Mary Pickford, the movie actress who'd starred in so many of the films Vita had been to see, such as her favourite: *My Best Girl*. And she was married to the gorgeous Douglas Fairbanks. Vita was in awe of her and even had one of Mary Pickford's quotes written on a postcard on the mirror at home: 'You may have a fresh start any moment you choose, for this thing we call "failure" is not the falling down, but the staying down.'

And here she was: the sweetheart of the silver screen, right in front of her. Vita watched as the two women chattered excitedly as they went into the building and, as the doorman stepped inside after them, Vita dashed across the pavement to the Guerlain shop next to Jenny's building. She was keeping an eye out for the girl from Dreyfus, and looked at the beautiful bottles of perfume on display in the window in front of her, her mind whirring. She simply *had* to get into the building. This was where she was meant to be – she could feel it.

Then she saw the girl in the navy cape in the reflection of the window. She was crossing the street, through the traffic. She rushed towards the front of the building and Vita had to spring into action to intercept her, grabbing her arm.

The girl turned round, looking startled. Then, seeing it was Vita, she seemed to slump with relief.

'You forgot this,' Vita said, handing over the material.

The girl took it from her gratefully. 'Oh, it's you. I went back to the shop. And they told me they'd given it to you.' Her eyes looked red-rimmed, as if she'd been crying. And Vita saw that she'd suspected Vita had stolen the fabric. 'You have no idea how much trouble I'd be in, if I'd lost it. Thank you for returning it.'

Vita smiled. 'It was no problem.'

'Madame Sacerdote is so lovely, you see, but she has a

commission that we have to rush out this afternoon. Well, I must go. Thank you again.' She smiled and turned away, already stepping through the black gates.

Wanting to pinch herself because she was *actually doing this*, Vita followed her through. There was no sign of the doorman. 'Have you worked here long?' she asked, and the girl paused on the first step of the sweeping stone stairway, surprised that Vita was following her. 'Only I wondered if Madame Sacerdote might be hiring,' Vita went on, trying not to be distracted by the plush interior of the building, which opened out at the top of the staircase into a large, sunny atrium. 'You see, if she would take me, I would work *so* hard.' She blushed furiously now at being so effusive and for sounding so desperate.

'Your French is very good.'

Vita smiled. 'I try to practise it,' she said, grateful for Madame Vertbois's fastidious teaching.

'I'm not sure if Madame needs anyone else . . .'

Vita looked at her, her heart hammering. 'You could ask, though?' She smiled and the girl sighed, clearly unsure how to get rid of Vita without being rude. Vita's eyes flicked towards the material the girl was holding. She owed Vita a favour and they both knew it.

The girl hesitated and then nodded. 'Come in then,' she said, 'for a minute. You can wait.'

20

Madame Sacerdote

Vita waited for an hour and a half on the hard stone bench in the atrium of the building, before she saw Mary Pickford coming out of the lift and walking across the atrium to the door. Vita held her breath as the actress looked over towards her and smiled, and Vita thought how beautiful she was. She watched as the doorman escorted her out of the building back to her chauffeur-driven car on the pavement. Then she saw the girl from earlier beckoning Vita from the stairway.

She hurried across the floor and followed the girl up a wide stone staircase, and then up another, carpeted in light pink, until they came to a foyer, where two enormous pink rose trees were in bloom in large pots.

Vita hardly had time to take it all in before they walked through a doorway, the glass etched with a round flower pattern saying '1909' in the middle. Madame Sacerdote had clearly been established for some time.

The girl, who now introduced herself as Agatha, led Vita through a plush reception area, then on through an ornate door into a huge salon, which faced onto the Champs-Élysées. The room had a high white ceiling, with elaborate cornicing and a fancy chandelier, but everything below it was decorated in muted grey tones, which gave a wonderful sense of modernity and freshness to the traditional room. The carpet was a soft grey, the wallpaper was grey, and at one end were low chairs and sofas upholstered in grey velvet with narrow gold braid. It was all so simple and tasteful, and so very classy.

At the end of the room was a set of long glass doors, blocked by pleated grey curtains, but now they opened and a woman walked through them, carrying a coat with a huge fur collar and giant fur-trimmed sleeves. She placed the multi-coloured coat gently over the sofa, as if setting down a sleeping child, then looked up and saw Agatha and Vita.

'Is this the English girl?' she asked, walking towards them, and Vita realized the woman must be Jenny Sacerdote herself. She was the one who'd greeted Mary Pickford from the car, and Vita realized that the actress must have been in this very salon only moments ago.

Jenny Sacerdote was wearing a black skirt with a white blouse tucked in, and a blue bow-tie at the neck. She had short dark hair, styled away from her face, and a stern expression, but as she approached Vita she smiled and her face seemed to soften. She extended her hand to Vita.

'I found her at Dreyfus,' Agatha said. She sounded nervous.

'You did us a favour today,' Madame Sacerdote said.

'It was a pleasure.'

The woman stood back and placed her hands akimbo, looking Vita up and down, and Vita blushed.

'Agatha tells me that you are looking for a job,' she said in English. 'What is it that you do?'

Vita felt breathless with excitement. She smiled at Agatha,

who gave her a little wave and walked over to the doors, and Vita was left alone with Jenny Sacerdote.

She took a breath. She could not afford to mess this up. Not when she was inside an office on the Champs-Élysées in front of this impressive designer.

'I'm interested in the way fabric works to help dancers move,' Vita said. 'I help with the dancers' costumes at Les Folies Bergère, you see, but my real passion is underwear – lingerie. But I want to learn everything – everything there is to know about designing. It's all I've wanted to do, since I was a small girl.'

'Oh?'

And seeing that Madame Sacerdote seemed genuinely interested, Vita gushed on, telling her about W&T and the order for Top Drawer. But just as she was starting to explain how she'd left London, another woman opened the doors behind the sofa and wedged them open, and Madame Sacerdote's attention was lost.

'Oh, we have a rehearsal for some of our pieces. Would you like to stay?' Jenny asked Vita, who nodded enthusiastically. 'Sit there and watch,' she said, showing Vita to the stiff chair next to the sofa. She took off her coat and sat with it folded over her knees. She stared up at the walls and ceiling, then saw that Madame Sacerdote was watching her. 'Do you like my salon, Vita?'

'Oh yes, very much. It's very modern.'

'My friend Robert Mallet-Stevens was the architect.'

Vita nodded, as if she knew who this was and was impressed. But being here made her feel as if she knew nothing – less than nothing – about this glamorous world.

For the next fifteen minutes, it seemed to Vita as if she were in a dream. Model after model came out, to be inspected by Jenny's critical eye. And the clothes . . . oh, the clothes were simply mesmerizing.

But the best part of all was that Madame Sacerdote was soon involving Vita herself.

'You like these?' she asked, seeing Vita sitting to the front of her chair as two models walked past in pretty afternoon dresses.

'Very much.'

'I send out more than a hundred and twenty dresses like this a day.'

'That many?' Vita asked.

'Yes. All over the world. To Russia, England, America,' Madame Sacerdote said, waving her hand as if it wasn't a big deal. 'Everyone works very hard here. I have a loyal team.'

She nodded to the next model to come forward, and the girl strode over the grey carpet in a tailored skirt that was short and wide, in thick grey fabric. She was wearing very fetching high boots.

'Russian leather,' Jenny commented, seeing that Vita had noticed them. 'The best. And with this skirt, it works, don't you think?'

'Absolutely,' Vita said, entranced. 'I like the silhouette,' she added as the model turned, just as absorbed in what she was seeing as Madame Sacerdote.

'You're right. It's a clean cut,' Madame Sacerdote agreed. 'Ah, and see this . . . this is one of my bestsellers,' she said proudly. 'The *Généralissime*.'

Vita watched the model strut down towards the end of the room in a military coat in soldier-blue cloth.

Now another model, with startlingly blonde hair, walked up in an oyster silk dress, with a woman in a black dress following behind, adding a few more pins to the row on her lapel. The model stopped in front of Jenny, and Vita admired the elegant sleeveless evening dress, with its low V-neckline. It was snug around the hips, then fell to a skirt that was cut from the knee on one side in a long ruffle to the ankle on the other. It was so stylish and was absolutely made for dancing.

The woman attending the model now had a rapid conversation with Jenny, before presenting several samples of braiding that was clearly meant for the dress. Jenny selected a length of braid that was covered in tiny hand-sewn pearls and edged in the finest gold thread.

'Vita, come,' Madame Sacerdote said and Vita sprang up from her chair, leaving her coat. 'This is Laure. She runs my studio,' she said, introducing the woman, who nodded at Vita. 'Now . . . where shall we put this,' she asked, holding up a length of the gorgeous braid, and Vita stood back and assessed the dress. 'Show me. Where would you put it?'

'I think from the shoulder to the hip,' Vita suggested assertively, taking the braid from Madame Sacerdote and draping it in an elegant line down across the model. 'And maybe some more fanning across here,' she said, taking the pin from the assistant and pinning it on the model's hip, then pulling the braid across. 'I don't want to cut it, but maybe two more rows going down.'

'Well,' Madame Sacerdote said, with a smile and a meaningful look at Laure, 'I could not agree more.' She spoke some more to Laure, who produced a pair of scissors from her belt, then Madame Sacerdote pinned the braid on the dress, in just the way Vita had suggested. Then she stood back and gave a satisfied smile.

'You have a good eye,' she told Vita, who positively glowed with the compliment.

'Oh, Madame Sacerdote, I would love nothing more than to work for you.'

'I see,' she replied, sounding interested. 'Well, I do need some more juniors. I would need a reference,' she said. 'We never take anyone on without one. And a sample of your work, and then . . .' She looked at Vita, as if sizing her up. 'Then we'll see.'

21

Let's Fall in Love

Vita spent the rest of the day and the ones that followed in a state of panicked excitement. She replayed her meeting with Madame Sacerdote over and over in her mind, wanting to pinch herself and prove it had actually happened. Paul had been right, after all. It had simply been a matter of getting through the door and being tenacious.

Something about being at Maison Jenny had inspired Vita into being the best version of herself. And having been that person, if only fleetingly, it had thrown into contrast how Madame Rubier treated her at Les Folies.

She knew, without a doubt, that she had to get back to that wonderful salon. *That* was where she belonged, because dear Madame Sacerdote could teach her so much. And her clothes! The clothes were to die for.

Now her mind was buzzing with fresh designs for her own underwear samples. And with a new purpose in mind, she felt focused in a way that she hadn't been since London. She'd managed to get some more material offcuts from Dreyfus and had turned the living room into a studio, using the kitchen table to cut the cloth, which was deeply satisfying, now that Madame Vertbois had lent her a sharp pair of shears. Even better, Julianne had given her a sewing machine that she never used, and Vita worked late into the night, trying to perfect a matching lingerie ensemble.

On Friday, when she heard there was a letter for her behind the bar at Les Folies, she immediately thought of Percy, hoping that he might have got in touch, but when she hurried through the foyer to get it, the note turned out to be from Fletch: *Do you think we could slip away from the party later? Just for a little while on our own?*

She smiled, clutching the note to her chest, recognizing the longing in his words that she felt, too. Tonight was Julianne's birthday and they were all going to a bar after the show to celebrate. She knew Nancy suspected that Vita and Fletch's 'fling' was progressing, but she continued to be dismissive when Nancy pried for details. She stuck with the line that they were friends and nothing more, keen to deflect Nancy's attention.

And it was this, more than anything, that made her realize how much Nancy had changed. Because once she might have confided in her – sought her approval and advice even – but these days Vita couldn't be sure how Nancy would react. Because if Nancy was high, she'd start teasing Vita in public.

It was gone eleven by the time they were all crowded around Julianne in the little booth opposite the long wooden bar, and Vita remembered going to the American Bar in the Savoy Theatre with the girls, after the shows at the Zip. This bar, however, was decidedly less salubrious, with dark wooden panelling and low red-fringed lampshades that glowed in the reflection of the giant gilt mirror on the wall. The air was thick with cigarette smoke, and they drank shots of the peach liqueur that Julianne liked.

There was a battered upright piano in the corner, the front of it removed to reveal the hammers, and now a man in a hat sat on the small stool in front of it and started playing popular songs. Soon the girls had crowded round for a sing-song. And then, just as he'd struck up with 'Let's Do It, Let's Fall in Love', which was Vita's current favourite song, Fletch and the other guys from the band walked in. She saw him over by the door and, when her eyes connected with his, he smiled at her singing, 'Let's fall in love.'

She felt heat flush through her and her neck go red, as she tried to ignore the fact that Fletch was here. She waved a perfunctory hello, but when the song finished and Nancy pointed out loudly that 'the boys' were here, Vita knew Nancy was watching her and scrutinizing her every move, as Fletch kissed her on the cheek and their hands touched for a fleeting second. She pulled away, but as soon as Nancy had turned, she surreptitiously sought out Fletch's hand and squeezed it in her own and he winked at her.

They drank more, and then Bobo brought over an ice-bucket with champagne to the long wooden table they had taken in the corner. Julianne started opening her presents, which were in a pile in the middle, between the dripping candles. She got to Vita's gift last and took out the knickers she had made – a pair in red silk. The girls passed them around, all of them keen to tell Vita how much they admired them. She saw Bobo laughing and looking embarrassed.

Still, it felt good to go up in the girls' estimation. And Nancy was full of it, declaring that this was nothing new, and that Vita's Top Drawer underwear had been *her* idea. Her sniping comments about Vita being a nobody seemed to have been forgotten for now.

Then, feeling more confident, Vita told the girls about meeting Madame Sacerdote.

'That's swell, Vita,' Fletch said, and she knew he meant it.

'Well, it was fun, I'm sure, Vita,' Nancy said, 'but you simply can't work there.'

'Why not?'

'We need you at Les Folies. *I* need you,' she declared, as if Vita were a fool for not realizing this. And Vita saw, suddenly, that this was the truth. Nancy being needy *was* what had held her back.

'She's right,' Simone said. 'We all need you, Vita.'

'Madame Rubier wants to give you a better job,' Julianne said. 'She told us the other day.'

'Did she?' Vita asked. This was certainly news to her.

'Oh yes. You mustn't go anywhere else,' Julianne said. 'You're one of us.'

'Well, I'm not going anywhere yet,' she said, glancing at Nancy. 'I have to get a reference, and I don't know how.' And it was true. There was nobody she could ask, and she didn't dare ask Madame Rubier. 'But if I could, it would be such a big opportunity.'

Nancy wrinkled her nose and, changing the subject, called for more drinks. Vita glanced at Fletch and saw that he was listening in on this exchange, and his eyes stayed locked with hers for a long moment. It was as if there were an invisible string between them and they were getting closer and closer.

And then, at just gone midnight, he flicked his head towards the door and Vita backed out, away from the girls until, sure that she hadn't been seen, she sneaked out of the door and met him outside.

'You didn't bring your coat,' he said, and she nodded at Fletch, chilly now that the night air was hitting her.

'If I had, they'd have asked questions,' she explained, pulling him away from the bar entrance to the street. Then she glanced over her shoulder. Nancy was coming out of the bar, swaying a little and calling her name.

Vita made Fletch duck down out of sight behind Bobo's car, which had the neck of his double bass sticking out of the window. She raised her head a little to see through the windscreen, as Nancy threw her cigarette on the pavement and went back through the revolving wooden door to the bar.

'She sure as hell doesn't like to let you go, does she?' he said.

'She's just . . .' Vita began, but she didn't want to justify Nancy's jealous behaviour tonight. She wanted to get away.

She nodded to the road and Fletch put his arm around her, then they ran across the cobbles and hurried towards the boulevard de Clichy – the red-light district. They walked along the central avenue of the wide street, and Vita tried to ignore the women who lolled in the doorways to the seedy casinos and bars.

'Where are we going?' she asked Fletch, suddenly unsure of herself. He'd wanted to see her alone, but now they were some way from the bar.

'Well, somewhere inside. You're cold. We could go back to my place? Just for a while? It's not far from here, and we could at least be alone there,' he said, staring at her.

'Let's do it,' she said, and he ran across the road to hail a taxi.

22

Shadows on the Ceiling

They hardly spoke as the cab rattled up to Montmartre and then climbed up east to the Goutte d'Or area in the eighteenth arrondissement. Vita considered herself and Nancy to live on the very furthest reaches of the city and she had never been this far out, knowing that the streets around the Château Rouge were known as 'Little Africa' because of the immigrants who had settled there.

She was worried now about how far they were away from her friends back in the bar. Her definition of 'not far' and Fletch's seemed to be very different, but along with the fear came a mounting excitement, the thrill of doing something so utterly daring . . . of being truly alone together. She knew it was probably wrong to feel it, but she acknowledged now the low, needy ache inside her as she glanced across at Fletch and saw his noble profile. She wondered how it would feel to touch his hair, his shoulders, his back – and how it might feel if he kissed her again. Only this time they might not get interrupted.

Fletch spoke perfect French as he instructed the cab driver to stop, and he held out his hand to Vita to help her onto the pavement near a large roundabout. She stepped out and

115

stared at the dusty hoardings on the sides of the tall brick buildings advertising soap powder.

Here the blocks of apartments were larger, but even more rundown than the cobbled streets she was used to, and the neighbourhood smelt different, too. In the glow of the orange-yellow street lamps she could see a water hydrant leaking onto the street, sending a swill of dirty water down the drain.

She looked across the road to some scrubby trees and saw an elderly black couple walking a small dog. They looked up curiously at her, and then at Fletch. On the corner there was a huddle of young men in suits, laughing, but they fell silent as Vita passed with Fletch, who nodded to them. She felt their eyes on her back as she walked along with him.

They hurried further up the wide street, passing unusual vegetable stalls that were still open at this late hour. There were barbers, too, and record shops and a chemist with strange-looking bottles in the window. Vita slowed to look, but Fletch took her hand, keen to hurry her along. From the open door of a bar she could hear a soulful songstress, and when she looked through the etched glass window, the bar was packed with black people. There wasn't a white person in sight, and she caught the eye of a woman who frowned at her, and Vita felt the hairs on the back of her neck standing up.

She'd never felt like this in her life before: so *other*. So alien. Was this how Fletch felt, when he played in bars and clubs? Was this the kind of shocking and, yes, indignant self-awareness he had to deal with on a daily basis? And she knew then that it was, and suddenly she understood what he'd been describing in America.

How awful that people couldn't just get along – that they couldn't get past the colour of each other's skin. She squeezed Fletch's hand, a new kind of respect for him welling up inside her.

Soon Fletch stopped by a dusty doorway.

'This is me,' he said.

She nodded, but this felt very real, and she knew that crossing over the threshold would be significant in ways she couldn't yet understand. She knew, though, that after meeting Madame Sacerdote, it really *was* possible to be a brave person. She'd spent far too long second-guessing herself and hiding away. She needed to do this. She *wanted* to do this.

'You don't have to come, Vita,' he said.

'I know,' she replied. 'I want to.'

Fletch walked in through the door, which opened into a cobbled yard and then into a square surrounded by tall buildings of apartments, with balconies looking down into it. They walked along one side of it, then Fletch took out a key from his pocket and opened a door in the corner.

'It's not much,' he said, as she walked inside. 'Just a room.'

He went to a table next to the low bed and lit a candle, and in the soft lighting she could see a picture framed by the bed of an elderly woman standing next to a palm tree – his mother, she presumed. The bed was neatly made, with a brown blanket tucked over the white sheets, the pillowcases ironed. Manuscript music was spread out over the bed, and Fletch hurriedly scraped it into a pile and put it on the small table next to a wooden clock. Above the table was a framed picture of a man playing the trumpet, his eyes screwed up, his cheeks puffed out. On the back of the door Vita could see another suit hanging on a hook. There was a small sink with a single tap and a chipped mirror.

She stood for a moment looking round, seeing the stain of damp on the brown wallpaper, the threadbare rug on the boards, but even though it was so minimal, it still felt so intoxicatingly *other*. She was in a man's room. *Fletch's* room.

They stood for a moment, staring at each other in the flickering candlelight. Then he stepped towards her and took her hands in his.

'You're shaking,' he said. 'Here, let's have a drink.' He went to the small cupboard next to the table and retrieved two glasses and a bottle. He poured her a hefty slug of bourbon and one for himself, then they clinked glasses and she downed hers in one, wincing at the sharpness of the alcohol. She laughed, handing him back the glass.

'That's good. I don't usually – I mean . . .' she began.

He nodded, understanding. He touched her hair, pushing some of it over her ear, and then smiled gently. Vita lifted his hand now and they pressed their palms together, their eyes locking. It felt so natural, so innocent, and yet so charged with meaning. She closed her eyes and leant in towards him, and his lips touched hers in the softest kiss.

And she understood then that there was no point in fighting it. Neither of them had come here for conversation, but for something else entirely, and she surrendered to the feeling of desire that she had to fight so hard to suppress in public. Even so, she whispered, 'We shouldn't do this. We should be getting back.'

'I know,' Fletch said, before kissing her more deeply. Vita ran her hands over his shoulders, feeling his rippling muscles, her stomach back-flipping as he pressed against her. She felt herself weaken as his hands started fumbling with the small buttons on the front of her dress.

She knew she should stop him. She should put her hand over his and tell him to be a gentleman. But she didn't. She didn't want him to be a gentleman – not at all.

Soon she stood before him, naked from the waist up, and he touched her breasts, his fingertip brushing the top of her erect nipples, and a deep moan of desire escaped her. And then he was holding her, kissing her, touching her everywhere and, before she knew it, they were entwined on the bed.

Afterwards they lay together watching the shadows on the ceiling, as they both caught their breath. Vita grinned and looked across at Fletch, and he held her hand.

'I've never been with a white woman,' he told her.

'Or me with a black man.'

They both laughed at the absurdity of these statements, because the colour of their skin mattered so little. Especially now. She ran her hands down the springy hair on his chest and felt his taut stomach muscles twitch.

And as he moaned, she felt another wave of delirious desire overcome her. And becoming more daring than she'd ever been, she moved to sit astride him, holding his hands in hers above his head.

'What are you doing to me, woman?' Fletch breathed.

'We should go,' she said, but even as she said it, she leant down to kiss him.

23

The Morning After
the Night Before

Vita woke up with a start, wincing at the bright sunshine coming through the blinds, hearing pigeons cooing outside the window and children skipping in the yard, singing a song in French. There was a ball bouncing against the wall, too, and her head pounded with it.

But now another sensation kicked in and that word she never used, but which Nancy favoured, flew out of her mouth as she sat bolt upright. 'Fuck!'

She clamped her hand to her head, nausea rising in her as she saw that she was naked and her brain tried to compute the magnitude of what she'd done.

She'd spent the whole night with Fletch. How had it happened? How could it be *morning*? They were going to go back to the bar . . . they'd *agreed*. She'd said she simply wanted to cuddle Fletch for five minutes more, after they'd done what they'd done for the third time, but they'd obviously both fallen fast asleep. She turned to Fletch, watching him sleeping on the pillow next to her, and her breath caught in her throat and panic made her heart hammer.

It wasn't just the fact of it: that incredible night of physical pleasure, which had been beyond anything she'd ever even begun to imagine. *That* was bad enough, but now that it was morning, Nancy would clearly know her secret – not to mention all the girls at Les Folies. They had a matinee performance today and she must already be late. They'd all know by now that she hadn't been home.

Stealthily and as silently as she could, she swung her legs out of bed, reaching for something to cover her shameful nudity.

Last night, she remembered, she'd felt the same way that she had done after she'd made love with Archie. It had been as if Fletch had woken up her body after a very long sleep. But now she felt wretched, and not only because she felt bad about Archie. She felt like she'd committed a terrible, terrible sin.

'Where are you going?' Fletch asked sleepily, his hand reaching out across the crumpled sheets. Vita flinched away.

'I've got to go. I didn't mean to fall asleep,' she said, standing and turning, her dress clutched to the front of her body. 'It's the morning.'

'Oh!' Fletch said, suddenly awake.

'I've got to . . . where are my . . . ?' Vita started, not meeting his gaze as she began scurrying around the room attempting to collect her clothing. She was trying hard not to cry, but now a tear fell. And then Fletch was next to her, his strong arms around her.

'Don't be scared, Vita,' he said. His voice was serious and she looked at him now, realizing that he was right: this feeling *was* terror. She was terrified about what they'd done, what she'd felt, what it all meant. 'I don't want you to regret last night, because I sure as hell don't.' He smiled at her and wiped away her tears. 'Now, by all means get dressed, but when we leave, we'll leave together,' he said. 'You don't have to run out on me just yet. And besides, I don't want you to face the mob alone.'

She gave a little yelp, remembering the streets last night and how alien she'd felt. She couldn't begin to imagine what it would be like in daylight. Surely she'd be so conspicuous that everyone would know where she'd been and what she'd done?

'I'm kidding,' he said, stretching – looking so comfortable in his own skin.

Was he, though?

'You don't regret it, do you? Last night?' he checked.

'No,' she mumbled, but she couldn't be sure. She felt this enormous weight in her chest of something she couldn't name, because a part of it was definitely the shock of being in a room with a naked man.

'Good.' He pulled her towards him and she relented, letting him embrace her, but then she wriggled free, keen to get dressed. Fletch whistled, going to the small sink. She watched him from the corner of her eye as she pulled on her stockings. He reminded her of a languid, powerful panther.

He was still humming as he turned on the tap and filled the sink with water. Then, as the taps clanked – in a way that was far worse than the taps in her own and Nancy's apartment – he sang a jazz riff, so that the taps provided the percussion; and, despite her panic, she couldn't help but laugh. She tried not to look at his taut, firm buttocks.

'That's better,' he said, lathering up his face with foam

and looking at her in the mirror. 'There's that beautiful smile of yours.'

And then she remembered how she'd fantasized about this moment in Solange's apartment – how Fletch might look, naked, in the morning – and she marvelled that somehow she'd manifested this precise situation.

'What you thinking?' he asked, seeing that she'd stopped still, her arms frozen, as she dressed.

'Oh – nothing. It's just I can't help finding you so . . .'

'You're not so bad yourself,' he teased and she laughed, the tension easing a little. 'Seriously, you're so different from the other girls. You have this style about you. An air of classiness. You're not brash like the others,' Fletch continued.

Dressed now, she walked towards him and touched the pink scar by his shoulder, wondering what others he meant. Did he mean the other dancing girls, or his other girlfriends? She couldn't imagine Fletch had become such a skilled lover by accident. She wondered now who else had touched his smooth skin like this. She wasn't jealous, more curious about the secret club she'd found herself joining. But she sensed that Fletch wasn't going to want to talk about his other conquests, and she respected him for not asking about her own. She didn't want to tell him about Archie.

'What's this scar from?' she asked.

'The war. A mortar shell. I was thrown ten feet off the ground. I couldn't hear for a week afterwards. My backpack took most of the shrapnel, and the guy behind me . . . well, he bought it, sadly.'

'It must have been horrible.'

'It was. But it's over, and I'm one of the lucky ones.'

'You're so brave,' Vita said, putting her arms around his waist and looking at him in the mirror. The shaving foam was half off now, but Fletch laughed, holding the cut-throat razor. She pressed her face against his back, knowing that this was a goodbye. Knowing she must never do this again.

'You're a very distracting lady,' he said. 'You know that?'

He took her hand and slid it boldly downwards, and then her stomach did that melting thing as he guided her hand around his hardness. The razor clattered to the sink and he let out a low moan.

'You're impossible,' she said, trying to remove her hand, but he had his own hand over hers and she felt emboldened and excited by the power she had over him. With his other hand, he picked up the cloth and wiped his face clear of most of the shaving soap, then turned round and picked her up, as easily as if she were a child.

'I've got to go, Fletch,' she said, but even as she said it, her legs wrapped around him as he carried her to the bed, and she knew it would be impossible to resist.

Afterwards, out of breath and sweating, Fletch turned and smiled at her.

'Now we really do have to go,' he said and she laughed.

This time, when she got out of bed, Vita realized she didn't feel so bad. This time it felt they were both in it together. Soon they were dressed and ready to leave. Fletch squeezed her hand for a moment, before picking up the brown trumpet case.

'Here we go,' he said, taking a breath and unlocking the door. He poked his head out and looked both ways, before ushering her towards the yard.

Now, in the daylight, she could see there were pots planted up with red geraniums and rows of bright washing on the clothes line strung between the balconies. A black woman looked over the balcony above and Fletch tipped his hat to her, but her eyes widened when she saw Vita.

She felt her cheeks burning, and the woman's eyes on her as they walked together towards the street.

24

Chuchotements

'I was going to call the police,' Nancy said, as Vita quickly made her way downstairs from the stage door in Les Folies Bergère, all too aware that she was still wearing her clothes from last night and had only just made it to the theatre in time for the matinee performance. Nancy was wearing Vita's coat and she felt a surge of relief that her friend had taken it home from the club.

When she'd mentioned to Fletch how worried she was about facing the girls, he told her that what had happened between them was private and special, and none of the girls' business. Vita protested that they must have worked out that she and Fletch had left the party together, but Fletch told her to stand her ground. Besides, even if they did suspect, none of them were in a position to judge her. They weren't exactly as pure as the driven snow themselves, he'd argued, and Vita had managed to convince herself that if she got a chance to talk to Nancy privately, then Nancy might be proud of her for going through the very 'fling' that she'd suggested.

But now, as Nancy pushed herself away from the wall where she'd been smoking in the corridor outside the dressing room, Vita realized that she wasn't going to be able to make light of her absence. Nancy wasn't proud or excited, or going to bond in the way Vita had hoped she might over last night's adventure. In fact she knew Nancy well enough to realize that the pinched expression on her face meant she had a demon hangover, and Vita braced herself.

'No, you weren't,' Vita said, blushing.

'I was. I was going to call the police,' she said. 'I was going out of my mind with worry. You can't just disappear like that, Vita.'

On the one hand, Vita was pleased that Nancy had actually missed her, but she was annoyed that she was getting this verbal dressing-down – especially here. Nancy put Vita through all manner of worries *all* the time, and this was the first time *ever* that she had done anything unusual.

'I fell asleep at Fletch's. *By accident*,' she said, defensively. 'Don't look like that, Nancy. It's hardly the crime of the century.'

'So, he wore you out that much, huh?' Nancy said, raising her eyebrows. 'I heard he has . . . *stamina*. Well, sweet cheeks, I hope he was worth it.'

Vita, stung that Nancy seemed to know about Fletch's prowess as a lover, followed her into the cramped dressing room. A rail of costumes dominated the centre of the room and around the edges there were tables against every wall, the surfaces crowded with make-up and accessories, the mirrors surrounded by buzzing electric lights.

'Panic over! Look who's back,' Nancy said flamboyantly to Simone and Collette, who were both in the corner, their hair wrapped in flesh-coloured turbans as they put on their make-up.

'Oh, Vita, you're back,' Julianne said, turning from the clothes rail. She pulled a sulky face. 'You left the party.'

'I know . . . I'm sorry,' Vita began, but she saw Julianne's raised eyebrows at Nancy, as if all her suspicions had been confirmed, and she knew right then that her night with Fletch had been discussed. It was just the kind of juicy gossip that was going to spread like wildfire amongst the girls, but she resented Nancy for fanning the flames. Collette and Simone were pretending not to whisper to each other.

Now Vita glanced over and met Collette's eyes in the mirror as she applied some glitter along her cheekbones.

'*Chuchotements, chuchotements,*' Vita said, angrily. *Whispering, whispering.* She started clearing up the dressing room, putting the dresses back on their hangers and returning them to the rail in the middle, feeling hot tears smarting. Nancy came over and gave her a look and Vita hoped she'd soften, but there was clearly no sympathy to be had.

'It's hardly the biggest sin in the world,' Vita said, in her own angry whisper to Nancy. Besides, what did they all care? She was practically invisible at Les Folies.

'Except that . . .'

'Except that *what*?'

Nancy pulled a face. 'Solange is a bit upset.'

'Solange? Why?'

'She and Fletch . . . they've had an on-off thing for a while.'

Vita felt her throat go dry. Fletch and Solange? What *kind* of thing? But Nancy's dancing eyes gave it away.

No wonder Solange had invited Fletch to her party. No wonder she'd called him down from the roof. And that's why he knew the roof existed. Because he'd been up there serenading *her*, too.

'You could have told me.'

'I didn't know. I swear. I only found out last night, when you and Fletch went missing in action and Solange realized what was going on.' She lowered her voice and leant in. 'There was a . . . scene.'

Vita felt her cheeks pulsing. She had so wanted to be discreet with Fletch, but now she'd upset Solange. And she felt soiled, too – annoyed that she and Solange had shared the same lover. And, worse, that she could so easily imagine Solange in Fletch's tangled bed sheets. Solange with her fancy apartment and amazing body.

Why hadn't Fletch told her? Going out with someone else's boyfriend was against the unspoken rules of the sisterhood. No wonder the girls were scandalized.

'I would never – if I'd known . . .' she whispered to Nancy, her eyes filling with indignant tears. But then she saw the look of triumph on Nancy's face and realized that Nancy was probably lying and had known all along about Fletch and Solange, and she'd deliberately encouraged Vita.

She remembered something Percy had once said about Nancy – that she was trouble: the kind of person who liked to detonate things and then leave a mess. Which was exactly what she'd done. Yet again.

And she remembered this particular feeling, too: this feeling of being betrayed by Nancy. Because she'd felt it before. When she'd discovered that Georgie and Nancy were friends. That viperous girl, Georgie – Archie's family friend – who'd deliberately set Archie up with Vita.

She felt furious then, and was furious now at Nancy's meddling. Nancy couldn't help playing with fire – couldn't help causing a drama. It was typical of her to twist the private situation between Vita and Fletch so that *she* was the centre of attention. And she didn't give a damn about who got hurt in the process.

Vita had felt so close to everyone last night – so much a part of the gang at Les Folies – but now she suddenly felt like an outsider. She'd clearly crossed a very big line, which was even more disorientating, because in their carefree, louche circle she hadn't been aware there had even *been* a line to cross.

She busied herself with the costume rail, determined to get on with her job and ignore Nancy, but her hands were shaking. Whatever she said – however she defended her behaviour – wasn't going work. She thought about Fletch and what had happened between them last night, but now, with a bit of distance, she felt shocked – and surprised, too, that she'd let herself go like that. It had been so carnal, so exposing . . . and so damned, deliciously *good*, but now she felt as if she'd been out of her mind.

More of the girls gathered in the dressing room, amid the usual high-pitched banter as they got prepared for the show. Vita kept her head down, hoping not to see Solange. With everyone worrying about the new pirate-themed costumes, hopefully there wasn't time. She helped fit Collette's sequinned waistcoat with the gold buckles, teamed with shorts and black fishnet stockings and a red headband, but Collette didn't speak or meet her eye.

Madame Rubier came into the dressing room now, and

Vita remembered what Julianne had said last night. Was it true that the stern wardrobe mistress had finally noticed her? She was tiny – an ex-dancer herself, the girls had told her – and she had a haughty air that reminded Vita of Edith.

Vita tried smiling at her now, but Madame Rubier walked straight over to where she was standing and roughly snatched the pile of pretend scabbards and daggers out of Vita's arms. Vita, shocked, tried clinging on to them.

'You can leave those.'

'But . . .'

She leant in close. 'We don't really need you here.' She looked down her nose at Vita, who realized exactly what had happened. She must have heard about Vita and Fletch and didn't approve. 'Am I not clear? You are dismissed, Vita.'

Vita let go of the daggers and they fell on the floor and everyone went silent. Madame Rubier looked at them on the floor and tutted, but Vita was too angry to care. She looked over at Simone and Julianne by the mirrors, but they turned quickly away.

'What's going on?' Nancy asked as Vita made for the door, brushing her shoulder.

'She says I'm dismissed.'

'What?'

'Madame Rubier has fired me.'

'But . . .' Nancy looked shocked and stared at Madame Rubier.

'I have hired someone else,' Madame Rubier said, in stilted English, for Nancy's benefit. So the old bag *did* speak English after all. 'Do not come here again.'

'You mean me?' Nancy asked, shocked, and Vita felt her

heart sink. Surely Nancy hadn't been fired, too, because of her?

But Madame Rubier shook her head. 'No . . . just her,' she clarified, then waved her hand to dismiss Vita.

'Sorry, old girl,' Nancy said, squeezing her arm, but Vita shook her off.

25

Old Friends

Edith came out of Charing Cross station and breathed in the London fumes, taking in the noise, the people, the traffic, and enjoying the sensation that this place, which had once felt so much like home, was now simply somewhere she was passing through.

Her parents' house in Leatherhead certainly hadn't felt like home, either. Having just visited them for the first time in years, she'd been very pleased to see that her mother had brought out the best china in the drawing room for Edith's visit, and it was this gesture, more than anything else, that had signalled to Edith that she'd finally won some respect.

She had felt so outcast when her parents had cut her off, after the business with the Askew chap, feeling the full sting of the social stigma they'd imposed upon her by doing so. But now . . . *now* she was finally vindicated. She knew her invitation had come about only because her parents had realized how much money the Dartons had, and Edith had enjoyed rubbing their noses in her success and wealth.

That said, her father still lived in the Dark Ages. When he'd called her into his study for a 'little talk', he'd actually made quite a long speech about how it was unseemly for her to work, and that her husband should be supporting her, and that business was for men, not for women. Even so, she had left feeling triumphant, the access to her savings account restored, the balance having significantly increased in the past few years, thanks to her father's stockbroking prowess.

She set off across the busy pedestrian crossing, past the Lyons Corner House and up towards Covent Garden, with a bounce in her step, her mind mulling over the plan that she'd come up with on the train.

Several of their clients had started to ask when new stock was coming out, and she needed to increase their market share of the lingerie department at Withshaw and Taylor, because so many other shops took their buying ideas from the iconic store. Now that she'd created a market, the market was hungry for their goods, and she and Clement had to feed it . . . soon. Of course Edith and Clement had promised the customers new designs, but they had been working from only one blueprint – Vita's.

The three designers they'd taken on had all failed to innovate, and Edith had even had a go herself, but her efforts had been useless and she'd started to have a lot more respect for Vita's vision. Or, as she'd come to believe, maybe it had been Percy's vision. Maybe Percy had been the one with the talent all along. And that was exactly what she was going to find out.

Percy's studio was tucked behind Covent Garden in a cobbled mews, but although she could see the lights were on inside, when she knocked there was no response. Deciding that Percy must be coming back soon, Edith decided to wait.

The mews, she noticed, had become smarter in the last few years and there was a new Italian café next to the pub. Now she sat in the window of the café and turned up her nose at the small cup of coffee the waiter presented her with, marvelling that these foreigners liked coffee at all, and feeling slightly soiled that the dark-skinned waiter was smiling at her. She reassured herself that the Italians were wasting their time. They'd never make any money from a café like this. The British liked tea, and this place and all the cafés like it wouldn't last. She regretted not stopping for refreshments at Lyons Corner House.

But her window seat gave her an opportunity to watch the front of Percy's studio and thankfully, after one cup of the grim-tasting coffee, she saw Percy approaching from the end of the road, carrying with difficulty two fabric tailors' dummies. She smiled at how funny he looked manhandling them. And she remembered, in a sudden rush, how Percy had brought some fabulous costumes to the Zip Club for the girls and had been so jolly, and how much fun it had been getting ready for the show.

For the first time in ages she experienced a real pang for those carefree heady days – for the camaraderie of the troupe, the applause, the champagne and the dancing, not to mention the thrill of her illicit affair with the club's owner, Jack. She'd been happy to see the back of that chapter of her life, but now she missed the girls and the buzz of it all. She missed having friends.

And then she remembered, with a stab of resentment, how her friends had turned out not to be friends at all. And that Vita had stolen Nancy away and the pair of them had waltzed off, without giving her a second thought. Well, Vita was a fool, she reminded herself. She was a fool to pretend not to be Anna Darton.

She might want to fritter her life away, doing God-knows-what with Nancy, Edith thought, but she'd discovered a business ambition within herself that burnt like fire in her belly. She would show Clement, his mother, everyone – and one day even Vita, too – that she wasn't so easily dismissed.

Quickly she left her seat in the window and, arranging her cloche hat, set off towards Percy, but seeing that his hands were full and he hadn't noticed her, she veered right into his path. One of the tailors' dummies wobbled and Edith caught it before it hit the cobbles.

'Oh, I'm so terribly sorry,' she said, and then she paused dramatically. 'Percy? Percy, is it really you?'

'Oh, goodness,' Percy said. 'Hello. You look well, Edith.'

'Thank you,' she said, stepping back and smiling, as if in delight and shock, thinking that Percy hadn't changed at all. He was wearing a jaunty paisley cravat and a knitted pullover over his white shirt, with a floppy bow-tie at the neck. He had thicker, round tortoiseshell-framed glasses, and she noticed several pins poking out haphazardly from the wool of his pullover.

She also noticed that something of his boyishness had gone and he looked older. He also looked wary, and she wondered how much he knew – about her and Clement, and about Vita, too. For a second she felt scared about this confrontation, but she was determined to bluff it out.

'I'd completely forgotten . . . Your studio is around here somewhere, isn't it?'

'Yes, just down there.' Percy nodded and then said, 'Why don't you come along? I'm going there now. It would be nice to catch up.'

'Here, let me help,' she said, offering to take one of the dummies, but Percy insisted that he was fine, and Edith walked alongside him the short distance to the studio.

'That is a very smart suit,' he commented, as he unlocked the door to the studio.

She could tell he was rapidly adjusting his opinion of her, and she smiled sweetly. Percy always had such good taste, and the way her lilac crêpe was nipped in at all the right places, whilst still being à la mode, was satisfying.

'Oh, this old thing,' Edith said as they stepped through the inset door and Percy set the dummies down inside.

Now that she ran a business herself, Edith marvelled that Percy could work in such chaos. Vita had loved it here, but Edith found it claustrophobic and disorganized and, if anything, since she'd last been here, it had become worse. Why Percy couldn't sort out all these old costumes was beyond her.

'Are you living in London?' he asked. 'Still dancing?'

'Oh no. Not any more,' she said elusively, then smiled, a feeling of triumph surging in her chest. *He really didn't know. He didn't know that she was married. Or to whom.* 'But I miss the old days. Do you ever hear from the girls?' she asked innocently, as she walked by the long workbench, running her hand along the smooth wood, then picking up a piece of gauze material that was covered in sequins.

'Not many of them. Jemima got married. Betsy, too. She's expecting a baby, so I hear.'

This was hardly surprising. Betsy had wanted nothing more than to get married and settle down. 'Well, good for them.' She paused for a fraction of a second, her heart in her throat. She simply had to know what Percy knew. And so, sounding as nonchalant as she could, she asked, 'I often wonder what happened to Nancy?'

'Nancy? She's with Vita in Paris,' Percy said.

'Paris?' Edith exclaimed, pretending to be shocked. 'Oh, actually, that's right – I vaguely heard something . . .'

Percy didn't know that she'd given her ticket to Vita, or that she'd married Clement. Today was getting better and better.

'Is Vita in touch?'

'I had a postcard,' Percy said, nodding to the wall. 'I keep meaning to get back to her, but I've been so busy.'

'May I?' Edith asked and Percy nodded. She walked over to the board and took down the sepia photograph of Notre-Dame cathedral and turned it over. She read the back of the card carefully, trying to keep her face neutral, but her heart was hammering. 'She wants to start her underwear business again?'

'She was so talented,' Percy said, with a sad sigh. 'It's a shame she ran away. I often wonder what happened to that Withshaw and Taylor order.'

'Oh, I remember that!' she said with a light laugh, hoping that Percy hadn't noticed the flush starting up in her cheeks. 'We did the presentation. That was *fun*. You should have been there. We all sang,' she laughed. '"Top Drawer, Top Drawer, you need look no further for . . ." I can't remember the rest. You should have been there.'

Percy put his hands in his pockets and looked at his shoes. 'Did you hear what happened?' he asked. 'To me, I mean?'

'No?'

'There was a man . . . who wanted to get hold of Vita.'

He meant Clement.

'What man?'

'I don't know why he was so desperate to find her, but . . .' Percy paused, his voice catching. 'He was very dangerous. And – well, let's just say it's taken me a while to get back on my feet. The whole business cost me . . . in many ways.'

'Oh dear. But you're fine now?' Edith clarified.

Percy looked up at her with furrowed eyebrows. 'I guess I am, although my life has had to change. I have . . . struggled.'

'And this man? You haven't heard from him?'

'No, but I worry for Vita. I hope she can stay away from him.'

'I'm sure she can. You know Vita. She's very devious, when she wants to be. Percy, I have always wondered whether she took all the credit for the underwear business when in actual fact it was you?'

'Me? Oh no, no. Not at all. *She* was the one with the talent and the vision. I simply pointed her in the right direction.'

'Is that so? You weren't tempted to start the underwear empire yourself?'

Percy laughed. 'No, Edith. I'm hardly the person for it. I have this to keep me occupied. And as I say, my health . . . well, I don't think I'll be working in the theatre much longer.'

'You sound like you need a holiday.'

Percy let out a sad laugh. 'I'm sure I do.'

'You should take a leaf out of Vita's book. It seems she's on a permanent holiday with Nancy,' Edith said, flapping the postcard in her hand and then putting it down.

'They're not on holiday,' Percy said defensively, 'they're working at Les Folies Bergère.'

'Oh, well,' Edith said. 'Fancy that.'

'If I get in touch, I'll tell her I ran into you.'

'Oh, you don't need to,' Edith said, waving her hand. 'She and I were never good friends. And honestly, Percy, I'd think twice before contacting them. Vita was always such trouble. I'd stay well away, if I were you.'

Percy gave her a nod and a strange look, then the bell on the door went and a stressed-out messenger boy from the Adelphi Theatre came through the door and Edith made her excuses, blowing Percy an air-kiss and saying she'd make her own way out.

Back in the cobbled mews, Edith took a deep breath on the pavement, waiting for her heart rate to slow down.

'*Ciao, bella,*' called the waiter from the café opposite, but Edith ignored him. *Dreadful foreigner.*

26

Café de Flore

Vita waited nervously in the covered awning of the Café de Flore, sipping the glass of water and replacing it on the round marble table in front of her. She could do with something stronger, but she didn't have the money for a carafe of wine. In fact, without her job, she was starting to wonder how on earth she was going to get by. Nancy was no use. She never had any money and, besides, Vita refused to ask her for anything – not after what had happened. She still wasn't actually *speaking* to Nancy. Not that Nancy had noticed.

She looked around her at the eclectic crowd: the usual ragtag bunch of writers and some older women who were eating alone, happy to flirt with the waiters in their white shirts and black aprons, who rushed between the tables.

The woman at the next table was wearing a peacock-blue jacket with an emerald brooch pinned to her lapel. Vita watched her load her fork with crispy schnitzel and a buttery potato, and her stomach let out an unseemly growl of hunger.

It had been four long days since she'd left Fletch's apartment and had lost her job at Les Folies, and the humiliation of it still stung. She'd hardly seen Nancy, who had stayed out late after two performances. Alone in the apartment, Vita had paced, feeling wretched and cut off from her friends.

Eventually, deciding she had to do something, she called the only other friend she had in the city. But when she'd dug out the card from her purse and had used Madame Vertbois's telephone to place a call to Paul Kilkenny, the man who'd answered had told Vita that Paul wasn't back for a few days. The man had sounded dismissive, and Vita wasn't at all sure that he'd taken her message.

Then last night Nancy had come in 'early' at eleven-thirty, but she'd been high – although she was pretending she wasn't. They'd started to discuss Vita's situation, but Nancy had been annoyingly flippant.

'It'll blow over,' she'd said, failing to grasp how much it mattered to Vita that her reputation had been shot to pieces.

'It won't,' Vita had replied.

'I don't see the problem. You didn't like old Rubier anyway.'

That might have been true, but it wasn't the point. 'You were the one who told me to have a fling with Fletch,' Vita had said, feeling put out.

'I know, and I'm pleased you did,' Nancy had replied, stumbling into the chair. 'But you have to be subtle about these things, that's all.'

'Subtle?' Vita had snapped, looking down at Nancy, seeing what a mess she was in. Nancy didn't even know the meaning of the word.

'Don't be so cross, little one,' Nancy had slurred. 'You were going to leave anyway. I thought you were going to work for that woman,' and she'd flapped her unlit cigarette in the air.

She meant Madame Sacerdote, of course. Vita had thoroughly intended to work for her, but with each passing day her confidence was waning. Why would Jenny Sacerdote take on someone like her? Besides, who could Vita call on to give her a reference, now that the door at Les Folies was firmly shut?

She'd smarted about it all night, and this morning she was only slightly mollified to realize that Nancy must have felt bad about their exchange, because when Vita had come in from walking Mr Wild, she'd found a note Nancy had left on the table, saying that Fletch had asked if she would meet him at the Café de Flore today for lunch.

She almost hadn't come, not really trusting Nancy as a reliable messenger, but being alone in the apartment with her thoughts as company was driving her crazy. And besides, she and Nancy had no food. *Is Fletch intending to buy me lunch?* she wondered. Could he afford it? Because she certainly couldn't afford to buy it for herself.

And if they did try to have a pleasant lunch, what would they talk about? And what would Fletch think Vita agreeing to meet him meant? That they were a couple now? And *were* they? She couldn't be sure it was what she wanted. Not after finding out about Solange.

She noticed a man at the back of the awning now, near the wall, reading a newspaper. He looked South American or Spanish, with a bushy moustache and oiled hair. He was smoking a cigarette and he stared at Vita for a moment too long and she turned away, feeling uncomfortable. But still she could feel his gaze on her, when Fletch arrived.

'Vita, you're here,' he said, as if he hadn't expected her to show up. She smiled weakly, as he sat down and leant forward to kiss her cheek. She heard the Spanish man shake out his paper in noisy disapproval.

Fletch was wearing a white shirt, open at the neck, and a black cardigan. He wasn't carrying Mabel and, without this crucial signifier that he was a musician, he looked odd and out of place, as if he might be a janitor, she thought meanly. He smiled widely at her, as if everything was normal, but Vita felt panic dart through her.

She'd hoped that seeing Fletch would answer some of the questions that had been churning round and round in her mind, but seeing him now like this, in the cold light of day, made her feel even more ashamed of the way she'd behaved in his room. Had she really done those things with him? And was he expecting it to happen again? Because it couldn't. Not after the damage that had already been done.

'I didn't think this was your kind of place,' she said.

'It's around the corner from one of the rehearsal studios. I'm in a new band,' he replied, putting his hat on the table. Then he leant forward with a grin. 'Although there's talk of having the afternoon off.'

Vita squirmed in her seat. If he meant that he wanted to spend the afternoon with her, then he was very much mistaken. But even so, she felt her pulse racing as she looked at his hand on the table, remembering how he'd touched her, and where . . .

'It's so good to see you. How have you been? I've missed you,' he said.

His brown eyes stared directly at her and Vita put her head down. She should never have come. This was absolutely the wrong place to have this kind of meeting. *As if they could suddenly have a friendly lunch.*

'What the matter?' Fletch said, finally realizing how flustered she was.

'Nothing.'

'Nothing?'

'You should have told me about Solange,' she blurted out, trying and failing to mask the jealousy and hurt she'd been feeling. How much of a fool she felt. And how humiliated she was, too, about losing her job over him.

'Oh,' Fletch said, nodding slowly and exhaling. 'Solange,' he repeated, as if the very word spelt trouble. 'I don't know what she thinks is going on, but there ain't nothing between us. Not like between you and me. And you gotta believe me, Vita, I didn't know she'd get you fired. She's kind of headstrong. I guess that women who feel kinda scorned can tend to be a bit . . . nasty.' He said this as if it were Solange's problem and nothing at all to do with him.

Vita took a second. So it was Solange who'd got her fired. She'd suspected as much, but it still hurt to hear Fletch say it so flippantly.

'If I'd known about you and her . . .'

'Listen. I'm serious, Vita. Solange don't mean nothing to me. Not like you,' he said in an intense whisper, reaching out and putting his hand over hers. She glanced at the next table, seeing that the woman had noticed the contact and her eyes were looking disapprovingly at Vita, who slid her hand out from under Fletch's. He looked up at her, his eyes searching hers, but she flicked her gaze away and pressed her lips together.

'You see, Fletch, I've been thinking and . . .'

Fletch leant forward. 'I've been thinking, too. Non-stop, as it happens. About you and the other night.' He whistled softly and grinned at her. 'That was really somethin'.'

He knew so little about her. He had no idea that Archie had been her only other lover, but now Fletch assumed – who knew what he assumed? – but certainly that she was *that* sort of girl. She stole a glance at him and looked at his disarming smile, and saw now that he thought they were going to carry on being lovers. She shook her head, hoping he'd stop talking like this, but he leant forward again.

'I never thought a girl like you and a boy like me – that we could be so good together. And to hell with what anyone thinks. If it works, it works. Don't you remember, Vita?' he probed further, and she felt his hand on her leg under the table.

She jumped and pulled away and, at that moment, she saw a man rushing past on the pavement. He was looking jaunty in a navy-blue suit with garish white spats and he came to a dramatic stop, then reversed, and Vita looked up and saw that it was Paul. He stopped, clutching his hat to his chest, and waved.

'Vita!' he called and grinned at her and, in a moment, he was next to their table. 'Oh, Vita!'

She stood up, and she and Fletch shook hands awkwardly with Paul, although for a second she thought he was going to kiss her cheek.

'I got your message,' he said with a big grin. 'I just got

146

back to town and I knew I'd run into you somewhere,' he went on, before looking across at Fletch. 'What you done? Your hair? You look different. You been staying out of trouble?'

Was it really that obvious that something about her had changed? Maybe it was because she was blushing. 'Where have you been?' she asked, keen to change the subject. She could sense Fletch bristling.

'Oh, here and there. Mostly out in the countryside,' he said, but didn't elaborate on who he'd been with. 'I did some sketches. I'll show them to you.'

She nodded and then, in the awkward pause that followed, she said, 'This is my friend, Fletch. He's a musician at the club.'

'Les Folies, right? You're both there?' Paul asked.

'Not me . . . any more. Sadly, I find myself unemployed,' Vita added, raising an eyebrow at Fletch.

'Oh, good. So you're free,' Paul replied, as if it were great news and not the disaster it actually was. 'Then we're going on that museum trip. You promised, remember? Was that why you were calling? To make a time, because look at this – it's all worked out perfectly.' He spread his arms out at her and she laughed nervously, looking between him and Fletch. 'So, how are you fixed this afternoon?' Paul continued.

'Well, I . . .' she began, glancing at Fletch.

'Good. It's settled then,' Paul said, clapping his hands together. 'I'll meet you at the Louvre at two, sharp. I've got to see the barber before then. Nice to meet you,' he finished, tipping his hat to Fletch.

'That's Paul all over,' Vita said, shaking her head and

sitting back down opposite Fletch. 'He's like a whirlwind.' She watched him scooting down the street in a great rush, but Fletch looked annoyed.

'Well,' he said, drumming his long fingers on the marble tabletop. 'So, you've got plans now for this afternoon? A nice little date lined up at a gallery. With your arty boyfriend . . .'

Vita did a double-take, astonished at his bitter tone. Why was he behaving like a jealous schoolboy? He could see perfectly well that she'd been bamboozled into the arrangement.

'Don't be like that. He's only a friend,' Vita said defensively. 'I hardly know him.'

'Solange is just a friend,' Fletch said, pointedly.

'Yes, but . . .'

'But what?'

'I don't sleep with my friends,' she said in a cross whisper.

'Only your enemies, huh?' Fletch said, standing up. He shook his head and picked up his hat.

'Fletch, wait,' she said. 'Where are you going?'

'Let's spare ourselves the awkward conversation, Vita. You and me don't seem to be on the same vibe.'

She looked at him, not altogether sure what a vibe was. 'But what about lunch?'

'I ain't hungry no more,' he said.

148

27

The *Mona Lisa*'s smile

Vita was still fuming about her encounter with Fletch as she made her way to the Louvre that afternoon. *This is why I've been single for so long*, she thought indignantly. *This* was why she'd sworn off men since Archie Fenwick. Because men were *impossible*.

She'd wanted to be the one to let Fletch down gently, but the way he'd behaved had infuriated her. How *dare* he suggest that she and Paul were in any way the same as him and Solange? She and Paul were friends, and he was kind and decent and interesting, and she was damned well going to enjoy her time with him.

It was only as she arrived in the giant square in front of the Louvre, its sandy-coloured gravel bright in the sunshine, that she realized that meeting Paul here might be more difficult than she'd imagined. She walked along the side of the impressive building, looking up at the ornate windows, and found the back of the queue of people waiting at the ticket booth. Did Paul mean for her to meet him inside?

But just as she was worrying about scraping together the money for a ticket, Paul appeared from the front of the queue, waving wildly and jumping up to be seen above the crowd, and Vita felt a wave of relief. He'd had his hair cut and it made him look even more boyish.

'I've got tickets. Come on,' he called. Without giving her time to back out, he led her by the elbow to the door and straight to the front of the queue, where they were ushered inside by the doorman.

She'd been to a few art galleries before, but Vita had not imagined the splendour of the Louvre, and before long, as they strolled through the marble hallways with their high vaulted ceilings, the outside world and all her worries seemed to fade away.

'Come and see the sculptures,' Paul suggested, leading her down a long corridor. He seemed to know his way around, but she wanted to slow down and take in the magnificent oils. But it felt good to be with him, because with Paul she felt as if she were on another adventure . . . but the right sort this time.

It was as if there were two parts to her life – the life with Nancy and the club, and the late nights and parties, and Fletch, too; and this other life, which had nothing to do with Nancy and was filled with art and creativity. And Paul belonged to this world, and it was a relief that even if it was just for an afternoon, she felt as if she belonged, too.

'Look at this one,' he said, staring at a marble torso of a woman. 'It's one thing to draw and paint, but to *make* things – there's a talent. Conjuring something up: something real, something you can hold.'

'You could take up sculpture,' she suggested, laughing that he was eyeing up the breasts of the statue. 'If you really want to study the female form.'

Paul laughed, embarrassed that she'd caught him ogling the statue. 'Let's go and see *Lisa*.'

Vita laughed at him abbreviating the painting's name – as if he personally knew the famous subject.

There was a crowd, and they had to mill around until they had space to stand in front of the great masterpiece.

'What do you think she's thinking?' Vita asked.

'That the chair she's sitting on is uncomfortable,' Paul offered. 'Or maybe she's thinking about what she wants to eat for lunch.'

'Or she has a secret plan,' Vita suggested. 'I see what they mean about her eyes. How they follow you around.'

'Is it how you imagined?'

'Not as big.'

'Size doesn't matter,' he said confidently, and she wondered if he was referring to himself. 'You know how much it's insured for?'

Paul told her and Vita whistled, impressed.

'Although this one could be a fake,' he said. 'There are always rumours about forgeries.'

'It'd have to be a good forgery,' she said. 'It's convinced me.'

'You'd be surprised how many things in this world are not what they seem,' he replied. 'Come on. I want to show you my favourite painting.'

He led her away through another two cavernous halls and then took a right and they were in a smaller chamber. It was empty and there was a brown bench in the middle, and Paul went over to it and they sat down.

'Now *there's* a portrait,' Paul said, and Vita studied the

picture of a woman on a horse. She didn't really care for it much herself, but Paul seemed to like it.

'Oh, look. Someone has left a case. That's odd,' Vita said. 'What do you think is in it?' she asked.

'I don't know. Money? A gun?'

She laughed at the absurd suggestions.

Or maybe it's an instrument, she thought, thinking of Fletch and Mabel. 'Someone will be missing it by now,' she said. 'There was a man around here somewhere . . .' She swivelled round, looking for the uniformed guard who patrolled the museum.

'Oh, don't worry – I'll hand it in on the way out,' Paul said.

They got up and started to stroll to the far end of the gallery and she followed Paul, presuming that he must know the quickest way to the exit.

As they strolled, she told him about how she'd met Agatha and had returned the material to Maison Jenny.

'Vita, that's swell,' Paul said. 'Tenacity. See, I told you – you are in the right place for fashion.'

'It's no use. I need a referee, and I don't have one. Maison Jenny would never take someone like me without one.'

'They should snap you up.'

'I'm not the right sort.' She told him about the strict-looking doorman.

Paul drummed his fingers on the case and she looked at him curiously. 'Nonsense! People are people.'

'Oh no, they're not,' Vita said.

'Yes, they are,' Paul insisted. 'Believe me, I know. And what I also know is that appearance is everything.' He narrowed his eyes, and she could tell he had an idea.

'What are you talking about?'

'You know that car?'

'Which car?'

'You know we saw that big, fancy car? The one you took a picture of me with.'

'Yes. What about it?'

'Say I could hire it for an hour? Or a car like it?'

'Don't be absurd.'

'There's always a way. Those fancy chauffeurs, they lurk around all day . . . bored. I bet there'll be one not three streets away from here.'

'Paul, you're not making any sense.'

'Let's go,' he said, linking arms with Vita and walking quickly towards the arrow sign pointing the way out.

'But what about the case?'

'I'll drop it into the police station on my way back.'

'From where?'

'From making an impression. Come on, Vita. Take a chance.'

28

St Hilda's

Mrs Anne Lanyard, the headmistress at St Hilda's, seemed like a friendly enough woman, Edith thought, as she showed her and the child into her office on the final part of their school tour. The spacious room was panelled in oak, with lists of names and sporting achievements inscribed in gold all the way up to the ceiling, and the heavy oak furniture was old-fashioned – rather like the headmistress herself.

Mrs Lanyard could do with some styling, Edith thought, as her dark-aubergine suit made her look lumpy and her jowls were covered in caked face powder, but maybe this was how the headmistress of a place like this *should* look. Edith so rarely got to discover the world away from Darton that she often imagined she would stumble across the kind of glamour and style that she longed for, but she knew that she certainly wasn't going to find it here.

Even though Clement rarely remarked on her beauty these days, others did and Edith had become quite used to turning heads wherever she went. At first, she'd enjoyed the attention, but increasingly she felt a little freakish, as if she had been lifted out of the glamour of London and plonked here, where people didn't have the faintest clue about fashion or style.

It seemed to her that everyone and everything in the North was desperately old-fashioned and staid. The people she met were so set in their ways, so sure of their place, that Edith felt now, as she often did, as if she were trailblazing, in her white designer dress that she'd had copied from a sketch in *Vogue*.

As they were shown to seats near the desk, Edith looked out of the arched window behind the desk to the playing fields beyond, where a group of girls were playing lacrosse. From what she'd seen so far of the school, she'd been impressed. She only had experience of schools in Surrey near her parents' house, so finding this boarding school near Manchester had taken meticulous research, but she had no doubt that it was the best and that her money would be well spent.

She still couldn't believe she was doing this – that she was actually paying for Clement's daughter to come here. She was quite astonished by her own generosity, and relieved that she'd been able to pay the term's fees up front from her personal savings account. She could, of course, have sent the girl somewhere far, far away, to keep her out of sight and out of mind. She could have got rid of her altogether. She was sure there were ways of making sickly-looking children disappear.

But then she'd taken a step back from her jealous fuming and, thinking more logically and long-term, she'd had a change of heart. Surely the more intelligent thing to do would be to keep the child where she could control her? What if she invested in the child's future? Might such a strategy pay off, in the long run?

This whole plan had taken weeks to coordinate properly and come to fruition. It had taken ages to find the right moment to get away from the mill, and to take Susan away to St Hilda's, outside Manchester, without her mother, Marianne, finding out. Or Clement, for that matter. Edith was sticking to her vow of never discussing her husband's lover or their bastard child with him. Fortunately, Clement was away for a few days at the races, so she'd grabbed the opportunity to bring Susan here. He didn't need to know about any of this until it was strictly necessary. If he didn't know, he wouldn't have a chance to object – or interfere. Not when every aspect of this clever plan would be to their mutual advantage.

She was beginning to understand that she was able to make more strategic decisions than Clement, who, whilst he was ambitious and driven, seemed to be ruled by his temper and former grudges. Like his father before him, Clement was prone to getting distracted and becoming unfocused.

Since Darius had died, Edith had lost count of the business decisions she'd quietly engineered that had kept the mill on track. Clement never told her in so many words, but she knew that she'd become fundamental to the management of the staff, the strategy, the buying decisions. She might not have her own desk – yet – but her feet were well and truly under the table.

And during this time Edith had secretly dedicated herself to finding out everything she could about her husband's lover. The other girls in the mill, from what she could gather, found Marianne Chastain snooty and difficult, although everyone agreed that she was a doting mother to Susan. But soon

Edith's findings had started to explain Marianne's sense of superiority – her French heritage, her milliner mother – and it had been this part of the puzzle that had set Edith thinking and had started her on this ambitious plan. And now that it was becoming a reality, she wanted to pinch herself. Even though she said it herself: she was a genius.

'Well, it's been lovely showing you both around the school,' the headmistress gushed, bringing Edith back to herself.

This was just Step One. She mustn't get ahead of herself.

'Thank you very much for showing us everything,' Susan said. She looked smaller than Edith remembered, and Edith realized that the uniform she'd bought would be way too big.

'Oh, what a lovely, polite daughter you have,' Mrs Lanyard said with a smile. Edith could see that the kind woman had taken a shine to Susan, although she herself found the child rather aloof and strange. She'd only spent a morning with Susan, but it was plenty. The girl had this weird way of observing her, which made Edith feel uncomfortable, and the sooner she was away from her, the better.

'No, no, she's not my daughter,' Edith corrected the headmistress, although she touched the girl proprietorially on the shoulder, and Susan blinked as she gazed up at Edith, who looked away.

'You're a lucky girl, coming here,' Mrs Lanyard told Susan. 'You will get a fine education. Do you want to come and meet your new friends?'

'I'd like that very much.'

'Do you need me to stay?' Edith checked. She glanced at her silver watch, knowing that she must make the half-past train, in order to get back to Darton before Marianne left the mill and became suspicious.

'No, it's not necessary. We can take things from here. I will leave you for a moment to say your goodbyes.'

She left the room and Susan's eyes – as pale blue as Clement's – locked with Edith's. 'I am so grateful to you, Mrs Darton, for this opportunity,' she said in a small, husky voice. 'I know you said that Mother wanted this for me and it was too hard for her to say goodbye, but it will be hard for us both to be apart. Could you give her this for me, please?' She took a letter out of her pocket and thrust it into Edith's hands. Had this been what she'd been writing on the silent trip here on the train? Edith had thought she'd been drawing. She thought the child had believed her lie that this plan had been sanctioned by Marianne.

'Be good,' Edith told her, slipping the letter into her snakeskin handbag.

'Mrs Darton, I . . .' Susan began, and Edith saw that her eyes were filling with tears.

'Stop that silly nonsense at once,' Edith scolded. 'Half the children at the mill would cut off their right arms to have the opportunity you have here.' Edith winced at her own choice of words. The child's grandmother had lost her right arm in an unfortunate accident at the mill. She stared down at the child. 'Your mother – and you – will thank me one day.'

She nodded, retrieving her gloves from her handbag and putting them on, before turning and heading for the door. She felt the child's eyes on her back as she turned the brass handle and, when she closed the door, Susan was still standing there, looking ghostly and mournful and alone by the desk.

On the train back to Darton, an hour later, Edith ripped open the carefully sealed envelope, unfolded Susan's letter and read the childish script, still surprised that she could even write. She'd tried to tell her mother what had happened this morning – that the trip to Manchester had come as a complete surprise, but that Mrs Darton had been 'kind', a compliment not lost on Edith. *I love you, Mother*, the child had signed off.

How wonderful it would be to be on the receiving end of that kind of unconditional love, Edith thought. She'd never had it. Not from her parents, and not, she realized, from Clement, who might give her security, but love – this kind of love – was a different matter altogether.

Maybe it had been discovering that Susan was Clement's child, but Edith had begun to realize that she needed one of her own very soon, to cement her place at Darton. If she bore Clement an heir, then whatever happened, Vita could never come back in the future and claim any part of Darton. And a child loving her, like Susan loved her own mother – well, that would be something to look forward to, wouldn't it?

But conceiving the son she longed for was easier said than done, when Clement's behaviour in the bedroom was so erratic. He'd been different since Darius had died, as if some kind of anger had left him. He wasn't so quick to lose his temper, although maybe that was her own steadying influence. Lately, however, the dominating games that he'd once played had stopped, and behind their bedroom door he'd treated Edith, more often than not, as he did at the factory: with cool detachment.

When their couplings happened, less frequently now, they were still violent and Clement seemed to go somewhere else, hardly looking at her as he pinned her to the bed. Afterwards he left immediately to go to his own bedroom, and Edith was left, feeling bruised and sore. She wondered whether he'd found another mistress.

Well, he certainly won't have the old one, she thought, tucking the letter safely away in her purse. No, neither Clement nor Marianne would know about this letter – or about St Hilda's. Edith would make sure of that.

She'd been envisaging the confrontation with Marianne for so long that Edith was not remotely nervous as she went up the stairs to the factory office and asked the secretary to fetch Miss Chastain a few hours later.

Edith waited, sitting behind Darius's old mahogany desk, rearranging the pile of headed paper in the tray. She was never allowed to sit here when Clement was in the office, but now she made herself comfortable, enjoying the sense of rightful ownership. Then she rubbed her hands over the skirt of her white dress, feeling them perspiring, and took a deep breath as the glass office door opened and Marianne came through.

She was wearing one of the workers' dark-blue overalls, a loose strand of long, blonde hair escaping from the matching blue headscarf. The clogs on her feet clip-clopped across the tiled office floor to the desk and stopped, but Edith didn't stand.

'What is this about, Mrs Darton?' Marianne asked. Her hands were red-raw and she wrung them together. She'd obviously been put to work with the chemicals and the dyes. She looked stressed and exhausted, and Edith tried to see objectively what Clement had found so attractive about her.

And then she realized. It was the defiance in her that must have appealed. There was this poise about the angle of Marianne's head that made her seem superior, and Edith felt the same way she had when Susan had stared at her. As if she were being assessed.

The woman had a nerve, Edith thought, after the scene she'd caused at Darius's funeral. Did she think she was *better* in some way than Edith? Because she'd got herself pregnant with Clement's child? Edith forced herself to keep a level head, much as she despised the woman.

'I have a proposition,' Edith said. There was no point in sugar-coating what she had to say, but she tried to keep her tone neutral. After all, she needed Marianne to comply, in order to pull off her plan.

'What kind of proposition?' Marianne was suspicious. 'Where is Clem— Mr Darton?'

Edith bristled. *As if she had a right to know.* 'Let me be clear, Miss Chastain. You and I are going to come to a *private* arrangement. Between us. Woman-to-woman. This does not involve *my* husband. And you will never speak of it to him.'

Marianne blushed. 'What kind of arrangement?'

Edith took a breath and spread her hands out on the desk. The opal engagement ring on her finger and the gold wedding band were clearly on show. She saw Marianne's eyes flick towards her hands.

'I am going to send both you and your daughter away – as you stated was your wish, when we last spoke.'

Marianne's eyes widened, then she looked confused. 'You're saying that we could live together somewhere else?'

'Oh no. Not together. Susan will be away at school.'

Marianne took a moment to compute this, and Edith felt a glow of satisfaction, seeing the incomprehension on her face.

'At school? What do you mean? Where?' Her voice was suddenly small – frightened, or maybe suspicious, Edith couldn't tell.

'Does that matter? Don't you want her to get a good education?'

'Yes, but . . .'

'Well then. Boarding school will be the making of her. We're both agreed. You don't need to concern yourself with the details.'

'Boarding school? But . . . but you can't send her away and not tell me where.' The poor woman still thought she had some power. Her eyes were frantic as she quickly tried a different, more compliant approach. 'I appreciate you taking an interest, but—'

'I don't think you understand. This is not a *choice*.'

'But . . . we need to discuss—I need to prepare Susan.'

'That won't be necessary. She has already left.'

Marianne was silent for a moment. 'Left?'

'Yes. Lily, is it, who you left in charge?' Marianne's face went pale. 'She's a very persuadable person.' Edith still baulked at the level of bribe she'd given the young girl – a train ticket to Cornwall, so that she could be with the farmhand she'd taken a shine to. Oh yes, Edith was good at finding out what made people tick.

'What have you done with Susan?' Marianne's voice rose in hysteria, but Edith had been expecting this. The woman came towards the table, her hands banging on the edge, her eyes filling with furious tears. 'You can't take her . . . you can't. Mrs Darton, please—'

'Pull yourself together, Miss Chastain. Sit down and pay attention,' Edith snapped in her fiercest voice.

'Oh, my baby. What have you done with my baby?'

The woman was sobbing now and she buckled into the chair. She sniffed loudly, wiping her eyes on the sleeve of her smock and trying to compose herself. 'Oh, *mon Dieu, mon Dieu* . . .' she muttered, her breath raggedy now.

'I said: calm down! *Do* you want to see your daughter again?'

'Of course,' Marianne said, trying to compose herself.

'Then you will do exactly as I say.'

There was a beat as Marianne tried again to compose herself.

'What do you want me to do, Mrs Darton?' she said in a quivering voice. 'I'll do anything – anything at all. Just let me have Susan back.'

'Well, that depends.'

'On what?'

'On a task I have for you,' Edith said, spreading her fingers on the edge of the desk.

'What task?'

'I'm sending you away, on . . . let's call it a fact-finding mission.'

'But where? Where are you sending me?'

29

Pay Day

Vita walked through the door of number seventy on the Champs-Élysées, her satchel swinging. Georges, the doorman, wished her a good morning and tipped his hat. How odd that she'd once been so terrified of him, she thought with a smile, as she took the steps two at a time up to the Salon.

'*Bonjour*, Vita,' Beatrice, Jenny's receptionist, said as Vita pushed through the door with its etched-glass inscription. Beatrice was in her late fifties – a portly, yet stylish woman, who ran Madame Jenny's operation with gentle efficiency. This morning she was in a mauve dress with a silk tie around the neck, and was watering the two plinths of pink roses that flanked the desk. Madame Jenny loved her pink roses, and Vita stopped to breathe in their heady scent. '*Tu es de nouveau en avance.*' You're early again.

Vita smiled. How could she stay in bed, when there was so much here at work? Besides, she'd already walked Mr Wild and, if she stayed in the flat, she'd have to deal with Nancy, and she couldn't face yet another showdown.

Nancy wasn't at all happy that Vita was working such long hours. She was annoyed that the two of them hardly saw each other these days, lamenting that Les Folies wasn't as much fun without her. Secretly, Vita suspected this was because the other girls wouldn't put up with Nancy's demands.

But Les Folies and all the constant dramas with the girls already seemed like a distant memory to Vita. Swapping her nocturnal existence for a proper day-job had made her feel so much happier and healthier. In fact she loved every single second of the long days in the studios on the Champs-Élysées. If she'd been allowed to spend the night here, she happily would have.

She started towards the door that led through to the studios, but Beatrice stopped her.

'Wait. I have something for you,' she said, setting down the metal watering can and going behind her desk.

Vita had been working here for four magical weeks now, ever since Paul had brought her from the Louvre in the borrowed car and made a great show of telling Madame Jenny (as Vita now addressed her) how wonderful Vita was, what a hard worker and 'all-round terrific girl'.

Paul had insisted that Vita pick up the samples of her lingerie from home on the way here, and the car had looked preposterous outside her apartment. Yet, looking back, she'd been borne along on Paul's conviction that she had to make the right entrance.

He'd been correct, of course, as they'd had no problem waltzing into the building, right past Georges, with Paul acting so grandiosely, as if he owned the place. Vita had been stunned that he would take such a risk, but he had silenced her giggles as they set off up the stairs.

'Believe me, concierges like him are the eyes and ears of the place. If we get past him, then we're in. He'll be the one who gives you a reference, far more than me. Because now he thinks you have friends with fancy cars.'

'Well, if only he knew!' Vita had whispered.

'Exactly. Appearance is everything.'

'Paul, I don't know why you're doing this for me,' Vita had said, even though she was so grateful.

'For the craic,' he said, and she looked confused. 'For the fun of it. And because I'm a sucker for a damsel in distress. This is what I mean, Vita. Taking a risk – it makes you feel alive.'

Upstairs, when they'd arrived in the reception area, Beatrice had been about to relent and make an appointment for Vita to see Madame Jenny, when the great designer herself walked through from the salon with Laure. And Paul had set to work charming them both, too.

At first Vita had been worried that his effusiveness might blow her chances, and she'd been quaking with nerves as she'd stood in the reception area and Madame Sacerdote cast her eye over the silk camiknickers and bra. But Paul had been right. Vita had felt completely alive.

But then she'd seen Madame Sacerdote holding up her bra to the light, and Vita had felt something inside her shrink, as she'd just seen her own pitiful attempts in the hands of someone so skilled. Laure had looked at them next, talking in a low voice to Jenny – words not meant for Vita to hear – and Vita had felt even worse.

'The sewing isn't that good, I'm afraid,' she had begun, feeling her chances slipping away and cursing herself for allowing Paul to bamboozle her.

But Madame Jenny had smiled, her eyes softening. 'If you want to know a secret: I can barely sew myself. I leave that to my very talented, how you say – I always forget the word in English – the sewer . . .'

'Seamstress.'

'Seamstress,' Jenny had agreed, and Vita had relaxed a little. 'No, what is important is the idea behind this, which I like very much.'

'Thank you,' Vita had said. 'The whole idea came about because I wanted something supportive that I could move in, when I was dancing – in London,' she'd added.

'That's very sensible. All of my designs are from the same principle. Elegance and movement. That is the key. I can tell, Vita, that you and I share the same designing instincts.'

It must be Madame Jenny's French, Vita thought. *The compliment of saying I have comparable instincts – she can't really mean it, can she?*

'When can you start?' she'd asked Vita.

'Right away,' Vita had said, glancing at Paul, who had winked.

'Why don't you start tomorrow? Agatha will take you to meet my draper, and you can work with her. There's a lot to be done and you mustn't get in the way, but make yourself useful. Laure here will be in charge, if you have any problems. I'll give you a trial for a week. And then we'll see. Let's hope you're as hard a worker as your friend says you are,' she'd added, with a wry nod at Paul, who had made a grand flourish of signing the visitors' book, which Vita thought was a step too far.

Vita, remembering the moment, idly looked now in the pages of the visitors' book on the reception desk for Paul's entry, as Beatrice rummaged in the desk drawer. It seemed to Vita that Madame Jenny's salon was the very epicentre of fashion, a kind of Mecca of luxury and Parisian elegance. Here amongst the thick, gold-edged pages were the names of royalty – Her Majesty the Queen of Egypt, Her Majesty the Empress of Japan – as well as celebrities, such as the mother and sister of Fred Astaire, the singer and actress Suzy Solidor and, excitingly for Vita, the curly-haired queen of the movies whom Vita had seen when she'd followed Agatha here: Mary Pickford. She'd been in again last week, and Madame Jenny was making her a little black dress with a bijou pleated hemline, long straight sleeves and a white piqué collar and bow-tie.

If she was ever going to learn about the fashion business, Vita thought, then Jenny Sacerdote had to be *the* best person in Paris to teach her.

'Ah, here we are,' Beatrice said now, handing over the envelope to Vita, who gave up looking for Paul's entry. She took the envelope from Beatrice and opened it and saw a sheaf of franc notes. 'It's your pay for the month, but Madame Jenny was keen that you had some extra, for the additional hours you've worked.'

Vita felt a swell of pride. So Madame Jenny had noticed her, after all. She thanked Beatrice, feeling a profound sense of pleasure at having earnt her own money – money that had nothing to do with Nancy. Money that was solely hers. All hers. She couldn't help running her fingertip over the notes. Then, embarrassed that Beatrice was watching her, she tucked the envelope safely in her satchel.

'Is Agatha here yet?' Vita asked.

'No. Laure is, though,' Beatrice said, nodding her head towards the studios. 'It's the big day. Ask her if she needs anything.'

168

30

The Wedding Dress

Vita pushed through the doors into Maison Jenny's studios. This early in the morning, the workbenches were empty, the machines quiet, but it wouldn't be long before everyone arrived and the busy day would begin.

There were dozens of women in the team, and most of them had worked for Jenny for years – even from when she had her first studio near the Place Vendôme. They were all fiercely loyal and keen that Vita, as a newcomer, should prove herself. None more so than Laure, who had kept a watchful eye on everything she did.

With Agatha as her guide, Vita had set to work absorbing every detail of the fascinating business, and there hadn't been a single moment when she hadn't been amazed by Madame Jenny's operation.

First, there were Madame Jenny's pencil sketches, and Vita passed some of them hanging framed on the walls, next to boards pinned with scraps of fabric and typed lists of supplies and schedules. How anyone could draw a female form so perfectly, yet show off the design of the garments, astonished Vita. When she'd first arrived, she'd flicked through the sketchbooks again and again, loving the lines – the way

Madame Jenny's ideas were so seemingly simple and yet so elegant. Vita looked at one sketch now, her favourite, of a skirt with a simple low waistband and a long-sleeved top with a high tie-neck.

There were some very skilled artists amongst the girls, including Agatha, who showed Vita how she turned Jenny's sketches into elegant watercolours, with the stylish charcoal transformed into vibrant colours.

But then the magic of turning the painting into an actual garment occurred, and Vita watched the enviable skill of the pattern-cutters, who taught her the way every kind of garment could be split into different pieces, and how the pieces were cut out of stiff brown card, then held on the material with little brass weights.

Each garment seemed to Vita to be a work of art, but they were fun, too, and so modern. Like the pink party dress that was based on a tennis dress; a midnight-blue dress with a slashed neckline; and a coat with a majestic collar.

It was all the details, too, that Vita loved: the little tortoise-shell buttons, the fox-fur for the collars, the ostrich-feather trims and the silk ties. Everything in the workshop was so tactile: sumptuous soft silk from Ceylon, lace from Calais and crisp *broderie anglaise* from England. Vita had been able to impress the other seamstresses and junior designers with her knowledge of fabric – her background at the mill finally becoming useful – but nothing had prepared her for such wonders.

Although Madame Jenny took special commissions, the bulk of the work came from the clients who came to view her collection. On those days the models would go out into the salon wearing the various pieces of the season, and the clients would order their sizes. Such was the demand for Maison Jenny dresses that Vita was soon thrown in at the deep end, helping to cut out the pieces for the most popular '*petite robe simple*', as the journalists called the must-have piece: a plain, straight black dress, narrow and short, which could work as daytime wear, with pearls added for the evening. *Who knew*, thought Vita, *that a little black dress could have such appeal?*

Her job quickly expanded, from simply watching to delivering the pattern pieces to the long, high cutting benches, where she helped weight them on the gorgeous fabrics. Once they'd been cut out, she'd carefully deliver the pieces to the seamstresses, and Vita marvelled at how fast and accurately they worked. When the dresses came back to be finished, her work really began. Soon she had become nimble at sewing on the hooks and eyes and carefully pressing the fabric with a hot iron. Then Agatha taught her how to fold the garment into the softest tissue paper, wrap it in pink ribbon and box it up.

It seemed they couldn't get the orders out fast enough, and each time Vita delivered a finished dress to Beatrice, for her to send out, she tried to imagine the wearer and the places that the dress would appear. It was so thrilling to have this connection to the outside world.

Laure, however, was always working on the bespoke commissions, and this week she'd been working with Jenny on the wedding dress of the season, for a princess who was coming in today for the final fitting. The dress was made entirely from ivory lace, with cap sleeves and a loose bodice to a dropped waist, then a front skirt to the knee and an underskirt that fanned out into a train.

At the far end of the studio Laure was hemming the lace, which had been cut in a scalloped pattern, and was kneeling on the sheet that covered the floor. She was wearing white gloves, so that the lace didn't get damaged.

'It looks wonderful,' Vita told her, and Laure got up and stretched, pressing the white gloves into the small of her back. She was probably in her thirties – certainly younger than Madame Jenny – but had a permanent frown line between her eyebrows. Vita wondered if she had a family at home, but didn't know much about Laure's private life. That's *if* she had a life beyond Maison Jenny.

'I'm too old for this,' Laure said.

Vita gave her a sympathetic look. The clients didn't have the faintest idea of the physical effort that went into each garment.

'Oh, but look at it! It's wonderful. Wouldn't you love to get married in a dress like this?' Vita said dreamily. She wondered if Maud had worn a dress like this when she'd married Archie. She guessed she'd never know.

'Maybe you will one day,' Laure said.

Vita laughed. 'Me? I don't think so.'

'Why not? You're a very attractive young girl.'

Vita blushed, amazed that Laure would make such an observation. *Was* she attractive? Is that what people thought of her? She knew Fletch had found her attractive, but that had been different. And Archie? Well, who could believe a word that man said . . . But to hear this from Laure? Well, it was certainly a boost to her self-esteem.

'What about the man . . . ?'

'Which man?'

'The one who gave you the reference?' Laure asked, winding the cotton around the spool she was holding.

'Paul. Paul Kilkenny?'

Laure's eyes connected with Vita's, and she saw then that Laure hadn't believed that Paul was who he implied he was. Perhaps Vita's entrance with him had been rather at odds with the person she'd been in the last few weeks – one who was eager and hungry for work.

'Oh, he's just a friend,' Vita said.

'I see,' Laure replied. 'Do you have lots of rich friends? People of influence like that?'

Vita almost laughed. Paul – a man of influence? It had all been such a good act, but it had clearly worked. Although now, as Laure looked at her, Vita realized she'd had this feeling once before – with Edith, who hadn't believed her story, either.

31

The Photography Shop

The following Saturday, Vita walked out of the photography shop on the rue de Bretagne in the Marais with Mr Wild. Her prints would be ready at eleven, so she was killing time by visiting the Marché des Enfants Rouges, the nearby covered market.

It was one of Vita's favourite places in Paris, and this morning she smiled as she walked past the men playing dominoes and smoking at the low tables of the Moroccan café, where one of the waiters was pouring an ornate silver teapot with a flourish, a steaming stream of sweet tea falling into the patterned glasses.

Inside the bustling market she wandered down the narrow aisles, listening to the friendly banter between the stallholders and watching the locals with their wicker baskets, who haggled over fresh green beans, mounds of pink-and-white borlotti beans, curly purple lettuces and plump tomatoes, strings of brown onions and knots of white garlic bulbs. She heard the clank of iron weights on the old scales as a stall-holder weighed out a dish full of waxy potatoes, above the chatter of people meeting and shopping together.

The air was filled with the waft of garlicky oil, which

came from a man selling cooked snails, and with the aroma of cheese from the stall she passed next, with great wheels of blue-veined cheese on display with their gnarled grey rinds, along with ones she'd never seen before: goat's cheeses with dewy white surfaces, and creamy Brie that oozed out onto a wooden board. A woman with a gappy smile threw down a small piece of cheese to Mr Wild and he guzzled it greedily.

A few stalls down, an old man in a grey wool beret at the honey stall enticed Vita to try some of his lavender honey, breaking open a hot baguette to let her try a piece, and she let the sweet treat dissolve over her tongue.

Further on she passed the fish stall, with bream heads gawping toothily next to piles of grey prawns, rows of red mullet and mounds of shiny brown cockles; the men behind the counter wore white hats, raising their voices over the clamour of customers. Down the next aisle she admired the flowers on the plant stall and bought a bunch of peonies for Nancy. Their pink-and-purple buds were tight now, but she knew that in a week or so they'd burst open beautifully into colour. Maybe they would cheer Nancy up.

Laying her flowers in newspaper in her basket, Vita turned, feeling the short hairs on the back of her neck standing up. It was a familiar sensation, but not one she welcomed – this weird sense of being followed – and she quickly looked down the aisles. She told herself to stop being so stupid. There was no one of interest there.

In fact she must stop being so suspicious and guarded. Because at long last she was free. And maybe she should become a bit more trusting of the world. Everything that had happened in London – it was over. Nancy had been right. She'd made a completely new life in Paris, and she was safe. And Paris . . . oh, Paris was simply wonderful.

After picking up some choux pastries from the baker's stall, she headed back through the market to the photography shop, pausing outside to browse through the racks of pictures in the wooden crates. But the feeling that she was being watched persisted.

There were all sorts of photographs in the boxes on the table outside the shop and she flicked through some of the images – of windswept beaches and people on old-fashioned bicycles; a man with a euphonium; and a few of soldiers after the war, their haunted eyes staring into the camera.

In the window were photographic prints of some of the movie stars Vita recognized, such as Clara Bow, and she put her hand to her hair, thinking that she must have it styled again, when she had time. Nancy had taken her to a hairdresser in London, where she'd first had her hair cut short and shingled, but it had grown quite a bit since then. Nancy, in a bid to save money, had snipped at Vita's hair herself, but it was hardly a professional cut. She needed to keep up her smart image, if she was going to get Madame Jenny to notice her more, and she resolved to find a hairdresser this afternoon to style her hair like Louise Brooks's bob.

She pushed against the shop door, with its notice stating that the photographer would take portraits. She wondered if she might get her own image done. Or maybe a portrait of Mr Wild, for Nancy. She smiled to herself, thinking how much Nancy would like that. 'Come on,' she told the little dog, pulling him in through the door.

The proprietor came through a curtain at the back, smiled in recognition and, a moment later, slid the little brown envelope across the counter.

Vita opened her purse and counted out the money, but not before she'd seen through the curtain that there was a studio at the back. There was a camera on a tripod and a big fabric hood. The proprietor quickly shut the curtain and the studio was blocked from view.

Too excited to wait any longer, Vita opened the envelope and pulled out the photographs that had been developed from her little box camera. There was Notre-Dame cathedral and the shot she'd taken of the fishermen . . .

'Vita?'

She looked up to see Julianne from Les Folies walking through from the studio. She was adjusting the front button on her dress, for all the world as if she'd just put it on.

'Julianne. What are you doing here?'

Julianne blushed. 'I do a little modelling on the side,' she said in a low whisper. 'Don't look so shocked, Vita. It's very tasteful and it's good money.'

But Vita *was* shocked. However far she went, she never seemed to be that far away from a woman selling her body for money.

'You could model, too,' Julianne said. 'You have a fine bone structure and the right . . .' She looked down at Vita's chest, and Vita blushed.

'I don't think so,' she said, realizing now how different her world at Madame Jenny's was. But, worried that she'd sounded superior, she smiled away her embarrassment. 'But thank you.' And then, hurrying on, 'Tell me, how is everyone? What's going on at Les Folies?'

She wondered if Julianne would tell her about Fletch and Solange and braced herself.

'We miss you,' Julianne said, and Vita smiled. 'But, Vita, listen. I don't want to be – how you say? – indiscreet, but could you have a word with Nancy?'

'A word?'

Julianne leant in close. 'Between us, she is on the verge of being . . .' She drew her hand across her sinewy neck. 'She is on her last warning.'

Vita sighed. 'Oh.'

'She turns up late, and she's always,' Julianne put her finger pointedly on her nose, 'you know. We all like to party, but . . .' She shrugged. 'Nancy takes it too far. She's no good without her little wife,' she teased, touching Vita's arm.

32

The Fluke Photograph

Vita knew that she had to have a serious talk with Nancy, but by the time she got back to the apartment, Nancy had already left to go to Les Folies, and Vita didn't hear her come in until much later that night. She woke with a start, hearing a crash as Nancy stumbled into the table in the hallway and cursed. Vita groaned and turned over on her side in her thin bed, bracing herself for Nancy's entrance. Mr Wild scuttled into the room and jumped on the bed, and Vita gently pushed him into the crook of her knees between her and the wall, to protect him from Nancy.

'Vita. Vita, you awake?' Nancy slurred from the doorway and even though she was several feet away, Vita could smell the alcohol on her breath. 'Mr Wild . . . here, boy,' she whispered, and the little dog dutifully jumped up onto Vita's hip, panting happily. Nancy walked over and grabbed Mr Wild from the bed, but the dog squeaked, demanding to be put down. 'Have it your own way then,' she said angrily and the dog yelped and scuttled back to his bed in the corridor.

In the kitchen Vita heard Nancy rattling the nearly-empty bottles in their meagre drinks collection, wanting more liquor. Vita felt guilty for pretending to sleep, but knew what Nancy was like when she was this drunk. Their conversation would have to wait until she was more sober.

But Nancy remained unwakeable for the whole of Sunday and in the end, after clearing up and trying to air the stuffy flat, Vita went out angrily for a walk with Mr Wild, muttering furiously to herself about Nancy's irresponsible ways. Why should she and the small dog waste a precious sunny day indoors when she'd been in the back office at Madame Jenny's all week?

She headed to the Tuileries to walk Mr Wild along the manicured pathways, but as she stopped to watch some children on the carousel, the anger that she felt towards Nancy gave way to pity and then to self-blame.

Who was she, to get angry with Nancy? It wasn't as if this was a surprise. Nancy had always taken things too far. She'd always been the life and soul of the party, and Vita smiled now, recalling the times Nancy had grabbed her hand and barged her way into private parties and nightclubs, taking little notice of doormen or officious people with guest lists. It had always been the case that Nancy had demanded to be at the very epicentre of the fun. And that Vita should be by her side.

Maybe Nancy was acting up because she felt abandoned. They'd been in each other's pockets ever since they'd met in London, and whilst it was true that Nancy had always been needy, Vita knew it came from a place of genuine affection. And now she remembered how generous Nancy had been in London – dressing Vita in her cast-off clothes, fussing over her hair and make-up, and telling Vita constantly how pretty she was and how funny. In fact until recently Nancy had always shown that most wonderful of qualities – she'd made Vita feel like the very best version of herself.

So now, taking a longer view of her current situation, Vita could begin to see that just because she was living her own life in such a different way now, that didn't mean Nancy had to. Being angry was a waste of energy, Vita told herself. She needed to try a different approach with Nancy. And, full of resolve to be both more patient and kinder, she headed back to the apartment. Nancy had always been her friend – her *best* friend; they had to reconnect somehow, and then Vita could establish some ground-rules about how they lived together more harmoniously.

But Nancy was out, and Vita ate the dinner that she'd made alone, flipping angrily through the magazine on the table in the small kitchenette, feeling as if she'd gone on another huge loop of emotion and was back at the beginning, feeling resentful and cross again.

On Monday morning, Vita got up early to walk Mr Wild before going to work and woke Nancy, roughly.

'I've left you some fruit and vegetables,' she said. 'And some stew. You need to eat properly, Nancy.'

Nancy groaned, and Vita recoiled at the smell of stale sweat, smoke and whiskey.

'You must start looking after yourself,' she implored.

'What do you care?' Nancy said, or at least that's what Vita thought she said.

'Let's go out together. This week. How about Thursday? After the show?' she suggested. 'We'll go dancing. It'll be just like it used to be.'

'If you want,' Nancy said. 'Now leave me to sleep.'

'It's a date then,' Vita replied, creeping out, but not before she'd seen Nancy turn over in bed, her bony shoulder exposed, a bruise on her inner arm. She thought about Julianne's warning, and alarm bells started ringing in her head. What on earth was Nancy getting herself into?

She was still worrying about Nancy when she arrived at work, but she was soon absorbed in the tasks of the day, and it was almost lunchtime before there was a small lull and the girls had a five-minute break. Vita took the photographs out of the pocket of her skirt to show Agatha, and soon some of the others were crowding around.

Laure, curious about them, came to look, too. 'What are those?' she asked.

'Vita's photographs,' Agatha said. 'She has a very good eye.'

'Oh, and look – there's Paul,' Vita laughed, as if she'd stumbled on the photograph by chance. She smiled genuinely at the image, which made it look for all the world as if Paul had just stepped out of the grand car and was coming forward to greet her. The chauffeur was standing in the background, but in the second that Vita had pressed the shutter, his gaze had been on Paul. The effect was miraculous – because it made the photograph, which had been such a fluke, so convincing. She handed the photograph round and saw Agatha pass it to Laure, who pulled up her glasses onto her nose, from where they hung on the chain around her neck, and studied the image.

'It seems Vita has friends in high places after all,' she said.

33

Petite Protégée

Perhaps the photograph had been enough to set Laure's mind at rest about Vita's credentials, because that afternoon Laure took Vita away from her ironing duties and beckoned her over to the long cutting bench.

'You know about this?' she asked, showing Vita the corset on the model. Vita nodded. She'd been admiring the fine lacework and the intricate boning, and she touched the stunning garment now, feeling how soft the lace was and how perfectly the little brass eyes were positioned.

'Jenny would like something softer to present, too. We thought one of your brassieres would work.'

Madame Jenny wants to show a client one of my designs?

'I have some preliminary pattern pieces here,' Laure explained, showing Vita what she'd cut out so far, 'but I shall leave it to you to alter them.'

'Alter them?'

'Make something that you think works,' Laure said, with a casual flip of her hand, as if this were an easy task and not, as Vita suspected, a very big test.

Vita nodded, her mind racing at a hundred miles an hour as she looked at the challenge ahead.

'But how shall I cut it out?' she asked Laure. 'What fabric shall I use?'

Laure reached under the bench and pulled out a bolt of pale-ivory silk, and Vita knew how expensive it was.

'What if I make a mistake?' she asked, worried that it would be a very expensive error. 'That silk, it's . . .'

'Then don't make a mistake, Vita,' Laure said.

It took three whole days for Vita to complete the bra, and she fitted it on Cleo, one of the models, who declared how comfortable it was. Madame Jenny came with Laure to inspect it.

'This is very good,' she told Vita, tugging at the centre front to see how it fitted. 'Very good.'

'Thank you,' Vita replied, wanting to slump with relief. She cast her own critical eye over the bra and was pleased with what she'd achieved. It was slightly different from the bras she'd designed when she'd presented Top Drawer. More refined and a better fit. 'Laure helped me,' she admitted.

'Only a little bit,' Laure said, and Vita felt this was high praise.

'Vita, I don't think you realize how talented you are,' Jenny said.

Laure nodded and smiled at Vita. 'She doesn't.'

'What you've done here is incredibly difficult.'

'I don't think so.'

'Well, as I said when we first met, you have exceptional instincts. I can see that one day you could have your own fashion house.'

Vita felt a deep flush starting inside her. Madame Jenny

couldn't possibly mean that, could she? She felt dizzy with the magnitude of her faith in her.

'So I feel it is my duty to teach you everything I know. Tell me, my little protégée, what is it you want to learn next?' She and Laure stared at Vita expectantly, and Vita realized that she had to be bold.

'What I really want is to be back in the salon,' she said. 'I want to meet the clients.'

'Is that so?'

'I want to learn what you do, Madame Jenny,' Vita went on. 'I would like to be your . . .' she groped for the word in French, 'shadow.'

Jenny Sacerdote smiled, her eyes twinkling. 'Well, actually, as it happens, we have an American in tomorrow, so your English will help.'

Vita wanted to patter her feet in excitement at this clear promotion, but she kept a straight face and nodded.

'You will like Irving,' she said, 'although his daughter, Daphne, is rather a tricky customer. But I have a feeling she'll respond to you.'

34

Irving King

'Tricky customer' Daphne King arrived at eleven-thirty the next day with her father. Laure had insisted that Vita wear one of Jenny's dresses for the meeting. In the antechamber, just behind the glass doors to the salon, there was a huge rail of dresses and a changing room with a sumptuous pink silk curtain. Pewter-framed mirrors covered the wall, and Vita admired her reflection in one of them.

She'd opted for a dress with a pleated black skirt that fell to the knee, with a dropped waist. The top was straight and elegant, with a V-neck trimmed in simple black-and-white brocade, and there was a wide pale-yellow scarf that tied at the neck. Best of all were the shoes that Laure had given her to wear: black silk with a pearlized buckle.

Vita could hear Irving King's booming laugh as Laure pushed open the glass door at the far end of the salon. She waited for Laure to go first, but she held the door open for Vita.

'You're not coming?'

'No,' Laure said, with a rare smile, and Vita realized that for today she was going to be on her own with Jenny.

She took a breath and headed through the doors, feeling

the significance of the moment, feeling that she was ready for this: her destiny.

'I'm sure we'll be able to help,' Jenny was saying. 'Ah, here's Vita.'

Irving King stood from the low sofa, heaving himself up, and Vita was touched that he was gentlemanly enough to stand up for her. He was wearing a smart navy-blue suit with a wide white pinstripe, which was gregarious, but somehow managed to be stylish, too, especially with the jaunty silk tie. He was old, Vita noted, seeing his receding salt-and-paper hairline – almost certainly in his forties – but he had a kind of boyishness, and she thought he must have been very handsome as a young man. She knew from Laure that Irving King was a rich financial investor from the United States, and he seemed to exude worldliness and the high, glossy sheen that very rich people had. He'd been married twice and had children by his second wife, from whom he'd recently divorced. Now he and Daphne were in Paris for the whole summer, whilst Daphne attended finishing school and Irving kept a low profile, to let the dust settle. He was, Laure had warned Vita, 'a character'.

But he seemed perfectly pleasant, Vita thought, as she walked across the wide expanse of grey carpet towards him and saw him do a double-take when he noticed her. She felt a swing in her hips and, delighting in being out of her overalls and in this gorgeous dress, she imagined for a second that she was one of Jenny's models.

'Where have you been hiding this beauty?' Mr King asked Madame Jenny as Vita arrived next to them and he shook her hand, his kind blue eyes locking with hers. He smelt nice,

Vita noticed, of expensive cologne; and his hands were smooth, with very clean fingernails. He wore a chunky signet ring on his little finger. 'Daphne, honey?' he said, addressing the young girl who was standing sullenly by the sofa, looking out of the huge windows down onto the Champs-Élysées, as if she'd rather be anywhere else but here.

Daphne had a large hooked nose and plain mousy hair and was wearing a shapeless fawn coat, with her hands in her pockets; she was slumped on one hip, in a gesture of extreme boredom. She turned slowly and looked Vita up and down with disdain.

'Meet Daphne, my daughter,' Irving said, then in a stage whisper to Vita that everyone could hear, 'she's the worst shopper in Paris.'

'Daddy!' Daphne admonished him, with an ugly scowl. 'That's not true.'

'I'm telling you, we've been to every goddamned shop in this city – pardon my French,' he said, 'and she can't find a single thing she likes.'

'Then you're in the right place,' Madame Jenny said, clearly amused. She looked towards the door as Beatrice came through and handed her a note. 'Excuse me for one moment – I shall back in a minute,' she said, following Beatrice out. 'Vita will look after you.'

Madame Jenny retreated, her eyebrows rising at Vita, who was left alone in the salon.

35

Daphne's Problem

Vita was determined she wasn't going to come across the way she felt inside, which was both intimidated and very, very nervous.

'Hello,' Vita said, smiling at Daphne. *The girl could really do with some make-up advice*, she thought, *and with having those bushy eyebrows plucked*. 'It's nice to meet you.'

'Ah, you're English,' Irving King said. 'So good to speak the mother-tongue. See, I told you this would be easy, Daffers.'

'Daddy!' the girl snapped, then shot an embarrassed look at Vita, who gave her a sympathetic smile.

'Where are you from?' he asked.

'England.'

'I can hear that. Where exactly?'

'Oh, you wouldn't have heard of it. Lancashire. A place called Darton?' she told him, amazed that this was more information than she usually gave anyone, but what harm would it really do to share it with Mr King? She felt that some personal details were probably required to break the ice.

'Lancashire. Very beautiful. Hills?' he said, as if going through a bullet-pointed memo, and she got the impression

189

that Irving King was the kind of man who knew about a lot of things. 'And cotton mills?'

'That's right. My father has a mill.'

Irving beamed, as if he'd passed some kind of test. 'Oh, really. How interesting. What kind of textiles?'

'I don't know these days,' Vita stumbled, worried that she'd already given away more information than was safe. Darton – everything about her life there – was in the past, and very separate from her life in Paris. Why had she brought it up? Because she was so nervous? Or because she wanted Irving King to think she was well connected? Whatever the reason, she must stop this conversation at once.

'Whyever not?' There was something about his intense blue eyes that made Vita blurt out the truth.

'I wanted to pursue a different path. I . . . I . . . ran away.'

'You ran away, eh?' Irving said, his eyes twinkling with amusement. 'Don't you go getting ideas and running out on me, you hear me?' he said to Daphne.

'Like I'd dare,' she muttered.

Vita smothered a smile, amused by this father–daughter dynamic, although she could see that her admission had won some kind of respect from Daphne.

'I've only been as far as Liverpool myself,' he said. 'I went to visit some distant relatives, but I won't be doing that again in a hurry. The damned people came after me for money. The cheek of it!'

'He didn't refuse them,' Daphne informed Vita.

Irving sat down in the chair and crossed his legs. Vita noticed a patch of his leg, his skin tanned above the jaunty socks. 'So now they've all got new houses and they've named the pub after me, so I'm told. The Irving Arms. I think it's got a certain ring to it, don't you?'

'It does, yes.'

He sat back and Vita smiled fully this time. This was clearly a man who liked talking.

'Oh, that accent. Don't you love that accent! Darling, why don't you come over here and talk to . . .' he groped for her name.

'Vita . . . Casey. Mademoiselle Casey.'

'Oh, we're all on first-name terms,' Irving said. 'Call me Irving. I'm certainly not *Mademoiselle*-ing anyone,' he said.

Vita watched as Irving, clearly trying to remember to give Daphne a moment to speak, picked up a magazine from the table next to the sofa and started flipping through it.

'What are you looking for, Daphne?' Vita asked, taking her cue.

'I don't want anything boring,' the girl said, then flicked her eyes towards her father. 'He doesn't seem to understand.'

'But I do,' Vita said, giving another smile at Irving, to show she was in control. 'Come with me. Do you mind if I borrow her?'

'Where are we going?' Daphne asked, some of her bravado leaving her.

'I think it might be better to find out what you *don't* like, first.'

In the antechamber she showed Daphne to the rail of clothes that the models dressed from.

'Daddy says I'm too choosy.'

'Not at all. There's nothing wrong with knowing your own mind. I was exactly like you at your age . . . just not allowed any wonderful clothes.' For a second Vita wondered whether pointing out that Daphne was rather spoilt would backfire, so she hurried on, 'So, let's get practical. What do you actually *need*?' she asked.

'Daddy says I need something formal. There's this dreadful ball that I have to go to.'

'So, evening wear,' Vita said, looking purposefully through the dresses. She found what she was looking for and pulled out one of the sophisticated evening dresses from Jenny's collection. 'How about this?' she asked, holding up the dress and then turning it round, so that Daphne could see the cream chiffon detail and the loop of pearls, the fabric cut so cleverly that it looked like a straight skirt, but was slit, to allow for movement. 'Why don't you try it on? I think you'll look wonderful in it.'

Daphne's face fell as she looked at the dress and then she shook her head. 'I don't look wonderful in anything,' she replied, and Vita suddenly saw that the problem wasn't the clothes.

'What on earth do you mean?'

'I hate everything. I hate the way I look in all the clothes.' Her voice caught and she looked horrified at this admission, as her eyes connected with Vita's.

'Well, why don't you let me be the judge of that?' Vita said. She cajoled Daphne into the changing room and pulled the pink curtain across, then heard shuffling as Daphne got changed into the dress.

'Could you help me with the back, Vita?' she asked from the other side of the curtain, and Vita felt a warm glow that Daphne had remembered her name.

Daphne was in the dress, although Vita saw already that the waist would have to be altered to be bigger, but Daphne was holding the top of it protectively against her chest. She took a step backwards when she saw Vita and turned round.

'What are you wearing?' Vita asked, horrified by the ugly bandage-like garment wrapped around her chest.

'I have to do something,' Daphne said. 'Nobody wants . . . these.'

Vita turned her slowly round by the shoulder. She gently took the fabric of the dress, and Daphne, defeated, let it fall, so that Vita could see the full extent of the ugly sheath. Daphne looked down in utter disgust at her breasts.

'Well, firstly, it is a waste of energy to hate any part of your body,' Vita said, 'and secondly, I can help.'

'How?' Daphne asked.

'Do you mind?' Vita said, taking out from her pocket the tape she used for measuring and threading it around Daphne's back.

'What are you doing?' Daphne asked, as Vita came closer to grab the other end of the tape.

'When you come back, I will have made you something,' she said. 'The reason you hate what you look like is quite simple. Wait there.'

Vita rushed through to the studio and quickly found the bra she'd made earlier. She took it back to the antechamber and gave it to Daphne.

'Here, try this,' she said.

Daphne took it and Vita saw the admiration flash in her eyes, and then uncertainty. 'Go on,' Vita encouraged her. 'Take off what you're wearing and put this on instead, and you'll see what a huge difference it makes.'

Vita waited outside the curtain for a moment, hoping this plan would work and that the bra would fit. A moment later the curtain opened and Daphne came out.

'Look at you,' she said, showing Daphne her reflection in the mirror.

The bra was a little snug, and Vita knew she'd have to make it in a larger size, but it gave Daphne some shape, as well as support.

'You don't have to suffocate just because you have breasts,' Vita said. 'Be proud of what you have. I am. Now put the dress on,' she continued, pulling up the top of the dress and helping Daphne thread her arms through the holes. Vita did up the little button at the top and, together, they both admired Daphne in the pewter mirror. The fabric fell wonderfully.

'But I look . . .' Daphne began.

'You look beautiful,' Vita said, meaning it. 'If you had a dress like this made, we'd make the waist a little looser,' she said, examining the back.

'I'm too fat for it,' Daphne said. 'I knew I would be.'

'It's the fault of the dress – not you,' Vita said firmly. 'How was the dress supposed to guess your waist measurement accurately?'

Daphne let out a little laugh.

'But the length, the colour and the shape? They're all spot-on, wouldn't you say?'

Daphne nodded.

'Well then, why don't you go and show your father.'

Irving was delighted when Vita presented Daphne. 'Daffers!' he exclaimed. 'Oh . . . look at you.'

Vita grinned at Daphne, who did a self-conscious little twirl.

'Walk in it,' she encouraged her, pushing Daphne a little way up the grey carpet. 'See how it feels.'

She smiled at Irving as Daphne, suddenly more confident, trotted towards him doing a few little Charleston moves, and Irving clapped his hands and laughed.

36

Bricktop's

The weather broke into heavy rain showers later in the week and Vita shivered, as she waited by the stage door of Les Folies for Nancy after the show on Thursday night, her umbrella dripping. She felt too embarrassed to go and wait in the dressing room – unsure if Madame Rubier would let her back in. Besides, she really didn't want to run into Fletch and Solange. She stamped her feet and shivered, batting away the tiredness. Cars splashed over the cobbles, their lights blurring in the rain.

She'd been working very long hours this week. Irving King had ordered no fewer than ten pieces from the collection for Daphne, and Jenny had laughed and clapped when he'd left the building and then hugged Vita.

'You are coming in the salon again,' she told Vita, who admitted that Daphne had left wearing the bra Vita had given her and thought Laure would be furious, but Madame Jenny waved her hand. 'A small price to pay, my dear. I will tell Laure.'

With so much work on, Vita had to stay after hours to make a replacement for the brassiere she'd given Daphne. She hoped it would make as much difference to the young girl as she thought it would, not just for Daphne's sake, but because Jenny herself had been so impressed with the way Vita had handled the situation.

And, of course, there was Irving, too. Vita remembered him now, standing up in boyish delight; and, in this private moment away from the salon, she allowed herself to study the thought that had been nagging at her all week. The thought that Irving had been . . . well, attractive. Older, of course, and definitely out of her league, but there'd been something about him that had made her open up – had made her feel like herself.

Now the door opened next to her and Julianne, Collette and Nancy came out, and her romantic ideas about Irving suddenly seemed preposterous. These were her friends. Irving – people like him, with money and class – belonged to a different world, a different society. One that she didn't belong to at all, she reminded herself.

'Oh, you came,' Nancy said, looking surprised. 'I didn't think you would.'

Vita couldn't help feeling defensive immediately, hating the way Nancy made her feel as if she'd been a neglectful friend. Why wouldn't she have come? It had been her idea, after all. But she didn't say anything, simply scanned Nancy's face for clues as to her mood.

'How was the show?' Vita asked, but Julianne and Collette were already huddling under an umbrella, on a familiar post-show high, and keen to get to the club for a drink. They didn't answer, calling out instead, over the patter of the rain, that they'd see Nancy and Vita there.

'Hang on,' Nancy said distractedly, scanning the parked cars and then running along the pavement, her coat pulled up over her head as protection.

'What are you doing?' Vita called, but Nancy didn't answer. Instead Vita watched as Nancy knocked on the window of one of the parked cars. She spoke to the driver through the open window and he passed her something, then Nancy put one hand out defensively. Vita took a step towards her, realizing that there might be trouble. But now Nancy turned and walked back towards her, shouting something at the car, which pulled away from the kerb with an angry rev of its engine.

Vita had been hoping that tonight would be like old times. She was getting used to Nancy being grumpy and brittle when she was hungover in the apartment, but she'd assumed Nancy was her old gregarious self in public and that the moodiness was simply for Vita's benefit.

But now, as she watched Nancy huddling under the shelter of her coat, her face was set in a scowl, and Vita saw that Nancy's legs were too thin, her cheeks hollow. Her make-up was not masking the fact that there were deep circles etched beneath her eyes, and Vita felt a shudder of alarm at the contrast between this Nancy and the Nancy in her mind's eye – the one with a bounce in her step and a sparkle in her eye.

'Who was that?' Vita asked.

'Nobody,' Nancy said, her eyes dull and angry. 'Have you brought any money? We should get a cab.'

But there were no cabs to be had, and they hurried along the pavement together as the cars splashed on the cobbles, and they had to sidestep them to stop their feet getting wet.

Vita longed to quiz Nancy about the altercation with the person in the car, but she knew she didn't really need to ask. She remembered Julianne's warning in the photography shop.

That person in the car must have been some kind of dealer. Someone Nancy was buying her dreadful powder from.

'I hate this ghastly weather,' Nancy said. 'No cabs anywhere.'

Vita tried to distract her from running out from the kerb every few seconds to try to hail one, and in the rain every cab was full.

'Let's just walk,' Vita suggested. 'It's only rain. Anyway, we'll soon be there and it'll give us a chance to talk.'

Nancy seemed to acquiesce to this plan, and soon put on her coat normally and was next to Vita, walking underneath the umbrella. Vita hoped Nancy would hook her arm onto hers, as she used to, but she kept to herself, crossing her arms over her body and tucking her hands into her armpits.

'What do you want to talk about?' Nancy asked. 'We can talk about how Madame Vertbois – that bitch – is going to throw us out of the apartment, if you want.'

'Is she?' Vita asked, surprised.

'I owe her too much. That's what she says.'

Vita took a second to compute this. She'd always given Nancy most of her wages towards her share of the rent, with Nancy insisting that the cheap rent was perfectly affordable and that, with her salary and Vita's, they could live pretty well. If she owed Madame Vertbois money, then what had she been doing with Vita's share of the rent? But Vita already knew the answer and, annoying as it was, she sensed that now wasn't the time to go to war with Nancy over domestic issues.

'Then I'll pay what we owe.'

Nancy glanced at her sideways. 'Really? It's a lot. You must be getting well paid,' she said, not masking the bitterness in her voice.

'Not very well, but enough. I hardly spend anything, as you know,' Vita said, 'and I know I owe you so much.'

This wasn't strictly true, but she felt she should say it, and she saw that Nancy had softened a little bit, so she continued enthusiastically, 'Oh, Nancy, it's so wonderful to be working at Maison Jenny. When we came to Paris,' she said, trying to jog Nancy's memory, 'remember how you said I could make it here – that this was the place to be?'

'Did I?'

'Yes, and you were right. I'm finally doing what I should be doing.'

She told her about Daphne, and how Madame Jenny had been so pleased Vita had made her wear a bra, but Nancy seemed distracted.

'Sounds swell,' she said, but sarcastically, and Vita felt her hackles rising that Nancy was acting in such a jealous way. Why couldn't she be a proper friend and be pleased that she was pursuing her dream?

They walked from the street into Bricktop's, and Vita paused to shake out the umbrella. The club's entrance glowed with red light as they made their way down a few steps to the low-ceilinged room. The band was playing a lazy tune – the banjo, trumpet and clarinet overlapping over the splash of the drums. In the heavy, smoky atmosphere, couples were dancing.

Vita wanted to carry on talking to Nancy, but she walked into the throng, shedding her coat and letting it drop, so that Vita had to catch it. Feeling the familiar sensation of being her servant, Vita told her to wait, but Nancy shouldered her way through the crowd to the bar.

Vita queued alone and gave their coats in at the coat-check, then finally made it to the bar. Nancy already had a rim of sticky white powder around her nostril. Her pupils looked large and grey in the low lighting. They were supposed to be having a night out, and Nancy was already high. Vita made a subtle gesture to her own nose and Nancy looked at her quizzically, then understood. Vita looked down as Nancy wiped her nose. If she was embarrassed that Vita had to draw attention to it, she didn't show it. Instead it was Vita who felt ashamed. Ashamed that Nancy no longer cared enough to check that her drug habit was discreet.

'Oh, look, there's lover boy,' Nancy said, keen to change the subject and nodding. And Vita saw Fletch on the dance floor with a girl she didn't recognize. Nancy must have known that he would be here, and must have deliberately wanted to cause a scene. Well, she wouldn't let her, Vita told herself. She shrugged, as if seeing Fletch were no big deal.

'What happened to Solange?' Vita asked.

'She's gone,' Nancy said. 'Back to Brazil, I think.'

Fletch had clearly wasted no time in filling the void, Vita noted, seeing the girl with the heavily made-up eyes draping herself over him. She noticed the elegant curve of her muscles under her deep-brown skin. Another dancer, then.

'Hey, Vita,' Fletch said, as he passed. His eyes locked for a long moment with hers. 'It's good to see you.' And she could tell he meant it. She thought back to the scene outside the café, when he'd got the wrong idea about Paul. She knew Fletch had been hurt that she hadn't been willing to give their relationship a chance, and now her stomach squirmed as she watched the girl in his arms and remembered how extraordinary his body was.

Is it guilt, jealousy . . . or humiliation? she wondered. Vita couldn't tell, but she also couldn't tear her eyes away from Fletch, as he bent down to whisper in the girl's ear. She put her hand on Fletch's shoulder and her eyes were cold as they met Vita's.

Nancy looked at her and gave a scornful laugh. 'Don't go getting, airs, Vita. It's not pretty.'

This was a typical comment of Nancy's, but she said it with a nasty edge and there was no smile in her voice. 'Oh, look. As if by magic.'

Nancy saw that the waiter behind the bar had placed two cocktails on a tray. And now, with his back turned, Nancy reached past Vita and grabbed one, knocking it back. Liquor spilled down her face.

The waiter turned and started shouting at Nancy, but she grabbed the other cocktail and downed it too, slamming the empty glass on the bar with a manic grin. Then she pinched Vita's arm and pulled her towards the dance floor.

'Stop it,' Vita shouted. 'You can't do that.' She mouthed an apology to the barman over her shoulder.

'You're such a prude these days,' Nancy snapped, starting to dance, her sweaty, bony hand clamped around Vita's. But there was a cruelty in her eyes and Vita felt her pinching her waist.

'Nancy, stop it,' she implored, trying to pull away.

'You never want to play with me.'

'Not like this, no. Not when you're high and—'

'You want to dance with Fletch, don't you?' Nancy hissed in her ear, not listening to her. Her eyes narrowed with that searching, jealous look that Vita knew meant trouble.

'No,' she said, trying to make Nancy understand.

'That's it, isn't it? You love him, not me,' she said, jabbing Vita painfully in the chest.

Vita felt fury rearing up. 'Oh, for God's sake, Nancy,' she shouted. 'When will you ever stop this ridiculous nonsense? Stop being so jealous. Can't you see I'm worried about you? That you can't carry on like this?'

She'd overstepped the mark. She could see it immediately. She knew better than to stand up to Nancy, especially when she was tight. And now Nancy's face formed a nasty sneer, then she turned and strutted away from her.

'Where are you going?' Vita called.

'Away from you. I hate you,' Nancy said. 'I thought you were my friend, but you just used me . . .'

'Nancy, wait!' Vita called, but Nancy was already stumbling up the stairs to the street. Vita followed, seeing the rain lashing down on the greasy cobbles.

Nancy walked straight out into the rain and immediately her hair was plastered to her face. She turned to face Vita. 'You've even stolen Mr Wild from me,' she said.

'Nancy, wait,' Vita replied, huddling under the club's canopy. 'Come back.'

'Go to hell, Vita,' Nancy said, her arms out wide in a grand gesture as she walked backwards into the road.

She didn't see the car. It slewed to a stop, but not in time. It hit Nancy, who jack-knifed over the bonnet and fell off the other side onto the cobbles with a sickening thud.

37

The Kindness of Strangers

'Nancy!' Vita screamed, running out into the street. The car had sped away from the accident, disappearing round the corner. 'Hey! Hey, come back,' she yelled.

She knelt on the road beside Nancy, who was deathly pale, a trickle of blood seeping from her hairline.

'Nancy! Nancy, can you hear me?' Vita sobbed. 'Help . . . Someone help,' she screamed. 'Help!'

Suddenly she was aware of a woman by her side.

'I saw it all. Wait there – I will get help,' she said in English.

'Go to the club. Get Fletch,' Vita said, hardly taking in the woman and pointing to the door of the club. She watched her run to the club door in her blue trench coat.

Vita shifted on the cobbles, feeling her knees starting to bleed. 'Oh, Nancy. Nancy,' she sobbed, leaning over her friend. 'Oh God.'

A moment later the woman was back, and then Fletch was there and two more men had come out of the club.

'Leave her. Don't move her body.' The woman, who Vita now saw must be in her twenties, pushed Vita aside and felt Nancy's pulse. 'She's alive. Just concussed, I think.'

'Vita, what happened?' Fletch asked, coming to her side.

'She ran out into the road. Oh, Fletch,' she said, burying her face in his lapel, 'this is my fault. I should have seen the warning signs. I knew she was going off the rails, but I never thought . . .'

'Here,' he said, taking off his jacket and putting it round her shoulders. Her teeth started chattering.

One of the other two men bent down over Nancy in the road.

'Should she go to hospital?' Vita asked, aware that her dress was plastered to her body.

'Miss. Miss, can you move?' the blonde-haired woman in the trench coat asked. Vita had assumed she was French, but she spoke flawless English.

Nancy groaned and then rolled over, and Vita held her breath, trying to suck in her tears. She watched as Nancy slowly pushed herself up. The woman helped her.

'Careful. Don't move too suddenly,' she said.

'What happened?' Nancy asked Vita. She held her head and then pulled her hand away and there was blood. 'Ow!'

'Oh, Nancy, thank God. Thank God you're all right,' Vita sobbed.

'Get me inside,' Nancy replied, already moving to her feet painfully.

Vita let Fletch lift her, and the other men supported her as, limping, she made her way back to the club.

Downstairs, Vita sat in the office with Nancy as she held a tea-towel of ice to her head. The bartender whose drinks she'd stolen gave Vita the kind of look that said this was

Nancy's own stupid fault. Vita's hands were shaking as she studied Nancy's face. Her eyes were closed.

'I think you should go to the hospital. You should be checked over by a proper doctor.'

'Stop fussing, Vita.'

'Then I'm taking you home,' Vita said.

Nancy opened her eyes. 'No. I want to stay. You said we'd have a night out.'

Vita shook her head, exasperated. Nancy seemed to have forgotten her drunken outburst and the reason she'd run into the road in the first place.

Her ankle was badly swollen, and Fletch had told Bobo to get the car. He helped Vita get Nancy outside again. To her surprise, Vita saw the woman in the trench coat and beret still standing outside the club, her hands in her pockets. She looked like a detective from a film, Vita thought.

'You're still here,' Vita said.

'I stayed to make sure your friend was better,' the woman said.

'That's so kind. She's . . . well, I think she'll live. Thank you.'

'I'm glad I was there. Glad I was able to help,' the woman replied, and Vita smiled at her. Then, studying her face for the first time, she searched her memory and cocked her head.

'You seem familiar. Have we met before?'

'No,' the woman said. 'I don't think so. I haven't been in Paris long.'

'Oh, I see.'

'I'd better be going,' she said, but she didn't move.

'Where do you live?' Vita asked. 'We could take you there on the way home? Our friend is giving us a lift. We live on the rue d'Orsel, near Sacré-Coeur. Do you live anywhere near there?'

'No, no, I'm in the other direction. Thank you anyway.'

'Oh, well, then.' Vita nodded. She would have liked to help the woman, but now Bobo was honking the car's horn, and she and Fletch helped Nancy into the back.

38

A Bad Patient

Nancy had a big lump on her forehead, her shoulder was very bruised and her knees were scraped raw. There was no possibility of her going back to Les Folies for at least another week. Vita sat on her bed in their apartment, seeing Mr Wild's expression of pure joy at being allowed onto the bed to cuddle Nancy all day long.

She was worried for her friend, who seemed to have no idea why she'd run out into the road. Nancy's eyes had dark shadows beneath them and her hands trembled. She coughed, too, her chest weak from all the smoking and from the chill she'd caught.

'Ow!' Nancy gasped, putting her hand on her chest after a particularly prolonged fit. 'Pass me a cigarette.'

'No, they just make your cough worse.'

'Nonsense – pass them to me,' Nancy demanded, 'there's one in the silver case,' she said, waving her hand at the dresser.

Vita, hating herself for being so weak, relented.

'Only this one,' she said, fetching the cigarette case and giving it to Nancy. 'But you're not allowed to smoke all day whilst I'm out at work.' She went over to the small window.

'Leave it. I don't like it open. I don't want to hear the outside world when I'm stuck in here.'

'But what about Mr Wild? He'll suffocate.'

'You're fine, aren't you, my baby?' Nancy said, but she only tickled his ears and didn't use her Mr Wild voice. Vita wondered if Nancy remembered what she'd said about Vita having stolen Mr Wild from her. She hoped the dog's affection now was putting that ridiculous thought out of her mind.

'You need to rest. You heard the doctor. If you don't rest, then you won't get better.'

'Oh, Vita, don't go to work,' Nancy lamented from the bed. 'Stay with me. I don't like being alone without you.'

'You've got Mr Wild.'

Vita felt torn. She knew she should stay, but Daphne, whom she'd missed on Friday, was in for her last fitting today and she needed to be there.

'Then get me a drink,' Nancy moaned, and Vita knew that far more than her company, this was what Nancy longed for.

'We discussed this,' Vita said patiently. 'Didn't we?'

Nancy looked put out.

'You agreed to stop – to stop everything after the accident, remember?'

But Nancy cast her eyes down, still reluctant to admit that she had a problem.

'I'll be home early,' Vita said, 'and I'll give the key to Madame Vertbois. She can check on you at lunchtime.'

'I hate her. I'll send her away.'

'Please don't. You need to rest your ankle, otherwise you won't be able to dance.'

Madame Vertbois reluctantly agreed to the plan, but only after Vita had given her most of her wages as a down-payment on what Nancy owed.

'I don't know why a nice girl like you is with her,' Madame Vertbois said, pointing her chin at the stairs. 'Girls like her are trouble.'

She's right, of course, but what can I do? Vita wondered as she caught the metro to the Champs-Élysées. She knew Nancy didn't want her to leave the apartment, but it was the only thing that would take Vita's mind off Nancy, and seeing over and over again in her mind her thin body rolling over the top of the car. And hearing that sickening thud. She was lucky the accident hadn't been so much worse.

Vita was late, and as she hurried along the wide pavement to the door of number seventy, she saw that Fletch was waiting by the tree outside Maison Jenny's.

'I was going to come to the apartment, but it was easier to come here,' he said. 'How is she? Nancy, I mean?'

'She's a bad patient, but she'll live. Thank you for helping.'

'It's the least I could do,' he said, and he put his hand on her arm. And Vita remembered what a decent and kind person Fletch was, and this was what had drawn her to him in the first place. She had a sudden flashback to his small room, and she blushed and wondered if he was thinking about it, too. Maybe he was, she thought, because there was a beat of silence as he stared into her eyes. She pressed her lips together.

And then she remembered his jacket. That must be the real reason he was here. She realized he probably didn't have too many good jackets, and saw that the one he was wearing now was frayed and didn't match his trousers.

'Oh, your jacket,' she said, clamping her hand over her mouth. 'I'm so sorry. I will bring it back to you.'

'Are you all right, Vita?' It was Laure. She was walking from the gate of the building to the tree, her face set in a frown. Georges, the doorman, was approaching, too.

'Yes, I'm . . .' She looked desperately at Fletch. He stared at her, wanting her to introduce him, to legitimize him.

'Move along,' Georges said aggressively in French, and Fletch stepped backwards.

'Really, Georges, it's fine,' Vita replied, stepping between them, but it wasn't fine. She could see how Georges must perceive Fletch and she wanted to explain, but now Laure grabbed hold of Vita's arm protectively, already turning her back to the building.

'You mustn't talk to people like him,' she muttered, and Vita was about to protest when she realized how Laure couldn't possibly understand her old life at Les Folies, or that Fletch might be a friend. She recognized Laure's prickly prejudice and knew that Laure would think less of her – far less – if she knew the truth.

Vita glanced over her shoulder at Fletch, her look desperate, wanting him to understand, but she could see that she'd hurt him.

'That thing – leave it for me. Really . . . don't let me bother you, ma'am,' he said, walking backwards away from her. And Vita cursed herself for not handling the situation better.

'Who was that dreadful man?' Laure asked, her voice loaded with suspicion, and worry, too.

'It doesn't matter,' Vita said, but she felt sudden tears choking her.

'If he bothers you again, Miss Vita,' Georges said, looking sternly after Fletch, who was crossing the road between the cars, 'you let me know right away.'

39

The International Call

Edith sat at her dressing table, smoothing her blonde hair into the sculpted curves that she wore flattened to her head. She reached into her dressing-gown pocket for the diamond hair clip and her fingers found the envelope and she pulled it out.

It was a letter from Mrs Lanyard, the headmistress at St Hilda's, and an accompanying note written by Susan to her mother. The child had complained of bullying and of dreadful, heart-wrenching homesickness, but the headmistress had assured Edith in her letter that this was normal and there was nothing to worry about. She had suggested that perhaps, though, some communication from her mother would soothe the child and help Susan to sleep.

Edith tucked the letter back into its envelope and returned it to the stack hidden in the bureau, just as Clement came out of his bedroom into their shared dressing room.

'Are you feeling well?' he asked, by way of greeting. She wondered if he was going to approach her and kiss her. At one time he used to kiss her in the mornings, but for some months now he'd kept his distance.

'Yes. Why shouldn't I be?'

'You look pale. Are you . . . ? I mean, you're not . . . yet, are you?' Clement asked in a clipped tone.

It was unusual for him to ask her such a personal question and Edith felt herself flushing. She had plucked up all her courage and had discussed the idea of having children with him a few weeks ago, and he'd seemed to be agreeable to the idea, especially when she'd pointed out that with a legitimate male heir, his sister could never come back and claim any part of the Darton fortune. He didn't seem to understand, however, the nuts and bolts of how it might actually happen.

'I . . . no, I'm not,' she said, feeling as if this was her fault, but feeling angry, too.

'Then go and see a doctor,' he said.

'I will,' she muttered, and he grunted.

There was a knock on the dressing-room door. 'What is it?' he barked as Martha stuck her head round the door, prompting a furious eye-roll from Clement. He hated Martha disturbing them in their private rooms. 'There is a phone call for you, Mrs Darton,' she said.

Edith picked up the green-marble telephone receiver from the gold stand on her dressing table.

'Hello?'

She heard the crackle of the line and then the operator saying, 'Call from Paris. Putting you through.'

'Who is it?' Clement called, and Edith swallowed hard. Was *nothing* private in this household?

She put her hand over the mouthpiece. 'It's my mother,' she said, and he shook his head, clearly not wanting to overhear their conversation.

'I'll see you in the car,' he said, then shut the bedroom door and she heard him as he trotted down the wooden staircase.

'How dare you call here?' Edith said, in a cross whisper, as Marianne came on the line.

'Mrs Darton, please . . . if you could only tell me about Susan—'

'You should not call the house. You must write. As I instructed.'

'But I'm desperate to know about Susan – please, you must understand. She's my daughter. She's all I have.'

'I've told you all you need to know. She's at boarding school and doing very well.'

'But she's never been away from home. I'm so worried . . .'

'They keep the children very busy. I doubt she has time to be homesick.'

'But . . .'

'Miss Chastain, you do your job, and then I will put you in touch with her. That is the deal we agreed upon.'

'But this whole thing – it just seems so wrong.'

Edith could tell that Marianne's voice was choking up and she felt a surge of anger. What was *wrong* was Marianne's affair with her husband. *That* was wrong. There was nothing wrong about some subtle investigating. Why was the woman causing such a fuss?

'Have you found her?'

There was a pause.

'Well?' Edith demanded.

'Yes.'

Edith relaxed and allowed herself a small smile as she

pressed the perfect blonde curl down, in her reflection in the mirror.

'And . . . ?'

'Miss Darton – I mean, Vita – is living with her friend, Nancy, as you thought she would be. It's taken some days, but I've found the apartment. They have a little dog.'

Mr Wild. That awful creature, Edith thought.

'Where does she go? What is she doing?' Edith demanded. These were, after all, the details she needed to know, the reason she'd dispatched Marianne in the first place. She'd hoped the woman would be happy to be back in France. Who wouldn't want an expenses-paid trip to Paris? And yet Marianne was sullen . . . reluctant.

'Mrs Darton, please . . .'

'Marianne,' Edith said crossly, 'I asked you a question.'

'She walks the dog everywhere. But Mrs Darton, please, I feel so dreadful. She seems very nice and . . .'

'You met her?'

There was a small pause. The line crackled and then Marianne spoke again. 'Nancy, well . . . she had an accident and I was there. I'd followed them from Les Folies.'

'What happened?'

'They'd gone to a club, and then Nancy – she ran into the road.'

Edith wanted to growl with frustration. This woman was impossible. Why wasn't she giving her more details?

'Why did she do that?'

'I don't know. They were having an argument. There was an accident. Nancy got hit by a car. That's all I know. Can I come back now? Please? I'll—'

'No, that is not enough.' In her reflection, Edith saw that her eyes were shining and she cocked her head, appreciating how fine she looked this morning. A fight? Nancy and Vita were fighting? That was good news. 'I want more.'

'But how?'

'You've got to get into her apartment. Infiltrate her life.'

'Into the apartment?' Marianne sounded shocked. Edith shook her head, astonished that this woman needed spoon-feeding instructions. She certainly had no initiative.

'Yes. Now that you know her, it should be easy. If you know where she lives.'

'But what do you want me to do?'

Edith looked at her reflection and then licked her lips. 'Be friendly. And then get Nancy out of the picture.'

'How?'

'Think of something. Nancy is very gullible – she believes in clairvoyants. And she's a drunk. If she ran out into the road, then she's probably half-mad already. If she's like she was in London, half the time she has no memory of what she's been doing. And get rid of that dreadful dog.'

'The dog?'

Edith let out an exasperated sigh. 'Be inventive. Use your initiative. Prove to me how serious you are about seeing your daughter again,' she snapped.

'I can't, I . . .' Marianne was crying now.

'If you do this . . . If you do as I say, then I will ask the school to let Susan write to you.'

Marianne sniffed and Edith could tell she was mollified. 'Will you?' she asked.

'Yes,' Edith lied, looking at the letters in her bureau. It

wouldn't be so hard to copy the child's writing, would it? She could manage that, although she had so many better things to do with her time. But if it keep Marianne compliant, then it would be worth it.

Marianne composed herself, and Edith was grudgingly satisfied that this small promise had smoothed things over.

'Now then, is there anything else you can tell me? Anything at all?'

Marianne coughed a little. 'I followed Miss Darton – Vita – to where she works.'

'To work? At Les Folies Bergère?'

'No, not there.'

'Oh? Well then, where? What is she doing?'

'She's working for Madame Jenny Sacerdote. A designer on the Champs-Élysées.'

Vita was working for a designer? Edith tried to compute this news. Her plan was for Marianne to infiltrate Vita's life, so that Edith would be able to know exactly what she was doing – exactly what she was designing. She hadn't expected Vita to be able to pursue her fashion ambitions, not without contacts or money, but Vita was tenacious, if nothing else, Edith remembered.

'I need to know everything. And this isn't enough, Marianne. What else can you tell me?'

'There was something . . .'

'Something?'

'There was a man.'

'What man?'

'A black man – a Negro,' Marianne whispered.

Edith gripped the phone. This was interesting. 'Go on.'

'They were at a club together when Nancy ran in front of the car, and I saw him again outside Madame Sacerdote's. I can't be sure, but there was something about him and Miss Darton.'

'Vita,' Edith corrected. 'How do you mean – something?'

'They seemed . . . intimate.'

'Can you come?' Clement said, suddenly opening the door to the bedroom and making Edith jump. 'Your cat has eaten another of mother's canaries.'

'I have to go. Write to me,' Edith said hurriedly.

'But Mrs Darton. The letter?'

'Do the thing I asked and you'll get it,' Edith said, then replaced the receiver with a thud.

40

Chocolate Eclairs

'Look at those,' Vita said, as she went through to the reception area with the latest dress from the studio. Beatrice's desk was obscured by a huge bouquet of peonies and white lilies.

'They're from Irving King,' Beatrice said, reading the card. 'They just came. They are to thank us for helping Daphne. But I suspect, Vita, that they are really for you.'

Vita blushed, remembering the roses Archie had sent once to her dressing room at the Zip Club in London. How long ago that seemed now.

'I don't think so,' she said.

'No, you definitely have an admirer there,' Beatrice said with a knowing smile.

In the studio, word about the flowers was clearly out.

'So, Irving King?' Agatha said, as she threaded a needle, and Vita realized that some of the others were straining to hear her response. 'Those flowers for you . . .'

'Not for me – for all of us,' she said defensively, addressing the others, too.

But Agatha laughed. 'You like him. Don't deny it, Vita. You're blushing.'

'He's old,' Vita said, leaning in close, over the bench.

'So what?' Agatha said. 'He's rich and interested. And I wouldn't say he's unattractive?'

There were murmurs of agreement from the other girls and Vita sighed, knowing she was blushing at their teasing.

'I will bet you a chocolate eclair from Pâtisserie Stohrer that he asks you out,' Agatha said.

The girls often talked about their favourite treats, and Vita shook on it. For Agatha, chocolate eclairs were the best treat in Paris. For Laure, it was macarons from Ladurée; for Beatrice, the little marzipan confectionery from a shop near the Pont Neuf.

And so it happened that Vita found herself on rue Montorgueil in the queue for eclairs at Stohrer's the next morning, thinking about how she'd lost her bet with Agatha. Because, as her friend had predicted, Vita did have a date with the irrepressible Irving King.

Her mouth was watering at the sumptuous array of maca-rons and elaborate cream pastries on display. She read the sign on the wall, about this being the oldest *pâtisserie* in Paris, having been founded by Louis XV's pastry chef. She could tell that the craftsmen who worked here clearly loved their trade, and she watched now as the man serving her loaded the eclairs in the cardboard cake-box. She appreciated the pride he took in his job, just as she loved being part of the team at Madame Jenny's. She only wished Nancy could understand how wonderful it felt for her to belong like this. How everyone in the studio was interested in her date with Irving.

She watched the box being wrapped in ribbon, smiling

to herself as she remembered how Irving had turned up unannounced yesterday afternoon, when Vita had been talking to Madame Jenny about her ideas for bras. Beatrice called them both to the reception area.

'I was passing,' Irving had said, holding his hat nervously. 'And the thing is, I'm going to a drinks party at the American Embassy tomorrow night,' he'd hurried on, 'and my date can't make it.'

Jenny had smiled and nodded.

'So I was wondering if . . .'

'Yes?'

' . . . if Vita would come. Jenny, what do you think? Do you think Vita would come out with me?'

'Vita is a grown woman,' Madame Jenny had replied, looking at her. 'She can make her own decisions. What she does outside these walls is of no concern to me.'

She had nodded to Beatrice and they had moved into the salon together, leaving Irving and Vita alone.

'How did Daphne get on at the ball?' Vita had asked, keen to change the subject, stalling for time.

'Daffers looked swell,' he said. 'She even agreed to the makeover you suggested, although it cost me a damned fortune. You've never seen so many lotions and potions.'

Vita had laughed.

'Well, I'll tell you all about it tomorrow. I'll pick you up – say, seven. It's formal, so . . .'

Vita paid for the eclairs now and left Stohrer's, then wandered up through the market past L'Escargot, with a spring in her step. Back on the Champs-Élysées, Georges, the doorman, tipped his hat to Vita.

'What have you got there?' he asked, nodding to the ribbon-wrapped cake-box that she was carrying. 'You'll make yourself popular.'

But Laure wasn't so keen on Vita having one of the eclairs. 'You can't eat those,' she scolded. 'Not if you're going out tonight. Not if you want to look good.'

'What will you wear, though?' Agatha asked, biting into the eclair with a smug smile, and Vita looked on jealously. Her date with Irving had better be worth the sacrifice.

The debate went on all day, until Madame Jenny herself told Vita to wear the midnight-blue evening dress. Vita knew it was a special honour and that the dress was worth a fortune, but when she tried it on, everyone applauded. Madame Jenny stood back and admired her.

'Are you really sure I can wear it?' Vita asked, examining the vision of sophistication in the mirror. It really was true: clothes could entirely change the way you felt about yourself. She felt older, wiser and protected, too – the dress giving her a level of class that she was worried she might be lacking amongst Irving's friends.

'Of course. You will be a good ambassador for Maison Jenny, Vita,' she said, and Vita was determined that she would be.

'Vita, there's a telephone call for you,' Beatrice said, coming into the antechamber, and Vita pulled a face at Jenny and Laure. It would be very embarrassing if it was Irving saying that he'd changed his mind.

Out in the reception area, Vita followed Beatrice to the desk, picking up the skirt of the dress, loving how it felt as it swished around her legs. She was expecting a compliment from Beatrice, too, who was usually so effusive, but Beatrice looked serious as she nodded at the receiver lying on the desk.

Vita, who had been feeling like a princess, felt nervous now as she picked up the receiver.

'Hello?' she asked. '*Bonjour?*'

'Vita?'

Vita clutched the telephone receiver, recognizing the voice. It wasn't Irving at all, and now her heart hammered with an altogether different kind of worry.

'Madame Vertbois?'

'Vita, you have to come back,' she said, in hurried French. 'Right now.'

41

The Men in White Coats

By the time she'd made it back to their apartment in a cab, Vita could see a white hospital van on the corner of the rue d'Orsel, its back doors open. Inside the building, the janitor and a few residents were standing outside Madame Vertbois's office, huddled around each other in the way that only people who had received bad news did. They looked anxiously up the stairs, and then a murmur shuddered through the crowd as they saw Vita.

'What's happened?' she asked, already feeling scared.

'Vita, oh, you're here,' Madame Vertbois said, breaking away and coming to hold Vita's hand. Her face looked crumpled and worried. She'd told Vita that something terrible had happened; and all the way here, Vita's mind had been racing. She thought that maybe Nancy and the concierge had had an argument, but she saw now that it was something much, much worse.

'What is it? What's happened? On the phone you said . . . Just tell me, please. I've been going out of my mind with worry.'

'It's your friend,' another woman said now, and Vita realized with a jolt of recognition that it was the woman

225

from the other day – the woman in the trench coat and beret, the one who'd been outside the club and had helped when Nancy had been hit by the car. What on earth was she doing here?

'Oh . . . it's you,' Vita said.

'I came to see if your friend was better. You told me where you lived, you see, and I was worried,' the woman stumbled on.

She *had* told the woman where she lived, Vita remembered.

'And I found myself in the neighbourhood and I asked about an English dancer, and the man in the shop, he told me that you and Nancy lived here.'

She looked anxious, her blonde hair scraped back. Even without make-up, and with her face pale, she was a striking woman. *What was her name?* Vita wondered. Had she ever known it?

'It's just as well she came when she did,' Madame Vertbois cut her off, looking at the woman with gratitude. They had clearly had a long conversation before Vita got here, and she stared at the two women, seeing a worried look pass between them.

'Madame Vertbois let me in, you see,' the woman explained to Vita. 'She let me come up here and look in on the dog.'

Madame Vertbois didn't look at Vita. She knew it was wrong to trust strangers.

'She gave you the keys?'

'Yes, and I went up and Nancy—'

'What about her? What's happened? Tell me!'

The woman bit her lip. 'Well . . . she was drunk, so very

drunk. And she said she'd taken pills to end it all. She said it was because of the dog . . .'

Vita couldn't take in what the woman was saying.

She looked desperately up the stairs, but Madame Vertbois held her back, because now, coming down the flight of stairs, were two ambulance men, carrying a body on a stretcher.

'Oh God, oh no!' Vita panicked. It wasn't – it couldn't be . . .

'Nancy was distraught,' the blonde woman said. 'She said she couldn't live without him. She said she was sorry.'

'Without who?'

'The dog. He . . . well, he was – he was . . . oh, I'm so sorry.'

'The dog is dead,' Madame Vertbois said, without ceremony.

'Dead?'

Madame Vertbois was clearly shaken and carried on in French to Vita. 'I called my son. He got the ambulance.'

'Mr Wild is dead?'

'He looked very peaceful,' the blonde woman offered with a sympathetic shrug, but Vita was staring at Nancy on the stretcher, her eyes pooling with tears.

The two men in white overcoats lifted Nancy's stretcher down the final part of the staircase now, and Vita saw that Nancy's face was deathly pale, her dark hair plastered with sweat dried onto her face. A big mask was over her nose, with the other end attached to a cylinder, which one of the men was holding.

'Is she . . . ?' Vita asked, but the blonde woman spoke in

rapid French to the ambulance men and one of them replied in a rough voice.

'They pumped her stomach, and now they've given her something to calm her,' the woman said. 'She was quite hysterical.'

'Oh,' Vita gasped, instinctively reaching out to touch Nancy, but the ambulance men were obviously keen to get her outside. 'Where are they taking her?' she asked Madame Vertbois. 'Who are these men?'

'They are from Sainte-Anne's,' the woman answered. 'The hospital for . . . it's for people with problems.' She tapped her temple. 'It's quicker to call them than the ordinary hospital, and your friend clearly needs specialist care.'

Vita followed the men outside and watched as they pushed the stretcher into the ambulance's open doors.

'Let me come, too,' Vita said, keen to step into the van, but the man barred her way.

'*Non, mademoiselle*,' he said. '*Non*.'

'But I've got to go with her,' Vita said, turning to the blonde woman, who spoke to the man again in rapid French, but he shook his head and she watched desperately as the white doors shut on Nancy.

'She will be perfectly safe,' the woman told Vita. 'Don't worry. They'll look after her.'

'I can't let her go alone.'

'You must. They have strict visiting rules, and they say you won't be able to go until the morning. Things will look better by then.'

Vita stood on the pavement as the ambulance drove round the corner. She saw that the shop owners and neighbours had come out to watch, and Madame Vertbois went out into the street and shouted at them. Vita felt the blonde woman's arms go around her.

'Come on,' she said, 'come inside, Vita.'

She wondered how the woman already knew her name, but didn't have time to worry about that now. Madame Vertbois must have told her.

She let herself be guided into the building. The janitor was walking down the stairs, carrying something in the brown blanket that usually lay over the back of their sofa.

Vita hurried up the first few stairs and pulled back the corner of the blanket.

'Oh, Mr Wild,' she said, her hand recoiling from the soft fur. The janitor shook his head, covering the little dog back up.

'Take him away,' Madame Vertbois said to the janitor, and Vita saw a grim look pass between them.

42

Potions and Pills

Vita felt as if her heart were breaking as she sank onto the steps, her evening dress pooling around her. She felt the blonde woman's arm going round her shoulder. 'It's over – come on, Vita dear,' she said. 'Let's get you upstairs.'

Vita shook her head. 'I don't want to go up there. I can't.'

'I'll come with you,' the woman said, saying something to Madame Vertbois that Vita didn't hear.

Just as she'd been when Nancy had had the accident, the blonde woman was competent and calm. Vita was pleased to have her arm around her as they made their way up the stairs.

She let out a sob as they got to the apartment and she saw the open door and that Mr Wild's little bed was empty, his collar on the cushion. 'I don't understand,' Vita said, picking up the collar. 'I don't understand what happened to him?'

'The dog was on the bed. Maybe . . . maybe your friend Nancy – she . . . well, I think she suffocated him.'

Vita shook her head and walked into the kitchen, where she slumped onto a chair at the table. 'Oh, this is awful.

So awful,' she said. 'Thank goodness you found her in time.'

'You've had a dreadful shock. Would you like a drink?' the woman asked and Vita nodded.

'There's brandy,' she said, trying to compose herself. 'Under the sink. I hide it there from Nancy.'

The woman poured a glass for Vita, and then Vita told her to take one for herself and they sat at the little kitchen table.

The woman put her hands over Vita's. 'It will be better soon,' she said. 'Believe me, your friend – she's in the right place to get help.'

'I should have been here.' She thought back to earlier: how optimistic and excited she'd been. Even before she'd arrived home, she had thought she might still have time to meet Mr King, but that wasn't going to happen now. Not now that Mr Wild was . . .

'I wondered why you were all dressed up,' the woman said with a kind smile. 'That dress is quite wonderful.'

Vita looked down at the beautiful dress, thinking of how she'd stood Irving up and how terrible that was, and how Jenny would be so annoyed that Vita had let him down. *So much for being an ambassador*, she thought bitterly. She'd embarrassed everyone.

'Sorry, I'm being so rude. I don't even know your name,' she said, as the woman slid a glass towards her.

'Oh, it's Marianne, although my friends call me Marie,' the woman said. They both smiled sadly now.

'Well, thank you, Marianne,' Vita replied, but she heard her voice catch again and tried to compose herself.

'It's Marie,' she repeated, with a kind smile. Vita clinked glasses with her and took a sip of the brandy, but it didn't help. She felt utterly wretched. And poor Marie: what must she think of all this, and this horrible situation?

'I think I should go. It's getting late,' Marie said, pushing her chair back. She hadn't touched the brandy.

'Of course.'

'You have a nice apartment here,' she said, her hands on the cane-backed chair. She wasn't wearing a wedding ring. 'I wish I was staying somewhere like this.'

'What's your place like?' Vita asked, realizing now that she'd asked Marie very few questions. She barely knew anything about her, and yet she felt as if they already knew each other. She was someone who understood about Nancy, when very few other people did.

'It's . . . well, I share with a couple, and they're not very nice. But when you come to a new city, it's hard.'

Vita had a flashback to how it had been in London when she'd first arrived, having run away from Darton and Clement, and from everyone and everything she knew. How she'd found herself in a horrible boarding house with those ghastly people, Mr and Mrs Jackson, and all of her money had been stolen. And she'd been sick – so terribly sick – without anyone to look after her. If it hadn't been for Nancy, who knows where she might have ended up. Selling her body to survive, perhaps, like the whores who'd lived next door.

'But I have no choice until I find a job . . .' Marie sighed again.

'You could stay here,' Vita offered.

232

There was a beat as Marie's pale face registered her offer.

'What did you say?'

'You could stay here,' Vita repeated. 'For tonight, at least. Without Nancy, or Mr Wild, I'm not sure I can face being alone.' Her voice wobbled and more tears came. 'It's the least I can do to repay you for your help. If it wasn't for you . . .' Marie touched her shoulder in a comforting way as Vita cried. 'How could she possibly want to kill herself? Nancy, of all people?'

'You can't ever really know someone,' Marie said, taking her coat off. She sat back down and held Vita's hand. 'Was she an unhappy person?'

'Sometimes, but more often than not, she was the life and soul of the party.'

'I'm so sorry,' Marie said, stroking her hand.

'She must have felt so dreadful about Mr Wild. She loved him so very much, but to do that . . .'

She felt Marie's arms go round her.

'It's all right,' she said, as Vita cried. 'I'm here now.' And slowly, eventually, soothed by Marie's gentle words, Vita felt her tears subsiding and she managed to calm down.

'Why don't you let me make you something to eat?' Marie said. 'If you don't mind, that is?'

Vita shook her head, glad that Marie was here. Glad that she was taking charge.

Later Vita made up her own bed for Marie, and took Nancy's room herself. She felt it would be wrong to put Marie in there, after what had happened. She cleared Nancy's bedroom of the pots of pills and the empty bottles of spirits, with the ghost of Nancy and Mr Wild in every corner. She put her hand on the pillow where Nancy's head had been, seeing one of her dark hairs. Then she sat on the bed, clutching the pillow to her chest, grief for her friend – and for Mr Wild – making it impossible to breathe.

'Oh, Nancy,' she sobbed. 'What have you done?'

43

Sainte-Anne's

Vita slept only for an hour at dawn, then called into work the next morning from Madame Vertbois's office and explained what had happened. Beatrice told Vita that she'd better take the day off, but Vita knew she was being kind, when there was so much work to do. The others didn't let their personal lives get in the way of their busy schedule at Maison Jenny, but what other choice did Vita have?

Beatrice said she'd get a message to Irving King to try to explain what had happened last night, but Vita knew Madame Jenny would be so disappointed that she'd put her friend above their prestigious client. People like Irving King didn't take kindly to being stood up at such short notice, and she knew that she wouldn't be asked out again.

Madame Vertbois's instructions to get to Sainte-Anne's hospital were written on a sheet of paper in loopy fountain pen, and Marie told her that the quickest way to the four-teenth arrondissement was by bus. For someone who'd only been in Paris a short while, she seemed to be very know-ledgeable, and Vita was glad of the guidance. Marie had even offered to come with her, but Vita said she'd better go alone.

But as she sat on the bus, looking down at the choppy

grey water as it crossed the river, Vita wished she'd let Marie accompany her. She thought of her new friend alone in the apartment, feeling worried now for a second that she'd placed so much trust in a stranger. But Marie seemed like a kind soul, Vita reassured herself. And besides, there was very little in the apartment that she could steal. *Apart from Mr Wild*, Vita thought, and then her eyes filled with tears as she remembered what had happened. *Poor, poor Mr Wild.*

With a heavy heart, she got off the bus at her stop and started walking down to rue Cabanis to the hospital, which specialized in neurology and psychiatry – words Vita had barely known until this morning, when Marie explained them to her. But knowing them brought no comfort, only a sense of horror and shame. She remembered how, long ago, a few of the men from the mill returning from the war had been admitted to Calderstones hospital in Whalley, not far from Darton in Lancashire. She'd been past it once with her father, and he'd called it the 'loony bin', and she'd glimpsed the high walls and stark brick buildings and thought of what he'd told her. 'When people go mad, they lock them in there and throw away the key,' he'd said, as if this were meant to be reassuring.

Now, as she arrived at the high iron gates set in a pale stone arch, Vita experienced that same sense of dread. Every instinct told her to run away, but there was incredulity, too. Surely Nancy didn't belong in a place like this? Not tough, crazy, wonderful Nancy. Had she really tried to end it all? Had she taken pills to kill herself? Out of shame?

Vita had to *do* something. She had to get her friend out of here, by any means necessary. The nagging feeling that this was all a horrible mistake persisted. Not so long ago Nancy had been high-kicking on the stage of Les Folies Bergère, and now she was locked behind these high walls. How had it all gone so wrong, so fast?

When she was finally admitted to the waiting area, the nurse behind the desk seemed to deliberately misunderstand Vita's French, and once again she wished she'd let Marie come with her to translate. She remembered going to the police station to plead for Percy's release after his arrest, and now she felt the same – as if she were beating her fist against a locked door.

She sat on one of the hard chairs that were bolted to the white floor and watched the doctors in their white coats, and the nurses in their long aprons and white headscarves, come and go through the swing doors. Occasionally, when the double doors opened, Vita could hear distant screams. Finally – and it felt like hours later – she was told to follow a harassed-looking nurse to Nancy's ward.

She tried not to look at the other patients, but it was hard to ignore them. There was an old woman, her head lolling to one side, and Vita nearly jumped out of her skin as one of the other patients – a younger woman who looked quite crazed, her hair standing up on end as if she'd been electrocuted – leapt out of bed to run at her, only to be stopped by the limits of her tether. The nurse frowned at Vita's shocked reaction. She didn't seem remotely bothered, but Vita was terrified. What was this place?

'She's over there,' the nurse said, pointing to the end bed of the cavernous ward, with light coming in from a high, barred window. She let Vita walk over the final part of the shiny floor alone, following the shaft of light, until she could see a lump in the bed behind the green canvas bed-screen. More and more of Nancy came into view, until Vita saw her friend propped up on pillows on the bed, her arms by her side, a drip going into one of her thin arms. Vita stopped for a moment, taking in the pitiful sight.

Vita had always admired Nancy for being so full of life, determined to be the brightest light, to reach the highest high, but here she was, pale and dimmed, broken and exhausted. She looked like a little girl.

Nancy's bloodshot eyes flicked over her as Vita approached and there was a flash of confusion, then she reached out. Vita sat on the bed beside Nancy, and as Nancy pulled her forward, she lay awkwardly, hugging her friend, her nose curling at the sour smell of her.

Nancy let out a whimper, and Vita pulled back and put her hand on Nancy's cool cheek.

'I'm here,' Vita said, trying to sound reassuring, but her eyes were prickling with tears at the sight of her friend.

'You've got to get me out of here,' Nancy said in a choked whisper. 'Vita, you hear me? You've got to help. I don't know why they brought me here. Oh, Vita. Vita, what am I doing here? How has this happened?'

Nancy was many things – manipulative, emotional, exuberant – but this was the first time Vita had ever seen her look scared. All her brashness had gone. All her bravado had vanished, and it was this that broke Vita's heart the most.

'Don't you remember what happened?' Vita asked. 'Yesterday?'

'Sort of – there was . . .' Nancy was searching her memory,

then what little colour there was in her cheeks drained away. 'Is it true? About Mr Wild? I dreamt he was dead.'

There was a beat as she met Vita's eyes. 'I'm so sorry,' Vita said, feeling her throat tightening and tears falling now, as she looked at the awful comprehension dawning on Nancy's face. 'You didn't know what was happening: you'd had too much to drink and you must have mixed up your pills,' she hurried on.

'No, I can't have done. I was asleep, and then there was someone there. I don't know who it was, but he . . . she had Mr Wild. I'm sure he was eating something.'

Vita couldn't bear to look at her friend's anguished face, and she thought of poor Marie finding Nancy in such a mess – discovering the little dead dog beneath the covers.

'No, Mr Wild was dead.'

'So it's true? I . . . I *killed Mr Wild*?' Nancy's voice was a scratchy whisper.

'Shhh, don't say it like that.'

'You told me not to have him on the bed – you told me I'd suffocate him.'

'Don't . . . It was an accident, Nancy.'

'Oh, Mr Wild.'

Vita held her as she grieved.

'Listen, I know it's awful, but Mr Wild had a good life. He was happy and he was loved. But you,' Vita said, and then for emphasis put her finger on Nancy's bony chest, 'you can't go checking out on me, too,' Vita told her. 'You silly thing. I don't know what you were thinking when you took all those pills, but that is why you're here, because you tried to . . .'

Nancy looked terrified. 'Did I? I don't remember.'

'That's what Marie said.'

'Marie?'

'The one who found you. Who helped you.'

'I don't remember,' Nancy said, her eyes filling with tears. 'Please don't leave me in here. Please take me home,' she begged. 'The men here, they're horrible and they don't speak a word of English. They won't tell me what's going on, or what they're doing. I shouldn't be here. I'm not sick, Vita. I didn't mean to—'

'Shhh,' Vita soothed, but Nancy couldn't be soothed.

It wasn't long before a nurse came and explained that Vita had to leave and that Nancy was being taken for 'an evaluation'.

'But I'm not sick,' she protested again, as the nurse helped her get out of bed and into a wheelchair.

'Then they'll discharge you,' Vita said, but she knew she didn't sound as convincing as Nancy wanted her to.

'I don't care what you have to do, Vita,' she said, desperately, clinging on to her wrist, 'but if you are my friend – if you love me like I love you – then you will find a way . . . *any* way to get me out of here.'

44

An Angel

Leaving Nancy in the hospital had to be one of the worst things she'd ever done, and Vita returned home feeling worried and depressed. The doctors could shed no light on when Nancy might be discharged, and Vita dreaded the thought of having to go there again to visit. She'd tried explaining to the staff that she would take Nancy home and care for her there, but they wouldn't listen and sent Vita away, telling her they were in charge now.

She was so wrapped up in her thoughts that she'd almost forgotten about Marie, but when she climbed the stairs to the apartment, her heart contracted with longing as she instinctively waited for the sound of Mr Wild's welcome.

Marie was in the kitchen, wearing a blue-and-white striped apron and lifting an earthenware pot out of the tiny oven. Something inside it had sizzled. It smelt delicious.

'I hope you don't mind,' Marie said. 'It is such a treat to do some home cooking.'

They hardly ever cooked at home, and Vita was astonished now at the scene of domestic competence in front of her. Marie must have been out shopping early to make all of this. There were even a few flowers in a glass on the table.

Grateful and weary, she sat on the chair and told Marie all about the horrible morning she'd had, and how desperate Nancy was. Marie served the chicken stew in the best bowls from the back of the cupboard and cut a chunk of rustic bread. But the contrast between where Nancy was and this was too much, and Vita felt shaky. Marie put her hand on her shoulder.

'It's no wonder you're upset,' she said. 'Eat something and you'll feel better.'

'Nancy doesn't think she did anything wrong,' Vita said.

'Then I'm afraid she really *is* in trouble,' Marie said sympathetically, and Vita felt tears coming. Marie gave her a freshly laundered handkerchief and eventually, taking a deep breath, Vita started to eat. Soon the warming stew was making her feel much better.

'I'm so sorry,' Vita said, 'I feel dreadful that you've had to witness all this.'

'I'm glad I was here. Glad I could help,' she replied.

'You've been there twice now. You must be some kind of guardian angel.'

Marie smiled, but Vita couldn't read her look. 'Oh, I forgot. This came for you earlier,' Marie said, pulling a telegram from her apron pocket, and Vita wondered if she'd already read it. 'Madame Vertbois brought it up. She seems like a very kind woman.'

Vita could tell that Marie and Madame Vertbois were on good terms. It was unusual for the old woman to be so friendly, and Vita thought Marie must be a good person, if she'd passed Madame Vertbois's judgemental scrutiny.

The telegram was from Irving King, insisting that he take her out for dinner tonight. Vita slid it across the table for Marie to read.

'That's wonderful. You should go,' she said.

'I can't. It's wrong. I can't go, with everything that's happened to Nancy. Besides, I'm too sad about Mr Wild.'

'Listen, Nancy might want to end things, but that doesn't mean your life has to stop, too. And anyway, didn't you say you were worried that you'd let everyone down at Madame Sacerdote's? Might this not be a way of putting things right?'

'I suppose so, but I'd feel guilty for going out and enjoying myself, after everything that's happened.'

'Don't,' Marie said, with a kind smile. 'Nancy is safe. She's being treated. Have a sleep this afternoon and then go out and enjoy yourself. You need a break.'

Vita felt relieved again that Marie was here and seemed to have the ability to talk sense. In the most awful of circumstances, she seemed to have found a friend – a friend who understood how she felt – and she was glad that Marie was staying. It might be a selfish thought, but it was nice to be the one being looked after, for once.

She watched as Marie ate quickly and efficiently, then cleared away the bowls from the table. Then she took off the apron, folding it up and smoothing out the wrinkles. 'I really must be going,' she said. 'It has been wonderful meeting you, Vita, even under these difficult circumstances, but I have imposed on your hospitality too much, as it is.'

'Nonsense,' Vita said.

'It's been lovely being here, and not in that dreadful room, but . . . well, I should leave you.'

'Please stay,' Vita said suddenly. She didn't want to be alone. Not without Nancy.

'I can't,' Marie shook her head. 'It would be wrong.'

'It's not wrong,' Vita insisted, seeing how bashful Marie was. 'You'd be helping me. Honestly.'

'If you're sure?'

'I'm sure. I like having company, and I don't want you to have to go back to that dreadful room.'

Marie closed her eyes for a moment, as if saying a prayer of thanks.

'Do you need to get your things?' Vita asked, realizing that she didn't know where Marie lived – or very much about her at all.

She nodded. 'I will. Later on.'

They chatted for a while, and Marie told Vita how she'd come to Paris to work in a shop, but when she got here the job was no longer available. She said she had no family to speak of and, as she spoke about her lonely struggle, Vita started to feel sorry for her.

There was a small pause. 'Actually, Vita, can I ask you something?'

'Of course.'

'I wasn't snooping, I promise, but I found a basket in your room and . . . and I know it was wrong, but when I moved it, it fell open and I saw what was inside.'

Vita saw Marie's cheeks flush as she quickly hurried out of the kitchen and returned with some of the items from Vita's sewing basket.

'These were on the top,' she said, holding up the half-finished brassieres.

'Oh, those,' Vita said, with a sad shrug. 'My little side-project.'

'They're wonderful. Where did you get them?'

'I make them. Bras, I mean. I should do more, but I've been so busy with work.'

'These are fantastic,' Marie said, holding up a bra in black silk that Vita had made, on which she'd sewn a few sequins. 'Unusual, I think. Who are they for?'

'Everyone,' Vita said. 'Ordinary women. Women like us.'

'Really? But it's so . . . It looks like something a showgirl would wear.'

'Exactly,' Vita said. 'That's the whole point. Shouldn't every woman have access to some of the risqué outfits the girls wear at Les Folies?' She was glad to be talking about her passion, and not about Nancy. 'Bras with sequins or pearls. Bras not only to hold up these,' she said, cupping her breasts, 'but for fun?'

Marie laughed. 'Would women dare?'

'Of course they would, given half a chance. Because that's the whole point: underwear is secret. You could wear this bra under the most formal of dresses and feel – I don't know – a little bit naughty.'

'I see what you mean,' Marie said, but she still sounded unsure.

'Back in England, when I was younger, I used to dye my petticoats with beetroot, just for fun. I didn't care what anyone else thought, or even if they saw it – I wanted to feel that I was doing something for me.'

Marie looked surprised. 'I haven't ever thought of clothes that way. I hardly take any notice of what I look like.'

'Don't you? Well, you should. You're a very pretty woman, if you don't mind me saying so. But it's not about what I – or anyone else – think; it's about what you yourself think.'

'I haven't thought about it like that,' Marie said quietly. 'I'm not the same as you. I wish . . .' She shook her head again and her words fizzled out, and Vita wondered if she was on the verge of confessing some truth about herself, but felt instinctively that she shouldn't push it.

'Why don't we finish this one together? I'll fit it for you,' Vita offered. 'And then you can wear it and see what you think.'

45

The Date with Irving

Later, having spent the afternoon with Marie, showing her the brassieres and sharing her plans, Vita was feeling in a much happier mood as she sat with Irving at the corner table of La Tour d'Argent. The historic restaurant on the quai de la Tournelle and the rue du Cardinal Lemoine had polished wooden panels, bright chandeliers and crisp white tablecloths. As they sat together at the softly lit corner table, the rest of the world – and in particular that awful hospital – seemed very far away.

Irving, who'd clearly been here before, had ordered wine from the extensive cellar to go with oysters, to be followed by foie gras, as well as duck; he'd told Vita that the ducks were numbered – an old tradition that the restaurant kept going. She wondered if she was going to be able to keep up with his lavish appetite. She'd suspected, from his size, that Irving was something of a *bon vivant* – and now she had the proof.

'Did you know that this was the first place ever to use forks?' he said, picking up one of the fancy silver forks next to his gilt-edged plate. 'It was to stop gentlemen staining their immaculate ruffs,' he went on, pretending to ruffle an imaginary neck-piece, and Vita laughed.

She'd been nervous when she first arrived, wondering how she would chat to Irving, or whether they had anything at all in common, but he was surprisingly easy to be with.

He was wearing a very smart tuxedo and, away from Daphne, he didn't look as old as she'd remembered. His hair was oiled and he was clean-shaven, with the kind of soft, tanned skin that looked pampered, and Vita imagined that he indulged in a daily shave at a barber's.

Now, as the dozen oysters arrived, served on crushed ice on a silver plate, Vita remembered dining at Kettner's in London with Archie, and the first time she'd had oysters.

Determined to put Archie out of her mind, she took a few oysters and put them on her gold-rimmed china plate, then squeezed the half-lemon that was neatly wrapped in muslin and watched the corners of the oysters wrinkling up, as if they were curling up their toes squeamishly. Then, with a silver fork, she separated the plump flesh from its pearly shell and gently slid the salty contents into her mouth, before chewing and wincing at the tart sensation.

'Marvellous, don't you think?' Irving asked, grinning at her. 'I love a girl who can stomach her oysters,' he added, and she wondered if she'd passed some kind of test. 'Try it with the Pouilly-Fuissé,' he said and she took a sip of the very fine wine. 'Sublime, don't you think?'

Vita smiled, keen to make a good impression and to right the wrong of standing Irving up. She'd already told him what had happened to Nancy, and he'd been very understanding. To her relief, he reported that he hadn't been at all worried about attending the function alone. She'd been silly to worry, she realized. Irving was a man, and it was different for them.

If their roles had been reversed and it had been Irving standing *her* up, she'd never have gone to a function like that alone, but he hadn't seemed bothered in the slightest.

'So tell me more about this friend, Nancy,' Irving said, sitting back as if waiting for the story, and she put her fork and napkin down, her appetite deserting her as she thought of poor little Mr Wild. Her eyes welled with tears as she told Irving what had happened to their beloved little dog.

'Vita,' he said, looking at her fully now, his eyes kind, 'that is so dreadful.'

She could tell that he meant it, but even so, she didn't want him to think badly of Nancy, so she told him about how Nancy had rescued her in London and how they'd danced at the Zip Club. She left out various less salubrious parts of their history, but, as she painted a picture of their friendship, it felt good to conjure up the person Nancy had been, rather than the pale, terrified person she'd left hours ago in that hospital bed.

'And now . . . well, now she's stuck in that place, for I don't know how long. Nancy can't bear it there. She doesn't speak any French, and she's confused and alone.' Vita looked up to the ceiling, trying to stop her tears from falling. 'I can't help feeling it's my fault. That I should have done more.'

Irving nodded and she realized what a great listener he'd been.

'Oh, darling,' he said, surprising her with the sudden term of endearment, 'how terrible it must be for you.' She smiled at him, so glad that he understood. She did feel much better, having unburdened herself to him. 'Let me help,' Irving said.

'Help?'

'To get your friend out of there. I don't know why she wasn't sent to an infirmary. Once you get put into one of those psychiatric places, they're the devil to get out of.'

'I know,' Vita said. 'That's what I'm worried about.'

'Let's get her home to the States. To her family. Where she belongs.'

'Nancy won't want that. She hasn't spoken to them for years. She'd kill me if I got in touch with them now. I called her lawyer, Goldie, earlier, but he said he couldn't help. He said Nancy's fund was empty and her family wouldn't help, and that a hospital was the best place for her. That might be the case, but Larry Goldblum hasn't been inside Sainte-Anne's.'

'Then let's send her to California. I have friends there who know of discreet clinics, with palm trees and views over the ocean, where types like Nancy can . . . well . . . dry out. You know, it's where people from the movies go – to take a break. It's really very nice. More of a hotel than a hospital.'

'But how could I possibly afford it? Nancy's trust fund has all but gone, and her parents certainly won't pay.'

'I can pay.' Irving shrugged. 'It's only money.'

'That's easy for you to say.'

'Of course it is, but I have plenty, and I like nothing more than spending it on things that make people I care about happy.'

Did that mean Irving cared about her? Vita smiled at him, sensing that he'd said too much with this admission. But he was sweet, she thought. And so very well-meaning. And then she thought of Nancy's desperate plea for Vita to do anything to get her out.

'I couldn't possibly ask you to do that.'

'Hush, hush,' he said, 'I will hear no more about it. Let me make some enquiries and arrangements.'

'But . . .'

'Honestly, it would be an honour. I like nothing more than fixing a problem.'

Vita bit her lip. His offer was wonderful – miraculous, in fact – but how could she ever repay such a favour?

As if sensing this, Irving went on, 'I'm sure there will be a way in which you can make it up to me. Keeping Daphne happy – well that's worth its weight in gold.'

'That's hardly a chore. She's a lovely girl.'

'She's easier than her sister.'

'Hermione?' Vita said. She'd heard about Daphne's younger sister.

'She's rather taken her mother's side in our divorce.'

Vita nodded. She didn't want to pry, but she hoped she could lend a listening ear.

'I took the rap, but really it was Alicia who left me. She said she didn't love me any more and wanted to be alone. I should have known there was someone else, but I didn't want to see it,' Irving said, with a sigh.

'Oh, I'm sorry.'

'A Paris divorce is all the rage. She rented an apartment, to prove that she lived here, and then in two weeks – pah! It was all done. No delay, no peeping detectives. She got her inspiration from Rudolph Valentino's wife.'

'How very modern.'

'Quite. And everyone should be moving on, except for the fact that my youngest daughter, Hermione, thinks I'm cruel.'

Vita couldn't imagine Irving being cruel. He was like a big teddy bear. He waved his hand, batting away the emotion that crossed his face now.

'I'm rather ashamed to be confiding in you.'

'Please don't be. I've been telling you all of my troubles.'

'It's still painful, but I get a sense of life moving on at last,' he said. 'We should drink to that,' he continued, and his eyes connected with hers as they clinked glasses.

Despite the dreadful week she'd had, and her worries over Nancy, Vita soon felt the wine doing its magic. She felt that, in sharing their troubles, she and Irving had formed a special kind of bond. She felt a warm, fuzzy glow and when the delicious dinner came to an end and Irving suggested that they go to Zelli's for a nightcap, she didn't object.

46

Zelli's

The Royal Box – Joe Zelli's club – was already buzzing, even though it only opened at midnight, and Vita and Irving had to wait in a small queue to get in.

Compared to Les Folies and the late-night clubs and bars Vita was used to, this was altogether a different sort of scene. She stood a little taller, glad that she hadn't worn Madame Jenny's evening dress, which still hung on Nancy's door, but a short dress – an old party dress of Nancy's that she'd altered. She'd added some offcuts of ostrich-feather trim from the studio. She rather liked the contrast of the fetching collar with the short dress length, but among all the women here, in their furs and beaded evening dresses, she hoped it didn't look too home-made.

Joe Zelli was in an immaculate tuxedo and had dark-brown hair and very chubby cheeks. 'Irving, you old rogue,' he boomed, pumping Irving's hand as they got to the door. 'Hey, hey. You!' he called to the waiter, clicking his fingers. 'The Royal Box for the Prince. I'll be up to see you later, old chap. Busy night tonight.'

'Goodness,' Vita exclaimed, as the waiter hurried over, and Joe told them to follow him to what she suspected was the best table in the house. 'Does he really think you're a prince?'

'No,' Irving chuckled. 'He says that to everyone.'

The decor was almost Moorish, Vita thought, looking through the smoke at the large rectangular dance hall, which was packed with dancing couples and, around the edge, tables stacked high with ice-buckets and bottles. She saw now that the entrance was mirrored, and above them was a balcony, which was clearly where the waiter was leading them now. As they headed for the stairs, they passed a wall of framed caricatures in black charcoal.

'Is that you?' Vita exclaimed, seeing a picture of Irving, although his nose looked unnecessarily large.

He laughed. 'I guess it is. There's this little guy, Zito, who draws all the guests.'

'That's Salvador Dalí,' Vita said, 'I recognize the moustache.' She dawdled, looking at the fabulous caricatures, recognizing the familiar features of the glamorous Kiki, whom Nancy and the girls called the 'Queen of Montparnasse'.

They were shown to their 'box' – a booth on the balcony, from where they could look down at the guests. Then a very tall waitress came over, wearing the skimpiest of dresses, cinched in at the waist. She was American and greeted Irving warmly. 'Hi, Irving,' she said in a languid voice, draping her hand on his shoulder, which seemed a very intimate gesture. Vita noted some other equally beautiful women cruising between the tables. 'Who's your lucky friend?'

'Lucibelle, I'd like you to meet Miss Casey,' he said, and the girl smiled.

'Welcome,' she said, taking her hand away from Irving's shoulder. 'The usual?' she added to him.

'Sure. Thanks, honey.'

Vita wondered how often he came here, to have his caricature on the wall and to be on first-name terms with the staff – and, more notably, they with him. And, as she'd suspected, this had to be the best table in the house, with a view over the entire club.

A moment later Lucibelle had brought an enormous bottle of champagne, and the telephone on the white tablecloth rang. Irving grinned, picked it up and then bellowed with laughter.

'How you doing?' He stood up, leant over the balcony and waved. He put his hand over the receiver. 'You can call between the boxes. It's Scott. Look, over there,' Irving said, pointing at another box, where a handsome man in a tux was waving.

'Well, come over, old chap. Come and say hello.'

'You're very popular,' Vita observed, and Irving laughed as he replaced the receiver. Lucibelle popped the champagne cork and began to pour the liquid into their glasses.

She hadn't been expecting Irving to be so fun-loving or so well connected. She'd thought, being Daphne's father, that he'd be far more grown-up, far more like she perceived her own father, Darius Darton. But now, in his favourite club, she was seeing Irving King in an altogether new light. He grinned and clinked glasses with her and Vita smiled back.

'Hello,' a man said and Irving stood up.

'Ah, Scotty, old boy,' Irving said, shaking his hand and

cupping his shoulder. 'Vita, this is Fitzgerald. He's a writer. You'll have heard of him, I'm sure?'

'Now, now, Irving. Don't put her on the spot,' Mr Fitzgerald said, and Vita had to try very hard not to gawp at him.

'The writer,' Vita said as she shook his hand, wanting to kick herself for not being more sophisticated. She thought of how Archie Fenwick would eat his hat if he could be here now. Scott Fitzgerald drew up a chair and sat down, and Lucibelle brought over another glass.

'I thought you were disappearing for the summer,' Irving said.

'Ah yes, the Riviera beckons,' he replied, lighting a cigarette.

Vita tried not to study him too obviously, as he and Irving chatted about how Scott and his wife would be leaving on the train at the end of the week. 'We'll be expecting a visit from you,' he told Irving, then added to Vita, 'he has a knack of always turning up when there's a party about to start.'

'Is that so?' Vita said, looking at Irving, who rolled his eyes bashfully.

'So I hear Le Monsieur is in tonight,' Scott said, lowering his voice to a confidential whisper.

'That's why Joe is so busy then,' Irving said.

'I've heard that name before,' Vita said, suddenly remembering that she'd arrived at Chez Joséphine just as Le Monsieur and his set had left. 'Who is he?' she asked Irving.

'That's the thing. No one really knows,' Fitzgerald said, with a laugh.

'I wish I knew,' Irving said. 'He's got the finest poker game in Paris. But it's invite-only.'

Vita made a mental note to ask Irving about this mysterious character, it being the second time she'd heard about him. The conversation continued about Joe Zelli being under the thumb of his French wife, who did the books, and how he'd taken to riding the limo that he kept, out to his chateau in the countryside. The club business was obviously very lucrative. Then the telephone on the table rang again and Irving handed the phone to Scott.

'I'm coming, darling,' Scott said, replacing the receiver. 'Zelda,' he explained. 'Duty calls,' and he stood up and drained the glass, before wishing them a good evening.

47

Dancing

Vita, still a little star-struck by Scott Fitzgerald, didn't have a moment to discuss Irving's famous friend, because three more couples came to the table to pay their respects, and each time Irving pulled an apologetic face at Vita. He clearly knew all the American society people in Paris, and the women looked at Vita curiously. It was obviously quite a coup to be seen out with the rich, poker-playing business tycoon.

'Can we dance?' Vita asked eventually when they got a moment alone, feeling a little self-conscious at all the scrutiny. 'I'm beginning to think it'll be the only way I can get you on my own.'

Irving laughed. 'Well, if you put it like that, how could I refuse?'

Irving, it turned out, was a good dancer and was soon leading her around the dance floor. She liked the way his big, soft hand folded around hers and, although he was tall and rather large, she seemed to fit against him and felt protected in his embrace. It was this, perhaps, that was the most surprising thing of all – she *liked* dancing with him.

Irving held her close, talking in her ear. 'It's nice to be out – to have someone to have fun with.'

258

'I'm sure you don't have any problem having fun,' Vita said, thinking about all the people who'd already come to say hello.

'But it's not the same when you're on your own. Alicia – my God! – she'd have never come here. She gave me a hard time. The *whole* time. Money can't buy you everything, Vita, let me tell you.'

'She never danced?'

'Never. She's so . . . well, so po-faced,' he said, and Vita laughed at the way he said it. She couldn't imagine Irving being with anyone serious.

'Then she missed out,' Vita said, scooching in closer as they wended their way through the couples.

'Listen to me,' Irving said in a self-admonishing way, 'running my mouth off about my past. What must you think? I'm never normally like this,' he said, as if he were confused himself.

'I don't mind. I like hearing about your life. It's interesting.'

'You're very easy to talk to, Vita,' he said, and for a second their eyes connected and they both smiled.

She felt her heart jolt a little, wondering if she'd been too intimate – whether she'd given Irving the wrong idea about her. And what was the wrong idea? *Was* this wrong? She couldn't imagine what Nancy would say, if she could see her, but that was part of Irving's appeal: he was her own discovery and was nothing to do with the club, or the girls, or Nancy. He felt fresh, as well as safe, and she let herself admit that she'd had an unexpectedly lovely evening. If he asked her out again, she'd definitely say yes.

And then as they danced past the band, Vita looked

through the smoke, hearing a trumpet taking over from the clarinet, and she felt an icy spike of fear. She knew Fletch played in various bands, but surely he wasn't here?

She tried to steer them away, but now, as she stole a worried glance towards the band, for a brief second she stared into the familiar eyes of the trumpet player and her stomach flipped. It *was* him.

She saw Fletch's eyes widen, as he took in the sight of her dancing with Irving. And now she flushed, remembering how Laure had reacted to him; remembering, to her horror, that she hadn't returned Fletch's jacket. And because she hadn't, he was bound to seek her out and want to talk to her. And he would probably have heard about what happened to Nancy, too . . .

Panic rose within her and, with it, a horrible, nagging sense of guilt – not just that she was here with Irving, but that she was out, clearly having fun, when her best friend was in hospital.

The song finished and Irving clapped the band.

'Shall we dance some more?'

'No, no, that's my fix,' Vita said quickly, turning away from Fletch. 'Let's go back to the table.'

She hurried up the stairs, keen to distance herself, hoping that upstairs, in the Royal Box, she'd be safe. She knew she was being a coward, but she remembered Laure, and Georges the doorman, too, and how they'd reacted when they'd seen Fletch outside Madame Sacerdote's. But this – here – was so much worse. She knew, with absolute certainty, that a man like Irving King would be horrified if he suspected what had happened between her and Fletch. And now her fling with him seemed even more outrageous, and reckless too, and the shameful memory of it throbbed beneath the surface of her skin, making her breathless with nerves.

But Irving didn't notice any of the inner turmoil Vita was feeling, and she was grateful when the telephone on their table rang again and he laughed and then excused himself, telling her to wait while he went to get some friends to join them.

Left alone for a moment, Vita looked around, wondering if this was the moment to go to the powder room, but as she was about to stand up, Fletch was suddenly by the table. She looked around frantically. Surely he wasn't allowed up here?

'You're going out with him? That old guy? That fat man?' he asked, without even saying hello.

'He's not fat.'

Fletch gave her a look and, with him standing so near, she could smell him and her stomach flipped, remembering what they'd done on his bed, remembering his muscle-bound chest.

'You're better than that, Vita,' he said.

It had been bad enough having Fletch be jealous of Paul, but this was too much. He had no right to lay any claim on her. Not when he was out dancing with other girls the whole time.

'You have no right—'

'He don't deserve you,' Fletch said, whispering and leaning in close, and the nearness of him, the scent of him, made memories come flooding back. 'Please, Vita, can't you see that you're just falling into being who they want you to be?'

She felt her face flushing. 'You can't say that.'

'I know you. I know you're better than this. Than all these racist people. You gave me a chance, and we could – if we tried – we could be together . . . change the world. It ain't too late, Vita. I still got feelings for you. What we had, girl . . .'

Then suddenly Irving was behind Fletch.

'Get your hands off her,' Irving roared, grabbing Fletch's shoulder and twisting him round. He threw a feeble punch, but Fletch caught his wrist. Irving yelped, as Fletch squeezed. 'I'll have you whipped,' Irving shouted.

'This is not America, sir,' Fletch said coolly, squaring up to him, before shoving him backwards into the table behind. There was the sound of glasses smashing and the couple at the table stood up.

'Both of you, please, stop it,' Vita implored, jumping in between Fletch and Irving and pushing them apart.

Irving looked like he was going to explode.

'You know him?' Irving asked.

'This is Fletch – my . . . he plays in the band at Les Folies,' Vita said, trying not to cry.

Fletch backed away, his eyes burning with fury, then turned and strutted towards the swing door, punched it violently and walked through. Vita apologized to the couple, who sat down again, and then Lucibelle was suddenly there with a dustpan to sweep up the broken glass.

'Never let one of those . . . niggers,' Irving hissed, 'touch you. Ever again. You hear me?'

'Irving, please. He's just someone I knew once,' Vita said, but her voice shook. She hated herself for not defending

262

Fletch, but she couldn't, without causing even more of a scene.

'A filthy scoundrel like him should know his place. I'll have Joe know that he came up here.'

'Please don't,' Vita begged, but Irving had already picked up the phone on their table. She put her hand over the telephone. 'Please, Irving – please leave it. I don't want a fuss,' she said in a hushed whisper, looking around at the other diners. 'Let's enjoy ourselves.'

'Vita, I'm sorry, but he can't just come up to our box like that,' he said. 'A filthy Negro.'

'Irving,' she said more forcefully, offended by his tone and his clear sense of superiority. 'Please don't say ugly things like that. This is Paris, not America. Please let's not ruin the start of a beautiful friendship,' she implored. 'I can't help who I am. I can't help it that I was a dancing girl – that I know people. People like Fletch . . .' she trailed off, seeing that he'd never understand. 'He meant no harm.'

Irving sighed, deflating, and then some friends arrived and the moment wasn't mentioned again, but Vita felt shaken up by the whole incident. She felt ashamed, too. Ashamed that she'd gone down in Fletch's estimation.

48

Female Bonding

Vita woke up to the smell of coffee and lay in Nancy's bed, listening to her pottering around the apartment, before remembering where Nancy actually was and what had happened, and that it wasn't Nancy, but Marie in the kitchen. Then she put her hand to her head, remembering last night and groaning.

Despite Vita asking him not to, Irving had told Joe Zelli all about the altercation with Fletch, when he'd come up to their table. He'd done it in a jovial way, but she knew, without a shadow of a doubt, that Fletch would almost certainly have lost his job with the band because of her. And now she felt wretched, on Fletch's account, and worried that the whole scene might have ruined things with Irving. She'd been so busy trying to be a lady, trying to fit into his set, and Fletch had been a stark reminder of who she'd previously been mixing with and where she'd come from.

It might not be the start of a beautiful friendship, but it was certainly the start of a fiendish hangover, she thought, as she clambered out from beneath Nancy's satin eiderdown and made for the kitchen.

'*Bonjour*,' Marie called, and Vita saw that the kitchen

was cleaner than it had ever been. Now, wearing Nancy's dressing gown and with her head thumping, she felt an uncomfortable role reversal.

'It's very tidy in here,' Vita said.

'I hope you don't mind. I like organizing things. I can't help myself,' Marie said with a self-deprecating laugh. 'You came in very late,' she said. 'How was it?'

'Fun – we had fun, but . . .' Vita sat at the table, wincing at her headache.

Marie observed her as she poured coffee from the white enamel pot into little bowls.

'There's a "but"?'

Vita rubbed her face. 'It doesn't matter.'

'It looks like it does,' Marie said gently.

Vita took a breath. 'We . . . we were dancing, and then I saw someone in the band that I knew. Fletch.'

'Fletch from the club? The one who was there when Nancy had her accident?'

Vita was surprised that Marie remembered his name, when it had been such an intense situation. She wasn't sure she'd remember the details of Marie's life so clearly. Not that she knew very many details.

'What happened?'

'He was playing in the band, and he saw me and came up to our table and spoke to me, and Irving got . . . well, he got the wrong end of the stick.'

'The wrong end of the stick,' Marie repeated, and Vita covered her face.

'What is it, Vita? You can tell me,' Marie said gently.

'I can't.'

'Yes, you can. We're friends now. You can trust me.'

Vita opened her fingers and looked up at her. Is that what they were? Friends? She supposed they were, and this fact, this word – *friend* – felt like everything she needed right now. Because she needed someone she could trust. Someone she could confide in. Who wouldn't judge her, but could help her out of this situation.

So she took a deep breath and said, 'The thing is, Fletch and I, we were – you know . . .' Their eyes locked, then Marie's blonde eyebrows shot upwards in surprise.

'You and Fletch,' Marie clarified slowly, 'were . . . lovers?'

And now the awful truth coming out of Marie's mouth made Vita's one night with Fletch seem so sordid and awful, in retrospect, that she felt another terrible stab of shame.

'It was just one time and . . . oh, Marie, how I wish it hadn't happened. But seeing him in the club, I panicked and there was a scene. I dread to think what Irving would say, if he ever knew. Oh God, if he ever knew . . .' She covered her face with her hands again.

'Then he will never find out,' Marie said. 'We all do things we regret, believe me.'

Vita was grateful for her understanding. Grateful that she wasn't being judged. She was so glad to have unburdened herself, because she could see that Marie understood how conflicted she had felt . . . and still felt.

'Were you really lovers?' Marie asked.

Vita nodded. 'Are you very shocked?'

'No. We really can't help who we find attractive,' Marie said. 'Or why. But you should put it behind you, and pursue things with Irving. If a man like him is taking you out, then embrace it. You don't want to be left on the shelf.'

Vita laughed, surprised, and remembering Betsy and Jane and their conversations at the Zip. 'You sound like an old woman. How old are you anyway?' she asked, realizing she didn't know.

'Does it matter?'

'No, but . . .' Vita frowned, confused once again by Marie, who always seemed to deflect her questions.

Marie shrugged. 'You should be careful. Otherwise a man like Irving King, he'll use you and then . . .'

'I don't think I'll be seeing Irving again.'

'Oh yes, you will. Of course you will,' Marie said with confidence. 'If he's that jealous, then he likes you.'

Vita thought of Irving and how keen he'd been when they'd parted to put the whole thing behind them. Maybe Marie was right.

'So now that you know my dark secrets,' she said, trying to make light of it, 'what about you? Have you had . . . I mean, is there anyone special in your life?'

'There was someone. Back in England.'

'Oh?'

Marie shook her head. 'He didn't treat me very well. It's over now.'

Vita wanted to press her for more details, intrigued by this small chink of information, but Marie smiled sadly.

'I'll tell you about it sometime,' she said with great resolve. 'I want to, but . . .'

'But?'

'It's not the right time now. Shouldn't you be getting on,

if you're going to see Nancy? Here, I wrote down the visiting hours for the weekend.'

Vita looked at the clock on the shelf and put her coffee bowl down with a clatter. Marie was right. She had to get a move on.

And now she remembered how Irving had said last night that he'd help. Would his offer still stand this morning, after what had happened with Fletch? And even if it did, would it be wrong to tell Nancy? To give her false hope?

'Shall I come with you?' Marie offered, and Vita smiled gratefully, glad that they really were friends now.

49

Unwelcome News

Edith glanced at her watch, knowing that this appointment had already taken longer than she'd expected and that she must be getting back to Darton. She looked at the dark-green walls of the doctor's office and the framed pencil sketches of female wombs.

She'd hoped that the private gynaecologist she'd paid for might provide her with some reassurance, but now, after his rather thorough and somewhat unpleasant examination, he sat on the other side of his green leather-topped desk and she could tell, by the way he made a spire out of his fingers in front of his beard, that he was bracing himself to deliver bad news.

'I will be blunt, Mrs Darton, although what I have to say may be painful. I'm afraid that untreated disease plays havoc, if ignored.'

She gave him a look, forcing herself not to wince at his words – at the shame they implied. He was too discreet to ask her where she might have contracted such a disease, but she baulked at the thought that he might think she was responsible for it.

'Go on.'

'And I'm afraid that this . . . condition has exacerbated what, I suspect, was always the case.' He sighed again, as if bracing himself. 'That it's highly unlikely you'll ever be able to have children.'

There was a beat, as Edith absorbed these dreaded words and cursed the doctor for enunciating what she herself had suspected over the last few months. She'd known that something terrible was wrong, but to hear it said was still a blow.

'Are you absolutely sure?' Edith asked, keeping her face as neutral as possible.

'Yes, I'm afraid I am. In fact my advice would be to have a procedure to take everything out – all your reproductive organs.'

'Is that necessary?'

'To avoid complications further along the line, then yes.'

'How long would it take?'

'The procedure?'

'I mean, altogether. Including the recovery time. I do not wish to be away from my work for very long.'

Dr Willoughby looked confused, but Edith held his stare. She couldn't possibly risk being away from Darton for any length of time. She was on constant alert to intercept any post that Marianne sent from France. She couldn't risk Clement opening it. She'd also had to bribe Bobby, the manager at the sorting office, to hold back any post that came from abroad for any of the workers in Darton, so that Edith could vet those letters, too. She wouldn't put it past Marianne to contact one of her former colleagues and tell tales on where she was and what she was doing.

'You'd need to give yourself time to recover. A few weeks.'

'I don't have a few weeks,' Edith said, getting up and looking at her watch. 'Good day, Doctor.'

'But, Mrs Darton, at least consider it? Talk to your husband—'

But Edith was already out of the door.

Outside on the wide Manchester street, she put up her large umbrella and walked purposefully down the steep steps of the granite-tiled building, watching her driver get out of the black car and hold the door open for her. She didn't acknowledge him, but shoved her umbrella at him.

She sat in the back as the car pulled away from the pavement and looked at the raindrops on the glass. Now, away from the doctor, Edith allowed herself to feel the emotion that she'd fought so hard to hide, and felt a tear slide down her cheek. It couldn't be true, could it – what the doctor had said? Surely there must be some mistake. How could he know with such certainty?

She swallowed hard, forcing the emotion away and swiping angrily at her tears. She summoned the steely hardness that she knew was necessary to cover the shame and upset. But now doubts nagged at her and she wished she had a friend. She wished she had someone – anyone – to confide in; but most of all she wished she still had Nancy.

She knew enough to realize that sex in married relationships wasn't at all like it was in the few racy novels she and Nancy had read when they'd been debutantes in London, but now she wondered just how badly behaved with women her husband was, compared to other men. She hadn't presumed that Clement would be faithful to her. Her father hadn't been faithful to her mother, but that hadn't stopped them having a good relationship and she'd hoped that she and Clement would form a deeper bond.

That still left the awkward sex part, though, which had never been as satisfying with Clement as it had been with Jack Connelly, who had seemed to know his way around a woman's body. Clement, however, seemed very uncomfortable in bed. She'd thought it unusual at first that he never looked at her when they made love, and that he was so aggressive sometimes, but now the fact of her untreated disease put a different perspective on things. Her mind raced as to where the shameful disease might have originated. With Clement, obviously, but where had *he* caught it from. Marianne? The thought sickened her.

Or might it be someone else entirely. She thought of Clement's frequent trips to London and pictured the whores who lolled around the doorways in Green Park, near where he stayed in Mayfair, and her heart contracted at the thought of his careless infidelity. Did her husband not look at her in bed because he preferred those rouged women of the night? She'd thought he'd loved her when he married her, but maybe he would never love her in the way she'd hoped he would.

She took a breath, summoning up the strength that she needed. But even so, why was this happening to her, when everyone else had what she wanted? Vita had a free life in Paris, Clement had mistresses and Marianne had a child. Why couldn't *she* have what she wanted? A baby. Just one small baby to call her own.

Now, knowing it would only make her more angry, she dug Marie's latest letter out of her handbag – the one she'd sent with Edith's passport, which she'd retrieved from Vita's apartment. The page was already worn from where Edith had folded and refolded it.

She read again Marianne's description of what was happening in Paris: the way Vita was being wined and dined by an older man, and how Marie seemed to be settling in as her companion and assistant. But the letter had a worrying, pleading tone:

> *I have done everything you asked, Mrs Darton. I have done that dreadful thing to a poor little animal, which plays so heavily on my conscience . . .*

Edith thought the woman had a cheek. She'd slept with Clement, and *that* hadn't seemed to play so heavily on her conscience. She'd borne him a child. Feeding that mangy little dog some of Nancy's narcotics, when it had been half-asphyxiated already, hardly counted, against that act of treachery.

> *I have even let Vita's dear friend, Nancy, believe that she is going mad.*

Edith had to agree that Marianne had been clever in that respect, calling the mental hospital, after finding Nancy drunk. The hefty bribe to the concierge of Vita's building had helped. She'd hoped Nancy would have to stay in the unsavoury hospital, which seemed to Edith a just and fair punishment for her duplicity.

*I feel so horrible to be lying to Miss Darton the
whole time, when she trusts me so much. If you could
only send me more news of Susan, as you promised . . .*

Edith looked out of the window of the car and crumpled
up the letter. She'd given Marianne just enough information
about Susan to keep her satisfied, but she'd have to send
something else soon. She cursed silently to herself, annoyed
that this situation was turning out to be far more complicated than she'd expected.

50

Cold-Shouldered

Nancy wasn't getting any better and they were still keeping her in hospital, while the worst effects of her sudden withdrawal from alcohol, cigarettes and drugs made her wretched with sickness. It was a pitiful sight, and Vita dreaded seeing her in such a state.

She was very glad that Marie was around to fill the void left by Nancy and Mr Wild. Maybe she was just being kind, Vita thought, but Marie seemed to be interested in her brassieres, and kept asking about her ideas and plans. It wasn't long before Vita was telling her about how she'd got her first meeting at Withshaw and Taylor, and about the presentation she'd done with the girls from the Zip. Marie wanted to know about them all – Jane and Betsy; Nancy, of course; and even snooty Edith.

Vita, glad to be talking about happier things than Nancy, also told Marie about Percy and how wonderful he'd been to her, and how he'd been the first one to spot that she wanted to be a designer. To her surprise, it turned out that Marie was not only practical, but an excellent seamstress, helping to stitch up the half-finished garments in the sewing box.

'Tell me about your family,' Vita asked on Saturday afternoon, as they sat surrounded by patterns and material; she tried to make it sound like a casual question and not one she'd been itching to ask all day. She knew so little about Marie. She was so reserved and self-contained, but Vita longed to find out all about her. And having shared so much about her own past, she thought it only fair that her new – albeit temporary – flatmate opened up a bit. 'Your said you mother was French?'

'She was from Reims,' Marie said. 'She trained as a milliner before she went to England.'

Vita wondered whether this was where Marie got her creative streak from. 'What about your father?'

Marie shrugged. 'I never knew him.'

Vita let this confession settle for a moment. Perhaps this lack of a father figure was why Marie seemed so distrustful of men.

'And what about your mother? Where does she live now?'

'She died,' Marie said and her face hardened.

'I'm so sorry.'

'She worked in a . . .' Marie paused, 'a place with machinery and . . .'

'Go on.'

'She had an accident at work and her arm was horrifically mangled. She couldn't work and . . .' Marie took a sharp intake of breath. She had a far-away look in her eyes. 'She wasn't treated well. Without her pay, we were living in poverty and she was in pain the whole time. The owners, they . . . they wouldn't take any responsibility, and she died on Christmas Day.'

'I'm so sorry,' Vita told Marie, meaning it. What an awful thing to have happened, although it was far from uncommon. Vita had read stories like this in the newspapers about factory workers all over the country, and she even remembered similar stories from Darton. Her father and brother, they were mill owners too and had always been dismissive of their workers – especially injured ones.

She thought now of Darton and of the workers' cottages on the hillside, and remembered the waif of a little girl who came to the hall one Christmas. The Darton family had been no better than the awful people Marie was describing now.

'Where did you say you were living in England?'

Marie shook her head and didn't answer, and Vita suspected that it was a huge, deep well of emotion, which Marie was struggling to put a lid on. She clearly wasn't going to open up any more, so Vita tried to lighten the sombre mood.

'If I ever have a workforce,' she said, 'I'll be like André Citroën and give my employees an extra month's pay at Christmas.' But Marie wasn't comforted by these words, and shortly afterwards Vita put on the radio to liven the mood with some jazz.

Marie didn't cheer up until they were out of the apartment, and Vita, keen to get their closeness back, linked arms with her new friend as they walked through the cobbled streets, stopping on the corner for a lemon-and-sugar crêpe for supper.

Then, showing Marie the familiar route that she always took with Nancy, they walked south, down to Les Folies.

Vita had decided to leave Fletch's jacket with the dancers. She'd talked it over with Marie, and they'd agreed that returning the jacket was the best possible way of getting Fletch out of her life for good. She couldn't risk him turning up at Maison Jenny again.

Besides, she had to get things back on track with Irving, and her promise to Nancy weighed heavily on her mind. Somehow she had to get Irving to come good on his offer to help. There was no other choice. She had to get Nancy out of that place as soon as she could, before she really *did* go mad. And it was this knowledge – that she was helping her friend – that gave Vita the confidence to walk through the stage door to see the girls before the show at Les Folies.

She could have left the jacket at the box office, although she'd been too cowardly to do so, for fear of bumping into Fletch in person; but now, as she stood in the familiar dressing room, she wished she'd been braver. There was a sudden hush as the dancers saw her, and she felt their hostility radiating towards her.

'You don't get to treat Fletch like that and then come round here,' Julianne said, snatching his jacket out of Vita's hand.

'He had every right to talk to you,' Collette said.

'I know, but . . .'

'And now he's lost his job with the band.'

Vita pressed her lips together. 'I tried to stop that happening,' she said.

'Well, it sounds to us like you didn't try very hard,' Collette responded. 'It sounds like you've got some fancy new designing job and you've forgotten who your real friends are.'

Vita felt tears springing to her eyes.

'Fletch is so angry and upset you'd do that to him. That you'd get your revenge like that,' Julianne said, her arms akimbo.

'Revenge?' Vita gulped. 'I wasn't getting *revenge*.'

'I'll make sure he gets this. And now I suggest you leave,' Julianne said, showing Vita the door. 'Oh, and Vita?'

She turned.

'Please don't use this as an address,' she continued, handing over a letter. It looked as if it had been opened.

Vita snatched it from Julianne and, chastened and upset, ran up the stairs to the back door.

'Oh, Marie,' she cried, falling into Marie's arms, 'they were so horrible. I should never have gone. What on earth was I thinking?'

'Forget them,' Marie said, soothingly. 'You've got me now.'

51

Passport Issue

The letter that had been at Les Folies was from Percy and was weeks out of date. He'd obviously written it in haste, explaining that he was passing through Paris and had hoped to see Vita when he visited the show. He'd said that he was on his way to visit a friend in Nice in the South of France, and Vita felt angry and upset that she'd missed him.

Over the following days she threw herself into her work at Maison Jenny, hoping to distract herself from the terrible situation Nancy was in. It helped that Madame Jenny, Laure, Agatha and all the girls were intrigued by Vita's date with Irving and, as she recounted each time the details about meeting Scott Fitzgerald, she embellished them a little bit more.

She was reminded of how the girls at the Zip Club had been when she'd first dated Archie Fenwick and, with things so bad with Nancy, she was grateful to have found such camaraderie again. She didn't tell them about Fletch, of course. It was too painful, and the reaction of the girls at Les Folies still made her feel ashamed and upset.

But despite talking up her date and how lovely it had been, she worried secretly that it might be the one and only date she'd ever go on with Irving King. Maybe, after the scene with Fletch the other night, he'd want nothing more to do with her. And what then? Maybe he'd stop buying dresses for Daphne. And she realized how terrible this would be – not just for Madame Jenny, but for her, too.

On Tuesday, Beatrice came through to the studio to inform Vita that there was a telephone call for her. For a horrible moment Vita thought it might be another call about Nancy, but when she picked up the receiver on Beatrice's desk, it was Irving.

'I'm very sorry about the other night, and what happened,' he said.

'Don't be,' she replied, relieved to hear his voice and that he sounded apologetic.

'You see, I'm a bit of a jealous old thing,' he admitted, with a self-deprecating laugh. 'It wasn't *him* so much . . . as anyone. But honestly, I promise, it will never happen again.'

She smiled, relief flooding through her. Marie had been right. He *did* like her after all. And 'again' – did that mean Irving wanted to take her out again?

'Listen, I've made some enquiries,' he said. 'Can you get me your friend's passport?'

'Nancy's?'

'Yes. My secretary can book her on a passage, but only if we book it with the travel agent today – and only if we hurry. I'm at Maison Jenny this afternoon with Daphne, for her fitting. If you get the passport for me by then, I'll be able to arrange it.'

Vita smiled for a moment as she replaced the receiver.

'Mr King?' Beatrice enquired, and Vita nodded.

'Yes, he's in later this afternoon. May I make another call?'

'Be quick, Vita,' Beatrice said. 'At this rate you'll need your own telephone line.'

Vita laughed and quickly placed a call to Madame Vertbois to get a message to Marie.

Then she replaced the receiver and planted a kiss on Beatrice's cheek, shocking the old woman. She went back to the studio, thinking of this afternoon and wondering if Madame Jenny would let her wear the black dress with the white top that she had been working on. Just to impress Irving. He was her only way of helping Nancy, and she was determined that this meeting would go well.

52

Boys and Girls

At noon Vita waited impatiently for Marie at the end of the Champs-Élysées by the Arc de Triomphe. Marie had agreed to come and meet Vita to give her Nancy's passport. She said she was unfamiliar with the Champs-Élysées and had seemed nervous about coming to the offices, so Vita had said she'd meet her here.

Marie arrived and Vita saw that she was wearing her trench coat again, but her hair was falling out of her chignon and her rouge and lipstick were hastily applied. Marie didn't ever seem to want to make much of herself, Vita thought, and wondered if this was how she herself had appeared to Nancy, when Nancy first met her in London. Back then, when she'd been Anna Darton, Nancy had been positively itching to give her a makeover, and now Vita felt the same urge with Marie. But she knew she wasn't as forthright as Nancy and wouldn't have the nerve to take Marie in hand, as Nancy had done with her. There was something a little bit reserved and distant about Marie – a quality Vita couldn't quite place her finger on – and even though they were getting closer, she suspected they'd never quite be friends in the way that she and Nancy had been. Vita found herself wanting to be closer, though, wishing to put a smile on Marie's face. There was something so sad about her – something that Vita suspected concerned more than simply the circumstances surrounding her upbringing.

After Marie had kissed Vita on both cheeks, they crossed through the traffic on the Place de l'Étoile to where a family was looking at the impressive arch. There were some children playing on the gravel and Marie stopped, gazing at the little girl with a wistful smile on her face.

'She's sweet,' Marie said.

Then the little boy chased the girl and pulled her hair. 'But he's not,' Vita added. 'You know, I had a brother just like that.'

'A brother?' Vita looked up to see Marie's eyes burning with intensity. 'You've never mentioned him.'

'Oh, believe me, you wouldn't ever want to meet him. He is more different from me in every way than you can possibly imagine. Even the thought of him makes me scared.'

'Scared?'

'He's a monster. He always has been. If you ask me, there's something wrong with him. We had the same upbringing, the same parents, but he's . . . I don't know,' she said, trying to find a way of describing Clement. 'He burns with jealousy and hatred – and for no real reason. He'd happily do whatever he could to destroy me.'

Marie suddenly turned away and seemed skittish and nervous. Vita had been expecting her to comment on her revelation about Clement, but instead Marie reached into her bag. Not for the first time, Vita wondered why it was that Marie often avoided personal conversations. She was so easy to talk to, but sometimes she closed up and retreated, like a wild animal.

'Here,' Marie said. She handed over the leather folder. 'Is this it? It was in the cabinet by the bed, as you said.'

'Thank you,' Vita said, relieved, taking the leather folder and untying the string binder. She looked inside and pulled out Nancy's passport, opening it and checking the dates, then put it back inside, but something caught her attention. 'That's odd,' she said.

'What is?'

'My passport isn't there. Well, it's not actually mine. I travelled here with Nancy and . . .' She trailed off.

'Shouldn't you have your own passport?' Marie asked.

'It's complicated,' Vita said. She'd confided so much in Marie already, but Marie hadn't responded well to her confession about Clement, and Vita didn't want to divulge the details of why she'd fled and taken Edith's passport.

'This is France, Vita,' Marie said. 'And believe me, getting such things can take some time. What would happen, say, if you needed to do something official?'

'Something official? Oh, Marie, you're so serious.'

'What would happen if you wanted to get married?'

Vita laughed. 'Married?'

'You might do. And then you'd have a problem.'

Vita nodded, absorbing her advice. 'Let's start with problem number one,' she said. She had to keep focused on Nancy.

They walked through the Arc de Triomphe and then it was time for Vita to be getting back to work. They strolled together down the Champs-Élysées, and Vita asked Marie what she was going to do for the rest of the day. She often wondered how her friend filled her time.

'I'll be out looking for work again,' she said, without much enthusiasm. 'Do you think Madame Jenny might have a job for me? As a seamstress perhaps?'

'I could ask.'

'Oh, Vita, would you? I would be so grateful. And wouldn't it be wonderful if we could be in the same building?' she said. 'And together all of the time?'

Vita smiled, but felt a pang of alarm. Nancy had always been so needy. Was Marie going to be the same?

53

A Little Black Dress

That afternoon, as Daphne went to try on the signature black dress they'd made for her in the studio, Vita was alone with Irving in the salon. It felt illicit, sharing a personal moment like this, and their voices lowered as he briefly took her hand in his and she noticed his chunky gold signet ring. She wanted to know whether he'd told Daphne about their date, but sensed that he'd kept it to himself.

'Thank you for helping with Nancy, Irving. You have no idea how much it means to me,' Vita said.

'It's not first-class travel, I'm afraid.'

'That doesn't matter,' Vita said, handing over Nancy's passport. But now the reality of Nancy going home to the States on a ship – alone – felt altogether too real and she experienced a shudder of foreboding. And it wasn't simply fear for Nancy, but because, as Irving's eyes met hers, she couldn't help feeling that this transaction would have consequences.

'I'm not sure she'll be all right on a ship by herself,' Vita said, imagining Nancy alone and scared in a cabin.

'Oh, don't worry. There'll be a private nurse from the clinic travelling with her.'

Vita put her hand on her chest, imagining a robust matron who would look after Nancy and at least get her to eat. 'Oh, I'm so relieved.'

'I hear he's a wonderful chap. Nancy will be in safe hands.'

A chap? Vita wondered how that news would be received by Nancy.

'I can see what you're thinking: that it's odd there's a male nurse. I thought the same.'

'Not at all. I'm sure he's a fine fellow.'

'They'll have to get used to each other, because the crossing takes two weeks.'

'That long?' She thought about the other passengers, and how Nancy was likely to get bored and start causing trouble.

'In a few years' time we'll be able to fly to America in less than a day. You mark my words, Vita – that's what Charlie-boy says. After he did it in the *Spirit of St Louis* last year.'

'You know Charles Lindbergh?' Vita asked, impressed. She had noticed the other night how Irving liked to name-drop.

'Yes, of course. Great chap. I'm investing heavily in air travel, you know.'

Now Daphne walked in from the far end of the studio wearing the black dress, looking down and admiring the skirt. Irving smiled appreciatively at Vita.

'She looks quite the young lady, doesn't she?' he said proudly and Vita nodded.

'What are you talking about, Daddy?' Daphne asked suspiciously.

'Nothing. I was telling Vita about Charles Lindbergh.'

'I prefer Lady Lindy,' Daphne said and Vita was confused. 'She's got a much more interesting story, if you ask me.' She did a little twirl on the carpet and then came towards them. 'I mean Amelia Earhart,' she clarified, seeing Vita's confusion.

'Male nurses, female pilots – the world is topsy-turvy,' Irving said to Vita.

'I saw it in the newspaper only last week. She got a tickertape parade all the way down Broadway,' Daphne said. 'First woman to cross the Atlantic.' She looked pointedly at Irving, who looked bashful.

'Well, I guess it just shows that you girls can do anything you set your mind to,' Irving said, then smiled at Daphne. 'Particularly dressed like that.'

Daphne had now arrived at the sofa and did a little pose, and both Irving and Vita laughed.

'I have to have it, Daddy,' Daphne said. 'Everyone should have a little black dress like this. Isn't it so sophisticated?'

54

A Bittersweet Farewell

A week later Irving had been as good as his word and he
came personally to pick up Vita from Maison Jenny's, so that
they could see Nancy off at the Gare du Nord. Vita knew
that Madame Jenny was only letting her have the time off
as a special favour to Irving, but she felt embarrassed that
her private life was, once again, encroaching on her professional career.

Out on the Champs-Élysées, Irving sat in the driver's seat
of his enormous open-topped Rolls-Royce, wearing leather
driving gloves and a long wool coat with a fur collar, despite
the warm day. Vita sat beside him, embarrassed at how
ostentatious the car was and how many people stopped to
stare at them, as they made their way across town to the
train station.

She could tell that Irving wanted this to be another jolly
adventure, and while she was very grateful to him for having
secured a passage for Nancy back to America, it was hardly
a happy occasion. In fact Vita was feeling increasingly
wretched at the prospect of saying goodbye to her friend.

It didn't help that Nancy had wanted to come back to
the apartment to get ready for the journey, but Vita had

refused to let her. She'd used the excuse that Nancy still had that nasty chest infection, and had persuaded the staff at the hospital to make her stay there until the last possible minute. But now she felt guilty that they hadn't had more time together; and guilty, too, that the real reason she hadn't wanted Nancy to come home was because Marie was living in the apartment, and Nancy was bound to cause a fuss about it.

On the few occasions Marie had come to visit Nancy at Sainte-Anne's, Nancy had been offhand and surly, and had told Vita she didn't trust her new friend. Nancy was clearly embarrassed that Marie had been the one to find her at that horrifying, traumatic moment, and it perplexed Vita that when Nancy owed Marie such a huge debt, she couldn't be more gracious.

Keen to avoid a stressful situation, Vita had taken a suitcase crammed full of the most practical of Nancy's clothes, along with the fur coat that had been a gift from Archie Fenwick, to the hospital last night. Nancy would have much better use for it on the Atlantic crossing than Vita would have in Paris, but it hadn't comforted Nancy, who was distraught about leaving.

Rolf, the nurse from the Californian clinic who was accompanying Nancy, had come to the hospital to meet Vita. He was blond and tanned, and he'd told Vita that his meeting with Nancy had been 'interesting'. Vita wasn't sure what he'd meant and, when she'd asked him, he'd shrugged and said it was normal for clients to be nervous and he understood that Nancy wasn't looking forward to the long crossing.

Now, as the car approached the crowded street outside

the huge station, Irving honked his horn and shouted to the porters, so that they could drive through the throng. Vita knew some people loved stations and the romance of international travel, but she found them stressful and over-whelming.

'We're meeting them on the concourse,' Vita reminded Irving, holding on to her hat, her stomach twisting with nerves. Because what if Nancy had changed her mind and refused to come? What if Rolf was no match for her and hadn't managed to get her to the station in time for the steamer train? She looked anxiously at her watch, knowing all too well how capricious Nancy could be, and how awful it would be if she let Irving down.

Under the clock in the vast concourse beneath the steel-vaulted ceiling Vita recognized Archie's fur coat before she recognized Nancy, who looked disorientated and small as she stood by her suitcase, looking round for Vita. She pressed a handkerchief to her mouth as she coughed. She looked pale and ill.

Vita waved and rushed over, and Irving followed, pulling off his gloves. He shook hands with Nancy, who spoke a little to thank him, before collapsing into a coughing fit. Rolf gave her some medicine and she turned away to take it, from a tiny green glass vial, and Vita gave Irving a worried look. Taking the hint, Irving busied himself getting the luggage to the train, and Vita and Nancy were left alone.

'You sure you don't mind me having your coat?' Nancy asked.

'Not at all. It might be windy on the crossing,' she told her friend, putting her hands on the collar, 'but think of the sea air. It'll do wonders for that cough of yours. And think of the ship – the lounges and dining rooms.'

'Oh, Vita, I don't want to go,' Nancy said. 'You remember we were once in the Café de Paris and I told you how they modelled it on the *Lusitania*?'

'Of course I remember.'

'The *Lusitania* sank.'

'The ship is not going to sink.'

'How do you know?' Nancy asked, her voice quivering. 'I'm scared, Vita. I don't want to go alone.'

'You have Rolf.'

'My prison guard.'

'It's not like that.'

Nancy looked over at her young male travelling companion, who was shaking hands with Irving. He had very white teeth. Vita wouldn't mind betting that Nancy would run rings around him in no time.

'Come with me. Please, Vita. You've always wanted to go to New York, remember? We can go there together. Start again.'

'I can't. Not now. Not when things are going so well at Madame Sacerdote's. You wanted me to make it in Paris, remember? And I think I have a chance, Nancy. A real chance.'

Nancy put her hand on Vita's face. 'You always were going to shine so brightly.'

'With your help,' Vita reminded her. 'Listen, go to the clinic and as soon as you're better, you can come back. I could even come to find you in America and we'll return in style. First-class.' She said this confidently, making a promise she had no idea whether she'd be able to keep, but she also knew that committing to a future arrangement was the only way to appease Nancy.

'I can't believe you're sending me away.'

'I'm not sending you,' Vita said defensively. It was typical of Nancy to twist things around. 'You have to go. To get better. Don't you remember what happened? What you tried to do? Because of the drinking and the drugs.'

'Oh, Vita, stop.'

'If you'd rather stay at Sainte-Anne's . . .'

'No, but you don't understand. These past few weeks have been utter torment. It's like I don't even know my own mind. I keep thinking about Mr Wild. How I just can't believe I—'

'Shhh, darling. Don't. Please, you'll set me off.'

Nancy nodded, her chin wobbling. She pressed a handkerchief into the corner of her eye. 'And what about him?' Nancy nodded to Irving, who had given the luggage to a porter who looked delighted to have been tipped so handsomely. Irving, seeing that they were looking at him, grinned broadly and waved, before tapping his watch. It was almost time to go. 'Is he your sugar daddy?'

'Sugar daddy?' Vita repeated, in an appalled whisper. 'Don't say it like that.' How could Nancy sound so mean, when Irving had been so kind? Maybe Nancy picked up on her look, because now she hugged Vita.

'I only want you to be happy, kiddo. And if he makes you happy, then you have my blessing. Whatever floats your boat.'

Rolf approached. 'It's time to go,' he said, beckoning to Nancy.

Vita hugged Nancy tight, burying her face in the collar of Archie's fur coat for the last time.

'Take care of yourself, Nancy,' she said, but her voice cracked.

'Goodbye, my little wife,' Nancy whispered, weeping now as Rolf took her arm and led her away towards the train. Vita watched her friend go, and all too soon she was engulfed by the crowd.

'Oh, Irving,' Vita said, letting him hug her tightly as she cried.

'She's going to the best place. Hey,' he said, 'don't cry.' He wiped her tears away gently and smiled, his eyes soft.

She thought about what Nancy had said and wondered now if Irving really did make her happy? He certainly made her feel safe, and that was something, wasn't it?

And, alone on the concourse with the porters rushing past, the whistles, the hiss of the steam engines and the sunlight coming in misty shafts through the glass panels in the roof, Vita found her tears stalling as Irving's face moved towards her.

Was this the price she'd paid for Nancy getting back to the States? *Probably*, she thought, but she didn't recoil as their lips met and she closed her eyes, waiting for the butterflies in her stomach that she'd felt with Archie, or the needy ache of desire that she'd felt with Fletch.

'Oh, Vita,' Irving breathed. 'Vita darling.'

And she put her arms around his neck and kissed him back. They *would* come, the butterflies . . . *wouldn't they*?

55

The Package

In the office at Darton Mill, Edith studied the contents of the latest package from Marianne in greater detail. It had been Edith's reward for sending Susan's 'letter' – a short, but glowing account of her life at school, and a plea for her mother to keep sending her there, saying how kind Mrs Darton (Edith had worried over this part) had been. Not a long letter. Not long enough to cause suspicion or give any details at all, but enough to keep Marianne in line.

Without Nancy in the picture – Vita's 'dear friend'; *oh, how that smarted* – Edith had hoped Vita wouldn't be able to cope and that, having lost her job at Les Folies and without any money, she'd have no choice but to buckle and come back home. She thought of how pleased Clement would be, when he discovered what Edith had done. And how appreciative of Edith he'd be to see the thing he most wanted in the world: his sister Anna, broken and cowed. And how joyous the revenge would be, when Vita realized how much her new friend Marie was betraying her. Then she'd get a taste of how it felt to be betrayed by a friend, as Edith had been betrayed by Nancy.

But Edith had underestimated Vita's resourcefulness. It

had come as quite a shock when Marie had reported that Vita had managed to get this King chap to dispatch Nancy to America.

And in the six weeks since Nancy had left, Vita seemed to be going from strength to strength – making a success of herself at this fashion house that Marianne spoke so highly of, whilst designing at home. Vita was too busy to notice that Marie was working every moment that she was out of the apartment, copying everything and sending samples back to Darton.

Now Edith watched as Ruth, one of the oldest of the mill workers, gingerly picked through the latest batch of silk and lace camiknickers.

'Where did you say you got these from again?' Clement asked, his brow wrinkling with suspicion as he nodded at the beautiful lingerie pieces that were laid out on the desk. Even after making money from Top Drawer, he was still embarrassed and ashamed to be associated with women's underwear.

And not just any women's underwear, but this new direction of Vita's: it was so stylish, so womanly, and Edith knew – she absolutely knew – Lance Kenton at Withshaw and Taylor was positively going to salivate when she presented this line at their next meeting in London.

She looked at Clement now and it was on the tip of her tongue to tell him that they came from Paris – to claim her moment of triumph – but she couldn't quite gauge his mood today. When she told him what she'd been doing and how she'd come across these designs, she wanted the revelation to impress him, to prove to him how clever she was.

'What does it matter. Can you copy these?' Edith asked Ruth.

'I'm sure we can, Miss, although they look quite complex. It was Marianne who was the most skilled at that sort of thing,' Ruth said.

Oh, the irony, Edith thought: that Ruth was holding something made by Marianne herself. If only she knew.

Ruth looked up guiltily, horrified that she'd mentioned Marianne in the office. Like everyone else at the mill, which was a hotbed of gossip, she knew of Marianne and Clement's relationship. Edith kept her face impassive. As far as Ruth was concerned, Edith thought Marianne was just another ex-colleague.

'Do you know where Marie has gone?' Clement asked. Edith baulked at him using his lover's nickname. How dare he reveal how close they were, in front of her? And in front of Ruth, too, who now looked cornered, as both Edith and Clement stared at her.

'Can't say, sir,' Ruth said.

'Can't or won't?' Clement asked, and Edith could hear the pent-up fury in his voice.

Ruth wrung her hands. 'Nobody has heard from her. Or little Susan. She just went. We haven't heard a peep – none of us. Marianne was always so closed off and kept herself to herself, especially after that terrible business with her mother . . .'

Clement turned his back on Edith and Ruth, the line of fabric taut between his shoulders. Marianne's mother's unfortunate accident at the mill was only one of many similar cases that Clement refused to discuss. Edith was hoping that the production line she had planned would make Darton Mill a safer place to work in the future.

'That will be all, Ruth,' she said. 'Take these down, and see what you can do.'

After Ruth had gone, Clement didn't speak for a moment. She wondered if he was going to mention Marianne again, but he didn't. And, pointedly, neither did she.

'So, Clement, we need to talk about further investment,' she said with a businesslike air, going to the desk and pulling out a letter that she'd received. 'I think it's time we sold some shares to raise capital for the new factory plans.'

Clement took the letter and read it. 'You'd want strangers involved in the business?'

'Not strangers. Money-men,' she said. 'Investors who can see the potential of our business and want to come along for the ride. With Arkwright opening those factories in India, the cotton-mill business will fold sooner than you think, unless we diversify. I've been reading all about it in the financial pages.'

Clement's eyebrows shot up. 'Have you?'

'I have told you before,' she said to him. 'Do not underestimate your wife.'

56

Le Procope

In the weeks that followed the first kiss with Irving, Vita wondered how she'd ever coped without Marie. It wasn't just that she kept the apartment clean and tidy and shopped, so that Vita could work long hours at Maison Jenny without having to worry about anything domestic. It was the wonderful way in which Marie had started sewing at home. In fact together they were forming quite a little cottage industry, and they often sewed and talked together late into the nights that Vita wasn't out with Irving. And even when Vita was out, Marie often stayed up so that Vita could give her all the details of her date.

If Marie minded living a vicarious life, she didn't let on. Vita had promised twice to ask Laure about the possibility of Marie getting a job, but she repeatedly put off finding the right moment. Because, with Marie's help, she was starting to see that Top Drawer really could take off again, and each time they discussed the designs and Marie finished a sample, she folded it carefully, wrapping it in tissue paper, and squirrelled it away in the large suitcase in the hall. Vita hadn't looked in there for a while, but she was sure that when she counted, there would be enough stock to go and make a presentation soon.

She was no stranger to seeing the bountiful fashion that was on offer in Paris, and her mind had started whirring about being part of the fashion scene in her own right. Not immediately, of course. Not while things were so great at Madame Jenny's, but sometime in the future. Madame Jenny's comment about her having her own fashion house one day filled Vita's head with lofty visions; and sometimes, at night, she lay awake remembering how she'd presented her bras to Withshaw and Taylor and, in her mind, she imagined showing her lingerie line to one of the shops on the rue du Faubourg Saint-Honoré.

She was often on her favourite shopping street with Irving, who had insisted that Vita had so few personal belongings that he was on a mission to 'kit her out', as he put it, insisting on buying her dresses and skirts and shoes. To her embarrassment, he'd even bought every single dress she'd borrowed from Maison Jenny, and Nancy's bedroom at the apartment was heaving with tissue-filled boxes and bags.

There were gifts, too – one for every time he saw her, each elaborately wrapped. Some were wonderful, like the blue shoes from Louis Vuitton and the paisley silk scarf from Guerlain, and some less so, like the old-fashioned and yet clearly expensive paste brooch, and the heavy lace fan that she and Marie giggled about. But she couldn't complain about Irving's old-fashioned style of wooing her.

It felt so nice to be wanted and to be courted by a gentleman. She knew that, like Marie, Agatha and the others at Maison Jenny were following each new date, each new present, with fascination, but Vita privately wondered if she was pursuing this relationship solely for the status it gave her at work. Madame Jenny was certainly very pleased that Vita and Irving's relationship was going from strength to strength. They had numerous pieces in the pipeline for Daphne, and several of Irving's friends' wives had been into Jenny's salon and placed large orders from the collection.

The only downside, as far as Vita could make out, were the inches going on around her waistline. Irving was such a *bon vivant*, and so determined that she should try everything he loved, that she was being overwhelmed by each rich new dining experience, and she was looking forward to him being away on his forthcoming business trip so that she could have some nights in with Marie, eating soup.

For someone who was so rich, Irving did very little work, it seemed to Vita – just the odd trip abroad to check on his business interests. He was heavily invested in all sorts of enterprises, he'd told her, and proudly showed her how he checked his stocks and shares in the papers, and she'd started to take an interest in them herself. One day, she'd told him, she'd own her own stocks and shares, and he'd asked her what in; she'd told him it would have to be a female enterprise, and he'd laughed.

When she'd questioned him about the exact way his investments worked, he'd told her that he liked doing business over a game of poker, whenever possible, as he could always fathom people out, he said. Everyone had a 'tell' that revealed when they were lying, he'd told her. And he was very good at spotting them – except when it came to his wives, he joked.

This week he was going on a trip to the casino in Baden-Baden in Germany and even though he wouldn't be gone for long, Irving insisted that he take her out for a farewell dinner.

Upstairs in the fancy dining room of Le Procope the walls were adorned with oil paintings and wonderful coloured tiles, and the proprietor – a friend of Irving's, of course – had amused Vita by telling her how, before he became emperor, Napoleon Bonaparte was a humble soldier and used to frequent this restaurant.

'And when he couldn't pay,' the head waiter said, in heavily accented English, 'then he would leave 'is 'at.'

'His hat,' Irving translated for Vita, amused and clearly having heard this story before. 'They have his hat in a case downstairs. I say, do go and fetch it – let's try it on,' he told the waiter, who shook his head.

'We don't let—' he began, but watched Irving lift his silver money-clip from his inside pocket and peel off a note, and the waiter hurried away. 'I will ask, sir.'

'Irving,' Vita laughed, 'you've put him in a terrible spin. You can't buy everything, you know.'

'Why not?' Irving shrugged. And soon the waiter came back with the large, dusty hat and presented it to Irving. He put it on, and Vita laughed and clapped her hands.

'Oh, you really do look so funny. I wish I had my camera.'

'Irving King, I thought it was you, you old devil,' she heard a voice say, and Vita turned to see a man approaching their table. 'What on earth are you doing with Napoleon's hat on?' The man had a plummy English accent and carried an all-too-familiar air of entitlement that made Vita's hackles rise.

Irving stood and shook the man's hand warmly. 'This is

Cassius Digby,' he said, introducing Vita, who turned to see the man and her stomach flipped over, because she'd seen him before, she was sure of it. Long ago, on the Serpentine lake, when she'd been in a boat with Archie.

'Diggers here is possibly the best card-shark in Paris.'

Diggers. It was *him. The same Cassius Digby that Archie knew.*

'Kind of you to say so, old boy,' the Englishman said.

Vita nodded mutely, before taking the hat from Irving and giving it back to the waiter.

She was sure he hadn't recognized her, but kept her eyes lowered as the waiter hurried away and she and Irving sat back down at the table, with Diggers standing over them. Diggers had ruined the moment she'd had with Archie on the Serpentine, and now he'd unwittingly done the same thing with Irving, when she'd so wanted to try on Napoleon's hat.

'Cassius here knows Le Monsieur,' Irving said, as if this were a very big deal. Vita didn't look up, but she was listening intently. 'I'm always asking him for an "in" on the game, but I hear these things take time,' he continued, in a not-too-subtle dig. 'Not something that money can buy,' he added, clearly for Vita's benefit.

'I'll do my best, old boy, I'll do my best,' Diggers said with an embarrassed laugh, and she sensed that this was a conversation they'd had before. And in that moment she squirmed at Irving's neediness and the all-too-familiar feeling of being excluded from the set. And she hated that it mattered to Irving, and that he was so enamoured with money and the English upper classes.

'So what have you been up to?' Irving asked, changing the subject.

'I bought a boat,' Diggers said. 'She's a beauty. You should come aboard,' he said. 'We'll be on it all summer.'

Irving laughed enthusiastically. 'We'll do that.'

And his eyes flashed briefly at Vita, and she realized how significant the way Irving had said 'we' was. She smiled weakly, feeling upset, because all she could think about was that Diggers knew Archie Fenwick, and Diggers knew Irving too.

It shouldn't be such a surprise, she told herself. She knew full well from her days in London, when she'd gone to society parties with Nancy, that the rich and well-to-do moved in the kind of circles where everyone knew everyone else – and their business, too. But she'd hoped to avoid all of that here in Paris. She'd hoped never to have to think about Archie Fenwick ever again. But somehow, with the arrival of Digby, she felt the tendrils of her past reaching out, and she had a horrible sense of her worlds colliding.

57

Bal Tabarin

Towards the end of the week that Irving was away, Paul Kilkenny came back to town. Vita was just showing out a client from the salon, and Paul was in reception on the low sofa. He sprang up when he saw Vita and grinned, and she flashed her eyes at him in warning. She didn't want him to say anything to blow her cover, not now that she'd convinced everyone at Maison Jenny that Paul was her rich friend.

'Paul,' she said in a low whisper. 'What are you doing here?'

'I was passing and thought I'd pop in to say that you're coming to Bal Tabarin,' he said.

'Am I?'

She smiled. It was typical of Paul to make such an assumption, and she felt that she really ought to refuse. Surely, having been taken out by Irving, she should reserve her evenings solely for him? Even though there was nothing official between them and he'd only kissed her twice, she *was* technically stepping out with him.

But then Irving was away, and Paul was her friend, and Vita had wanted to go to Bal Tabarin for ages. The famous nightclub on rue Victor-Massé had the best dancers, and she'd heard that Julianne from Les Folies had joined the line-up.

'The new show has started. I won't take any excuses,' Paul said.

He tipped his hat at Madame Jenny and her client, an Italian heiress who stared intently at Paul, and Vita noticed the bizarre moment. The heiress flapped her hand over her face as if flustered, and looked as if she were going to say something – introduce herself maybe – but instead she made for the stairs.

But later, on the rue Victor-Massé, Vita was still thinking about the effect Paul had had on Madame Jenny's client. Had she found him attractive? He certainly looked fashionable in his pale-blue suit, and Vita viewed him through new eyes – eyes that were thinking about what Marie might say, if she met him.

They were seated at a round table in front of the stage. Paul, it turned out, was friends with the new proprietor, the infamous Pierre Sandrini, whom he knew from the Moulin Rouge, and Vita was excited to see the sensationally popular show.

'I should have brought along my friend, Marie,' she told him. 'Maybe you two would get along?'

'Oh,' Paul said, with a strange look on his face, 'I wouldn't waste her time. I have no time for any of that business.'

'What business?'

'Oh, you know – romantic business,' he said, clicking his fingers for the waiter to bring them champagne. 'It's not my thing.'

The waiter hurried over with a silver ice-bucket and popped

the champagne cork, as Vita watched the couples on the dance floor. This declaration from Paul that romance wasn't his thing was unsettling. Did he mean romance with someone else, other than Vita? *Should I feel guilty for being out with Paul?* she wondered, knowing how jealous Irving was. She noticed a man coming towards them across the floor then, and Paul shook his head at him and the man stopped and retreated.

Paul cast his eyes down, and suddenly Vita felt a jolt of . . . what? She wasn't sure, but as she looked at Paul's pink cheeks while he studied the edge of the table, she remembered this feeling – because she'd felt it before with Percy – and slowly a whole new understanding started to dawn on her.

'Paul?' she said, and he looked up at her sheepishly and, as his eyes locked with hers, she nodded meaningfully. 'I saw that. I hadn't realized.'

'Hadn't you? But I saw you that day.'

'What day?'

'I was in the apartment with my . . . friend.'

'What are you talking about?'

'By the bookshop.'

And now Vita had a vague memory of the men in the window near Shakespeare and Company. That had been Paul?

'I didn't know it was you.'

'I thought you knew all along,' Paul said, and she saw his cheeks flushing and remembered the phone call she'd made to his apartment, and the man who had answered. 'Didn't you?'

'No!' she said, shocked, then she quickly recovered. 'Although it's none of my business, and you mustn't think I mind, because I don't.'

Paul nodded. 'Thank you. It's not something I can talk

about, or really share with anyone. You'd think it'd be louche here in Paris, but people . . . well, people still judge. And I know it's silly, but I worry that my reputation might get . . . damaged, if I were to be seen with the wrong sort. One has to be careful. That's why I always try to be seen in public with a member of the fairer sex.'

'Oh!' She laughed at his admission. 'So that's why you invited me to lunch and took me to the Louvre?'

'Vita, don't hate me,' he said in a low voice, leaning forward.

She put her hand over his. 'I'm worldly-wise, Paul, don't worry,' she replied. 'I don't mind covering for you.'

He clinked champagne glasses with her and gave her a smile that was filled with relief and gratitude. Vita took a long sip of her drink, determined not to be one of those judgemental people herself.

'And what about you, Vita?' he said. 'What about your romantic entanglements? Please tell me I'm not the only one with a complicated life?'

She told him about Irving and how they'd been dating.

'He's been so kind,' she told Paul, before explaining what had happened with poor Mr Wild, and how Irving had helped Nancy get a passage on the steamship to America. 'Nancy said the crossing was dreadful for the first few days. But now she's in a clinic in California.'

Paul frowned. 'And your friend, Mr King, is paying?'

'Well, yes,' she said, embarrassed. 'But he wanted to,' she hurried on. 'And Nancy has written and says it's marvellous. There were the crushing headaches at first, but she hasn't had a drink for weeks and weeks. Not that she can get one in America.'

'There are ways and means,' Paul said, with an amused smile.

'Between you and me, I'm delighted Prohibition is there, so she won't be tempted when she leaves the clinic.'

'And when will that be?'

'She says she's been having hypnotism, but she still can't really recall suffocating poor Mr Wild, so I think she'll be there a while longer.'

The waiter filled up her glass and she looked across the dance floor and saw there was a party being seated, and Paul raised his glass and two of the women waved.

'Oh, I recognize that man,' she said, feeling the hairs on the back of her neck standing up. 'He's a friend of Irving's. I met him at Le Procope.'

'Cassius Digby – Diggers. Owns a boat in the South of France.'

'How do you know him?' Vita asked, realizing once again that the circles of people she knew were overlapping.

'Everyone knows everyone in Paris,' Paul said, saluting Diggers with his glass. 'You must know that by now, Vita. It's a very small town. That's why one has to take care of one's reputation.'

'I hope he doesn't gossip about me being out with you,' she said, worrying now, 'when Irving is out of town.'

Paul laughed. 'Don't worry your pretty little head, Vita. You're safe with me.'

But am I safe? she wondered as the show started. It had been so much easier when she'd been in the shadows at Les Folies and nobody took the blindest bit of notice of her. But now, because of her relationship with Irving – and being here with Paul – she'd unwittingly stepped right into the heart of the most gossipy section of society.

The lights dimmed and there was applause, and the couples who were dancing took their seats and shortly the show started. Vita watched as the ballet dancers came onto the stage – their costumes, designed by Erté, drawing gasps of awe from the crowd. Within moments Vita was transported by the music and the beautiful tableaux the dancers made. But seeing them onstage made her miss Nancy and the girls at Les Folies and, sitting in the dark, she marvelled at how far she'd come. But where was she going? *Where is all this heading?* she wondered.

And was she really safe with Paul, now that she knew his secret? She looked across the enraptured audience towards Cassius Digby and saw that he was looking at her and raised his glass. She'd tell Irving about tonight as soon as he got home, she resolved. She hated the thought of people gossiping behind her back. She didn't want Irving ever to have any reason to doubt her.

58

Putting on the Ritz

Edith held on tightly to the snakeskin case she was carrying
containing all the samples, as she and Clement walked through
the doors of Withshaw and Taylor on Bond Street. They
passed through the millinery department, with the mannequin
heads modelling the latest hats.

'That's very à la mode, don't you think?' Edith said,
pointing out a soft beige cloche hat with a lovely bow of
beads, but Clement wasn't interested.

Instead he held her elbow, talking into her ear, as they
walked towards the busy lifts.

'Are you sure it's all right to present all of these when we
haven't made them?' he asked, and Edith bristled that he was
so distrusting of her plan.

'It will work. This will make us money. Trust me for once,
Clement.'

Clement pursed his lips, then put his hands in his pockets.

'And be civil,' she warned, as they got closer to the lift.

Miss Proust stood up as Edith and Clement entered the
area outside Lance Kenton's office on the seventh floor.

'Hello again, Miss Proust,' Edith said, gratified to see the
secretary looking her up and down, and she was glad she'd

worn her new suit. She now undid the tiny pearl buttons on the inside of her wrists and removed the soft leather gloves and her matching hat.

The glass office door opened and Lance Kenton, the buyer, came out. He was a greasy sort of man, Edith thought, but she allowed him to shake her hand and he bowed his head, looking into her eyes.

'Your wife is as stylish as ever, Mr Darton,' Lance Kenton said, by way of greeting.

Edith flashed a triumphant look at Clement. It always pleased her when other men noticed her in front of her husband.

'I have to tell you that business for the brassieres is booming,' he said. 'I'm hoping you have something new for me.'

'Oh yes, we certainly do,' Edith said, following him into the office.

Afterwards, even Clement had to admit that the meeting had been a huge success. Edith had used the opportunity to really spell out her plans for Darton, and the machinery they were investing in. And, back on the street, she felt ten foot tall.

'Where were you thinking of dining?' she asked Clement.

'My club.'

'But they don't allow women. Let's go somewhere else.'

In the end they ate in the Ritz's dining room, but Clement was sulky and quiet. Edith couldn't help looking round the room, waiting to be seen, wishing she was still a part of London society. She'd had so many friends here once, but now she felt on the fringes and left out, when she should be feeling right at the centre of things.

'Clement, why don't we go dancing?' she suggested. 'We could go to the Café de Paris?'

'I can't dance any more,' he said, and Edith cursed herself for reminding him of everything his sister had taken from him. 'You go, if you must, but I don't want to.'

Edith pressed her lips together, worried that her marriage was falling apart. They were so rarely away together and, more importantly, so rarely sharing the same bed that she thought it was a good opportunity to cement things with Clement. Outwardly, their marriage seemed perfectly respectable, and it mattered to her that other people thought so, too. They might be running the business together, but the more she tried to impress Clement, the further away he seemed to get from her. She tortured herself with the thought that he was missing Marianne, or that he'd seek his pleasure with other women.

Later, in the bedroom, she put on her prettiest lacy nightgown and brushed her hair, waiting for Clement to come in from the bathroom. He stood in the doorway looking at her, and Edith crossed her legs, drawing them up and trying to look alluring.

'It's been a long day. Why don't you come to bed,' she said, spreading her fingers out on the silken counterpane.

'There's no point,' he said. His words stung, but his look was even more brutal. 'I didn't tell you before we came, but Dr Willoughby from Manchester telephoned me.'

Edith felt a stab of icy dread. Why had she trusted the doctor? And why hadn't her patient confidentiality been respected? It would have been, if she'd been a man. 'Oh? What did he tell you?'

'That you're barren. If I'd known that, I'd never have married you,' he said, then he walked out and slammed the door.

Edith's heart pounded as she put down the hairbrush and looked at her lap, tears pooling in her eyes. She took a deep breath in and forced herself to keep focused. Clement didn't mean those cruel words, surely? It was his frustration with himself, and the disabilities inflicted on him by Vita, that were making him lash out at her now, she thought. She mustn't let that word 'barren' ruin everything.

But for this evening, it had, and she lay awake all night. In the small hours, she fretfully vowed that she would do whatever it took to win back her husband's respect. And once Edith had succeeded in ruining all of Vita's hopes – once she was broken, and Clement found out what his wife had done for him – then she would win his heart, wouldn't she? And he'd finally see what an asset Edith was.

59

Sweeping the Cobwebs
Off the Moon

When Irving came back from Baden-Baden he took Vita out for dinner with friends in Saint-Germain and afterwards they went dancing on the Quai Saint-Bernard. With the lights strung up between the trees, the couples dancing beneath them and the moonlight twinkling on the river, Vita could see why Paris was known as the city of romance. She felt fuzzy with the fine wine and the feeling that Irving was so pleased to see her.

He grinned down at her, his hand squeezing hers as they danced – albeit slowly. He sang along to the lyrics of 'Keep Sweeping the Cobwebs Off the Moon': 'So, shake all of your sorrow, take care of tomorrow and keep sweeping the cobwebs off the moon.'

'I didn't know you could sing, you old romantic,' she teased, although she felt embarrassed that she'd called him old.

'Oh, I missed you, Vita.'

'You were only gone for a week,' she laughed. She'd hardly had time to miss him in return.

'What have you been doing while I was away? Apart from working far too hard?'

She looked at him, knowing that he was already reading her, already looking for her 'tells'.

'I've been working – oh, and I went to Bal Tabarin with my friend Paul,' she told him. 'He had a spare ticket.'

She sensed him tensing.

'Now, Irving, don't you dare go getting jealous,' she told him, searching out his eyes. 'Paul and I are friends, and nothing more. Although he was a very bored friend, because all I talked about was you.'

He nodded. 'A good topic of conversation,' he said and she reached up and kissed him.

'I promise you, he's just a friend. I'm really not his type.'

'I don't believe you wouldn't be everyone's type,' Irving said, put out. 'You're so very lovely, Vita.'

'Oh, Irving, you *are* jealous. And here I am, being honest with you. If you're going to sulk, I won't tell you anything.'

He smiled at her bashfully.

'That's better,' she said, pleased with herself for scolding him.

'I can't help it. I want you all to myself,' he said.

'And you have me all to yourself,' she said. 'I promise.'

'Not if you go out with other people.'

She rolled her eyes, seeing there was only one way to set his mind at rest. 'Oh, you're impossible! If I were to tell you a secret, would you keep it?' she asked.

'Of course I would.'

'And if I told you something you didn't approve of, would you still keep it?'

'Vita, you're being very mysterious,' he said. 'Just tell me, for goodness' sake.'

So she told him about Paul being a homosexual, and told him about Percy, too.

'Don't look so shocked. It's not so very unusual. This is Paris – and anything goes, remember. That's why we're here.'

'I suppose,' he conceded. 'I don't have colourful friends like you.'

'You have more friends than anyone I know,' she said, laughing. 'And I bet you anything that at least one of them is – you know . . .'

'You think?' he asked, with a frown.

'I *know*. Honestly, Irving, you're so old-fashioned sometimes.'

Finally, knowing that he was no longer jealous, Vita relaxed and they danced some more. In the moonlight she thought Irving was rather good-looking. Maybe it was true what they said about absence making the heart grow fonder.

'Oh, I do so love this. I want a home filled with music,' he said and Vita thought how lovely that sounded.

'I'd like that, too. I'd like a piano. I had one once,' she said, but she shuddered, thinking of Darton Hall and the cold dining room and the out-of-tune grand piano. She'd always felt too intimidated to play it, for fear of the sound disturbing the silence of the house.

They danced until midnight, when Vita told Irving that she simply had to get some sleep if she was to work in the morning. But the summer night was so balmy and hot, and it was so lovely being out with Irving, that when he suggested they walk for a while, she agreed and she held on to his arm as they wandered up towards Saint-Germain.

'Come on. I've got a better idea,' Irving said suddenly,

going over to one of the horse-drawn carriages that were standing at the side of the road by the river, and talking to the driver. Vita went over and patted the dappled horse's mane.

'Your carriage awaits, milady,' Irving said in a silly English accent, and Vita climbed on board. Once he had settled in next to her, she linked her arm through his and Irving smiled down at her and patted her hand.

'Where are we going?' she asked as they set off.

'You'll see,' Irving said.

60

The Eiffel Tower

As the horse clopped along and they swayed behind in the rocking carriage, they chatted and Vita told Irving the latest news from Nancy, as three letters had arrived from America that morning. Marie, who had got into the habit of rushing down to Madame Vertbois first thing in the morning to collect the post, had brought them up, and now Vita snuggled into Irving and told him about them.

'What else did she say?' he asked.

'She says the clinic is, just as you said it would be, more like a hotel. She's met some famous actors already.'

'That's good.'

'She's exercising again.'

'Well, I'm glad she's getting better. You should go out and see her. You would love California. I could take you there.'

Vita laughed, thinking how typical it was of Irving to make such an outlandish offer.

'I can't,' she said, 'I've got to work. And even if I could go, it would be impossible.' She told him about how she'd travelled to France on Edith's passport. 'So, you see, I'm not terribly legitimate, I'm afraid.'

'You should have said before,' Irving said. 'I have a man who can sort that out.'

She believed he had ways and means of getting what he wanted – after magically procuring some last-minute tickets for Nancy for the crossing. But getting her a passport might be tricky. Especially when she wasn't even called Vita Casey.

'Oh, Irving, are you really going to solve all my problems?' she said.

'Of course I am. Every one of them. Until all the problems are gone,' he replied, and then he leant down and kissed her.

At this late hour there were only a few cars on the road, and it felt to Vita as they got nearer the Eiffel Tower that they had it all to themselves. Three of the four sides were lit up with an advert for Citroën, the car manufacturer.

'Is that where we're going?' she asked, and he grinned and nodded.

'It's best to see it from the Troc,' Irving explained and they clopped across the river, going right under the structure of the huge tower, and Vita gasped and laughed, holding on to her hat as she stared up and up through the steel girders. She'd never seen anything so wonderful.

The horse came to a stop on the edge of the Jardins du Trocadéro, with the fountains lit up, twelve or more spraying majestic plumes of water up towards the night sky. The Palais du Trocadéro glowed in the distance, lit up by spotlights on the lawn.

'I've actually never been this close to the Eiffel Tower before,' Vita said, still awed by the giant structure. 'I've been meaning to go up it, but . . .'

'You know, Vita, that I'm not a man to mince my words,' Irving said. 'So how about it?'

'How about what?'

And then, as she looked down, she saw that he was kneeling on the floor of the carriage.

'Irving!' she exclaimed.

'Vita, I want you to marry me. What do you say?'

She saw now that he'd retrieved a black velvet box from his pocket and had opened it up. The giant diamond ring glinted in the light.

'Won't you be a doll and make an old guy happy?'

She remembered now the flights of fancy she'd had as a child, wondering where she might be and who might be proposing to her. She'd never imagined that she'd be under the Eiffel Tower in Paris, being proposed to by a millionaire.

'Say yes, Vita,' he urged. 'I'm no good at being on my own. And besides, this thing is so uncomfortable to carry around in my pocket. Not to mention me ruining my trousers like this.'

Vita laughed and pulled him up, and they sat together on the seat. It was so typical of Irving to make it sound as if accepting something that was clearly worth a small fortune would be doing *him* a favour.

'But we hardly know each other. It's been such a short time,' she gasped, her eyes glued to the huge diamond.

'So what! When you know, you know. I knew straight away,' he said, 'the second I saw you walking towards me across Jenny's salon. We're right together.' He took a breath and she saw how emotional he was. 'That home full of music? I want you to be in it, Vita. Besides, it's not right for a man to be alone with two daughters – and they like you.'

'I haven't even *met* Hermione,' she pointed out.

'She'll think you're swell,' he said with a dismissive wave. 'What do you say? Come on, Vita. Say yes.'

She might not love Irving, but she certainly liked him, Vita thought. And that was enough, wasn't it? Nancy had told her that nobody married for love these days. That marrying for love was the worst thing you could do.

'Yes,' she said. 'Yes, you silly thing. I'll marry you.'

61

Sillage

The news of Vita's engagement to Irving spread rapidly, and over the following weeks she was inundated with congratulatory messages from the clients at Madame Jenny's. Laure had already started planning Vita's dress, and Agatha was utterly enthralled by the whole story of Vita's surprise engagement, swooning over the romance of her whirlwind courtship and the proposal under the Eiffel Tower. Vita wondered whether, in the telling, she'd embellished it rather too much.

She had always marvelled at the girls at the Zip wanting to get married while they were young and at their best, and was surprised that here in Paris, where things were so much more sophisticated, nothing was different, on this front at least. Her peers made no secret of the fact that they envied Vita her new status as wife-to-be and, while this was comforting in one way, in another way she felt panicky that everything was changing so fast. Sometimes, mainly when she was alone, Vita had a profound sense of unreality that this was actually happening to her.

Everyone seemed thrilled by the news, apart from Madame Jenny herself, who had declared – in a rare insight into her private life – that she had been married briefly once, but wouldn't be trying it again any time soon. She was already married to her salon and had no time for another husband.

And Vita sensed that Marie wasn't deliriously happy about it, either. She'd said all the right things about how she was happy for Vita, but Vita sensed that something was bothering her – maybe the thought that they wouldn't be living together any more after Vita was married. Irving had already thrown himself into the task of buying them their dream home.

On Saturday, Vita insisted that Marie leave the flat and come out with her, hoping that some time away from the apartment would get things back on track. Now, on their way through the perfume department on the ground floor of the Galeries Lafayette, she was hoping that the lavish store, with its plush hallways and goods from around the world, would cheer Marie up.

Vita twisted the giant ring on her finger, still trying to get used to the way it felt. She kept looking at her hand, terrified that she might lose the heavy ring.

'Isn't it weird having something so big on your hand?' Marie asked, with a frown.

'It is. But I think that's because it's loose. We're going to Cartier after this, to get it altered.' Vita smiled, a little embarrassed. 'But you must come, too, and we'll all go out for lunch.'

But Marie didn't commit herself to this plan, and Vita drew her over to the Givenchy stand, picking up the florid glass bottle and spraying some on her wrist.

'What about this one?' Vita said, holding up her arm for Marie to smell the perfume.

Marie nodded. 'I like that one. The French have a glorious word,' she said, smelling another bottle thoughtfully. '*Sillage*.'

'What's that?' Vita asked. '*Sillage*,' she repeated, rolling the word on her tongue.

'It means that you leave a little piece of yourself wherever you go. A little trail.'

'I like that,' Vita said. 'Oh, look at this lovely bottle. What about this one?' She offered her wrist to Marie, but Marie wrinkled her nose.

'Too strong,' she said. 'For you, I mean. You need something to match your personality.'

'And what is my personality, according to you, my dear Marie?' Vita asked, laughing.

'Not what one would expect,' Marie said, after some thought.

'What a strange thing to say,' Vita said. 'Come on, the lingerie department is upstairs. Let's go and see.'

They came out of the lift on the third floor to an understated lingerie department, where many of the items on sale were hidden away in wooden and glass cabinets. They'd often discussed how Vita and the girls had clinched the appointment at Withshaw and Taylor, and Marie had suggested that they get an appointment with the buyer here. Vita, thrilled that she'd taken such an interest in the newly revived Top Drawer, was keen to follow through on the idea.

'Ours are so much better than all of this. How many bras have we got?' she asked Marie. 'In the case, I mean? It must be almost full.' And then, not waiting for an answer and seeing a rather senior-looking assistant, she beckoned Marie over to the other counter. 'Come on, let's find out who we need to talk to.'

The assistant called over the manager of the department and soon, thanks to Marie's excellent French, Vita had the name of a person to speak to on Monday. Marie said that she'd stop by to make a firm appointment when Vita was at work.

'Oh, goodness,' Vita said with a happy sigh. 'Imagine getting Top Drawer in here,' she said. 'Oh, Marie, I can't wait to show off what we've done.'

'Me too,' Marie said, with a rare smile, and Vita linked arms with her. It was wonderful to have the girls at work, but Marie was now her best friend. And as soon as they had sold in their work and Top Drawer was official again, Vita was determined that Marie should be her partner in the business.

They were moving through the department now into the fashion hall.

'Let me buy you something to celebrate,' Vita said. 'A new dress.'

They stopped at the gorgeous ready-to-wear collections and Vita plucked a red dress from the rail and held it up against Marie.

'Oh, look. You must get this one. The colour is absolutely right,' she said.

'It's red.'

'I know. And a lovely shade of it, too.'

'I can't accept this, Vita,' Marie said, looking flustered and pushing the dress back towards her.

'But I want you to have it,' Vita said, put out by her reaction.

'No, no, I can't. I won't. I must go now.'

'But you can't go. We're meeting Irving,' Vita said. What on earth had got into her?

But Marie insisted, and in a moment she'd scurried away to the stairs and Vita had to wait alone for Irving by the store's entrance.

When he arrived, he didn't seem too disappointed that Marie had gone and wasn't there to meet him with Vita. But Vita was cross that her friend had behaved so oddly, just when they'd been getting on so well.

In Cartier, they stood by the gleaming glass counters and Irving pointed to a huge necklace. 'Won't you look at that,' he said.

The assistant approached now. 'It's the Patiala Necklace, sir,' he explained. 'They say it's one of the biggest diamonds in the world. It's a ceremonial necklace for a maharaja.'

'We'll take two,' Irving joked, and the assistant laughed. 'That's funny,' Irving said to Vita. 'Why the long face?'

'I can't work out Marie,' Vita said. 'Maybe she's jealous because I have so much, when she has so little.'

'She has you. That's not little,' Irving said, but he didn't understand, and Vita couldn't quite put her finger on why she felt so unsettled.

62

The Studio

If Vita had thought life was fast-paced before, now it seemed that she could hardly catch her breath. Irving made her meet him every lunchtime and after work, too, for celebratory drinks with friends or house viewings. It was simply exhausting.

On Wednesday he'd insisted that she meet him behind the rue du Faubourg Saint-Honoré to see a house that he said was definitely 'the one'. She arrived at the address to discover one of those little squares so unique to Paris, which was filled with neat flowerbeds, a green water fountain and a majestic sculpture of a horse, and was surrounded on all sides by the kind of smart colonnaded buildings that made onlookers swoon with envy.

And it was in the very finest building at the top of the square that Vita found herself climbing the wide marble stairs of the three-storey house, taking in the splendour of the huge glass dome, which flooded the stairway with golden light.

'And look in here,' Irving said, opening the modern panelled doorway to let Vita look inside the freshly painted room. 'This can be a guest room, or, I suppose, a nursery,' he said.

Vita stared at him. 'A nursery? But you already have children. And they're nearly grown up,' she pointed out.

'Don't *you* want children, Vita?' He studied her face as if there might be something wrong with her that he hadn't noticed before, and she laughed.

'I hadn't thought about it.'

'I thought every woman wants children. Above everything.'

'Is that so?' Vita said, shaking her head at his decree.

'Doesn't she?' he checked. He looked rather pained as he said this, as if this whole conversation were making him very uncomfortable. She could see the colour rising in his cheeks.

'Does it matter if she doesn't? Because shouldn't it be *her* choice?' she asked. 'The woman's, I mean. Shouldn't she be able to decide?'

Irving looked cornered, clearly not having considered this before.

'What if a woman wanted to . . .' she knew she was pushing her point, but she felt it was important, 'if she wanted to have a successful career instead of having children.'

'A career!' Irving laughed, and Vita frowned. For a man with daughters, who claimed to be 'modern', he could be exactly the reverse.

'Yes, a career,' Vita said seriously.

She thought about Madame Jenny and how she'd forged a successful career, and how she herself was inspired by her on a daily basis. Every day her job became more and more exciting, as Madame Jenny took on more and more of Vita's ideas. They had commissions stacked up until Christmas, and Vita couldn't wait to get back to the studio to start work on the new collection.

330

'Come on,' Irving said, grinning and taking her hand. 'There's more.'

She wanted to press her point, but knew she'd have to pick her moment. Irving was too exuberant right now and she laughed as they went up the rest of the stairs two at a time. He was soon breathless with exertion and panted as he threw open the door once they reached the top. She wished he'd become fitter, but his life was a constant quest to find the finest of everything – particularly when it came to food and alcohol.

'You need to get healthy,' she scolded, patting his chest and then squeezing past him into the vast room. She walked slowly across the parquet to the floor-to-ceiling windows.

'Oh, Irving,' she sighed. 'It's wonderful.'

'I wouldn't open the windows,' he said, 'the refurbishers are putting a guard up. It's rather a drop.'

Vita looked down from the French windows to the railings below, then out beyond the strip of road to the pretty square.

'Oh, look at the view,' she said. She could see the top of the Eiffel Tower above the grey-tiled rooftops.

'I knew you'd like it,' Irving said, coming and putting his arm around her from behind, so that their heads were side-by-side. His whiskers tickled her cheek, but she didn't pull away. 'You can stay here all day and look at the view to your heart's content.'

'All day? But what about Madame Sacerdote's?' she said. 'I'll be going there every day,' she reminded him.

Irving chuckled. 'You can't *work* any more, Vita.'

'Whyever not?'

'Because we'll be married,' he said, pulling away from her and turning so that he could see her face. He looked puzzled. 'Your place will be with me. At home. You'll be my wife,' he added with emphasis, as if this would be a job in itself.

Vita pulled away from his embrace. 'But I like working, Irving.'

'And that's very admirable. But Madame Jenny can spare you, and I can't.'

She could see that Irving was serious, and she felt a shiver of alarm for all she'd be losing if she gave up working with Madame Jenny. And what if Madame Jenny didn't want her, once she became Mrs Irving King? It hadn't occurred to her before, but with her new status, Vita would be stepping over the invisible line from worker to customer class. Everyone at Madame Jenny's would treat her differently. Everything was going to change, but she *wanted* to work. She didn't want to be idle. She didn't want to waste everything she'd learnt.

'But I don't want to give it up. Not unless . . . well, unless this chance with my lingerie takes off, and Marie and I can get Galeries Lafayette – or even a little boutique – to sell what we've made.'

Irving rubbed his forehead and she stiffened. Whenever she told him about her ambitions, he was always rather dismissive, but now that they were having this conversation, she knew how important it was to make him understand.

'What? What's the matter? You're a businessman,' she said. 'You work. Why can't I?'

'It's different. You're a woman.'

She fell silent. It *was* different for women, but the unfairness of it still stung.

But then she thought of Marie and turned round in the room, looking at the space, an idea taking hold.

'Yes, I'm a woman,' she said. 'One with a very good business idea, and this is the perfect space for a studio – my studio. To get the business really off the ground. You're always asking me what I want, and what I want – *all* I want – is this. A studio. A chance to make my dream happen.'

'A studio?'

'Yes,' Vita said, spreading her arms out and twirling in the light pouring in from the window. 'Marie can help me set it up, and this is just what we need. If you really don't want me to work for Madame Jenny, at least let me work for myself. And I'll be a perfect wife, I promise.'

Irving laughed. 'Is that what would make you happy?'

'Yes,' she said, going towards him. She kissed him on the lips, closing her eyes.

'Don't get me too excited,' he chuckled. 'Or I really won't be able to wait until we're married,' he whispered, kissing her more fully.

Vita let herself be kissed, and thought about the studio and how it would look, once she had benches in here and mirrors, machines and mannequins. Then she remembered that she was kissing her fiancé and scolded herself, trying to pay attention.

'I can't wait for our wedding night,' Irving whispered, with a bawdy chuckle, grabbing her buttock and giving it a hefty squeeze, making her jump.

'Me neither,' she said, baulking inwardly at the lie.

'Don't be nervous about . . . that,' he said meaningfully. He clearly assumed she was a virgin, and Vita squirmed at how many secrets she had, and how much there was in her past that he must never know about.

'We really should get planning,' he said and she nodded, daunted by the conversation about the wedding, which they'd been putting off. 'Because I was thinking . . . if you're not inviting your family, then let's not involve mine.'

The last time they'd discussed it, Irving had been intent on having the party to end all parties, and Vita had calculated that the wedding wouldn't happen until at least next summer. 'Not involve your family? But won't the girls be upset?'

'You know,' Irving said, 'why don't we just elope?'

'Elope?' she laughed. 'Where to?'

'Right here in Paris. We could get married at the registry office and then we could go to the Riviera for our honeymoon. I could show you Nice and all along the coast. We could drive,' Irving said.

'I guess,' Vita replied, trying to take in the enormity of this new plan.

'We could do it soon. The end of the month.'

'But how?' she asked, aghast at this sudden new timetable and what it might mean.

'I know discreet lawyers. If it's so easy to untie the knot, it shouldn't be so hard to tie it again.'

'Irving, you make marriage sound like it's a handkerchief.' *Or a Hermès scarf, more appropriately.*

'Oh, Vita darling. We don't have to take anything too seriously. All that matters is that we have fun,' he said, 'and enjoy being together. What could be so difficult about that?'

63

Big Business

In the office Edith closed the glass door, glad for a moment to be alone, and placed a call to the apartment block in Paris. After an age, the concierge finally picked up and, after an irritating exchange when the woman refused to understand Edith, it took another long time for Marianne to be fetched from the apartment.

'You haven't called,' Edith said angrily into the receiver. 'And I've been expecting another package.'

There was silence at the end of the line. Then a stifled breath.

'Marie?' Edith demanded. 'Marianne, are you quite all right? What's happened?'

'Nothing – only I can't stand it any more. It is only a matter of time before Vita finds out what I've done. And she's been so good to me. She and I have become friends.'

'You are not *friends*. You won't ever be *friends*. Not when she finds out what you've done – how you've betrayed her. Not to mention what you did to the dog.'

Marianne let out a wail. 'Don't, please don't. Mrs Darton, what you have made me do, it's so . . . You don't understand.'

But Edith understood perfectly. 'Pull yourself together. Remember why you're doing this. For Susan. For her future.'

Marianne let out a little sob. 'But I can't stand it any longer. Vita, she's getting married soon. There's a registrar booked. I'm going to be a witness,' she sobbed. 'And, Mrs Darton, when it's over, I'm going to tell her everything. I'm going to—'

'No, you are not. You are going to keep your mouth shut,' Edith said, shocked that Marianne would even consider betraying her like that. 'And I am going to come to Paris.' She paused, knowing that she had to play her trump card to salvage the situation. 'I'm going to come with Susan. To see you.'

Another long pause. A sniff. 'You will bring Susan to Paris?'

Edith winced, annoyed that she'd backed herself into a corner. The delight in Marianne's voice – the hope – was too much.

'I'm thinking about it, rather than Susan staying at school for the holidays.'

'Oh, Mrs Darton, if you could. If you would bring her and I could see her, then . . . then I would do anything you asked.'

Edith squeezed her lips together. 'Then we have a deal.'

'Vita will be on her honeymoon,' Marianne said, and Edith could tell how her brain was whirring with the arrangements. 'She can stay with me at the apartment.'

'I will consider it. But only if you tell me what's happening there. This silence really won't do.'

Edith couldn't help her reprimanding tone. The past few

weeks had been torturous without Marianne contacting her from Paris. She had been planning on rewarding Marianne with the news about W&T and how they'd significantly increased their orders. But now she wouldn't. Marianne didn't need to know how her subterfuge had put Darton back on course.

'I have been doing what you asked me to. I've been making the bras – all of her designs,' Marianne said, clearly eager to please Edith at long last.

'Good. There are lots of units?'

'Yes, I have all the stock. And Vita, she has an appointment in the Galeries Lafayette to present it all.'

'When?'

'In a few weeks. She says she'll have to postpone the appointment, now that the wedding has come forward. She says we'll go when she's back from her honeymoon.'

'Well then,' Edith said, 'that's perfect. Don't change the appointment. Keep it.'

'Keep it?'

'Yes, keep it. We'll go ourselves.'

She hung up quickly, seeing Clement coming up the iron stairs. He opened the door, clearly annoyed that it had been shut.

'Who were you talking to?' he asked.

'Nobody. You know, I was thinking I might go to Paris. To look at the fashions there. And maybe to get some of our stock into the shops,' she said.

Edith smiled sweetly at Clement, her heart beating fast. Was this the moment to tell him? That the designs they'd just sold to one of the finest department stores in England were his sister's? That she'd enacted the most perfect revenge on Vita that she could think of? All for him? And that this wonderful plan was continuing, with the opportunity in Paris?

But Clement stiffened. 'Paris?' he asked and there was a beat of silence.

'You don't need to worry about her,' Edith said soothingly, knowing that he was thinking of Vita. 'Anna, I mean. She's nothing. I doubt she's even there. And even if she is, she can't affect us, can she?'

'A man died because of her,' Clement said, not masking the contempt in his voice. He'd told her previously about the private detective he'd hired to track down his sister, when she'd first run away. Clement had clearly been fond of Rawlings and was upset he'd been killed by a bus – an accident that he blamed Vita for entirely. And although Edith knew only the sketchiest of details, it did sound as if Vita had run away in the nick of time. She'd certainly been in a terrible panic when Edith had given Vita her own ticket and passport to join Nancy on Le Train Bleu out of London. That simple exchange had been a stroke of genius on her own part, Edith thought, because if Vita hadn't gone, Edith wouldn't have got Top Drawer. Or any of this.

'I know, darling,' Edith said sympathetically to Clement.

'He was a good man. A man with a family. With principles. She should pay for what she's done.'

'Oh, I'm sure she will,' Edith said, 'one day soon.'

64

The Much-Anticipated
Wedding Night

With only Marie as a witness at the registry office, the wedding didn't really feel like much of a wedding at all to Vita. She knew Agatha had been disappointed that Vita wasn't having a grand ceremony and, to avoid upsetting anyone else, Vita hadn't told the girls at work when the actual wedding was taking place.

Irving had insisted this was for the best, because once they invited one person, they would have to invite everyone, and it was easiest to do the whole thing in a low-key kind of way. Even so, Vita was sad that Nancy wasn't there to witness her big moment. That said, most of the short ceremony had been unintelligible, the celebrant having such an appalling English accent and being clearly unable to read it, so he'd resorted to speaking the words in French. She and Irving had got the giggles by the end of it.

Afterwards they'd taken a *bateau-mouche* down the Seine for the wedding breakfast to mark the occasion, and there had been a lovely jazz band on board, and they'd danced and drunk champagne until it was time for Marie to leave.

'You are so wonderful,' Vita told her friend, feeling

emotional and slightly tipsy. She hugged Marie, then stroked the hair away from her face. If only Marie made a little more effort, she could be as lovely as she'd looked today. The pink dress and jacket that Vita had bought her showed off her slim figure and smooth skin.

'I'm not,' Marie said, her eyes leaving Vita's face now and her smile fading. 'I wish I was.'

Vita pulled a face and lifted Marie's chin, to look into her pale eyes. It was typical of her to deflect such attention. 'You have done so much for me. Really. Thank you for being such a good friend.'

Marie's eyes were full of tears and she only shook her head. 'Enjoy the hotel,' she managed. 'And your honeymoon.'

After they'd docked near the Pont Neuf and Marie had gone back to the apartment, Irving had hailed a cab to take Vita to the Georges V hotel, where he'd booked dinner and where they were spending their wedding night.

Vita for a fleeting moment wished she could skip dinner, lie on a bed and kick off her heels, but another part of her was stalling the moment when they'd be alone together in the bedroom. She'd got used to kissing Irving, of course, and there had been some intimate touching, but she'd never seen him naked and sensed they were both nervous about their wedding night – and the expectations they'd both placed on it. She wondered now whether Marie's advice not to sleep with Irving before their marriage had been entirely sensible.

In the plush dining room the staff were falling over themselves to treat the newly-weds like royalty, and Vita drank quickly and copiously. Now, though, as they walked into the lift that whisked them up to the sumptuous honeymoon suite, she realized she was drunk.

'Oh, darling,' she told Irving, 'I'm really quite gone.'

'We certainly drank a lot of champagne today,' he agreed, but it was different for him. The alcohol didn't seem to have touched him, and Vita realized blurrily that she shouldn't have tried to keep up with him.

They kissed as they went up in the lift, and Vita felt her stomach clenching with nerves, now that the moment was here. Perhaps Irving sensed this, because he squeezed her hand as they walked through the door to the huge bedroom, with its enormous bed covered in pale-green silk sheets. Someone had drawn the covers back and there were rose petals on the bed beneath the ornate silk canopy.

Vita went to the window and looked out at the magnificent view framed in the French windows, as Irving poured her another glass of champagne.

'Oh, Irving, look at this place. It's simply beautiful.'

'I'm glad you like it,' Irving said. 'Only the best for you, my dear Vita.'

'I would be quite happy not having all this, you know,' she said, putting her hand on his chest. 'I know you like to spoil me, but if we are ever poor . . .'

'We won't ever be poor,' he told her. 'You don't need to worry about that. Never again. In fact I have something for you. Two things.'

'What is it? Irving, you've given me too much already.' Her hand sprang to the diamond pendant he'd given her earlier on. It must be worth a fortune.

'Come here,' he said, patting the silk counterpane of the

bed. 'Firstly, here is your passport.' He handed over a Manila envelope and she smiled at him before opening it and pulling out the passport. If this were a counterfeit, then it was an exceedingly good one, Vita thought as she flicked through the embossed pages.

'Mrs Vita King,' she whispered, seeing her photograph next to her new name.

'It's proper and legal,' Irving assured her. 'I had to get it for you so we can travel everywhere . . . all over the world,' he said and she kissed him.

'Thank you, Irving, thank you.'

'That's not all. You see, I had no idea what to buy you as a wedding gift, and Marie suggested that you'd appreciate financial independence. She said every woman wants financial independence. She was quite forceful about it.'

'Marie was?'

'Yes, she gave me the idea.'

'What idea?

'Well, you like stocks and shares,' he said and handed her a folded sheet of thick paper. 'So I've bought you some of your own.'

It was a share certificate made out to Vita King. 'Who are Hillsafe Investments?' she asked, reading the fancy inscription.

'Let's call it a safety net,' he said. 'Just for you – should anything happen. They invest in all sorts of companies, so think of it as your own piece of pie.'

She folded up the share certificate, too fuzzy with champagne to take it all in. She kissed him. 'Thank you,' she whispered. Irving smelt of garlic and brandy, but she ignored it. 'Dear Irving. You are so thoughtful. I have nothing to give you in return.'

'Let's go to bed,' he said.

'Give me a minute, darling,' she replied, springing up and going to her leather trousseau, where she took out the ivory silk-and-lace ensemble. She went into the bathroom, where she slipped out of her Maison Jenny evening dress and changed quickly, before brushing her teeth. Then, taking a deep breath, she looked at her reflection in the mirror – she looked different: older, she thought – before whispering her new name. 'Mrs Irving King.'

She sprayed some perfume on her neck and forced herself to remember what Irving had told her earlier, just before they'd married: 'I may not be the best-looking chap, but I'm rich and I can make your dreams come true.'

And that was what she wanted, wasn't it?

Back in the bedroom, Irving had discarded his clothes over a chair and was under the covers, his knees up beneath the sheet. 'Let's try this thing,' he said, putting his cigar down on the ashtray next to the bed. 'Strip off,' he commanded.

She felt herself flushing, seeing him naked for the first time. How fleshy and hairy he was. She posed by the doorway, waiting for a compliment. Didn't he like the fine silk she was wearing?

'No,' he said gruffly. 'Slowly. Properly. You're a dancing girl,' he said, picking up on her look. 'Entice me.'

She did as he instructed, and Irving looked like he was concentrating hard. Soon she was naked and she climbed into the vast bed, pressing herself against him. He kissed her fully, then rolled over on top of her, and she felt the weight of him make the air leave her lungs. She closed her eyes as he moved between her legs, but a moment later he buried his face in her neck and she heard him curse.

For a moment she didn't realize what was going on, and then Irving moved away from her.

'Damned thing,' he said. He shuffled over to the edge of the vast bed and put his elbows on his knees and his head in his hands. 'I've ruined everything,' he muttered. 'This is why my wife left me. And you'll leave me, too.'

Vita, experiencing a new emotion that she couldn't describe, knelt up and massaged his shoulders, noticing the thick hair that sprouted beneath his shoulder blades. She stroked it. She could learn to love it in time, couldn't she?

'We just drank too much,' she soothed. 'It doesn't matter.'

'Oh, but it does.'

'We'll find a way.'

'Oh, Vita. Vita. You're everything to me,' he said, turning and burying his face in her breasts. 'Please don't leave me.'

65

Lavender Fields

Despite Vita's promise to find a way, it was impossible, when Irving drank so much every night. And two days later, after a tearful goodbye to the girls at Madame Jenny's, they left Paris for the South of France and had yet to consummate their marriage properly.

Irving filled up every second of their time with treats and surprises, but Vita knew there was something unspoken between them, and she wished she could talk to someone about it and work out how to fix it. She missed Marie and picked up the telephone several times to call her, but the thought of having a personal conversation when Marie was standing in Madame Vertbois's office put her off.

She curled up every night next to Irving, listening to him snoring like a bear, awake in the dark, wondering what to do – wondering what Nancy would say. Wondering what she'd done, and if marrying Irving really had been such a good idea.

Because what if the problem wasn't Irving, but her? What if, despite his protests, he didn't find *her* sexually attractive? What then?

But if the nights were plagued by fears, the days were

different. The days were so much fun. They took Le Train Bleu down to Nice, then a quaint little train to Marseille, where Irving had a man meet them in a very fancy British racing-green car with a retractable white roof.

Vita had been rather daunted by the idea of driving around with Irving for three weeks in a sports car, but he'd insisted that it was far too short a time to show her everything he wanted to.

And, sure enough, soon she was being borne along on Irving's enthusiasm, and there was no doubt that seeing the French countryside this way was magical. He even taught her to drive, and Vita loved the thrill of the open roads.

Soon she was insisting on driving every day, as they made their way up through the hills to villages where tanned women scrubbed at white shirts with soap. They stopped and stared when they saw Vita driving through their narrow streets. She drove on through the lavender fields, and they stopped for lunch in Aix-en-Provence, where they sipped cool rosé on the terrace of Les Deux Garçons and watched the painters in the Cours Mirabeau.

Irving said that he hoped they'd run into Picasso, and Vita laughed. She was quickly learning that Irving liked to feel that he was connected to anyone of note.

When it was his turn to drive again, she leant against his shoulder and stared at the passing landscape, under-standing why the painters came here to paint. In the morning light the fields had a golden, hazy glow to them, with the ocean in the distance a dazzling expanse of twink-ling blue.

They dined in Avignon, with Irving making her try a

plate of delicious steak tartare and the waiter was over-familiar. Irving admitted that he'd been here with his wife, Alicia, but added that she had been terribly fussy. Vita, wondering if this was either a repetition of history or a test, decided to indulge her new husband and let him teach her everything he wanted to. And so, continuing her gastronomic education, he took her to a vineyard, where they ate at a small table among the vines, and Irving bought a case of red, which he declared they'd drink on their tenth wedding anniversary.

And as the days progressed, Vita warmed to her new husband. Her initial instincts had been right, she realized: Irving really was just a boy trapped in a man's body. He had sophisticated tastes, of course, and liked to be seen having the best of everything, but underneath it all, he simply wanted to be loved. And she tried her best to love him, showing him as much affection as she could and cuddling into him, which made Irving's eyes go twinkly with delight. And she enjoyed the power she had to make him happy.

They wound their way back along the coast, stopping for nights in Saint-Tropez and Cannes. Irving wished to go to Antibes, but Vita said she wanted to stop in Nice for a few days, to see if she could find Percy. She'd made Irving promise that if they were to find him, he must not to pass judgement.

'Haven't you realized that you've changed me, my darling?' he said one night as they were dressing for dinner.

'Changed you?'

'Alicia said I could never change, but I'm trying to be modern. Like you. Hadn't you noticed?' he asked.

Vita laughed. 'Go on . . .'

'Well, it turns out that I can be kind to blacks, and I will tolerate your friend. Even if he is queer.'

'Oh, Irving,' Vita said, shaking her head, seeing how much he did want to be modern, but how far he still had to go. But at least it was a start, and she loved him for trying.

'You're making me a better person, Vita,' he insisted.

66

Success in Nice

Nice was majestic, Vita thought, as Irving drove into the glorious seaside town – the sea a dazzling jewel blue, the buildings grand and imposing along the seafront. They arrived at the Hotel Negresco with its pink dome on the Promenade des Anglais in the afternoon.

It had been Vita who had found out about the Negresco, from a woman she'd got chatting to in Le Majestic hotel in Cannes, and the concierge had booked them in.

Irving had grudgingly decided to go along with her plan, although now he looked put out as they drove through the gates and stopped the car by the steps. Vita knew that he didn't feel the hotel was smart enough, but Vita thought it was lovely.

As they made their way through the lobby, followed by the grey-suited bellboy who had brought some of their luggage from the car, Irving took off his gloves and stopped to read the sign on a wooden stand.

'It was a hospital in the war,' he said. 'And it looks like it never really recovered after that,' he added, but Vita disagreed, taking in the colossal crystal chandelier.

'Stop being a grouch because this was my idea,' she said,

taking his gloves and hitting Irving playfully on the wrist. 'You're going to have a wonderful time here. There's the casino just across the way.'

Upstairs in their suite, she watched as Irving tipped the bellboy, and then she pressed her husband against the door and kissed him.

'Don't think about it,' she instructed, reaching inside his trousers and then sinking to her knees. She was going to make this happen, no matter what.

And soon Irving was on the rug on his back and inside her. And, as she sat astride her husband, she closed her eyes and pictured Fletch, as Irving moaned and moaned. And then, with a great yell, he eventually achieved what they'd both been longing for.

The image of Fletch had been vivid in her mind and now, as Irving relaxed and grinned up at her, she felt a great unfinished yearning. Irving, however, was oblivious to it, laughing like a little boy at Christmas, as he tipped her over onto the floor and reached for a cigar. But did it really matter that he couldn't satisfy her, when he gave her so much of everything else?

'How about that?' he grinned.

'I told you. It's going to be fine.'

And she meant it. They would be fine. She was committed to her husband. Nothing could derail her.

67

Percy

Irving was so excited that he had managed to consummate their marriage that he insisted they go to the casino, this being his lucky day. Vita dressed up and waited for Irving to change and sat on the balcony, flipping through the pages of *Vogue*, happy to see an article about Maison Jenny. She studied the picture of Jenny and her team, all crowded into the studio, feeling a pang of sadness that she wasn't among them.

But she was here in the South of France, she assured herself. On her honeymoon. She was hardly in a position to complain. Even so, it felt as if she'd given up a lot, in her haste to marry Irving. She'd promised to be a good wife, in return for him letting her set up a studio in the new house, but was she really cut out to be the kind of attentive, simpering wife she suspected he wanted? She wasn't convinced that he really wanted her to have a career.

She gazed down at the view. The Negresco, like the other white hotels facing the sea, had large palm trees in front of it; across the promenade, before the sea, there were wrought-iron benches, and steps leading down to a stretch of white sand and then the sea itself. She could see why it was called the Côte d'Azur. The fashionable set walking in the shade of the palm trees, the seagulls swooping, the golden light on the hills in the distance – it was simply glorious.

'Irving, bring my camera,' she called, wanting to take a picture of it.

But just then she saw a man wandering along the promenade – a man with tortoiseshell glasses – and her heart skipped a beat for a moment. It was Percy. She was sure of it.

Without waiting for Irving, she flew out of the room, down the stairs and ran across the promenade, looking both ways, but Percy had gone.

'Damn it,' she cursed, realizing she must have missed him. If, indeed, it had been Percy.

But if it had been him, then he *was* here in Nice. It was a small town and Percy was hardly inconspicuous. She bit her lip, her heart swelling with excitement. How wonderful it would be to see her friend again.

Vita asked for Percy everywhere over the following few days – at the casino, the hotels, the flower market and the telephone exchange – and she kept a vigil at the window of the hotel room, determined not to miss him if he passed.

Irving thought she was being ridiculous. 'You've left enough messages all over town,' he pointed out. 'If your friend wanted to be found, then you'd have found him by now.'

Vita didn't want to believe him, but soon the time had come for them to leave Nice and go along the coast to the prestigious Grand-Hôtel du Cap-Ferrat, where Irving had booked the honeymoon suite.

She felt moody and out of sorts as they made their way to the hotel lobby, where Irving paid the bill. Vita was counting their Louis Vuitton brown suitcases, which had been brought down in the lift, when her attention was caught by the bellhop at the door, and she saw that he was pointing towards her.

And then she noticed that he was directing a man in a dapper light-brown suit with a boater hat, and her heart skipped a beat. It couldn't be, could it?

'Percy?' Vita called, leaving the suitcases and rushing across the lobby.

The man turned and took off his hat, and then Vita grinned and broke into a run. 'Oh, Percy, it *is* you!' she said.

Vita saw Irving turn from the desk as she rushed towards Percy and flung her arms around him. Percy seemed startled and she pulled back, scanning his face. He looked exactly the same as she remembered, although his hair was a little longer, but his familiar eyes shone behind his tortoiseshell glasses.

'I had a message that you were in town,' he said. 'I'm so glad I didn't miss you.'

'Oh, Percy, me too,' Vita said, 'but we're just leaving.'

'We?'

'Over here, darling,' Vita said, waving. 'Irving, this is Percy Blake. This is my husband,' Vita said proudly, and she watched confusion and then politeness cross Percy's face. The two men shook hands.

'Oh, we have so much catching up to do. And hardly any time.'

'Why don't I get the luggage in the car, and you can stay and talk,' Irving suggested.

'Let's go outside,' Vita said. 'It's such a glorious day and I shall be in the car for ages. Let's walk, shall we?'

She linked arms with Percy as they walked from the hotel, across the promenade and down the steps to the beach, and Vita took her sandals off as they walked on the sand. Percy told her that he was staying in Nice with a friend, in a villa along the coast. From the way he talked, Vita realized that this person was more than just a friend, and she was happy that he'd found someone to replace Edward. And in return, she told him about meeting Irving and about their wedding.

'It sounds to me as if you've landed on your feet,' Percy said. 'I always knew you would.'

Eventually they found the perfect patch of sand and Percy spread out his jacket and they sat down, looking out at the sea and the view of the promenade and the casino. They stared out to sea, and Vita realized that they'd talked about so much, but not about London or what had happened there.

'I'm sorry . . . about Edward,' she said. 'And London. I couldn't bear it that you got hurt.' She pictured Clement and that awful moment at the Zip Club when she realized that Clement had Percy's cane.

'You could have told me, Vita,' he said. 'About Clement.'

'I know. I should have, but you see, I had no idea that he was alive. I really thought I'd killed him.' And as they sat, with the waves lapping at the water's edge, Vita told him everything she should have told him before. About being Anna Darton and growing up in that terrible family, and about her argument with her father and Clement. She told him, too, about how she'd run away, and how Nancy had rescued her. 'That's why I went to such lengths to change my identity,' Vita explained. 'And why I kept quiet about my past. I never thought in a million years that Clement would track me down, or try to hurt anyone close to me.'

Percy listened and then described his own awful dealings with Clement: the violent attack when Clement had stolen Percy's treasured cane and the awful scene in the hotel room, where he'd been arrested.

'When the police came, I've never been so scared,' Percy said. 'They were so rough.'

'I came to find you, to get you out,' she told him, 'but they wouldn't let me see you. And Edward was no help. I tried, Percy, you've got to believe me.'

'I thought I was going to jail, and I contemplated ending it all.'

'Oh, Percy,' Vita said, her heart contracting with the thought of the pain Clement had caused him. 'I'm so sorry.'

'But then, quite mysteriously, all the charges were dropped and they let me go. I stayed with Wisey for a while, but then I got back on my feet and returned to the studio. I pretend, during the day, that none of it ever happened, but sometimes at night . . .'

She took his hand. 'I'm so sorry. I promise you that I will never have anything to do with Clement *ever* again.'

'I hope not,' Percy said, with a sad smile, and she saw that he'd forgiven her. 'So, enough about the past. Tell me everything. I gather Nancy has gone back to the States?'

'It's rather a sorry tale,' Vita said, hugging her knees to her chest. It was so wonderful to be here with Percy, and she realized how much she'd missed chatting to him. She filled him in about Les Folies and their Paris nightlife, and Nancy's descent into alcohol and drugs.

'Oh no. I always suspected something like that might happen,' Percy said, unsurprised.

'Irving managed to get her to a sanatorium in California. Oh, it's so awful talking about her,' she said, putting her hand on her chest. 'Poor, poor Nancy.'

'I'm sure Nancy will survive,' Percy said reassuringly. 'She's as tough as teak.'

'I hope so. Although losing Mr Wild was a terrible blow.'

They talked some more, and then Vita saw that Percy was looking at her dress and he reached out and took the material of the skirt and she laughed.

'Sorry,' he said, 'but it's such a lovely dress.'

She explained that it was one of three that Madame Jenny herself had given her as a wedding present. She told Percy all about working at Maison Jenny, and Percy was delighted that she was doing so well. And she told him, too, about Marie and how she'd started designing again, and had a collection together to present when she got home.

'That's marvellous, Vita,' Percy said. 'But . . .'

'What?'

'It's just that I did some investigating – about Top Drawer,' he said. And Vita frowned, hearing the note of caution in his voice.

'What about it?'

'Didn't you know? Top Drawer is already . . . out there.'

'What on earth do you mean?' Vita asked, startled and sitting up.

'W&T is stocking the bras in three different colours.'

Vita felt her heart pounding. 'Our design?'

'Yes. I had a good look – even though I appeared very suspicious, hanging around in the lingerie department, let me tell you.'

'You're *sure* they're the same bras?'

'Identical. Tiny alterations, because they've been machine-made. And machined properly.'

Her mind was racing. 'But how?'

'I don't know. Someone must have copied our designs. I have no idea how, though.'

Vita bit her lip, and then told Percy about giving the designs to Edith in return for the ticket to Paris.

'Edith?' Percy interrupted. 'You gave them to Edith?'

'Yes. That's how I got to be in Paris with Nancy.'

'But I bumped into Edith not so long ago. And she didn't mention anything about this at all.'

Vita listened as Percy described their encounter word-for-word.

'Do you think she was lying?' Percy said.

'Well, obviously she was lying. But why?' Vita put her head in her hands, trying to think. 'Did Edith say where she was living, or what she was doing?'

'No, but she looked very smart. She warned me not to get in touch with you, and I'm sorry I didn't sooner, Vita. What if she's behind this?'

Vita shook her head, trying to fathom out the implications of everything Percy had told her. She'd given Edith Top Drawer, in return for her freedom. But what did that mean? What part could Vita possibly play in Top Drawer now? Did

Edith expect her to go cap in hand to her? Did Edith want to be in charge of Vita? Or maybe it wasn't Edith at all. Maybe she'd given Vita's designs to someone else. It was all too much to take in.

'Nancy said Edith wouldn't do anything with the designs,' Vita commented.

'And everything Nancy says is true?' Percy asked, with a sceptical frown. He'd always taken Nancy with a pinch of salt.

'What if Edith took Top Drawer and made something of it?' Vita asked. 'I didn't think she would – didn't think she had what it took.'

'Well, maybe you underestimated her.'

Vita was aware that Irving would be waiting, and they walked back together to the hotel, with Vita stopping every so often to proclaim, 'Edith?'

And Percy seemed just as flummoxed by the whole idea of Edith running Top Drawer as she was. As they wandered across the sand, they discussed it some more.

'Whoever's behind it recognized a good idea,' Percy said. 'I told you that you were on to something.'

But Vita couldn't be consoled. It hurt far more than she'd thought it would that someone else had taken the credit for her work – her idea, her dream. But what could she do about it? She couldn't go back to England. Not now. Not only because of Irving, but because of Clement, too.

'I'll see what I can find out,' Percy said, 'but I won't be back in England for quite a while.'

When they got back to the promenade, Percy retrieved his bicycle.

'Don't be too disheartened about Top Drawer,' Percy told her. 'You've got plenty of good ideas. You can create your own lingerie line. It sounds as if what you've got going with this friend of yours . . .'

'Marie.'

'Yes, Marie – that sounds as if it could be just as good as Top Drawer. Better even.'

'I guess,' Vita said, but she couldn't shake the feeling that everything had changed.

'Follow your heart. Follow your dream. Don't give up,' Percy said and she nodded.

He touched her face and she held his hand against her cheek, not wanting to say goodbye. She'd missed Percy more than she could tell him, she realized.

'I'm glad you're happy, Vita,' he said. 'So very glad that you've found love.'

She nodded. 'Thank you.' She was pleased she'd painted such a good picture of her life with Irving, but now she felt tears behind her eyes.

'I guess it's just as well that you're happily married,' he said, as he got back onto his bicycle.

'Why's that?'

'Because I ran into your old flame, Archie Fenwick. He's writing his novel, apparently. He was here last night with friends.'

68

Cap Ferrat

Edith . . . Archie . . . Archie and Edith. Vita could barely walk back to the hotel, where Irving was already waiting for her in the car, with the final case being strapped to the rack on the back.

Archie was here. *Archie was here in the South of France; and Edith had taken her business.* Now, from being relaxed and happy, Vita was breathless with stress – or anticipation? She couldn't work it out.

'You all set, honey?' Irving called and she nodded, hardly able to look at him. 'Don't look so glum. You can drive, if you want.'

But as she sat in the driver's seat, she didn't want to start the car. She wanted to turn round and run after Percy. To grill him for more information about exactly where he'd seen Archie. Because now she couldn't help it – her mind was filled with what-ifs. What if Archie really was here? What if he was here in Nice, just as she was leaving?

'Are you quite all right? You finally got to see your friend – I thought you'd be happy,' Irving commented, and Vita shook herself, remembering where she was and what she was doing. Then she started up the engine and drove away from the hotel, and away from Nice. Away from the ghost of Archie Fenwick.

The road out to Cap Ferrat was breathtaking and Vita sped up, the car whizzing around the bends of the dramatic road, with the sea beside them a deep, sparkling blue.

'Steady on,' Irving shouted.

'Sorry,' she said, but her knuckles were white as she gripped the steering wheel.

'Hey, hey, slow down,' Irving shouted, and he pointed now to a new building on the cliff edge. 'You see that place?'

'Yes.'

'Coco Chanel is building her house there.'

Vita slowed some more and looked at the grand villa.

'Is she here?' Vita asked, thinking how wonderful it would be to meet the famous designer.

'She'll be on a yacht,' Irving said, 'with the Duke of Westminster, no doubt. But hey, if you fancy sailing, why don't I look up Diggers? We could go on his yacht?'

'Oh no, please don't,' Vita said.

'But why not, if he's around? There'll be a poker game, and you know how much I'm itching to play.'

By the time they made it to the famous Grand-Hôtel du Cap-Ferrat, Vita was exhausted, both emotionally and physically.

'Quite a journey,' Irving told the concierge, as they walked together through the marble hallway. 'My wife is a demon driver.'

Upstairs the honeymoon suite was possibly one of the most beautiful places Vita had ever been, but she could hardly take in the splendour of it all. She stood on the balcony, looking out at the long, manicured lawns leading down to a pool on the cliff edge, surrounded by striped bathing huts. The sea beyond had a golden glow to it – the famous light that all the painters loved. This was all theirs for the next few days, but Vita suddenly wished she was back in Paris with Marie. Back in her old life, where she could work out what everything meant.

'So what's up, Vita? You're very distracted,' Irving said.

She sighed and slumped into one of the armchairs by the open window. He sat down opposite, and she told him what Percy had said about Withshaw and Taylor stocking her bras.

Irving listened intently. 'Well, let that be a lesson to you. If you've got a good idea, then you'd better run with it. Otherwise someone else will get the jump on you.'

She nodded, annoyed that he was dispensing this advice, when she'd had to ask Marie to cancel their appointment at Galeries Lafayette because they were away. She felt another pang of guilt for being so idle here, when she had so much to get on with in Paris.

'When we get home, can I commission the carpenters to make the benches I want for the studio?' she asked him.

Irving laughed and kissed her. 'When we get home, you can do whatever you like. The house is a blank canvas. I'll give you the chequebook and get whatever you wish. Money is no object,' he said, and Vita went to him and hugged him.

'What's that for?' he said with a chuckle. She knew he probably thought she was keen to show how grateful she was for his generosity, but really the hug was to try to hold

362

on to him, to try to anchor herself, when her heart was in turmoil.

And as he led her to the bed, she told herself that she was safe with her new husband. She must forget all thoughts of Archie, and concentrate on her honeymoon. She had her future to look forward to.

69

The Man on the Quay

The Grand-Hôtel du Cap-Ferrat soon became a welcome sanctuary for Vita. She liked the pool and the lovely lounge, where she'd spent the last two afternoons with her sketchbook. She was busy designing again, her mind going over and over the fact that her bras were being sold by Withshaw and Taylor.

On the one hand, she was proud, and buoyed up, too, with the thought that her business idea was working; but on the other hand, it outraged her that it was *her* idea someone else was clearly making money from. Could Edith really have done that?

Well, whoever it was who'd got a head-start in England, Vita was not going to let them get the jump on her in Paris. This was *her* idea – hers alone. If anyone was going to get the credit for it, then it should be Vita.

But while her mind was fully occupied, when Irving suggested a few days later that they lunch in one of his favourite restaurants in Villefranche-sur-Mer, she knew he was bored. After their drive from Nice, he was keen to drive himself along the coast, and he teased Vita about how terrified he'd been on the way here. She laughed, enjoying the easy way they had of being together.

They'd talked a lot about the studio, and about Vita's business going forward, and she appreciated his encouragement. That said, Irving was of the opinion that she should go to Withshaw and Taylor and explain that the bras were hers, but she told him that was impossible. Mostly because she had no proof, but also because she didn't want to go back to England. Not now. Not ever. Not while Clement was still a threat.

She tried again to explain this to Irving over their sumptuous lunch of fresh lobster.

'Why don't I find him?' Irving offered. 'Have a manly chat. He's your brother, after all. I know you don't see eye to eye with your family, Vita, but this has got to stop, surely? You're a respectable married woman now. Surely it's time to set the record straight?'

'No,' Vita said. 'You mustn't. Clement's too dangerous.'

'I don't believe you,' Irving said. 'Nobody is that dangerous.'

'But people around him – they get hurt,' Vita said, thinking of the man who'd chased after her when she'd run away from Clement, when he'd found her at the Zip Club, and the thud of the bus. 'I couldn't bear anything to happen to you. I've told you before, I want nothing to do with my family. I'm making my own way, thank you very much.'

Vita wished he'd understand, but she saw that Irving couldn't, so she changed the subject. After lunch, she insisted that they walk it off, and they strolled along the quayside arm-in-arm and Vita admired the colourful fishing boats.

She'd brought her camera with her, and now she took some photographs, sighing to herself at the beauty of the place. But then, in the viewfinder, she saw a man at the far end of the quay. He was dressed in a light-blue short-sleeved shirt and cream slacks, with the slip-on canvas shoes that the fishermen wore. His skin was tanned, his hair streaked blond by the sun. He was walking towards them, his hands in his pockets, looking out towards the sea.

Vita felt her mouth go dry. *It couldn't be him, could it?* But as the man came closer, she saw that it was indeed him. It was Archie Fenwick. She told herself to run . . . to run as fast as she could.

'Let's go back,' she said.

'Oh no, it's so lovely here – let's walk to the end,' Irving suggested. 'Come on, you're always telling me to walk, and now I actually want to.'

Vita had no choice but to link arms with her husband, her heart hammering. She kept her face lowered, looking at her feet, and still Archie came closer and closer and she felt as if her cheeks were pounding and time was slowing down.

He hadn't noticed her and, as they walked past, she kept looking away from the sea, although it took every ounce of her strength not to turn and stare at him.

'Vita?' She heard his voice, and now Archie had retraced his steps and was standing in front of them, and she looked up at him. 'Vita?'

Her stomach seemed to turn to jelly as he took off his sunglasses and stared at her. Then he looked desperately at Irving, who put his hand over Vita's hand.

'What are *you* doing here?' Archie asked.

'I'm on my honeymoon,' she said, although her voice cracked and she masked it with a cough. 'Archie, this Irving

King,' she said, breaking her arm out of Irving's grasp and stepping back a little way, so that the two men could shake hands.

She could see that it was Archie's turn to blush now. 'So pleased to meet you,' he said, then he stood back, his arms akimbo. 'Married. Well, fancy that.'

'Archie is a friend from London,' Vita felt duty-bound to explain. 'Actually he's a friend of Cassius Digby.'

'You know Diggers?' Archie frowned at Vita and then at Irving.

'Sure,' Irving said. 'He was in Paris a while back. He's got a boat around here somewhere, hasn't he?'

'He has, that's right,' Archie said. 'He was heading up to Monte Carlo, last I heard. Where are you staying?' Archie said.

'The Grand-Hôtel du Cap-Ferrat. Best place on the whole Riviera,' Irving said. 'Honeymoon suite is top-notch.'

Archie nodded, his cheeks pink. 'Good – well, I'm glad. Congratulations to you both.'

'And you?' Irving asked, his direct manner startling Archie.

'Oh, I have a little apartment here,' he said. 'I'm here for a few weeks, finishing my novel.'

Irving looked at his watch and Archie's eyes searched out Vita's.

An awkward goodbye followed, and Archie hurried past them and up a lane between the buildings into the old town.

'Who was that?' Irving asked, as they walked on.

'Oh, just someone from way back.'

'Not an old flame?' Irving asked. 'Better not be, otherwise

there'll be pistols at dawn.' He was teasing her, Vita knew, but she turned away so that he couldn't see her face and pretended to look at the view.

'No, not at all.'

'It's all very well for these romantic young men to waft about the Riviera writing, but where's their grit, eh?'

'Quite,' Vita said.

70

Lilly

She didn't have a choice, she told herself, but even so Vita felt as if she were going to the gallows, as Irving helped her onto the tender that would take them out to Cassius's boat, *Lilly*, which was moored in the harbour. It had been so hot for the past few days that she could barely breathe, but now, as the small motor boat cut through the crystal-clear water, she felt the breeze on her face and turned towards it.

She didn't dare to hope – she didn't dare. But what if? What if Archie . . . ?

She had gone over and over their excruciating encounter on the quayside, which had left every part of her vibrating with longing. They'd exchanged so pitifully few sentences that she picked over them all for scraps of meaning.

Afterwards she'd tried to be breezy with Irving, backing up her lie that Archie was merely an acquaintance, but their vast suite of the splendid Grand-Hôtel du Cap-Ferrat now became the biggest stage of her life. She felt as if she were acting: her laughter and smiles all false, now that her mind was filled only with Archie. Archie, whom she had loved so passionately. The same Archie she hated, too. The Archie who was here – breathing the same air as her. The Archie who was writing in a little cottage, with . . . Maud? Was Maud here? Vita's mind raced. Was Maud now his muse, as Vita had hoped to be herself one day?

And then two days ago she'd been swimming in the pool on the cliff edge when she'd heard a noise coming from one of the striped bathing huts. She'd walked up the steps, drying off her hair on a towel.

'Hello?' she called tentatively, approaching the bathing hut, wondering if a cat or even a fox might have been hiding out in the cool interior.

And then Archie stepped out from the shadows, putting his finger to his lips to tell her to be quiet, and Vita gasped.

He put his hand on her arm and she backed away.

'You frightened me.' She looked around desperately, wondering if they were still alone by the pool, hoping to goodness that nobody had seen him. 'What on earth are you doing here?' she asked in a cross, lowered voice, even though she knew that they were alone.

How *dare* he come here! How dare Archie disturb her like this, when it had taken every ounce of her strength to stop thinking about him, day and night. He didn't deserve one minute of her time. Not one minute. Not after the way he'd treated her.

Archie looked crazed as he pulled her round to the back of the beach huts by the cliff steps.

'I had to see you. I rowed round. My boat is down there,' he said, nodding to the beach. Vita could see a tiny rowing boat bobbing next to the rocks. It was quite a way round the headland, and treacherous, too. He looked wild, his hair damp from the spray, his shirt plastered to his body. She felt an urge to put her hand on his chest, remembering how he'd looked naked, remembering how he'd touched her in the boathouse on that magical day long ago. Heat rose in her body at the memory, but she battled it down. She *would not* show Archie that she remembered.

But even so, her heart leapt at the risk he'd taken to see her.

'You can't be here,' Vita hissed. 'In fact I don't want to talk to you. I told you. I'm on my *honeymoon*.'

'But, Vita . . .'

'Don't! Don't you dare, Archie. Not after everything you've done. You have no right.'

'Vita, I'll do anything to spend time with you. *Anything*. Give me a chance to explain.'

'It's too late,' she said, refusing to meet his intense gaze.

'You don't mean that.'

'Irving is coming down for a swim any moment.'

If Archie heard her, he ignored it. 'Diggers has a big game on this weekend on board *Lilly*. I'll get an invite to your . . .' He couldn't say the word 'husband'. 'To . . . him, and then meet me there.'

'No.' She shook her head vigorously, her eyes filling with tears. Then she put her hands to her ears, wanting to block him out. 'No. Just go away. Leave me alone.'

'Vita.' His hand was on her arm and she whipped away from his touch, staggering backwards. Archie stood perfectly still, staring at her, and she stared back at him and her breath caught in her throat. Her stomach turned molten, and her heart was hammering as he stared at her with those eyes – those eyes she had loved so much. 'Please. I'm begging you.'

She pressed her lips together, biting them from the inside as she shook her head. Then she heard Irving's voice and sprang into action, pushing Archie towards the steps.

'Go – just go,' she said urgently.

And now Vita and Irving stood side-by-side in the tender as it gathered speed, and Irving grinned and dabbed his forehead with his handkerchief. He was wearing an open-necked sports shirt, and she could see that his chest was terribly burnt, but he wouldn't countenance protecting himself from the sun.

Vita smiled back, wondering if he had any sense of how tumultuous her thoughts had been, from that poolside moment until now. For a man who prided himself on looking for 'tells', Irving had failed to notice his wife going to hell and back.

Of course she'd begged him not to accept the invitation from Cassius Digby, but Irving had pooh-poohed all her reasons for not going.

Now, looking at the elegant lines of *Lilly*, with its teak decks and cream funnel, she felt like Anne Boleyn arriving at the Tower of London.

'You seem nervous,' Irving said.

'I told you before. It's been so lovely, being just the two of us,' she said. 'I don't want to meet lots of new people.'

But she knew Irving didn't feel the same. In fact this was exactly the kind of social engagement he adored. Not to mention the added delight of the poker game that he wanted to get stuck into. She knew he'd always been in awe of the aristocracy, and later, as they were introduced to the crowd gathered in the salon, Vita could see him lapping up the credentials of the elite company.

Vita smiled wanly as all the introductions were made, already on the lookout for Archie, although she felt the eyes of the other women on her and knew that she was being judged for being Irving's young wife.

Later, after they'd been shown to their cabin, they dressed for dinner and Irving was excited about joining the gathering, but Vita felt out of sorts as they went up to the salon. She fanned herself, feeling hot in the evening dress she'd worn. It was one of Jenny's pieces that Irving had bought for her wedding trousseau.

'Is this a Maison Jenny?' Heda asked. She was a plain woman in her fifties with a large double chin. She touched the chiffon sleeve of Vita's dress. 'So very elegant.'

'Thank you.'

'Isn't that where Irving found you? At Maison Jenny?' another woman asked, as if Vita were no more than a stray cat. She had wide-set eyes and cropped, dyed red hair and smoked with an air of entitlement that had always annoyed Vita, although other people seemed to find it irresistible. She was Belinda, Vita remembered from their introduction earlier. Belinda Getty. Her low-cut gown was embroidered with lavish beads, and Vita recognized it as one from the Chanel collection. It was worth a fortune.

Belinda removed the ebony cigarette-holder from her mouth and blew smoke towards the inlaid wooden ceiling.

'That's right. I was helping Daphne. Irving's daughter.'

'Oh, I know who Daphne is. You're so brave to take on

those children,' Belinda laughed, with a grimace at Heda. 'Particularly the younger one.'

Vita didn't want to let on that she had yet to meet Irving's younger daughter, Hermione.

'Yes . . . rather you than me, darling,' Belinda said, but her look wasn't friendly as she said it, and Vita wondered what she meant. Did Belinda have some kind of past with Irving? She smiled, a knowing feline grin, and the conversation moved on, but Vita was left feeling rattled.

Apart from hearing about Alicia, she had very little idea of Irving's former romantic life and wondered how many other women he'd dated before she'd started going out with him. He'd always been the one to be jealous, and the focus had always been on Vita and her past conquests. She'd never questioned him, assuming that there'd been Alicia and then, heartbroken, he hadn't had any other serious girlfriends until Vita. But maybe that wasn't the case at all.

She was still mulling over this when dinner was called. It was a lavish affair in a smart dining room, with a wonderful view of the harbour in the sunset. Vita sat quietly next to Irving, who was holding forth about his poker successes. She counted a full table of eighteen guests; when the spaces had all filled up and Archie didn't come for dinner, she started to relax a little.

He wasn't here. Not tonight, in any case. Which meant that tonight she was off the hook. She could relax, she told herself, realizing how much she'd been on tenterhooks. And if Archie wasn't here now, then maybe he wouldn't come at all.

71

Moonlight on the Water

The poker game took place in the *grand salon* and, unlike
the rest of the wives, who retired to the library for post-dinner
drinks, Vita joined the men to watch Irving play his first
hand.

'You here alone, Cassius?' Irving asked. 'You got yourself
a wife yet?'

Diggers laughed. 'Not one as good as yours,' he joked. 'If
only there were more out there like Vita.'

She smiled, but felt the hairs on the back of her neck
standing up as Diggers shuffled the pack and his eyes met
hers. 'I came with a friend, but he's not a poker player. He's
an artistic type and likes to keep himself to himself. He's
probably up on deck.'

Vita didn't move and forced herself not to react, suspecting
that Diggers was watching her closely. She refused to give
herself away, but her mind raced. Did he mean that Archie
was here? And was that a code for her to go and join him
on deck? Did that mean Diggers knew about her and Archie?
Not that there was anything between them now, but if he
knew about the past and told Irving? Vita couldn't let that
happen. Irving would be beside himself if he knew that she

and Archie had been lovers, especially when she'd already lied to his face.

Oh, this was such a mess. Such an agonizing mess. It was excruciating staying in the smoky salon as the men played and she pretended to be jollying Irving along. Eventually she couldn't bear it any longer.

'I'm going to get some air,' she told him, kissing the side of his head. 'Good luck, darling.'

'I don't need it,' Irving said, showing her his cards, and she could see that he had a good hand.

'You see, is that a bluff or a double bluff?' Cassius asked, laughing. 'Vita, are you in on the act?'

'You'll never know,' she said coyly and made for the door.

Outside, the lights of Monte Carlo glowed against the black hills in the distance. Vita, keen to avoid the wives, took the long way round to the top deck. She hadn't been lying when she said she needed some air. Her skin prickled in the welcome evening breeze and she breathed in deeply, then stood looking at the moon rising over the water. She cursed herself for agreeing to come, wishing that she'd stayed in Cap Ferrat in the safety of the hotel.

She heard music and laughter as a door opened and closed along the deck, and then it went quiet again. She should go back inside and join the other women, she told herself. She couldn't be out here alone. Not after what Diggers had implied – that Archie was on board somewhere on this yacht. Besides, what if Irving lost his hand and came looking for her?

And then she heard a noise behind her.

'Vita.'

She closed her eyes, hearing soft footsteps as Archie

came and stood beside her. He placed his hands on the rail, just an inch away from hers. His body was so close, she could sense his warmth, smell his familiar scent. She knew instinctively that she should move away, but standing here, side-by-side, felt so momentous. She thought of how she'd felt standing next to Irving in front of the French registrar only a few weeks ago. That had had none of the gravitas of this moment.

She tried to remember her planned speech: about how much Archie had hurt her; how vile his mother had been; how unforgiveable his behaviour was, using her as he had. She'd planned to tell him that she'd given him everything – all of herself – and he'd thrown her away, as if she meant nothing.

Instead she found herself drinking him in, like a desert flower drinking in rain. Archie Fenwick was here. Her Archie. Right here. Within touching distance. Her heart pounded so hard, she wondered if he could hear it, too. She could feel herself shaking and gripped the rail. The moment stretched and stretched, and a voice in her head was screaming at her to move, to run away, to get inside to safety, but she didn't move.

'Oh, Vita, I'm so glad you came,' he whispered. 'You have no idea.'

She let out the breath she'd been holding. 'I'm going inside,' she said, but still she didn't move. 'I don't want to be seen with you.'

'I understand,' Archie said, with the expression of a whipped dog.

She swallowed hard and kept her voice level as she asked, 'Does he know? Diggers? About us?'

'He won't say anything.'

So yes, he *did* know. Archie sounded flippantly confident, but Vita felt a dart of dread and closed her eyes.

'You don't understand,' she said, remembering Irving's jealous rages. It had been bad enough him seeing her with Fletch, but if he found out the truth about Archie . . . 'Oh God, I wish I hadn't come.'

But now as she turned towards him, her eyes locked with Archie's and the words dropped between them, like the lies they were.

'Oh, Vita,' he said, reaching out and putting his hand over hers. The gesture was so intimate, so possessive, and she pulled her hand away. He had no right to touch her like that, not after everything he'd put her through, but still her stomach did back-flips of delight. '*I'm* glad you're here. I needed to see you, to talk. That's all.'

'What do you wish to say to me?' she asked, her voice rising. 'Apart from "sorry". Although I'm not sure you could say it enough times to make up for how much you hurt me.'

'I didn't mean to,' he said. 'Oh, Vita, please, you've got to believe me.'

But she shook her head; her heart was hearing the words, but she forced herself to remember.

'You used me,' she said. 'You and your friend Georgie – you had a plan. What did your mother say?' she asked, trying to keep the scornful tears that now rose in her voice. '"I couldn't accept my son going into his marriage as a virgin.

And I wouldn't countenance him going to a prostitute. So I found the next best thing . . . you.'''

He hung his head. 'It wasn't like that. I'd seen you before any of that happened. At the Café de Paris. You remember? On the staircase? When we saw each other? I know you do, Vita. Look at me.'

There was a beat as she saw how much he meant it.

'You know what an awful meddler Georgie is,' he continued, imploring her to understand. 'And Mother? Well, I'm sorry she was . . . vile. What she said was unforgivable. *I* certainly haven't forgiven her. We haven't spoken since the wedding. She might have got Hartwell back, but I've washed my hands of her.'

Vita shook her head. She couldn't accept Archie's apology. She mustn't. She turned now, the gentle breeze from the sea blowing her hair, and she pulled it away from her face. She must go. She must walk away. He'd said what he wanted to say. And did she believe him? She ached for his words to be true, but knew she might get sucked in again. She'd fought for too long, too hard, to forget him. She wrapped her arms around herself, nodded once and then walked towards the light, her mind made up.

'Please don't walk away. Do you have any idea how much I've missed you? How I've thought about you every single day. That night on the roof? It was the best night of my life.'

'Don't, Archie,' she said in a husky whisper, turning back to look at him. 'Don't say those things. You can't do this. You can't just walk back into my life,' she said, indignant tears coming now as he walked towards her. She didn't want to be emotional, but she couldn't help it. 'You're married.'

'And so are you. And to *him*?'

'Don't you dare judge Irving,' Vita said angrily. 'He's been kind to me.'

'Kind? You married for kindness?'

'And you married for money. And for your mother.'

Their heads were inches apart, their eyes blazing, but now Archie grabbed her, pulling her towards him, and as she let out a helpless cry, he kissed her hard. For a second she felt weightless, as if her whole body was melting against his.

But then she gasped and, coming to her senses, pulled away and slapped his face – hard.

'Don't you dare,' she cried, backing away now, knowing this had been a terrible mistake. Knowing that what she must do was go back to her husband.

But Archie called out after her. 'I know you, Vita,' he said. 'You can't escape this.'

'You don't know me,' she countered. How could she begin to explain to Archie that everything she'd told him about herself was a lie?

She could see tears in his eyes. 'Vita,' he pleaded. 'I think of you all the time. I never *stop* thinking about you. I think about you so much, I often wonder if I can make myself appear in your thoughts. Do I . . . ever?'

If only he knew, she thought. If only Archie knew that for so long it had been exactly the same for her.

'It's too late,' she said, backing away and running towards the safety of the wives, where she could hide and drink away her broken heart.

72

A Hint of the Past

Irving came to bed at three in the morning, but Vita was still wide awake.

'I was looking for you in the lounge. It's quite a party in there,' he said, slurring slightly as he threw off his jacket. She noticed the patches of sweat under his arms. He reeked of brandy and cigars, and his cheeks were pink.

After her encounter with Archie, Vita had joined the wives in the salon, briefly, but she felt excluded from their conversation, so she'd come to bed early and had spent the last few hours in a state of nervous anxiety, replaying what had happened with Archie over and over. And remembering the kiss. Oh, the *kiss* . . .

'I wanted to read my book.'

'Oh, my sensible little wife,' he said. 'I so love you.'

'Did you win?' she asked.

'I was neck-and-neck with Diggers for a while, and then he won. But guess what?' Irving sat on the bed with a large harrumph, jolting her and overbalancing as he tried to take off his shoe. 'He's got me an "in" with Le Monsieur. There's a game at the casino tomorrow night. You don't mind if I play, do you?'

'No,' she said, hearing his excitement. 'I'd like to go to the casino.'

'Oh,' he said, wrinkling his nose. 'Little wife, I'm afraid it's men only. Diggers will be leading the charge. I think the girls are staying here. I've heard there are fireworks, so you'll be able to watch them from the yacht. You'll have the best view in the harbour.'

She nodded, annoyed that he was leaving her here. And as he got into bed next to her and she cuddled up to him, she vowed that she'd find something else to do tomorrow, to avoid being here alone with the wives. And with Archie.

Irving slept in late and Vita, feeling claustrophobic in the stuffy cabin, went up to the sun-deck for some air. Four of the women from last night were on the sun-loungers, their laughter and animated chatter stopping when they saw Vita. But before they did so, she thought she heard Heda saying, 'Someone to tame Irving, at long last. I mean . . . all those other women. *Poor* Alicia.'

Vita nodded a good morning, but she felt their gazes like a rebuke and walked the other way, although her mind was racing. Other women? What other women? What did they mean? She wished she'd had the confidence to challenge them, but she knew she couldn't. Not now.

When Irving got up, she could tell he was hungover, but even so, she felt sulky and annoyed.

'Can't we go out for the day?' she asked. 'Just the two of us?'

'I want to relax. Chat to Cassius,' he said with a yawn. 'I need to reserve my energy for tonight.'

Vita tutted and sighed, and Irving pulled her towards him. 'Vita darling, you're on one of the best luxury yachts in the world, with some of the finest women in society. I'm sure you can find a way to entertain yourself.'

'I don't think they like me,' Vita said.

'I'm sorry if it's awkward,' Irving replied, kissing her on the nose. 'You see, most of them know Alicia rather well.' Vita swallowed her feeling of humiliation. 'But you're my wife now,' he said. 'They'll have to get used to it.'

She looked at him, longing to ask him the questions that burnt in her mind – about his affairs, about the other women she'd heard the wives discussing – but knew she couldn't. Not now, and not ever. Irving had made it very clear that he liked earthly pleasures, so it shouldn't come as a surprise that meant women, too.

But now Vita felt unsure and exposed. What did those other wives know about him that she didn't? Irving seemed to adore her, but she saw now that it didn't necessarily follow that he'd be faithful to her. But then what about his problems in the bedroom department? Did those women know the truth about his inability to perform? Is that why Irving was so keen to show off his young wife? Because she made him look good?

73

The Library

If Archie didn't want to be seen on board *Lilly*, then he was doing a good job of it, as he didn't arrive for lunch, or later that afternoon after they'd played croquet on deck, or even after dinner, when the light started to fade and the tender took the men – all dressed in tuxedos – from the yacht back to shore. Vita was still annoyed that she wasn't going to get to see the famous casino.

She watched them go, then retired to the library in a bid to avoid the gossiping women, and to pick a book for her bedtime reading. In the library she allowed the butler to pour her a gin and tonic as she studied the books. There was the most wonderful collection on board, and Cassius Digby clearly had good taste.

She sat in one of the chairs, looking at a new edition of *Lady Chatterley's Lover* as the waiter retreated, but then he held open the door as Archie slipped through it. He was casually dressed, in slacks, a shirt and a paisley cravat. She looked at his tanned arms as he put his hands in his pockets.

'I thought you'd gone,' she said, trying to keep her voice neutral – or sounding annoyed at least.

'No.'

'Have you been spying on me? Is that why you're here?'

'Of course. I've been waiting for them to go. It's been torture.'

She sighed. 'I have nothing more to say, after last night.' She picked up the book and pretended to read.

'You know, I've finished my manuscript,' Archie said, walking towards her. 'It's called *Sylvine*. It's about a woman . . . No, it's not about a woman. It's about you.'

She looked up at him, her cheeks pulsing, the memory of last night's kiss branded on her memory.

'Good for you, Archie, but I don't want to hear it. In fact I don't think we can be alone like this,' she said, snapping the book shut and putting it down.

'Vita, please,' he said. Then he knelt down beside her. 'I'm lost without you. I hate being married to Maud, when all I can think about is you. So tell me that you're happy with Irving – that he's everything to you – and I'll go away and leave you in peace.'

She felt tears stinging her eyes. She looked up and away from him, willing them not to fall. Archie's finger touched her hand and, just as she had last night, she felt her whole body trembling. He knelt up and their faces were close.

'Look me in the eye. Tell me to go,' he whispered, but she couldn't. He reached out and held her chin, and then his face was coming towards hers and she was lost in a kiss that felt like home.

74

Fireworks

They sprang apart when the library door opened and the butler came back in.

'Would you like another drink, sir?' he asked Archie.

Vita rushed over towards the window, but her cheeks were burning. Had the butler seen them kissing?

What if he had? What then? What if everyone found out about her and Archie? She could barely believe this was happening. Her pulse was racing and she was breathless, as Archie gave the butler some money and sent him on his way.

'We can't do this,' she said in a shocked whisper, turning to him and putting her hand on her chest. 'Everyone will find out.'

'No, they won't. Come on,' he said, holding out his hand for her. 'Follow me.'

'Where are we going?' she whispered, as Archie held her hand and led her down the corridor and then up a couple of staircases. Out on deck, he peered round the corner, holding her hand in the shadows, then slipped round to where the lifeboats were attached to the deck.

'I have spent the entire day working out how we can be

alone and not be seen by anyone. And it's in here,' he said, nodding down to the lifeboat, which was roped to the side of the yacht. 'Come on.'

Her teeth were chattering, but not with the cold, as Vita let him help her over the rail, and soon they were on the rope ladder and he helped her down to the lifeboat, which swung slightly as they got into it. There was a pile of blankets and a bottle of champagne.

'It's quite a nest you've made here,' she said, amazed that he'd thought all this through. Amazed that he'd assumed she would come with him. But before she could protest, he kissed her again. And suddenly all the pent-up sexual desire she'd been storing seemed to throb through her body and, when he lay her down, his lips didn't leave hers.

'Oh, Vita,' he gasped, pulling up her skirt, and she felt a need like she'd never felt before. 'Vita, my love.'

Soon they were both half-naked, and then he was inside her and she wrapped her legs around him and she was lost, her whole being seeming to fuse with his. She'd never experienced this intensity before as they moved together in silent communion, staring into one another's eyes, her body yielding to his, melting into his. She saw him holding his breath and she too could barely breathe; his eyes closed and suddenly, at the same time as his, she felt her orgasm shuddering through her, as the fireworks lit up the sky above the harbour, the noise masking their cries of delight. Vita looked up, seeing Archie's face illuminated by the lights, and she didn't think about Irving. Only that she loved this man. She loved this man and she must lose him again.

Afterwards he kissed her as she nestled into his arms,

looking up at the stars. She felt as if this were the only place in the entire world she wanted to be.

'We should cut the ropes and drift off,' he said. 'How far could we get before anyone noticed?'

'Oh, Archie,' she sighed. 'Don't say that.'

'We wouldn't have any money,' he said, 'but we could live a simple life.'

'I don't care about money,' she said.

'Oh, Vita, let's do it. Let's just go and live together till we're old.'

'But . . .'

'There are no buts.'

'You know there are,' she said, leaning up on her elbow. 'You're married, and I am, too.'

'Then what are you saying? That we should only have this? Whatever "this" is? An affair?'

'No. This . . . this can't happen again.'

'You don't mean that.'

'I do. I really do. You see, it won't work. Irving will be on to us in a second. He reads people . . .'

'He doesn't read you. Not like I do,' Archie said.

He was right, but she persevered. 'And what would happen if Maud found out? You'd lose Hartwell, your friends, your chances of getting published.' She felt cruel spelling it out like that, but it was the truth. 'It has to be this way, Archie,' she said. 'It has to.'

'You can't mean that, Vita,' he said. 'In your heart you can't mean that, after tonight.'

'Archie, I've made a commitment to Irving. And you have to Maud. We had our chance.'

'And what now?'

'We get dressed and get back on board, without being seen, and I'll go to my cabin and you'll leave and . . .' her voice broke, 'and go home to Maud.'

He put his hand on her cheek and stared into her eyes. 'Is that what you want?'

She nodded, but she couldn't hold his gaze. Then Archie kissed her and she cried as she kissed him back. And then he was kissing her more, and she clung to him. And as they made love again, it was slow and more intense than she'd ever imagined possible.

'We will be together,' he whispered. 'Somehow. One day.'

75

At the Carousel

Edith had arrived in Paris late last night, determined to enjoy every second of her break away from Clement.

Oh, the joy of travelling alone. For the first time in a long time, Darton and all the worries about the new machinery and the impending strike action by the workers were solely Clement's problem for a blissful few days.

She'd had a splendid breakfast at the hotel – French croissants really were something special – and had wandered along the Champs-Élysées looking in all the shop windows, marvelling at the fashions and the stylish women everywhere. She'd even stopped outside Maison Jenny.

No wonder Vita had been inspired to design – everywhere she looked, everything was so *chic*. But all too soon she had to tear herself away from the shops because it was time to leave to meet Marianne in the Tuileries Gardens. She knew that Marianne had chosen the rendezvous point by the Italian carousel because she was expecting Edith to bring Susan. In truth, Edith did feel a slight pang of guilt for setting Marianne's hopes so high, but she'd really never had any intention of bringing that awful pale child.

For a start, travelling with her and putting up with her

sullen silence would have been unbearable. Not to mention seeing the reunion between mother and daughter, which Edith had no stomach for. Not now that she'd never experience that for herself. It still stung so bitterly that Marianne had borne Clement a child and that she never would.

She waited, listening to the breathy pipe-music and looking at the ornate medieval figurines that reminded her of the Punch & Judy shows of her youth. She started fanning herself, wishing she'd brought sunglasses, as the sun was so bright.

At first she didn't recognize the woman coming into view as Marianne. Her husband's lover was suntanned, her hair a halo of gold in the sun. She was wearing a stylish mint-green drop-waisted sailor dress, which showed off her slim figure and fine ankles.

'Hello, Marianne,' Edith said, as if they'd seen each other yesterday and not months ago, and trying to hide her shock at her altered appearance.

'Where is she?' Marianne asked, her eyes dancing with delight, looking hopefully at the rising and falling painted horses on the carousel. She walked closer, leaning over the looped railings, scanning the faces of the laughing children on top of the carousel horses, but none of them were Susan.

Edith watched her expression change.

'Mrs Darton?'

'She's not here.'

'But you said . . . you said you'd bring her.' Marianne sounded indignant and Edith felt her hackles rise. She didn't owe this woman anything.

'I've brought this instead,' Edith said curtly, opening her handbag and handing over her carefully crafted letter.

She'd been to the school before she'd come to Paris, to make sure that Susan was safely enrolled in the summer programme. She'd taken the liberty of bringing some school photographs to show Marianne, who now studied them carefully, her face almost touching the small rectangles of black-and-white paper. There was one of Susan on the lacrosse team, her spindly legs on show and a small gap between her and the rest of the team.

'She doesn't look—' Marianne began, but stopped, her eyes full of tears.

'She's doing very well, as I'm sure she says in her letter. She's filling out with all that exercise and fresh air, and she simply loves her lessons. She's very happy at you being here and working for me. It's a very satisfactory plan.'

'But . . .'

Edith gave Marianne a stern look and she lowered her eyes, clutching the photographs of Susan to her chest.

'I don't have long, and I'm very hot,' Edith said. 'I want to see the stock and get prepared for the meeting tomorrow.'

'As you wish,' Marianne said.

Edith couldn't believe that Vita and Nancy had had this wonderful city all to themselves – and all that *fun* – when she'd been in rain-soaked Darton. The feeling that she'd missed out gnawed at her as Edith walked up the stairs to Marianne's apartment, with the ghost of Vita and Nancy's laughter seeming to ring in her ears.

In the cramped apartment Edith fingered Vita's hats and

admired her clothes, as Marianne lifted the large brown leather suitcase onto the bed. She opened it and Edith inspected the contents. She pulled out the individually wrapped brassieres in their pink tissue, stunned – now that she was seeing this new stock in close-up – at how much more glamorous they were even than the latest Top Drawer stock they were producing in Darton.

'And this is what you've made so far?' she asked and Marianne nodded. She'd been so sullen all the way here and Edith wished she'd cheer up. On the metro she'd read the letter from Susan over and over again.

'I have to say, your workmanship is very good, Marianne,' she said, throwing the woman a bone. Edith had come all this way, armed with the letter and photos. The least Marianne could do was cheer up and be grateful.

'Vita has taught me such a lot. And she's paid me for each one of these.'

Edith curled her lip, annoyed that Marianne had mentioned the money. Vita might think she was keeping Marianne, but it was Edith who was paving the way for this whole arrangement to work.

'I hope you haven't forgotten, Marianne, that you work for me.'

'How can I?'

Edith was shocked by her bitter tone, and now she saw that Marianne's eyes were red with spiteful tears.

'Aren't you happy with the news from home?' she enquired.

'Yes, but . . .'

'What? What's the matter?'

'Frankly, Mrs Darton, the letters don't sound like Susan,' she said. 'She doesn't talk to me like that. Are you sure she wrote them?'

Edith felt a shiver of alarm. She'd perfected the childish writing, although it was demeaning to do so. To hear that her efforts hadn't worked was a blow.

'Of course I'm sure,' Edith snapped, a little too harshly, and she scowled at Marianne. 'You're being very obtuse. I'm happy to stop sending the letters, you know. I can easily cut off contact altogether.'

There was silence as Edith examined more of the bras. Marianne silently wrapped up the ones she'd looked at, putting them back in a neat order.

'I think we should take all of these to our meeting,' Edith said. 'I think they'll be snapped up.'

Marianne sighed. 'But . . . but what will happen when she finds out? Vita, I mean? Because she will, and she'll suspect me.'

How sad that Marianne craved Vita's respect and friendship so much.

'You're resourceful and clever, Marianne. You've proved that to me. Find a way of excusing what has happened. Blame someone else. Vita thinks you're her friend, and I need it to stay that way. I want you to stay close and keep your eyes on her. I want to know everything she says and everything she does.'

Marianne rubbed her eyes.

'How long will this last? How long do you expect me to be here? Only I'm desperate to see Susan.'

'I wish you wouldn't complain so much, Marianne. You

have a nice life here and your daughter is getting a good education.'

'But if this meeting works and they stock Vita's bras, what then? What about the money?'

'The money?'

Edith stared at Marianne, seeing clearly for the first time that the woman was a lot less stupid than she'd thought. Not only that, but she thought she had some kind of right to this whole enterprise.

'The money,' Edith said levelly, 'is what you owe me. Do you have any idea how expensive that school is?'

76

Post-Honeymoon Blues

Vita had found the perfect modern glass vase, which she'd positioned in front of the mirror on the table at the bottom of the sweeping staircase. She admired it now, hoping it would be the first thing Irving would see when he came in. She stood back and picked up the long-stemmed roses from the newspaper on the floor, to start arranging them.

She looked at herself briefly in the mirror, and at the marble steps going down to the grand foyer and front door of the new house behind her. It was six weeks since they'd returned from their honeymoon and had moved in officially, but it felt longer. Vita looked at her reflection more closely now and saw that she was grey and tired, and she resolved to go and change and do her make-up before Irving returned from his latest trip.

She had been warned by a few of Irving's friends' wives that there might be a post-honeymoon slump, but settling into life in the new house was trickier than Vita had expected.

She missed her job terribly and she'd asked Irving to reconsider letting her work at Madame Jenny's, but when she'd gone to visit the offices on the Champs-Élysées, she'd felt like an outsider. Everyone had treated her differently, now that she was married to Irving. She'd left feeling as if she were in the way, with Beatrice and Laure's good wishes ringing in her ears, but no invitation to return in a hurry – apart from as a customer.

Even Georges, the doorman, treated her more deferentially and, as she'd walked away, she'd felt bereft. She hadn't realized how much she'd got used to the camaraderie of the girls and being part of a team. She resented Irving for making her give up her promising career, especially when the days when he was at his club or away on business stretched before her.

Then last week, just after Irving had gone on his latest business trip, Hermione had turned up unexpectedly from school, with her childhood governess, Isadora, in tow. Irving, on the telephone, laughingly apologized to Vita that he'd forgotten to tell her, and that Vita should make his daughter and Isadora welcome. Isadora was a 'gem', he'd said, and the girls never went anywhere without her. Vita was to treat her like a member of the family. And it was fortuitous timing, he'd pointed out, since Vita had yet to hire any staff. Isadora could fill in. She was an excellent cook, Irving enthused, telling Vita to request her *boeuf bourguignon*.

It was hardly the introduction Vita had been hoping for, and she was soon out of her depth. Isadora told her the house simply wouldn't do and set to work, cleaning it from top to bottom, tutting at the builders' dust and turning her nose up when more furniture arrived. She kept muttering that Alicia would never have bought the things Vita did, and Vita was irritated that she was constantly being compared unfavourably to Irving's last wife.

Irving had once told her that his younger daughter was the spitting image of her mother, in both temperament and looks. Vita had assumed that Hermione's and Daphne's mother, Alicia, was a simpering kind of woman, who hadn't – in his own words – been 'in tune' with Irving, but as she was rapidly discovering, that wasn't the case at all. And if Alicia was anything like Hermione, then she was stubborn, hard and extremely difficult to win over. Daphne had been spoilt enough, but Hermione was on a whole other level, and Vita remembered the warning she'd received on *Lilly* from Belinda Getty.

But oh, how Vita tried. However, the fifteen-year-old with her blonde, quivering ringlets had refused to let herself even be kissed by her new stepmother when they'd first met. In the week since then, things had hardly improved, and Vita wondered how she'd cope in front of Irving, when he returned home later from his business trip.

Marie had assured her that everything was so new, and the change was so sudden, that it was bound to be difficult. It wasn't easy being a mother, she said, but Hermione would come round.

Vita tried to take comfort in Marie's words, but secretly she knew it wasn't her new role as Irving's wife, or being an unwanted stepmother, that was really bothering her. No, it was the constant gut-churning, sleep-depriving fact of what she'd done with Archie. It was so huge . . . so much so that half the time she could hardly breathe when she thought of him and their magical time on the Riviera.

She tried – over and over again – to find a plausible justification for what had happened, but there was no escaping the horrible way in which she'd betrayed her new husband. The absolutely unforgivable way in which she'd already broken her marriage vows. And the lie of it – the constant lie felt as if it were eating her from the inside out.

On their return from *Lilly*, Irving had seemed completely oblivious to her turmoil, and that had only made it worse. Lying next to him at night as he snored, Vita felt torn in two with guilt and longing, as her mind returned again and again to those precious hours with Archie. And her heart felt so painful, she was worried that she might be ill.

There hadn't been a choice, she told herself now, as she prodded the long-stemmed roses into the vase. Either to succumb to the overwhelming attraction she'd felt for Archie or to end their fleetingly rekindled relationship. As Nancy would have said, it was unfinished business and, in one sense, having had her questions answered was a relief. Archie *had* loved her. It hadn't been a lie. He'd felt the same as she did – possibly even more wretched, from everything he'd said.

So what had happened with Archie was consigned to the most treasured vaults of her memory. That crazy interlude could *never* happen again. She would just have to live on the memory of it. That would have to be enough.

It was easier in the daytime, of course, when she filled every hour that she could with shopping for the house and making it beautiful, like she was now. As promised, Irving had given her a large chequebook and told her to buy whatever pleased her, and for the past weeks she'd trawled endlessly through the streets of Paris, buying lamps and paintings and rugs, sideboards, dining furniture and art. She'd concentrated on making Hermione's room the nicest – not that she appreciated it at all.

But the purchases didn't bring Vita the satisfaction or joy she'd hoped. She was building a home – a fortress for her and Irving to live in – but now the future without Archie seemed like a prison sentence.

Sometimes Marie came shopping with her, but she'd been different since Vita had come back from her honeymoon, not in an obvious way, but she was definitely more reserved and a little distant. She sensed that Marie was sad they were no longer living together. Or maybe it was Vita's constant shopping that highlighted how different their lifestyles were.

Vita, of course, insisted on continuing to pay for the apartment at Madame Vertbois's where Marie was making her brassieres, but it must have been strange for Marie to be there alone. She didn't really seem to have a life beyond Vita.

And it was this that gave Vita the motivation to get the studio finished, so that Marie could come every day and they could work together. The pattern-cutting benches had been commissioned, and Vita had had carpenters working round the clock while Irving was away. She could hear the hammers upstairs, and she couldn't wait for the room to be finished to show Marie how wonderful it looked.

At least her business was starting up again, Vita consoled herself, putting the finishing touches to the flower arrangement and screwing up the newspaper. Finally there was a real chance to get things up and running, and her pieces out there, being seen and bought and enjoyed. It mattered that she made her mark in Paris and could prove to Madame Sacerdote that her faith in Vita hadn't been for nothing.

She couldn't wait for this meeting that Marie had arranged at the famous department store next week. Because with a commission under her belt, she would throw herself into her business and build a team of her own. And if she was a success at that, then her marriage wouldn't matter so much, would it?

77

Hermione

Vita was just clearing away the leaves and newspaper when Hermione came in through the front door with Isadora. They'd been out and were laughing, but they both stopped abruptly when they saw Vita on the half-landing.

Vita flushed in the intensity of Isadora's dark gaze, as the older woman shuffled towards the kitchen.

'Have you had a nice time?' she asked Hermione, with an attempt at a bright smile.

'It's none of your business,' Hermione countered, coming up the stairs towards her, and Vita flinched at the hostility in her voice.

'Please, Hermione,' Vita said. 'Can we not try to be friends? For your father's sake, if nothing else?'

'Why would I be friends with you? I told you. He only married you to annoy Mommy,' Hermione said, her green eyes narrowing scornfully.

Vita felt the words like physical barbs, but forced herself to stay calm.

'It's true,' the young girl said with utter conviction. 'Daphne says that Grandmama in New York says she'll never have you in her house. That you'll never get any of her money.'

'I don't want her money,' Vita said, stung that Hermione and Daphne between them had already soured her relationship with Irving's ageing mother, whom she had yet to meet.

'Of course you do. That's why you married Daddy. A gold-digger. That's what Mommy calls you.' She stared straight at Vita as she said this, seeking her reaction.

'I really don't have any interest in what your mother says,' Vita said coolly, trying to keep her voice level. 'It is of no concern to me. And as for being a gold-digger – for your information, I will be making my own money.'

Hermione made a grunting sound and stamped past her up the stairs. Vita watched her go to the room on the first floor and slam the door with unnecessary force.

Vita gripped the edge of the table, suddenly wanting to take the vase of flowers and hurl it up the stairs after the girl. She was still there, trying to compose herself, but feeling dizzy and nauseous, when Marie came through the front door.

'Oh, Marie,' Vita said, startled.

'It was open,' she said, looking back to the door. She was carrying the large brown suitcase. 'I heard a little bit of that,' she said with a sympathetic look. 'Are things no better?'

Vita was so grateful for her concern – for the fact that at least she had one friend. She shook her head, battling down tears, and Marie gave her a sympathetic look.

'Vita, you mustn't let her win. You mustn't let her have all the control.'

'You're right,' Vita nodded, taking a breath and trying to stop the tears. 'At least we can hide in the studio,' she said. 'Come and see. It's nearly finished. Are those all the pieces?' she asked. 'Here, let me take it.'

'No, it's fine,' Marie said, holding on to the suitcase. 'It's not heavy.'

'How many are in there – did you count?' Vita asked.

'Over a hundred,' Marie replied, her eyes bright.

Over a hundred, Vita thought, as she followed Marie with her precious cargo up the stairs. It was sweet that Marie was so attached to the case. The contents represented such a lot of hard work. Hard work that very soon would result in a commission, Vita was sure. Tomorrow they would work in the studio together for the first time, and it would be a whole fresh start.

78

The Pianola

Vita had suspected it, but the moment Irving came home later that evening, it was obvious that Hermione was going to do everything she possibly could to compete for his affection, practically sitting on his lap and putting on a babyish voice. All of which Irving lapped up, not seeming to notice what an act it was, or how Hermione was deliberately trying to annoy Vita.

Even worse, he was delighted to see Isadora, to whom he spoke in fluent Spanish, which made the old nanny completely melt, and she laughed and laughed and held on to Irving's arm. Vita realized that the two of them had lived together for many years, and when he invited Isadora to join them for dinner, Vita felt even more left out of their old jokes and memories.

Trying to win him over, she took Irving on a tour of the house to show him all the things she'd bought while he'd been away.

'And look in here,' Vita said, opening the door to the drawing room, where the low velvet suite was tastefully arranged around the glass table.

Irving cocked his head on one side.

'Don't you like it?' she asked.

'It's rather modern, isn't it?'

'I thought that was the point,' she said, realizing that he hated it.

'I told her it was ugly,' Hermione chipped in.

'If you like it, darling, then I will, too,' Irving said magnanimously.

Vita smarted at his criticism.

'It's hard to do everything without you,' she said. 'These rooms are so big. There's been so much to buy to make them look even vaguely homely.'

'But I told you – you're the one with the taste. I don't care.'

But he obviously did.

'I think it'll have to move a bit, though,' he said.

'Why?'

'I won a grand pianola in a poker game,' he said gleefully. 'It's new. And massive.'

'Oh, Daddy, that sounds fun,' Hermione said, her eyes shining triumphantly at Vita.

'A pianola?' Vita asked. She'd wanted to buy a piano, but Irving hadn't sounded keen.

'It's really quite marvellous, Vita. You change the papers in it, press the pedals and it plays all by itself.'

'Isn't that cheating?' she said.

She knew that he wanted her to be excited, but she felt annoyed that Irving hadn't noticed how much work she'd put into making their new home. Or that it had all been rather soured by Hermione.

* * *

The following morning Vita was up early. Up in the studio, she opened the large French windows and looked down at the sheer drop to the street. The builders had taken away the ironwork guard to paint it, but had yet to replace it, and she was relieved that poor little Mr Wild wasn't here. She still felt his absence strongly, especially on a day like today, when she might have taken him on a walk around the square.

She took a sharp breath in, recognizing what was happening, and forced herself – as she had to on an hourly basis – not to be morose or get lost in memories. She had to look forward, not to the past. This was going to be a new start, she told herself, looking round the studio and running her hand over the workbenches.

There was a knock on the door and Marie poked her head round the door.

'You don't have to knock. This is all ours now. Come in,' Vita said, smiling. It was always a relief to see Marie, who stopped her revelling in her memories. And now she saw that her friend was carrying the old sewing machine. 'You didn't have to bring everything over from the apartment,' she said. 'If I'd known, I would have come to help, or at least brought the car.'

'It wasn't necessary.'

'But I've ordered new machines,' Vita said. 'Three.'

'Why three?'

'Because once we have our order from Galeries Lafayette,' she said excitedly, rubbing her hands together, 'we're going to expand. You and I are going to take this business forward quickly, and we'll need a team.'

Marie looked startled at this, but she nodded. Vita heaved up the suitcase from under the bench. It was surprisingly light.

'So I was thinking: there should be enough in here to stock the line,' she said. 'But we'll have to get making more right away,' she added as she popped the lid. But as she opened it, expecting to see the neat, tissue-wrapped bras, she saw immediately that something was wrong. Very wrong.

The case was empty.

Vita flung the sheets of pink tissue into the air, searching desperately. 'Where are all the samples?'

'They were there yesterday,' Marie said. She hurried over and Vita could see that her cheeks were burning.

'You brought everything from the apartment?' Vita checked.

'Everything. You saw me.'

'Oh, my goodness,' Vita said. 'Where have they gone?'

'Oh, Vita,' Marie put her hands to her pink cheeks. 'What's happened? All of our hard work . . .'

Vita swallowed hard, the nausea rising. She clung on to Marie for a moment to steady herself.

It was only then that Vita noticed Hermione standing by the doorway, a smug smile on her face.

79

The Thief

Irving was in his study reading his newspaper when Vita burst in, dragging a reluctant Hermione after her. The study on the ground floor had a stylish stained-glass window and was mostly filled with Irving's huge mahogany desk, on which stood a framed photograph of Daphne and Hermione.

'What's all this?' he asked, taking the lit cigar from the ashtray and having a puff.

'Daddy, Daddy,' Hermione yelped. 'She's awful. She's saying terrible things. You mustn't believe her.'

'Irving, can you please help,' Vita commanded, and he grumpily put down his paper.

'I didn't take anything,' Hermione shouted. 'She's saying I'm a thief.'

'Then who did take it?' Vita said, trying not to raise her voice.

'I don't know.'

'What's going on?' Irving asked, clearly concerned now.

'Someone in this house has been in the studio and has stolen our samples. If it wasn't her,' she jabbed her finger at Hermione, 'then it must have been Isadora.'

'She didn't,' Hermione said, erupting into babyish tears. 'She wouldn't. How dare you accuse me. Or her. As if I care about your horrible brassieres.'

'Girls, girls,' Irving said, patting the air. 'Please.'

Vita growled with frustration. How dare he call her a girl. She was his *wife*. It infuriated her that he couldn't see what was going on here.

'I hate you,' Hermione screamed at Vita, before stamping out of the room and slamming the door.

'See!' Vita said.

'She's a child,' Irving said, looking perplexed. 'She doesn't mean it.'

'She does. You have no idea how awful the last week has been. How much she resents me.'

'I'm sure it can't have been—'

'Irving,' Vita said. 'If your daughter didn't have a hand in this, then it *must* have been Isadora. She's the only other person who has been up to the studio. I want her gone by the morning.'

'You can't sack Isadora,' Irving said. 'The girls love her.'

'You don't understand. The designs, everything – they've gone missing.'

'Are you sure? I mean, perhaps you've mislaid them. Perhaps Marie—'

'I haven't lost my mind, Irving,' Vita snapped. 'I had everything ready. It's weeks – months – of work. Poor Marie is distraught.'

She felt more tears rising, and Irving came round his desk to comfort her. 'Don't get upset,' he said. 'We'll find them.'

But Vita couldn't be comforted.

410

'Just get rid of her,' she said, as she sobbed against his chest.

'But what about Marie?' Irving said.

Vita pulled away from him, looking up into his face. 'What about her?'

'Well, I mean, she's the one with most access to the studio.'

'Marie *made* everything, Irving. She's more upset than I am.'

'I'm not so sure,' Irving said. 'As I've told you before, there are tells. Little tics that give people away.'

'What exactly are you saying?'

'Well, if you really want to know, I don't trust her.'

'You don't trust Marie?' Vita's voice rose hysterically. 'Marie *is my only friend.*'

'Calm down.'

'You don't understand,' she said, shaking him off. 'We've got a meeting at Galeries Lafayette next week. We'll never be able to replace what we've lost. Everything is ruined.'

80

Bone-Tired

Despite the sun-filled rooms and the soft furnishings, the atmosphere in the house turned ice-cold. Irving was upset when Isadora packed her bags and left the following morning in tears, protesting her innocence, her dark eyes full of blame. Hermione, furious with Irving and Vita, left shortly afterwards to go and stay with family friends. She had made a big show of calling Alicia in New York, and she was now coming back to Paris with Daphne on a mercy mission to rescue her daughter – a turn of events that hadn't pleased Irving at all. He was more than happy to have an ocean between him and his ex-wife.

'Oh, Alicia is going to love all this,' Irving said scornfully, when he heard her on the telephone in the hall.

Vita held her ground, though. She was still furious. She couldn't shake the feeling that it had been Hermione who had stolen everything from the studio. And then, at other times, she was sure it had been Isadora. To appease Irving she employed a girl called Celine, who, unlike Isadora, was compliant and obedient.

She felt most awful for Marie, though, who had told Vita that she'd had to cancel the meeting at Galeries Lafayette.

They couldn't begin to do justice to their idea with so few samples to present. Marie had tried to be positive about it, of course, saying that they needed to start again and design a completely new range, but Vita felt the setback keenly. They'd been so close, and now it would be months and months before the business could get off the ground.

It didn't help that Vita hardly had any energy at all. And on Thursday, when Irving wanted to go to Zelli's to cheer her up, she begged him to go without her, but Irving said it was out of the question for him to be seen out without her.

Up in their booth, Joe Zelli sent champagne to congratulate them on their wedding, but Vita was in no mood to celebrate. She didn't want to dance or drink, and Irving was annoyed that she wasn't joining in, like she used to.

On Friday morning she overslept and, when Irving woke her, he was already dressed.

'What time is it?' she asked blearily.

'Goodness, Vita, what is the matter with you?' Irving laughed. 'Haven't you remembered? I'm going away.'

She sat up in bed, feeling queasy and tired, as if she'd hardly slept at all. She'd always risen early and sprung out of bed, but now her legs felt like lead. 'Again? Where?'

'To London. Just a bit of business. It's only a couple of nights at the Ritz.'

She kissed him, trying not to show how his stale breath turned her stomach. 'Do you have to go?' she asked him.

'You could come with me, although it'd be very boring for you. I'm playing poker at the In & Out Club.'

Vita got up and dressed hurriedly, but when she tried on her skirt, she was annoyed to find that the waist was too small and the button wouldn't do up. 'It'll do me good to have some time off all that fine food,' she said. 'I've put on weight around my middle,' she said, 'and it's all your fault.'

'Then take it back to Jenny's and have it altered.'

'I wouldn't bother her with that. I'll do it myself. Or Marie will,' Vita said, and Irving looked annoyed. They'd never resolved their argument about Marie, who still came every day. She kept away from Irving up in the studio, working hard to replace the bras they'd lost, but Vita knew Irving was irritated that Marie was up there. He didn't understand that she was the only thing keeping Vita sane.

They had breakfast together and, when it was time for him to go, Irving held her closely. 'Oh, Vita, you do know that I love you just the way you are, don't you?' he said, but she didn't believe him. He wasn't going to love her if she was fat. 'I'm going to miss you.'

'And I you,' she said. 'Try to have fun.'

He chuckled and kissed her again. 'I'll try.'

Marie was already in the studio when Vita walked in. She was riffling through a drawer. She looked up at Vita, who stood with her hand on the door.

'Good morning,' she said. 'You haven't seen that magnifying glass by any chance, have you? I know it's in one of these drawers.'

Vita shook her head, feeling too queasy to question why Marie might need such a thing.

'I say, are you quite well, Vita?' Marie asked.

414

Vita shook her head and ran from the studio to the bathroom, and threw up her breakfast and cup of tea. When she came back, Marie looked at her.

'I think I've got some kind of illness,' Vita explained. Marie slid off the bench and led her to the sofa. 'I feel so tired.'

'Sit down. I'll call for Celine to bring you something.'

'Thanks,' Vita said, but she didn't want anything. She felt wretched.

'How many mornings have you been sick?' Marie asked.

'A few,' Vita admitted. 'I'm sure it'll pass.'

Marie shook her head. 'I don't think you're ill.'

'What do you mean?'

Marie sat beside her, holding her hand. 'Vita, I think you're pregnant.'

Vita took a sharp intake of breath and then burst into tears, great waves of anguish washing over her as Marie confirmed her very worst fears.

'Goodness, Vita, whatever is the matter? Why are you so upset? It's a good thing, isn't it?'

Vita shook her head, her eyes flooding with tears.

How could she ever begin to describe to Marie the guilt she felt – the awful, gnawing suspicion that it might be Archie's baby? She hoped it was Irving's, of course – that their one time in Nice had been enough. But then . . . then she thought of making love with Archie, and she felt sick at the thought that she might be carrying proof of the terrible sin she'd committed.

'Oh, Marie,' she said.

'What is it? Tell me,' her friend implored, but Vita shook her head.

'I can't.'

'Yes, you can,' Marie said gently. 'We're friends. You can tell me anything.'

81

Sowing the Seeds

Sometimes information could be as juicy as fruit, Edith thought, as she got ready for her evening out in London. And this particular nugget felt like a specially ripe cherry. One she couldn't help but savour over and over again.

Vita and Archie Fenwick.

Oh, the sweet joy of knowing what Vita had done – how fully she'd betrayed her husband, Edith thought as she pressed the new lipstick onto her lips and admired herself in her hotel mirror.

At first, when Marie had told Edith that Vita was pregnant, her initial reaction had been a bitter stab of jealousy, but this . . . this new revelation sweetened it considerably. Because it didn't take a genius to work out that Archie was quite possibly the father of Vita's baby, and now Edith had all the information she needed to destroy Vita for good. The prospect of it made her feel heady with delight.

It was almost too good to keep to herself. She thought of how much Clement would love to know this, too, but didn't tell him. She would in time, of course, but right now Clement had other things on his mind.

They'd been at a delightful party last night, but this

morning Clement had received a telegram from Harrison, the foreman, saying that the Darton workers were coming out in solidarity with Arkwright's workers across the valley. The last of the mills there were closing, now that Arkwright had moved his business to his factories in India. The Darton workers were worried that things were going to go the same way for them.

It was typical that they should wait until Clement and Edith were away to cause the maximum disruption. Edith was annoyed that Clement had refused to let her talk to the workers herself. She was sure that, with the investment she'd secured, they could restock the mill with new machines and machinists and double – if not treble – their production. But that would take time, and the workers weren't happy with their jobs being taken over by machines.

Edith had calculated that at least half the workforce would have to go, and she knew that, with the other cotton mills in Lancashire having closed, the prospects of finding employment were slim. But that wasn't her problem, she reminded herself. They could strike all they wanted, but it wouldn't change the facts. They were lucky they had jobs in the first place.

Clement was cross about the strike, too, but Edith didn't tell him it had played beautifully into her plans. After all, they were signing two new deals tomorrow and they couldn't both be in two places at once, so grudgingly Clement returned to Darton, which meant that Edith had London all to herself.

She checked herself in the mirror in the corridor, knowing that she was attracting attention. She was wearing a full-length white gown, and her blonde hair was curled and styled on her head, with the Darton pearls hanging in her daringly low-cut dress. Oh yes, tonight she was going to have some fun.

Edith sat alone at a round table in the dining room, looking across at the table in the bay window where Irving King sat. He didn't notice her at first, so Edith took a moment to observe her husband's brother-in-law. *Her* brother-in-law. It was weird to think that this man had no idea how they were connected. Or how much Edith knew about him and his wife.

'Hello, my dear,' Irving said, finally looking up, and Edith made a show of blushing and pretending to be embarrassed that she'd been caught staring. 'It looks like you're dining alone.'

'My friend . . .' Edith said, pretending to be exasperated, 'she's late.'

'Then won't you join me for some champagne?'

In her mind, from what Marie had said, Edith had the impression that Irving was a fat, brash American, but Vita's husband wasn't without his charms. She felt his eyes raking over her appreciatively as she joined him at his table.

They chatted for a while and she introduced herself as Edie, although she didn't reveal her surname. She'd taken off her wedding ring earlier and now saw Irving checking her hand.

'So tell me, Edie, about yourself. What are you interested in?' he asked.

It had been a long while since she'd been flirted with like this. A very long time. She'd forgotten how much fun it could be. *But she must stay on track*, Edith reminded herself. Even so, she had to bat down the temptation to tell Irving who she was. To tell him that she was a businesswoman and that he ought to respect her.

She smiled. 'Oh, I do this and that,' she said elusively. 'I read,' she added, with a slight laugh, as if she knew this was a ridiculous occupation.

Irving smiled. 'I'm not much of a reader myself. My wife is. She loves books.'

'Oh, you're married?' Edith said innocently.

'Oh yes. Vita, she's swell – the apple of my eye.'

'That's wonderful. You should give her the manuscript of this book I've just read,' Edith said. 'It's called *Sylvine*.'

'Who's it by? I'll pick up a copy.'

'Oh, it's not published yet. I got the manuscript fresh from an agent. I like to be the first to know what's good – you know?' She took a sip of champagne. 'To have my finger on the pulse of what's what.'

'That's very sensible,' Irving said.

'It's by this writer called . . .' She pretended to remember the name. 'Archie Fenwick.'

She said his name deliberately, enunciating it clearly, then sat back as the waiter topped up her glass.

'Fenwick. Fenwick . . .' Irving King said, looking up, his face crinkling as if trying to remember something. 'He sounds familiar. In fact, yes, we ran into him in the South of France.'

'Oh dear. I hope you locked your wife up,' Edith said. And she saw then that she'd caught him on her hook.

'How so?'

'He has a *terrible* reputation,' she said, leaning forward conspiratorially. 'He was involved in a scandal,' she said. 'He got caught up with a dancing girl from one of the clubs. His fiancée was furious.'

Irving sat up. 'What club?'

'Oh, I don't know the details,' Edith laughed, flapping her hand. 'The Zip, I think, although it's closed now. One of those dancing girls that put themselves around and sleep with all sorts of men – black, white, they don't care.'

Irving took a sip from his glass, but the merriment had gone from his eyes.

'He's touting his manuscript around the publishers now,' Edith continued. 'I have a friend who's thinking of publishing. I tell you what: why don't I lend you my copy?'

82

A Letter in the Sunshine

Vita still felt wretched, the morning sickness twisting her insides out, but she was determined to put on a brave face in front of Marie. Now that her friend had pointed out the reason why she was feeling so dreadful, she had spent every waking hour trying to reconcile herself with the thought that she was going to be a mother. She couldn't imagine what Irving would say when she told him. He'd be delighted, she hoped. And if he was happy, then she would be too, she told herself. She would make the most of it – just as soon as she stopped feeling so sick.

This morning Marie was later than usual and, after dressing, Vita made her way to the studio, but then the telephone in the hall rang and she walked down the stairs to pick it up. It was probably Irving calling, she thought. She hadn't heard from him since he'd left for London, and she suspected that he'd become embroiled in a rather long game of poker.

From her viewpoint in the hall, she could see that Celine was at the front door and that the pianola Irving had won was being delivered, its shiny black sides covered in brown blankets. The two workmen in fawn overalls were bringing it with difficulty into the hall, and Vita was worried that they were going to damage the marble.

'Careful,' she called out to them, then paid attention to the phone call. 'Hello.'

She heard the clunky connection and smiled, wanting to hear Irving's voice.

'Irving?' she asked, but it wasn't him. It was Marie. It sounded like she was somewhere noisy – for all the world as if she were in a station.

'Vita, I'm not coming today,' she said. Her voice sounded strange. 'Or tomorrow. Or maybe for the whole of the week.'

'What? Marie? Where are you?'

'I have to attend to a matter. A family matter.'

'But, Marie?'

'I'll explain. I promise. When I'm back. I'm sorry. I have to do something to make things right. Just trust me. I'll be back – and then . . . then I'll explain everything, I promise.'

Vita was out of sorts for the rest of the morning, directing the men to put the pianola in the drawing room, although the bulky, shiny thing rather ruined the whole sleek aesthetic.

It's as well Marie isn't here, she thought, with so many domestic arrangements to sort out. Even so, she couldn't help wondering what on earth had got into Marie, and why she hadn't previously mentioned her domestic crisis. It wasn't as if Vita didn't share everything with her, and it bothered her that Marie had a private life she knew nothing about.

What family matter could be so important that Marie had to go away? As far as Vita knew, her mother and father were dead, so why had she chosen to go now, when she knew how much Vita needed her? It felt as if everyone was deserting her, and the house seemed eerily quiet.

'Here's the post, Madame,' Celine said as she wandered through the hallway towards the kitchen. She handed Vita an envelope. 'It's a lovely day out there.'

'You're right. It is, isn't it?' she said.

She grabbed her sunglasses from the table in the hall and headed out of the front door. She looked at the pots that she'd had planted inside the railings, then wandered down the steps and across the road into the square.

The letter was from Nancy, and Vita wanted to savour it alone. In the square she sat on a bench by the fountain in the sunshine, reading her friend's giant scrawl, which spread over pages and pages.

It seemed that Nancy had left the clinic and was now on her way to New York. Vita smiled as she read her description of Los Angeles and how she'd been seeing a clairvoyant, and she remembered Nancy's devotion to Mystic Alice. She sounded very much like her old self. She wrote:

> You mustn't trust that girl, Marie – or whatever her name is. I'm telling you, Vita. She did something to Mr Wild, I'm sure of it.

Vita sighed, putting the letter in her pocket. It was typical of Nancy to blame someone else for that awful tragedy, but it annoyed her that both Irving and Nancy distrusted Marie so much. Marie had been so kind and gentle with Vita, when she'd told Marie how terrified she was about being pregnant.

How scared she was that, amongst other things, a baby would ruin her chances of getting her business off the ground.

She closed her eyes, thinking about the words she'd use when she wrote back to Nancy, to tell her about the baby.

The baby. *Oh, the baby.*

Vita put her hands over her stomach and tried to imagine what was happening inside her. This new life that she was now responsible for. Her baby. This unexpected gift.

She took a breath, trying to comprehend the magnitude of it. And now she allowed herself to mull over the thought that had been going round and round her head. If only she had a clairvoyant who could tell her for sure whether the baby was Archie's or Irving's.

But it must be Irving's, she thought, remembering the hotel room in Nice. It *must* be his baby. And a baby would be wonderful, wouldn't it? A baby would make everything right.

She heard the honk of a motorcar and shaded her eyes, seeing a grand car turning the corner into the square, and got up. She stood and watched Irving get out of the car and head up the steps towards their home, where Celine answered the door with a little curtsey.

She watched from the square, amazed for a second that the grand house was her home – with her new husband inside it.

She tucked Nancy's letter into her pocket and set off to find Irving. She would tell him the news today. Right now, she resolved. She'd tell him and let him be delighted. Because it *was* something to be delighted about, she told herself.

A baby.

83

The Girl with the Mole

Inside, Celine flicked her eyes up the stairs to indicate where Irving was, and Vita started up the marble stairs, thinking that she must change the flowers in the vase. Or maybe there was no need. She was sure Irving would be buying her a huge bouquet when he found out her news.

She looked into the drawing room, expecting him to be admiring the new pianola, but the room was just as she'd left it.

'Irving darling,' she called. 'Irving, where are you?'

He didn't answer, and she found him eventually in their bedroom. He was still wearing his jacket and was looking out of the window onto the square. He was very still.

'You're home,' she said, going up to him, wanting to hug him, glad that everything was perfect and she could tell him her news without anyone interrupting them.

'Vita,' he said, turning to face her, but he didn't move towards her and she stopped, taking in his sombre mood.

'What's happened?' she asked, her mind racing. 'Did you lose?'

'In a manner of speaking.'

Now she saw that he had something tucked under his arm,

and he chucked it towards her contemptuously and it landed on their bed. Vita saw that it was a thick Manila envelope.

'I didn't want to believe it,' he said. 'But I'm not stupid. Go on. Look inside.'

She picked up the envelope, her heart racing as she undid the string tie and pulled out the sheaf of pages. She looked at the front page, her stomach lurching as she saw the title – *Sylvine* – and the author: A. Fenwick.

'Where did you get this?' she whispered.

'Does it matter?' he asked. 'I expect you know already that this is about you. Don't lie to me, Vita.' His voice was raised and she closed her eyes.

'Archie and I, we were . . . it's so difficult to explain.'

'I think he's explained it all perfectly well.'

She'd never heard Irving sound like this. Now, she watched as he went over to the mantelpiece and, with a growl of fury, picked up the glass clock and smashed it on the floor. Vita yelped.

'You lied to me,' he shouted.

Vita put her hands to her head, frightened now. 'Please, Irving,' she implored, seeing his eye casting around for something else to smash.

'What will everyone think, when they know that it's you?'

'Irving, you're being ridiculous. I haven't read this, but it's a novel. It's fiction.'

'Oh no,' he sneered. 'You can't play that card with me. The girl with the mole on her arm? It's you, Vita. It's all you.'

'Please don't do this. You're working yourself up. Please can't we talk about it?'

'I can't look at you,' he spat, then brushed past her and hurried down the stairs.

'Irving, wait.'

She ran out onto the landing after him, but he was already halfway down the stairs.

'Please, Irving,' she implored, 'let me try and explain. Don't leave.' But he'd reached the front door and was roughly pushing Celine aside.

A second later, the door slammed hard, the reverberations reaching Vita like a punch. Holding on to the banisters, she felt her knees give way and she sank to the marble tiles with a low groan of despair.

84

Alicia Returns

Vita's eyes were pinched with tiredness. She hadn't slept, but had spent all night reading Archie's manuscript, and now she felt wretched and wrung out. On the one hand, the book was brilliant and had been written, she suspected, as a very long-winded apology. At times Archie's voice had been so clear that it felt as if he'd leapt off the page and had been talking solely to her. But much as she was moved and flattered that he had articulated his own thinly disguised feelings, it felt too exposing and far, far too real. She couldn't help reading it through the prism of her husband's obvious jealousy and upset; and Vita felt mortified that, for example, Archie had described her so accurately, and their love-making in the boathouse.

Perhaps he was blinded by love, but reading her life in print made Vita think that not only was Archie a great romantic, but a fool, too. He'd never get away with publishing this and keeping his own reputation intact. Maud, surely, would never allow it? What wife would let her husband publish such things?

As she came to the final pages, with the character in the novel declaring that his love for Sylvine would transcend everything and everyone – spouses included – Vita could understand why Irving was so upset. There was no mistaking, from these pages, that she and Archie had been lovers. But how had Irving got hold of his novel, when Archie had only just finished it? Someone must have given it to him. Someone who wanted to stir things up and cause trouble. Someone who knew about her and Archie. Someone like – she racked her brains – Archie's friend Georgie? Or Cassius Digby or those viperous wives? The image of Belinda Getty sprang sharply to mind.

Irving hadn't come back since he'd stormed out yesterday, and now Vita got up, feeling queasy and worried, wishing that Marie was here.

She tried to busy herself in the studio, but it was useless. She couldn't concentrate at all. And then, at four o'clock, she heard music and ran down the stairs to the drawing room.

Irving was sitting at the pianola, his head hanging as the keys moved in front of him. He was very drunk and looked like he too hadn't slept at all. His feet were moving, though, the paper drum turning inside the pianola, and the melancholic sound of Liszt's *Liebestraum* filled the room.

'Irving,' Vita begged. 'Stop playing. Let's talk.'

'Go away,' he slurred. The keys continued moving, the sombre tune only adding to the awful atmosphere between them.

'Please,' she said, standing closer to the piano, willing him to look up at her, but his head dropped and he only pedalled the pianola harder so that the tune sped up. It was somehow sinister, like an out-of-control fairground ride, and Vita felt frightened. She'd seen Irving drink, of course, but she'd never seen him drunk like this. 'Come and have some coffee,' she implored above the din.

'I don't want to talk to you. Ever again,' Irving slurred.

'You don't mean that.'

'I do.'

The drawing-room door opened and Celine came in.

'Irving!' Vita said, stepping closer now, attempting to close the lid of the pianola, which she knew would cut off the sound. Irving's hand stopped the lid, but as he did so, he stopped pedalling, so that the music ceased abruptly. In the moment of tense silence that followed, Vita addressed the maid, embarrassed that the young girl was witnessing this dreadful scene. 'What is it, Celine?'

'There's a Mrs King to see you,' she said in a small voice and, a moment later, an elegant woman in a large hat strode through the door, pushing Celine out of the way. She stood looking at Irving.

'Suitably dramatic music,' she said haughtily, with a harrumph, her eyes settling on Vita, who realized with a horrible jolt that this was Alicia.

Irving's ex-wife was in her late forties and exuded glamour. She was wearing a light-blue coat with a fur collar and white gloves. She was slim and tall with striking red hair, coiffed expertly under a stylish hat. Irving had made Alicia out to be mousy and boring, but Vita could see, from the haughty lift of her chin and the way she strutted in her high heels, that she was anything but.

'What do you want, Alicia?' Irving slurred, starting up the pianola again.

'Irving, stop that dreadful racket,' she commanded, 'and I'll tell you.'

'Say what you have to say and get out,' he muttered. 'If

this is about Hermione, then talk to my wife,' he said bitterly, flicking his head towards Vita.

'I've come because I have something important to say, Irving,' she said, ignoring Vita, who felt fury rising in her at the rudeness of the woman.

'Please . . . this is really not a good time—' Vita started in her sternest voice.

But Alicia ignored her, holding up her gloved hand to stop Vita speaking. She strode to the piano. 'Irving, stop it,' she shouted.

'No,' he shouted back.

'Very well,' she said, raising her voice over the pianola. 'It pains me to have to tell you that this . . .' she waved her hand in Vita's direction, 'this *girl* of yours has been taking you for a fool. Did you know she had an affair, right under your nose, on Cassius Digby's yacht? I've heard it twice now within our circles. Everyone is talking about it.'

The music continued.

'Irving! Irving, did you hear what I said? Pay attention. You're being made a fool of. This Fenwick chap is the father of her baby.'

Now the music stopped and there was a moment of thunderous silence. Vita wanted to speak, but she was rooted to the spot by the look Irving gave her. For a second the room seemed to spin a little and she grabbed hold of the pianola, heaving in a deep breath.

'The what?' he said.

'Didn't you know? She's pregnant. So I've heard,' Alicia said, a gleeful note in her voice.

How could Alicia possibly know? Vita felt the blood rush

432

from her face, as Irving stood up now. He stepped towards her, his eyes bloodshot, yet horribly intense.

'You're pregnant, Vita? You didn't tell me?'

'I was going to. You've been away. But the baby is yours,' she said, her words tripping over each other. 'Irving – the baby is yours.'

But he continued towards her alongside the pianola. 'You're lying. I can tell.'

'No, Irving, listen . . . please.'

Irving held up his hand. 'It was true,' he said in a whisper. 'It was all true. The book. And him . . .'

'Yes, on the yacht. Right under your nose,' Alicia said, butting in.

'Stop it,' Vita shouted at her.

She thought Irving was going to say something else, or maybe strike her, as he took two more steps towards her, but then he slowed, putting his hand to his chest, and his knees buckled.

'Irving,' she cried, trying to catch him as he fell to the floor, crashing into the glass table on the way. He was gasping, clutching his chest.

'Call for help,' Vita cried.

But Irving's ex-wife simply stood there above him, raising an eyebrow as Irving writhed in agony on the floor.

'Oh, really, Irving, this is most inconvenient.'

'Look what you've done. What you've said!' Vita shouted. 'How *could* you?'

'Actually, that wasn't even what I came to tell him,' Alicia said, pulling off her gloves by the fingertips as if she had all the time in the world.

85

A Visit from the Headmistress

In Darton Hall, Edith looked out of the landing window, shielding herself from view with the faded curtains. She could see a strange car on the drive and wondered who on earth would be calling. She wasn't expecting anyone, and Theresa Darton rarely had visitors – certainly not ones who came in official-looking cars like that.

'They're calling for you in the drawing room, Mrs Darton,' Martha said from the bottom of the stairs.

'Who's here?' she asked, but Martha scurried away, and Edith walked down the stairs, annoyed that her day had been interrupted when the new machines were due to arrive later on at the mill. That's *if* the lorries could get through the picket lines. Infuriatingly, the workers were still on strike, their placards shouting useless sentiments about fairness and pay. If only they could understand that modernization was critical and they were only standing in the way of the inevitable. It was so frustrating, when Edith needed to get the new machines installed, and then for everyone to get on with the designs she had planned. They had hefty Top Drawer orders to fulfil, and more in the pipeline. This unrest was most inconvenient.

On the way into the lounge Edith stooped to pet Victor the cat, but she sensed an odd atmosphere as soon as she crossed the threshold. Theresa Darton and Clement were sitting stiffly in the green leather wing-backed chairs, and Clement didn't stand when she came in, but glared at her. Edith looked at him quizzically and then saw that there was someone else in the room, sitting in the chair with its back to the door. And now that person turned to look towards the door, and Edith saw it was the headmistress from Susan's school.

What in God's name was Mrs Lanyard doing here? Had something happened to Susan? Why hadn't the damned woman contacted Edith privately, if there was a problem? This was going to be very difficult to explain to Clement. But she would find a way of fronting it out, Edith told herself, her mind whirring with the implications of the woman being here, as she shut the door and walked towards the low table between the arrangement of chairs in front of the fire. She could see the silver coffee pot on the tray, but the cups hadn't been touched.

'Mrs Lanyard, would you please be so kind as to tell my wife what you have just told us,' Clement said, standing up and going to the fireplace. Edith recognized the barely concealed rage in the pallor of his skin. His fist clenched and re-clenched, then he stuffed his hands in his pockets. Above him, the face of Darius Darton in the portrait that hung over the mantel glared down at her.

'I'm afraid Susan has gone missing from school,' the headmistress said, looking between Edith and Clement. She looked terrified.

Edith gritted her teeth, cursing herself for being caught out like this. She should have confessed everything when she had the chance, instead of putting it off again and again. *This was not how it was supposed to happen.* Her revelation about Susan, about Marianne . . . Vita . . . the designs . . . all of it was supposed to be triumphant. It wasn't supposed to be like this.

'It's true then? You've been schooling Susan?' Clement asked Edith and she didn't answer, her words faltering at the tone of his voice.

'She told a friend that she was going to find her mother,' Mrs Lanyard continued uncertainly.

'Marie?' Clement asked.

'Yes. It seems her mother has been away in Paris, and the poor child – she's been beside herself. Well, I wrote to you about it, didn't I, Mrs Darton?'

Clement glared at Edith and she felt her cheeks pulsing.

'Marie has been in Paris all this time?' he asked. She hated him then, for the way his question betrayed the fact that he'd missed her.

Again Edith didn't answer as Mrs Lanyard continued. 'Well, the poor child got a letter from Miss Chastain last week, saying that she'd only just found out that Susan was at St Hilda's. I had no idea the child had been brought to us without her mother's knowledge.'

There was a barbed, scolding tone to her voice, meant for Edith, but Edith's mind was racing too fast to be offended. How had Marie found out? How could Marie possibly know about St Hilda's, when Edith had been so careful to keep everything from her? It must have been the photographs – the school photographs. There must have been something, a St Hilda's emblem perhaps on one of them, a sign on one of the buildings that Edith had overlooked, because now Marie had found Susan . . .

'Last night Susan told one of the girls that she was running away to be reunited with her mother.' The headmistress looked between Edith, Clement and Theresa Darton, clearly losing the conviction in her story.

'Go on.' Clement's eyes gleamed with menace.

'Well, this is why I came. We take such matters very seriously, and we have to consider the safety of the child. I have to go on the only clues that I have, and Susan told her dorm-mate that her mother was working for Anna Darton in Paris, so I thought you would be able to shed some light as to—'

'Anna? Anna is in Paris? Oh . . . oh, Edith!' Theresa Darton let out an uncharacteristically shrill sound, startling Edith, who had been standing very still, terrified to make a move, as if she'd stumbled on a monster she didn't want to antagonize. But she knew now it was too late. 'You've known all along where Anna is?' Theresa Darton gasped. 'All this time?'

'I can explain,' Edith said, but her voice sounded strange – flustered and shaky. Her hands trembled and she clenched them together, looking between Theresa and Clement.

'Tell me this isn't true?' Clement said, his voice menacing and low. He stepped towards her, his eyes thunderous, and Edith staggered backwards, terrified. 'Those designs?' Clement said, his eyes locking with hers. 'They're hers?'

Edith nodded, her mind racing, but she knew that the

only way to salvage anything was to be honest. 'Please let me explain, Clement dear. That's why I sent Marianne. You see, I thought – I thought . . . well, I *reasoned*,' she began, but she could tell Clement was too cross to understand, and now the logic of her plan seemed muddled in her own head. She remembered how she'd felt so gleeful to be killing two birds with one stone – dispatching Marianne and having a spy in Paris – but now it was too hard to explain, when she felt pinned by her husband's dark gaze.

Now Clement strode over from the fireplace and came right up to her, his finger pointing in Edith's face, and she let out a little yelp. 'You – you . . .' he began, but he was too cross and his words fizzled out. 'What were you thinking?'

'I thought you'd be pleased. We needed designs and—'

'Mrs Darton, what about Susan?' Mrs Lanyard asked, startling Edith, who had been so held in Clement's gaze, as he tried to fathom the breadth and meaning of what she'd done, that she had momentarily forgotten the headmistress.

Now Clement's head turned slowly towards Mrs Lanyard. He grabbed hold of her arm and escorted her very firmly to the door. 'You'll be leaving now,' he said, his tone ominous.

'Mr Darton, I—' Mrs Lanyard's eyes were wide with shock as she passed Edith. Clement flung open the door and Martha, who'd clearly been listening, sprang back.

'Martha, please see Mrs Lanyard out,' he said. 'And then fetch my valise and call for the car at once.'

'Where are you going? You can't leave. The machines are arriving,' Edith said.

Clement turned and came back to her, putting his hand around her neck and pushing her backwards so that she fell into the armchair. Edith put her hands to her throat, where his rough gesture had choked her. Then he put his hands on the arms of the chair, his face right up against hers.

'You deal with it,' he hissed in her face, flecks of spittle landing on her skin. For a second she thought he was going to strike her, but then Clement turned his back on her and strode towards the door, flinging it open, walking through it and kicking Victor the cat, who yelped. Edith watched him from the chair, frozen.

'Oh, you stupid, stupid girl,' Theresa cried. 'Now look what you've done.'

86

Pushed Out

Vita felt wretched as she sat at her husband's bedside in the plush private hospital suite, where Irving had been taken after he'd collapsed. There hadn't been much improvement in his condition. He was still barely conscious and he lay, pale and grey beneath the white sheet, his breathing laboured. Alicia had made the phone call to bring him here as if it might be a hotel he was particularly fond of. She'd been quite calm about it, implying that it was all histrionics on Irving's part, when Vita could see that he was in terrible pain.

Having met her, Vita was beginning to understand how Irving had been bullied, and it didn't surprise her at all that Alicia had demanded a quick divorce. She was clearly a woman who got whatever she wanted. Vita couldn't stand her, but her own heavy hints that Alicia should leave this medical crisis to Vita had fallen on deaf ears.

She was very relieved that Alicia had stepped out of the room for a moment and, alone for the first time since the morning's events, Vita felt tears coming. She stood up from the hard metal chair and went to Irving's side, putting her hand over his, regret and anguish making her heart contract.

She was still reeling from Alicia's entrance earlier, and

how awful it had been when she'd told Irving about Archie, as if it were nothing more than idle gossip amongst their set. The way she'd said it made it sound as if Vita were a plaything of Irving's. And she remembered Hermione telling her that Irving had only married Vita to annoy Alicia. She'd thought Hermione was trying to be cruel, but now she had a sickening feeling that there was some truth in it after all.

Now the door opened and Vita dabbed at her eyes quickly, and a small bald man walked in, wearing a white coat. He introduced himself as Irving's physician, Dr Bernheim.

'Will he . . . will he be all right?' Vita asked, as the doctor went to the other side of the bed and held Irving's limp wrist, taking his pulse.

'I'm sorry – are you a friend of Irving's?'

Vita felt her cheeks burning. 'I'm his wife,' she said.

'Oh?' Dr Bernheim looked startled at this news.

'Irving and I were married. This summer.'

'I see. Well, congratulations, my dear,' he mumbled, then blushed. This was hardly a congratulatory situation.

'What do you think will happen?' Vita asked. 'Will he get better?'

'I hope so, but to be frank, this turn of events is hardly a shock.'

He went on to explain, in a low, subdued tone, that this had been on the cards for some time. He'd repeatedly warned Irving about the price he'd inevitably pay for his smoking, drinking and stresses at the poker table.

'Of course I'm sure you know about the high blood pressure that has affected him . . .' he looked at Vita now, although he seemed embarrassed, and lowered his voice, 'in the bedroom.'

Vita blushed and nodded mutely, shrivelling inside. She thought of their dreadful wedding night and their subsequent efforts, none of which had been as successful as that one time in Nice.

The doctor was about to say more, but now the door to the private room opened and Alicia and Hermione came in.

'Alicia,' Dr Bernheim said, his demeanour changing, his arms opening into an embrace. Alicia went up to him and kissed him on both cheeks.

'Thank you for sorting out the room, Saul,' Alicia said, as Hermione pushed past Vita to Irving's side. 'Although you clearly haven't been looking after Irving very well. If you'd done your job, he wouldn't be here. What do you make of his condition?'

Vita felt fury rising within her, at the gall of the woman. 'We were just discussing that. I really don't think the doctor should discuss it with you, when I'm his wife—'

'Oh, is that so?' Alicia snapped. The doctor looked alarmed.

'She's the one who made Daddy have a heart attack,' Hermione said now, pointing at Vita, who gulped, astonished that she'd said such a cruel thing. The doctor looked sternly across the bed at Vita.

'Exactly. If he dies, let it be noted that she is to blame,' Alicia continued. 'And by the way, if he does die, let me assure you that you won't get a penny of his money.'

'That's what this is all about? His money?' Vita retaliated in a low whisper. Surely Irving could hear this dreadful exchange? 'How could you be so callous? You . . . you – you need to leave! Both of you.'

'Oh, we're not going anywhere,' Alicia said.

'Please,' Vita begged. 'Irving is very sick. This is too much and it's not the place—'

'I take it you haven't heard about the lawyer?' Alicia said, tutting.

She now threw the folded paper she was carrying under her arm down on the bed and nodded for Vita to look at it. '*That* was what I came to talk to Irving about.'

'I don't understand,' Vita said, looking at the newspaper. The headlines were shouting about some barristers who had been sent to jail.

'It seems our divorce wasn't legal. Typical of Irving to cut corners.'

'But *you* found the lawyer,' Vita said, trying to take in what Alicia was saying.

'That's beside the point. Technically, Irving and I are still married. Which makes *your* marriage totally illegal. Null and void, in actual fact.'

'You can't—' Vita began.

'So I won't be leaving,' Alicia said, pulling towards her the chair that Vita had been sitting on, the noise of the metal scraping across the tiles, making Vita's hair stand on end. 'Irving needs me now. He needs his family.' She nodded to Hermione, who dutifully sat down on the chair. Then Alicia came and stood in front of Vita, between her and Irving, her arms folded.

The door opened again, and Daphne came in and flew into her mother's arms. 'Oh, Mommy, you're here,' she said. Alicia kissed the top of her head and then looked at Vita.

'Run away now,' she said. 'There's a good girl.'

443

87

Pyjamas

For the rest of the week Vita stayed in the studio alone. It was the only place that felt like hers, the only place she felt safe. She lost track of time, the sleepless nights bleeding into restless days. Having been ousted from the hospital by Alicia and warned to stay away, she couldn't go and visit Irving – although she'd made up her mind several times to get dressed and go back there. He was her husband. He was dear, kind Irving. Irving who loved her more than everything . . . he'd told her again and again. He needed her, surely?

But then she replayed over and over again the scene with Alicia and remembered how she hadn't stuck up for herself; and the feeling that it was all too late, and that she'd never have access to her husband again, made her feel winded and weak.

The newspapers were filled with the scandal of the barristers who had pushed through the Paris divorces. Vita scoured the details, hoping that Alicia's declaration wasn't true. Because if Alicia and Irving's divorce wasn't legal, then where did that leave her? What were her rights? Her status? Her name on her passport was Vita King. She was Vita King, wasn't she?

But maybe Alicia was wrong? And if she was, then maybe Vita should hold her ground and not let her nemesis win. Because as far as she was concerned, she and Irving were legally married, and this baby – this baby was Irving's, she was sure of it. Alicia had just been stirring up trouble, knowing how jealous Irving would be about Archie. She was peddling gossip . . . rumours . . .

Except that the rumours were true.

And once again the same question nagged at Vita: why, oh why, had she ever let Archie Fenwick back into her life? Not that she'd had a choice. He'd pursued her . . . and once again her reputation and her life were in tatters because of him.

On the fifth morning since her return from the hospital, Celine said there was a visitor, and Vita put on her robe and ran downstairs to find Isadora in the hallway. They'd parted on such awful terms, and now Vita saw resentment filling the old woman's face.

'I have come to collect some clothes for Mr King. Pyjamas, please, if you have them,' she said formally, with a tilt of her chin.

'Does that mean . . . ?' Vita asked hopefully. 'Is he awake? Tell me, please?' she implored. 'Is he getting better?'

Isadora nodded, but Vita could tell she wasn't going to be drawn. Her loyalty was clearly to Irving, not to mention to Alicia and the girls.

'Please, Isadora, can you give him a message for me? Can you ask him if he wants to see me?'

'He doesn't,' Isadora said straight away, her brown eyes looking Vita up and down. 'And to be frank, I doubt he'll want you here when he returns home to convalesce.'

Vita felt her barbed words and drew her gown more tightly around her. She had to leave? Leave her own home? But where would she go?

'Please fetch me his pyjamas.'

Seeing that Isadora wasn't inclined to talk, Vita nodded and went up to the bedroom, to Irving's bureau. But as she fetched his pyjamas from the drawer and ran her hands over the soft cotton, tears came and she sniffed. Irving had been so kind to her, so generous and sweet, and now he hated her.

'It's no use crying,' Isadora said, and Vita jumped, seeing that she'd crept into the bedroom behind her.

'I can't help it. Oh, Isadora, if you only knew how sorry I am. I'm sorry for everything. I'm sorry that you hate me, and that I accused you, but—'

'You should be sorry. No one touched anything of yours,' Isadora said, bringing Vita up short with a direct reference to the awful day she had been dismissed.

'It really wasn't you? Or Hermione?'

'No. Irving has been good to those children,' she said. 'He's brought them up as if they were his own. They would never do anything to hurt him. Or steal from him.'

Vita took a moment to take in what Isadora had just said. '*As if they were his own . . . ?* What do you mean?'

'Irving isn't their biological father,' Isadora said. 'He couldn't have children. Doctor Bernheim helped Alicia go to a very progressive clinic in Switzerland. And when she came home, she was pregnant with Daphne. Irving was so over-joyed, they had Hermione the same way.'

Vita felt herself exhale very slowly, as Isadora's knowing eyes connected with hers and the awful truth sank in. Irving wasn't the girls' father. She remembered the pained conversation she'd had with Irving about the nursery when he'd shown her around the apartment. He'd been trying to find out if she wanted a child, but she'd moved the conversation on. She hadn't given him a chance to tell her the truth.

Because now she understood. If Irving couldn't have children before, that meant that he *couldn't* be the father of her baby. Which meant Irving knew that if she was pregnant, then Vita had betrayed him.

That's why he collapsed. Because he must have known that Alicia was right – about Archie . . . about Vita herself.

She felt stunned as Isadora firmly took the pyjamas from her hands. The old woman turned in the doorway.

'He will not forgive you,' Isadora said. 'But you should have listened to him. He didn't trust that woman – your friend, Marianne. And neither did I. If you ask me, she's the one who took everything.'

88

The Mannequin

Vita felt chilled as she drove along the boulevard Haussmann, willing her suspicion not to be true, but the memory of Isadora's dark gaze was making it impossible not to act. Because if Isadora and Hermione hadn't taken the bras, then surely that left Marie being responsible in some way? The thought was too dreadful to contemplate, but she had to do something. She had to rule out the terrible suspicion that clawed at her.

She parked the car on the kerb outside Galeries Lafayette, infuriating the doorman, who told her to move on; but she pushed past him through the doors into the perfume department, amazed that people were here shopping and enjoying themselves as if they didn't have a care in the world. Had she been like that?

Yes, she remembered, she had. She felt the sting of the memory – of being here with Marie, and how full of promise her life had been, how splendid it had felt to be Irving's fiancée. How she had been so determined to be a good wife.

She remembered Marie telling her that her personality was 'not what one would expect'. Is that what Marie had said – or something like it? At the time it had seemed odd, but Vita had brushed over it; but now the memory of it chimed like a warning bell, along with questions – so many questions. What had Marie meant? And what had she expected Vita to be like? And why would she have had any expectation at all, if they were strangers? And how had it been that Marie had managed to infiltrate Vita's life so fully?

She took a long, deep breath and closed her eyes for a moment, just before she got out of the lift on the third floor. *Marie was her friend*, she reminded herself. This was Isadora and Alicia's doing – this intention to unsettle and undermine her. She shouldn't even be here. What was she hoping to find? What was she looking for? For a second she thought about pressing the button for the ground floor, in order to return to the car and drive away, but now the lift door pinged open and she stepped out into the lingerie department.

Everything was just as it had been previously, and she stood, taking in the plush carpet, the soft lighting, the uniformed assistants, the long wooden and glass benches, the soft curtains of the dressing room.

'Madame, are you quite well?' the assistant asked. Vita recognized the woman who'd made the appointment for herself and Marie.

'I . . .' Vita began, but her eye was drawn to a mannequin in pride of place – positioned to catch the attention of anyone coming out of the lift. It was a velveteen body on a fancy wooden plinth, dressed in a bra: a very familiar-looking bra.

Ignoring the assistant, Vita walked over to the mannequin, walking around it, looking at the stitching. There was no doubt. It was her design, and one of the bras Marie had made.

'Do you like that one?' the assistant asked. 'It's new. Would Madame like to try one?' She clicked her fingers and another assistant appeared. 'What size would you like us to put in the dressing room?' The other assistant went behind the desk and opened a wooden drawer. She started putting bras on the glass counter, wrapped in tissue paper. The ones that had been in Vita's case . . .

Vita felt winded. She turned to the assistant.

'I came here before,' she said, trying to make the woman understand her panicky French. 'I came here before, with my friend.'

'Oh,' the assistant said, as if finally placing Vita. 'I'm sorry, I thought you were a customer. Do forgive me. I remember now. Your friend, yes. She came again in the summer. She brought us lots of stock. It's selling fast.' She smiled, clearly pleased with her success.

Marie? Marie had done this? She'd come in the summer and sold all the stock, when Vita had been away? But why? Why hadn't she told her? Because she was too ashamed? Is that why she'd left Paris? Because she'd known Vita would find out?

She pictured Marie taking the case up the stairs to the studio. But Vita had never checked inside the case; she'd never actually seen the bras. It had been an empty case all along . . .

How had Marie risked it, knowing that Vita might have found out her lie any second? But of course Vita hadn't opened the case, because she'd trusted Marie. And Marie had been all too happy to let her blame Hermione and Isadora.

'She came with another woman, too.'

'Another woman?'

'Yes, with your friend. She seemed to be the one in charge. She was English as well. A blonde woman. Very stylish.'

Vita shook her head, putting her hands to her temples. *Marie had been working with someone else?*

'Madame? Madame? Can I help you?' the assistant called out, but Vita was already running for the stairs.

89

A Surprise at the Old Apartment

Vita didn't care that she was being beeped by several other drivers, as she cut through the traffic and sped through the streets up to Montparnasse, marvelling that she hadn't been here for so long. She slewed to a stop, jolting as a tyre mounted the pavement on the corner of rue d'Orsel and some pedestrians sprang out of the way. She got out and slammed the door, before pounding on the wooden door of number seven.

Madame Vertbois looked taken aback to see Vita, but she had no time for the old woman.

'Is she here?' Vita demanded, pushing past the concierge and making for the stairs.

'Vita, wait,' Madame Vertbois called, but Vita ignored her, sprinting up the stairs two at a time, tears blurring her vision.

'Marie. Marie?' she called, pounding on the door of her old apartment. The handle turned from the inside and Vita pushed against the door, forcing it open.

But it wasn't Marie. Instead a small girl staggered backwards against the hall table next to two suitcases. She stared at Vita with big, pale-blue eyes.

All the way here Vita had been preparing the dressing-down she was going to give Marie, the furious way in which she would demand an explanation. Because there *had* to be an explanation. But the presence of this strange child threw her off-balance.

'Where is Marie?' she demanded. 'Marie Chastain?'

Had Marie moved out?

'Maman isn't here,' the girl said.

Maman?

'Marie is . . . Marie is your mother?'

'Yes, Miss Darton.'

Miss Darton? Did the child just say 'Miss Darton'?

'How do you . . . ? How do you know my name?' Vita gasped.

The child tried to smile. 'You were kind to me once, when I came to Darton Hall at Christmas.'

Vita put her hand on her chest, the memory surfacing of that Christmas in Darton long ago, when a child had knocked on the door and Darius Darton had ordered the dogs to go after her.

Darton. The child.

This child was Marie's – and the child was from Darton? All this time she'd been in Paris, Marie had known about Darton, about who Vita really was . . .

She felt the air leaving her lungs, but then she heard a noise, a scratching from the bedroom. The little girl opened the door that had been Nancy's room and a small white dog ran out, yapping happily.

It ran over to Vita, before doing a little circle, and Vita thought she might faint. Because it was Mr Wild.

She picked up the dog to examine its face, but it was Mr

Wild all right. The little dog licked her face, then nuzzled her neck.

'I don't understand,' Vita cried. 'Oh, Mr Wild. Mr Wild.'

But Marie had told her he was dead – that Nancy had killed him. But . . . but she hadn't. Mr Wild was alive. It had all been a hoax, a lie. But why? Why would Marie do something so terrible?

Now Nancy's warning about Marie reared up, and Irving's, too. And, finally, Isadora's. Everything they'd said was true. Marie had betrayed both Vita and Nancy . . .

She remembered Marie standing outside the club when Nancy had run into the road. And afterwards, when Marie had come to the apartment and said that Nancy had killed Mr Wild. She'd deliberately sought out Vita and Nancy.

And now Vita had betrayed Nancy and sent her away, believing Marie and all the dreadful lies she'd told.

She backed away now, still holding Mr Wild, her heart pounding, her mind scrabbling for answers, but she felt as if she were falling down a scree slope, unable to get a grip. Then she turned and ran as fast as she could down the stairs.

'Where are you going, Vita?' Madame Vertbois called, but Vita ignored the duplicitous old woman. How long had she known? About Marie and her child?

She ran to the car and put Mr Wild in the front seat. And then, her hands trembling, she swerved into the traffic.

90

Marie Tries to Explain

Outside the house Vita parked, her breath still coming in raggedy gasps. She tried to calm down for a moment, turned off the engine and put her head on the wheel. She had to think. She had to think fast. And she needed help, because if Marie was connected to Darton, then she must be connected to Clement, too, which meant that very possibly Clement knew where she was. Which meant that she had to leave. She had to leave right away.

But how? And then she remembered. There was one person she could ask to help her.

She got out and set Mr Wild down on the pavement and he sniffed around, and then she saw Celine on the steps to the house, having heard the car.

'Oh, Mrs King,' she said. '*Un petit chien.*'

'Mr Wild – here!' Vita called and the dog obediently trotted up the steps.

'Can you give him some water, please, Celine?'

Celine picked up Mr Wild and followed Vita back inside, but she was already on her way to the telephone.

She pressed her finger on the jamb, impatient to get through to the operator. Then she demanded to be put through to Paul Kilkenny at the number he had given her. Vita waited, watching Celine and Mr Wild, her mind racing. How was Mr Wild alive? And the child – Marie's child – why oh why would Marie keep such a huge secret? They were friends, weren't they? But then she thought of what she'd seen in the store. No, they *weren't* friends. She barely knew Marie at all.

'Vita,' Paul said when he came on the line. 'Vita, this is a surprise. Have you called to say goodbye? I'm leaving for the States tomorrow.'

She didn't reply, but gripped the receiver instead. 'Paul, you know you said that if I was ever in trouble . . .' she began, but her heart was racing and she could hardly speak.

'Vita? Vita, are you quite all right? What's happened?'

But it was too much to explain. 'Can you come?' she asked, telling him her address. 'Quickly. Please.'

'Of course,' he said. 'That's very close to me. In fact, you're just around the corner. I'll be there in a jiffy.'

Relieved, Vita put the phone down, but Celine, who was holding Mr Wild, called out. 'Oh, I forgot to tell you. Marie is back. She's up in the studio.'

Vita could feel her heartbeat in her throat as she made it to the top of the stairs. In the studio the doors were open onto the street, and the room was filled with light. As Marie turned, smiling, she looked different, as if the worries of the world had lifted from her shoulders.

Vita felt her heart lurch at the sight of her friend – at Marie's familiar smile, at the face she'd trusted.

'Oh, Vita,' Marie said. 'I'm so glad to see you. It's been such an exhausting week, and I have so much to explain—'

'Get out,' Vita shouted. 'Just get out.'

Marie's face fell. 'Vita?'

She was too cross to let Marie speak, her words tumbling out in a shrill accusation. 'I saw them in Galeries Lafayette. I just went there – all of our work. *All* of it. You lied. *You* took the bras – all of them . . .'

Marie's smile faded. She swallowed, her eyebrows drawing together, her hands wringing. 'Oh, Vita, please, please understand. I was going to tell you. I was trying to find the right time.' Marie came towards her, but Vita shook her head and covered her ears.

'I don't want to hear it. I trusted you.' She was crying fully now, all the pent-up anger and frustration pouring out of her. 'How *could* you? How could you do this to me?'

'I didn't have a choice. Vita, if you would only sit down and let me explain.'

'And Mr Wild! I went to the apartment.'

'You did?'

'You said he was dead.'

'He ate Nancy's pills, that's all.' Marie sighed, looking ashamed.

'But you made Nancy think . . . What have you done, Marie? How could you? When I helped you?'

'Vita, please.' Marie's eyes were shining as they stared up at her. 'I can explain everything.'

She couldn't look at Marie, who stood, still nervously wringing her hands. There was a commotion downstairs, and Vita heard Celine talking to someone, and then the sound of someone coming upstairs. At first Vita thought it might be Paul, as the uneven, clumping steps got faster.

'I came from Darton because he married her,' Marie said, her eyes blazing. 'Clement, your brother. He married her – Edith – when he'd promised me, you see; he promised me . . .'

'*What?*' Vita shook her head, trying to understand. She stepped closer to Marie to hear her better, but her mind was spinning.

Edith? Edith was married to Clement?

'He promised me and Susan, his daughter.'

That child . . . the child she'd seen. The child was Clement's?

These two bombshells left Vita stunned.

She thought about the assistant at Galeries Lafayette, who had described another blonde woman. Edith – Edith had been here in Paris. With Marie.

'Vita, you've got to believe me. It was all Edith's fault. She wanted all the designs for Top Drawer, and I *had* to give them to her. She took my Susan, my baby, you see. You'll understand soon that a mother will do anything for her child. I had to get Susan back. And I didn't know where she was and then I saw the name of the school on one of the photographs Edith had given me when I studied it with the magnifying glass and I saw how I could make it right. If I went to get Susan . . . if I told Edith to go to hell, I could make everything right. Because, Vita, I realized long ago how wrong it was to trick you. And I wanted to tell you so badly.'

'You were working for Edith?'

So Percy had been right all along. Edith was behind Top Drawer.

458

'Not working for her – not willingly. Never willingly. She was forcing me. But you and me, Vita . . . we're friends. I realized that. I realized that I owed Edith and Clement nothing. Vita, we're such a good team together. We can work together properly now.'

Marie stopped suddenly, her face pale with shock. She was looking past Vita, who followed her gaze, her heart contracting as she saw a familiar figure filling the doorway. Clement stood there, leaning on his stick, his blond hair plastered to his forehead, his face shiny with sweat. He was wearing a thick-pinstriped suit, his neck bulging at the white collar. He stared at Vita and Marie, then came into the room.

'All this time,' he said. 'All this time, and you two . . .' He thrust his stick at Marie.

And Vita saw terror now in Marie's face.

'God damn you, Marie,' Clement said.

'Clement. Stop it,' Vita shouted.

'And you! You were here all this time.' He had reached them now, and Vita instinctively went to bar his way, but Clement struck her hard around the face. Marie screamed as Vita stumbled away.

'Leave me alone,' Marie shouted at him, and Vita watched as Clement's stick rattled to the floor. He grabbed Marie by the throat and she backed on tiptoe towards the open window.

Vita screamed, lunging for Clement's stick. She picked it up and whacked him hard on the back. He cried out and let go of Marie, who stepped back, but she was at the window ledge, and now Vita watched as she stood for a moment, trying to balance at the edge, her blue eyes wide with alarm.

Vita sprang forward to grab her arm, but it was too late. She screamed as Marie's fingers brushed hers, then watched as Marie fell backwards out of the window.

There was a sickening crunch.

'Marie!' she screamed.

Clement let out a strangled wail and went to lunge for Vita, but she escaped past him now, terrified. She ran as fast as she could down the stairs and out of the front door. Celine was screaming and pointing to the railings. Marie was lying on top of them, her body impaled, her head at an awful angle.

Vita scooped up Mr Wild, who was barking.

'Call the police,' she told Celine. 'Quickly.'

She rushed down the steps, holding Mr Wild, and saw that Paul was standing outside the house.

'She just fell,' he said. 'Oh, Vita, she fell right in front of my eyes.'

'Oh, Paul. Paul,' Vita sobbed, falling into his embrace.

And then Clement came out of the house. 'Look what you've done,' he shouted at Vita. He stumped towards her on his stick, his eyes murderous. 'I'm going to kill you. I'm going to fucking kill you.'

Paul drew out a gun from inside his jacket, pushing Vita behind him.

'Who is this guy? Say the word, Vita, and I'll pop him.'

Clement stopped and Paul moved round him, still pointing the gun at him, so that they could get to the car.

'Marie, Marie, Marie!' Vita was hyperventilating, looking

at her former friend's body, the blood pooling around the railings.

'She's gone, Vita,' Paul said. 'She's gone. There's nothing you can do. Get in the car.'

She fumbled with the door of the car, Mr Wild still in her arms, and then the door was open and she got into the driver's seat.

'Don't move a muscle,' she heard Paul say to Clement, with the gun still trained on him, as he walked round the car. Then Paul jumped in next to Vita and she started the engine, her hands shaking violently as she watched Clement stump into the street and lean over the bonnet of the car.

Vita yelped, throwing the car into reverse, and swerved backwards, away from her brother – away from the dreadful scene, as sirens started up in the distance.

91

News from Paris

Edith thought her head was going to explode as she battled through the throng to the factory entrance.

'Please – please, just stop it,' she implored the workers, covering her head as they shouted and jeered. She couldn't believe Clement had left her all by herself to deal with this.

Inside, she leant back against the doors, seeing the cavernous floor empty, the old looms having been stripped away. But the new machines had yet to get through the picket line.

She'd been so close to her victorious revelation about Vita and Paris, but the damned headmistress had ruined everything. Clement had left almost straight away for Paris, and Theresa Darton had railed at Edith about what a terrible, duplicitous wife she'd been to her son.

Since Clement had left, Edith hadn't heard a word from either him or Marianne, and she'd been racked with doubts and misgivings. She wished she'd had more chance to explain, so that Clement could see that she'd done what she'd done for him – for their business, for the success of Darton. And that her passion to succeed matched his own.

She knew that, in time, Clement would see how brilliant

her plan had been, but it worried her that he'd rushed off to Paris to find Vita, in a hot-headed and furious mood. And now Edith was annoyed because she'd hoped her victory over Vita might have been more definite. She'd hoped to be there to enjoy it, too.

Edith had heard about Vita's affair with Archie Fenwick from Belinda Getty, whom she'd met at Annabelle Morton's soirée when she'd been in London. When Belinda had found out that Edith had once been a dancer at the Zip Club, her tongue had loosened and she'd been all too eager to tell Edith about the scandal. Belinda had heard it from Cassius Digby's butler, who had been keen to take revenge on Cassius, after he'd been fired. When he'd been spurned, the butler had talked openly about all sorts of shenanigans on board *Lilly* – including how he'd seen Vita and Archie in the lifeboat, making love.

Edith had counselled Belinda to make sure that Alicia King found out about the juicy details of the affair, too. Then, the following night, she'd given Archie's manuscript to Irving, to seal Vita's fate. She had done more than enough to disgrace Vita and ruin both her marriage and her business.

She thought back to how Clement had been before he'd left – how angry. She'd been frightened, but also strangely aroused by how passionate he'd been. He was a man with depths she'd never realized; if only he'd understood how much she'd done to get him what he wanted.

Now she heard the phone ringing in the office upstairs, and she took the stairs two at a time. The phone kept on ringing until she snatched it up.

'Hello?' There was silence, then the line crackled. 'Hello?'

'It's me.'

Relief washed over her. Here was contact, at last.

'Clement? What's happened?'

'Marie – she's . . .' Clement's voice sounded strange. 'She's dead.'

'Dead?' Edith gasped.

'She fell,' Clement said. He sounded dazed. 'There are police.'

'*Police?* Where are you now?'

'At the hotel.'

'What about Vita?'

There was silence. Clement was clearly in shock. 'She's gone.'

Gone. How could she have gone? She should be broken. Disgraced. How could Vita have got away? What on earth was happening over there?

'What about the child? What about Susan?' Edith asked, trying to get Clement to focus.

'She wasn't there.'

'She'll be with Madame Vertbois. In Vita's apartment. You must go and get her, Clement. The rue d'Orsel. Number seven. Go now.'

'Edith, you did all of this . . .'

Edith tried to fathom out his tone. Did Clement mean that he thought she was responsible for Marie's demise?

'I did what I had to do to ruin Vita,' she said. 'That's what you wanted. And I got new designs for Top Drawer into the bargain. I thought you'd be pleased.'

There was another long silence. 'And the child? What about the child?' he said.

Edith noticed that he didn't say her name, or lay claim to her.

'She's yours. And she could be ours,' she said, taking a risk. Was it too soon to tell Clement this secret wish?

'What do you mean?'

'Clement, just focus. Find the child and bring her home. I need you here.'

92

The Truth about Paul

Vita felt numb. Numb and then sick.

In the hours since Marie's dreadful accident, she'd been to the police station to give her statement, and Paul had given his as a witness, too. She'd implicated Clement in Marie's death, but the police – frustrated with Vita for leaving the scene of the crime – had told her there wasn't much they could do.

There would in time, she was told, be questions about the building regulations and why there hadn't been a guard in front of the French windows, but for now Marie's death would be recorded as a tragic accident.

She still couldn't get over the horrible sight of Clement in her home. Or the awful truth that he knew Marie. That he was the father of that little girl. That he'd married Edith, who had manipulated Marie – and Vita, too – all the way from England.

All those lies. Lies, lies, lies. All of them Clement's fault. Clement and *Edith's* fault.

A blonde woman . . . the one in charge. The smiling face of the assistant in Galeries Lafayette swam into Vita's mind's eye. Edith had stolen her designs and taken her business.

Now Vita felt shaky as she parked outside the house.

'What if he's still there?' she asked Paul.

'I can handle him,' he replied, patting his jacket. She remembered him pulling out the gun.

'Why have you got a gun?' she asked.

'I wouldn't question it now, Vita. Not when it may come in handy.'

Paul got out of the car first and walked along the pavement, holding the gun outstretched. Vita followed, holding Mr Wild tightly.

Marie's body had gone from the railings. In the fading light, Celine was on her hands and knees with a bucket, wiping up the blood. The roses had been trampled flat. She screamed when she saw Paul with a gun.

'He's not here?' Vita asked. 'Clement? The man with the stick?'

Celine shook her head violently. 'No, he went away,' she said. 'Shortly after you. Before the police came. Hermione and Daphne telephoned. They are coming back with Mr King from the hospital. They will be here soon.'

Paul put his gun down, but Vita still shook as she walked into the house.

'Stay by the door,' she told Paul. She had to be quick. She didn't wish to confront Irving or the girls.

She went first to the study and searched in Irving's desk for her new passport. She found it, along with the envelope he'd given her on their wedding night. She opened it up and saw it contained the share certificate, and she remembered how Irving had told her that Marie had suggested he give her financial independence.

Maybe, just maybe, Marie had tried to be a good person. Maybe she had wanted to be a true friend to Vita, but it was too late now. It made her feel immeasurably sad that she'd never know the truth.

She picked up one of Irving's cigars, sniffing the Cuban leaf, then putting it back and closing the drawer. Then she took off her wedding and engagement rings, put them in an envelope and left them on the desk. She wanted to leave a note, but her heart was too full, her mind too fogged with the shock of everything that had happened, to find the right words.

Upstairs in her dressing room she ripped a few of her favourite dresses from the hangers in her wardrobe and stuffed them into Nancy's brown suitcase, which Marie had brought from the apartment. She didn't want to take one of the smart valises that Irving had bought. She didn't want to be reminded of her honeymoon.

Outside the bedroom, she stood on the balcony, looking up towards the studio, but couldn't bear to go back up there.

'Is that it?' Paul asked as she came down the stairs with the suitcase, and Vita nodded. He set Mr Wild down, then took the case and carried it outside. Then he put his fingers in his mouth and whistled.

'I thought we'd travel in style,' he said from the bottom of the steps, winking at Vita.

She didn't know what he meant, but then a fancy white car came round the corner and a chauffeur got out and opened the back door. Paul let Mr Wild jump onto the rear seat.

On the doorstep Vita hugged Celine and kissed both her cheeks. 'Tell Mr King that I've gone. Tell him I'm sorry.'

'Goodbye, Madame,' Celine said with a little curtsey. The poor girl looked wretched, her eyes red-raw from crying.

Vita got into the back of the car, then Paul got in from the other side. The chauffeur looked familiar and he tipped his hat and smiled at her.

Vita quieted Mr Wild next to her on the back seat. She didn't look up at the tall, narrow house and the window from which Marie had fallen to her death. She didn't look back as they left the square.

She opened the window to let Mr Wild get some air, and he panted in the gap as the streets of Paris slid past. And then something snagged at Vita's memory.

'This car?' she said, looking round properly at the interior. 'Isn't it the one we went to Madame Sacerdote's in? Did you borrow it again?'

Paul and the chauffeur laughed, but Vita didn't see what was so funny.

'No, it's mine. It was always mine.'

'It's yours?'

'Oh, come on, Vita, don't look like that.'

'But that day, when we met at Shakespeare and Company, we walked right past it.'

'And Renard here played along beautifully.'

The photograph that she'd shown Laure and Agatha at Madame Sacerdote's . . . Now it made sense. The look in Renard's eye. They'd been sharing a joke. 'You fooled me?'

'You were easy to fool.'

'I thought you were a starving artist.'

'Because that's what you wanted me to be.'

Vita felt put out.

'But if you're not an artist, then what are you?' Vita shook her head, her eyes narrowed at him, and Paul gave a self-deprecating shrug.

'This and that. They call me "Le Monsieur".'

There was a beat as Vita took this in. Paul – artist Paul – was . . .

'*You're* Le Monsieur? You're not an artist?'

'No,' he said. 'I'm surprised I got away with that one. I certainly wasn't very good at explaining art, was I?'

She remembered the lunch, and Paul saying that he liked all the greats. Now that she thought about it, he had a point.

'And the case in the Louvre?' she said, remembering suddenly how Paul had found a case, right by his favourite picture.

'Oh . . . that. It was just a cash drop-off,' he said with a shrug. 'All pre-arranged.'

Vita sat back in the seat, trying to take it all in.

'So it turns out that all of my best friends really aren't who they say they are,' she said stiffly, thinking of Marie. 'Or were.'

'Oh, don't take it so hard. I never meant to hurt you,' Paul said. 'You were so innocent – so good – I couldn't help but play along. I liked being Paul, the starving artist.'

'But you're actually Le Monsieur?' she checked.

'It's just a funny nickname that's stuck. I'm a bootlegger, really. I like to provide for people whatever they need. And that's mostly liquor.'

'That's why you went to Cognac?'

'Yes, for the brandy. The ship we're sailing on is loaded with barrels,' he said, 'for the good folk of New York.'

'Won't you get caught?' she asked.

He laughed. 'You think those customs officials don't like fine wine, Vita? Now don't you go worrying. The crossing will be perfectly grand, as long as you don't mind playing poker with the boys.'

Vita looked out of the window as Renard drove them around the Arc de Triomphe, trying to take everything in. She thought back to how she'd been that day when she'd first met Paul, and how she'd felt that Paris was about to lie within her grasp. And maybe, for one golden moment, it had been.

She thought of all the wonderful things that had happened here – of the Les Folies girls and Fletch, and of dear Madame Sacerdote. And she thought, too, of all the things she still couldn't begin to reconcile: Nancy, Marie, Edith, Clement, and now this: the fact that Paul was Le Monsieur.

'You'd be surprised how many things in this world are not what they seem,' she said quietly, remembering the very words Paul had said that day in the museum. 'You really had me fooled.'

93

A Loved Grandchild

In a move to keep the peace with her mother-in-law, Edith took it upon herself to explain to Theresa Darton that Clement was bringing the missing child – his child – home from Paris. She explained how she'd been schooling Susan, and that she was keen for Clement to adopt her. Theresa, to her surprise, softened at the mention of a granddaughter. Perhaps the lonely old woman wanted someone to love other than her canaries.

When Clement arrived home, however, the child didn't speak, and Susan was still mute when Theresa put her to bed in Vita's old room. Edith followed and quietly locked the child's door, to make sure she didn't run away in the night. Then, after a very stiff shot of brandy, she went downstairs to talk to Clement.

She'd already decided that the only option was to be completely honest. So she told him everything from the beginning: starting with her deal with Vita when she'd left for Paris from the Zip Club, to how she'd used Marianne to steal Vita's designs, and how, in the summer, she had clinched the order in Paris. Clement listened to it all, sipping a tumbler of brandy.

'So, you see, we have both lied to each other,' she said,

once her confession was over. 'And I didn't like lying. But, Clement, you gave me no choice.'

He shook his head, not looking at her.

'You are a cruel man,' she said. 'You have a lot of anger, but I think I understand you. Won't you let this be a start of a new phase? As business partners? As parents?'

'You really want that?' he asked. 'You want to raise that child?'

'I want to raise *your* child,' she said. 'But as you so hurtfully pointed out, I'm barren.'

He was silent for a moment, then he sighed. 'I'm sorry I said that, Edith.'

Edith nodded, not wanting to cry, but feeling tears in her chest. She'd never thought she'd ever hear Clement apologize, but it felt so good to hear it.

'Let's start again in the morning,' she said and he nodded.

For the first time in ages they slept in the same room in the same bed that night. She'd expected him to get up and leave, their difficult conversations still so fresh, but then she felt him spoon against her, pulling her body to his. He held her all night.

Now, in the kitchen, Theresa Darton bent over the small child.

'She's just like you,' Theresa said, looking at Clement and then back at Susan. Her eyes were shining, and Edith saw that she was happier than she'd ever seen her.

Martha came in. 'Mrs Darton, the gentleman is here,' she said.

Edith and Theresa both looked up, but Theresa gave way to the younger Mrs Darton.

'Show him into the drawing room. We'll be there in a moment,' Edith said.

'Let's go out and see my canaries,' Theresa said to Susan, leading her away. The small child said nothing, but let herself be led off. However, as she got to the door, she turned, her pale eyes staring into Edith's.

'She's a strange child,' Clement said.

'Yes, but she's a bright thing. She will serve us well.'

Clement nodded, and together they turned to go and meet the man from the investment fund.

'I hope you are feeling more settled, after our talk last night?' she said.

Clement looked at her. 'I've thought about what you said. I'm glad you did what you did, Edith. But I still hate her,' he said. 'Anna, I mean. I hate her and I always will.'

'I understand,' Edith replied, touching his arm.

She didn't say any more, but led Clement to the drawing room. Vita might have got away for now, but it was all over, she reassured herself. Marianne's accident had solved a big problem, too. Edith had got her husband back, and she'd got a child. An unusual way of getting one, she had to admit, but now she knew they would be parents together. And now that Top Drawer had taken off, Vita's business ambitions were ruined. Edith had won, and she'd got the revenge that her husband had so craved. Vita would never catch up now, no matter how hard she tried.

Mr Heal, from Hillsafe Investments, was a nervous man. He held on to his hat on his lap, as Edith poured him some tea.

'It's kind of you to come,' she said, although it had come

474

as a shock when he had requested a meeting. Perhaps the financiers had heard reports of the strikes and unrest at the mill. She hoped this genteel meeting would set things straight. She told Mr Heal about the new machinery that was coming, and about their recent successes in Paris, and he seemed pleased.

'So, Hillsafe Investments?' Clement asked. 'My wife tells me that you have many investors?'

'Yes, that's right, Mr Darton. It's a financial investment fund, which, I have to tell you, doesn't usually invest in this sort of enterprise,' Mr Heal said. 'However, my client was adamant about investing in Darton Mills.'

'I see,' Edith said, confused.

'And who exactly is your client?' Clement asked, frowning at Edith.

She felt a shiver of alarm. When a man from Hillsafe Investments had first made contact, Clement had been out and Edith had taken the call. Pleased that she was taking an active role in the future of Darton, she'd been the one to pursue the investment opportunity and she'd been so gratified when Clement had gone along with it and trusted her judgement. She'd told him that Hillsafe were reputable and trustworthy, but she realized now that she hadn't done proper due diligence. She'd taken everything for granted and just assumed that the investment fund was composed of many sources. Money-men, she'd been led to believe. A fund of anonymous shareholders. That's what she'd told Clement, when they'd done the deal.

'The shares were actually bought by our client – a . . . Mr King from Paris. However, I believe he transferred the shares directly to his wife.'

Edith felt as if an icicle had pierced her.

'Say that again?'

'There's a woman called . . .' Mr Heal paused, consulting a sheet in his leather folder. 'Yes, she's called Mrs Vita King.'

'Vita?' Clement said.

'Yes, that's right. Vita King. The stock is in her name. Although I'm not altogether sure that she knows that her husband had been so specific in investing in Darton. I'm just here on a courtesy call,' he said, smiling. 'Checking on the client's interest.'

Edith held her breath. 'Vita?' she whispered, as Clement's eyes met hers.

'Yes, that's right,' Mr Heal said. 'Vita King owns forty-nine per cent of Darton Mills.'

476

94

America-Bound

The ship's horn rang out as it slipped through the grey-green sea away from the coast. Vita watched the great blades of the motor churning the water below her. Mr Wild snuffled around the long coil of rope on the deck, and Vita pulled the shawl around her shoulders, observing the seagulls surf on the air. She watched the white cliffs of the French coast receding and bade a silent goodbye to Europe.

She said a quiet prayer into the wind now for poor Irving. If he got better, she hoped he'd mend his ways and be a little healthier. Although she could understand now why he'd got into the habit of drinking so much, having been married to that awful woman, Alicia. Perhaps he could get rid of Alicia properly this time, and maybe find himself a better wife.

She remembered how Nancy had said that marrying for love was a silly thing to do, but she'd been wrong. Marrying without properly loving someone was a disastrous thing to do, and Vita vowed she'd never do it again.

She thought of Alicia having to deal with the aftermath of Marie's death at the house, and braced herself as she pictured Marie on the railings and the awful way she'd met her death. And Vita thought now of the child . . . her niece, at the apartment. The girl who had looked so much like Clement. How was the poor child going to react when she found out that her mother was dead? She felt a pang of anguish – and guilt, too. Surely she owed it to Marie to have rescued Susan?

Or maybe not. Maybe her instinct to leave Europe had been the right one. She couldn't risk being entangled with Clement. Her brother's intention to destroy her had clearly not lessened over time.

Besides, she didn't owe Susan anything. Marie had never told her about her daughter. Astonishingly, Marie had kept Susan completely secret. And, wrapping her arms around her body, feeling a sudden chill, Vita marvelled once again at the level of Marie's deceit. But of course now everything made sense: Marie's distance from her, and the way she'd worked so hard. It had all been under duress, because of Edith.

Edith. Edith! Vita shook her head. She'd never have thought Edith could be so spiteful, so cunning, but she'd underestimated her old enemy. She'd taken Vita's ideas in London and, even when Vita had started out again in Paris, she'd taken her ideas there, too.

Well, she wouldn't win, Vita vowed. Top Drawer had been *her* idea. Somehow – and she didn't know exactly how or when – she would find a way of proving herself. She'd start again. And one day she'd come back and claim what was rightfully hers.

'Come on, let's go and find the boys,' she told Mr Wild, turning away from the cliffs and looking out towards the horizon. The sun was low now, and she shaded her eyes and looked at the golden water ahead and thought what a good picture it would make. Nancy's camera was down in the cabin in her bag, and she thought of all the pictures she had yet to develop.

She remembered how she'd seen Archie in the viewfinder of her camera on that glorious summer's day. How much she'd loved him then, and how much she loved him still. But he wasn't hers. She knew that now. He had a wife. He'd made his choice.

And besides, he belonged to that awful set – the people who'd ruined her marriage with their gossip. She wondered if that very gossip had reached Archie and Maud, and whether he knew of the rumour that Vita was carrying his child. What would Archie do when he found out? What would Maud do? Would Archie come for her in Paris and find that she'd gone? And was that really what she wanted?

No, Vita decided. What she really wanted was to be on a different continent from her brother. What she really wanted was to be reunited with Nancy, her true friend.

'You wait until she sees you,' Vita told the little dog, thinking how joyous the reunion between Mr Wild and Nancy was going to be.

When they'd got to the port yesterday Vita had sent a cable and had had a crackling conversation on the long-distance line. She had tearfully tried to explain about Marie – about how Nancy had been right, and that she should never have trusted her. And Nancy had been right about Edith, too: she did have disastrous taste in men. She'd married Clement.

'But it's good that Marie showed up when she did. Don't you see?' Nancy had shouted down the line.

'How is it good?' This was not how she'd been expecting Nancy to react.

'Because she did me a favour,' Nancy had yelled gleefully. 'I needed to sober up, and I'd just have got worse and worse. And California has been amazing. Oh, Vita, I can't wait until you come. We're going to go out and make our fortune in the talkies. I've met this fabulous producer . . .'

Vita had smiled, her heart warming as she heard that the old Nancy was most definitely back.

'But I'm getting ahead of myself. First, I'll see you in New York when you get there. I'm going to stay with my parents for a while.'

'You're speaking to them?'

'Oh yes, Vita. Yes! You're coming to stay, too. You'll love them.'

Vita wondered now what Nancy's parents would be like, and what Nancy would say when Vita told her that she was expecting a baby. Being a penniless single mother was hardly the best credential to present to Nancy's family, but she couldn't worry about that now. She'd have to deal with it when she got to New York. That's if she got there on this ship of Paul's, loaded with illegal brandy.

Vita pressed her hand to her abdomen and, to her surprise, felt a flutter inside her, like a little kick. She gasped, sensing that her baby wanted to make itself known, and closed her eyes, savouring the new sensation. Feeling, too, that she had been blessed, and that this little soul who had come into being under a sky full of fireworks was hers; and that if she made it to America, she'd do whatever it took to keep him or her safe.

'Hello, baby,' she whispered. 'Are you ready for the next adventure?'

Author's Note

I've had a hankering for this era ever since watching Woody Allen's 2011 film *Midnight in Paris*. I hope I have successfully conjured a flavour of Paris in 1928 for the reader without too many glaring inaccuracies. If there are any, I apologise, but this is fiction, after all. There have been many books I've used for my research, but chief amongst them is Mary McAuliffe's *When Paris Sizzled* as well as *Paris was Yesterday* by the New Yorker correspondent Janet Flanner. William Hurt's Audible narration of Ernest Hemingway's *The Sun Also Rises* was also very helpful, as was Dr James Fox's fantastic BBC4 documentary *Bright Lights, Brilliant Minds: A Tale of Three Cities*.

During my research, I wanted to find a designer whom Vita could work for in Paris and found a Vogue article about Jenny Sacerdote and her modern offices in the Champs-Élysées. To my surprise, I saw that the company still had a website, so I sent a cheeky request for more information. To my utter delight, the CEO of the company, Anne Vogt-Bordure, replied and I went to meet her in Paris, where she told me the remarkable story of Jenny Sacerdote and her rise from humble beginnings to become not only a worldwide celebrity, but also a hugely influential fashion designer, who, in 1928, won the Grand Prix de l'Élégance. By the way, it was actually Jenny Sacerdote who was responsible for inventing the little black dress. When the Second World War came, however, Jenny closed down her offices and the company ceased to exist.

But now, many years later, Anne, pursuing her interest in Jenny Sacerdote's life and career, has brought the brand back to life. In her workshops in Paris, she's making many of Jenny's original groundbreaking designs for a modern audience. I bought a red silk one – the inspiration for the braiding scene when Vita first gets an audience in Jenny's salon. I would like to take this opportunity to thank Anne for allowing me the artistic licence to put Jenny Sacerdote in the story and for her insight into Jenny's amazing world. Please do visit her site www.jennysacerdote.com.

Joanna Rees 2020

Acknowledgements

Firstly, and most importantly, thank you to all the readers out there who buy books, spread the word and pass on feedback. You are wonderful. Thank you to all the bookshops and libraries who support us authors and to all of my fabulous author friends, who re-tweet and generally provide comfort and solace. I'd also like to thank Wayne Brookes, my publisher at Pan Mac, and all the team there – particularly Ellis Keene and Samantha Fletcher, as well as Mairead Loftus, Anna Shora and Leanne Williams for bringing the book to a wider international audience. None of this would be possible without the support of my agent, Felicity Blunt at Curtis Brown, and thank you, too, to Rosie Pierce. For her invaluable editorial assistance, a huge shout-out to Susan Opie, as well as Shân Lancaster. Thanks, too, to my early readers, Dawn Howarth, Eve Tomlinson, Bronwin Wheatley and Louise Dumas, and to all of my friends who always support me. And to Jo Andrews for occasionally digging me out and making me play piano duets.

I'd like to thank my family, particularly my sister, Catherine Lloyd, who always reassures me that I can get to the end of a book. I'd also like to thank my daughters,

Tallulah, Roxie and Minty, who were all completely up for a Paris research trip and made our adventure so memorable. Finally, a massive thank you to Emlyn Rees, my husband, for chivvying me along, making me endless cups of tea, coming to Les Folies Bergère with me, learning to do the Charleston and teaching us all to play poker. I'm looking forward to seeing what we get up to next in the name of research.

The Runaway Daughter

By Joanna Rees

The first book in the A Stitch in Time series.

It's 1926 and Anna Darton is on the run from a terrible crime she was forced into committing. Alone and scared in London, salvation comes in the form of Nancy, a sassy American dancer at the notorious night-club, the Zip Club. Re-inventing herself as Vita Casey, Anna becomes part of the line-up and is thrown into a hedonistic world of dancing, parties, flapper girls and fashion.

When she meets the dashing Archie Fenwick, Vita buries her guilty conscience and she believes him when he says he will love her no matter what. But unbeknown to Vita, her secret past is fast catching up with her, and when the people closest to her start getting hurt, she is forced to confront it or risk losing everything she holds dear.